SEIZE ME

Club Genesis - Chicago, Book 3

USA Today Bestselling Author

Jenna Jacob

SEIZE
Me

USA Today Bestselling Author

JENNA JACOB

Seize Me

Club Genesis – Chicago, Book 3

Jenna Jacob

Published by Jenna Jacob

Copyright 2023 Dream Words, LLC

Edited by: Raw Book Editing: www.http://rawbookediting.com

ePub ISBN: 978-1-952111-42-6

Print ISBN: 978-1-952111-43-3

Previously published as *Master of My Mind*.

He climbed inside my mind and controlled my every craving.

I'm **Leagh Bennett**—kept woman. The unexpected death of my lover shatters me, but when his family discovers our relationship, their cruel vengeance nearly destroys me. Homeless, penniless, and grieving, I seek refuge at Club Genesis to mourn and face an unknown future alone.

When **Tony Delvaggio**, panty-melting psychologist and the club's savage hotshot, forces me to confront my anguish, I tell myself his probing questions are purely professional. But his whiskey-smooth suggestions break through my defenses and ignite desires I never knew existed. Frightened, I push Tony away. But he's relentless, delving into my psyche until I'm letting him even deeper into my body and my heart—where I've let no man before. His raw passion shocks and devastates me. And soon, I'm falling too hard to resist…

But when my past returns and danger threatens, I'm forced to choose between running again or surrendering my all and letting Tony… *Seize Me*.

Previously published as *Master of My Mind.*

Chapter One

I stood beneath the faded green awning, staring at the gleaming mahogany casket. The sparkling brass handles mocked the warmth that had been ripped from my soul. A cold rain splattered upon the canopy while somber-faced friends gathered beneath it to show their respect. Across the gravesite, seated in fabric covered folding chairs, I watched as the well-rehearsed tears spilled down the cheeks of his ex-wife. His hateful daughter tried to soothe the ice queen's theatrics. Neither woman was there to mourn the loss of the man I loved but to masquerade as grieving victims until the fat inheritance landed in their laps.

The monotone voice of the minister resonated in my ears. None of his words of comfort penetrated the numb void that had consumed me for days. I was all but dead inside; just as dead as my beloved Master, who would soon be lowered into the black earth hollowed out below him. And God help me, I wanted to go with him. Not because I wanted to die, but because I couldn't imagine life without him.

The honorable George Bartholomew Marston, State Supreme Court Justice for the past four decades, was being laid to rest. I felt as if I was outside my own body. Friends and family stood in a line before passing the casket one last time, placing blood-red roses atop the gleaming wooden box. I felt as if I'd been transported into a macabre movie, one I could barely watch but helplessly had to endure.

George's best friend and fellow judge, Reed Landes, stepped up to the coffin; his eyes were rimmed red, and the distinguished man's chin quivered. I swallowed back a sob. Pain wrapped its icy hands around my heart and squeezed. It was almost time to say goodbye; however, that was beyond my comprehension.

A firm, steady hand enveloped my shoulder. Glancing up, I gazed into the compassionate amber eyes of Mika LaBrache; friend, Dominant, and owner of the BDSM club, Genesis. I'd spent countless hours basking in my Master's adoration at Mika's club. His submissive, Julianna, dabbed at the tears on her cheek before smoothing a hand over her very pregnant belly. I couldn't ignore how life mirrored death. A new life grew inside her. A life that she and Mika would love, protect, and cherish—while the man who'd loved, protected, and cherished me was gone. It was so fucking unfair.

"It's time to lay your rose on the casket, Leagh." Julianna wrapped her fingers around my arm as I glanced down at the dark red rose gripped in my fist. Opening my hand, tiny red dots blossomed in the center of my palm. The thorns were smeared in crimson. It seemed like hours had passed since Trevor handed me the flower. Strange, I had no recollection of it piercing my flesh.

"I can't do it," I choked, swallowing back the tears I'd held inside for days. Even knowing a part of me would be interred with George forever did little to ease my devastation. Sucking in a ragged breath, I willed myself to remain strong. I refused to allow George's ex or daughter to revel in my pain or glean the depth of my love for him. They'd only use it as a weapon against me.

It had been humiliating enough, while standing on the church steps, when George's ex-wife demanded I be barred from the memorial service. Luckily, Drake, an imposing leather Dom from Genesis, leaned down and whispered something into the haughty bitch's ear. She'd sputtered and paled before she'd jerked her nose in the air and stormed inside the chapel. If it hadn't been for Drake's intervention, I never would have gathered the courage to attend the devotion. I'd shielded my grief from the hateful shrew then; I wasn't about to let her see a chink in my armor now.

With a nod of understanding, Mika lifted the rose from my palm and set it atop the copious pile of flowers adorning the casket. When he returned, Julianna wrapped her arm around my waist, attempting to lead me from the gravesite. My entire body froze. I couldn't move. I didn't want to. Stepping from beneath the awning meant I'd be forced to face a future without George. Even more unbearable was the fact that I would be leaving him alone, entombed in the cold black earth.

"Can you give us a little help here?" Mika murmured to Tony Delvaggio, the familiar Dom, Sadist, Dungeon Monitor, and resident shrink of Genesis.

He was a hulk of a man who always called me "brat" to my face— and meant it. The same one who set butterflies dipping and swooping in my stomach every time I caught him staring at me in the club. He was erotic beyond words, turning submissive heads—collared or not— every night at Genesis. Tony always sent my pulse racing, even now. It was ridiculous for him to affect me in such a way. Stupid even. I'd always been civil to the man, because he was a Dom and a friend of George's, but his intense nature made my skin itch in a very uncomfortable way.

Julianna stepped aside as Tony slid a thick arm around my shoulder. He was warm and solid. I tried to ignore the way he made my heart skitter.

"I've got her, Mika. You just keep Julianna and that little bun in the oven dry. We'll meet you back at the cars."

Tony raised his umbrella. It opened with a whoosh before he maneuvered me from beneath the canopy. Somehow, I put one foot in front of the other while I focused on Mika escorting Julianna up the hill. He held her close to his side—protective and adoring—enveloping her in comfort, reassurance, and love.

Anguish sliced deep. George was gone, yet Julianna still had all the things I longed for. Even though she was one of my closest friends, envy burned, spreading like a cancer through my veins. Tears stung my eyes as I cast my gaze toward the ground. The wet, brown grass blurred.

"Just a bit farther, Leagh," Tony encouraged. His voice was husky and deep.

Glancing up at the man, he smiled, but it didn't reach his eyes. Sorrow and pity replaced his usual piercing gaze. "Are you going back to the church for the luncheon?"

I shook my head. I couldn't stomach the thought of sharing a meal, let alone the same air, with George's pretentious ex-wife, Sloane, and his hateful, spoiled daughter, Hayden. "I just want to go home."

"No problem. I'll take you."

After settling me into his car, Tony jogged toward Mika. Through the rain splattered windshield, I watched the two men exchange a few words before Tony hurried back and climbed in behind the wheel. As he started the engine, I couldn't help but exhale a heavy sigh. The funeral was over. Yet the anxiety and fears that had eaten at me for the past four days weren't gone. They'd simply been replaced by new ones.

A long, unrelenting list spooled through my head. Most pressing, I had to find a job and a new place to live. Since Hayden was George's only heir, I wouldn't be welcome in his stately mansion after the will was read. Even though his elegant home on the shore of Lake Michigan had been my legal residence for the past two and a half years, his vile daughter would force me out as soon as she possibly could. I had a little reprieve, though. Reed Landes, the executor of George's estate, had assured me that I was welcome to stay until Master's affairs had been settled. But the clock was ticking, and time was running out. The fairy tale was at its end.

Staring out the foggy window, I watched the scenery rush past while I tempered the growing ache to crawl into bed, snuggle between the sheets, and absorb the waning vestiges of George's scent. Hold tight to his ghost for as long as possible before I had to find a way to say goodbye.

"If you need someone to talk to…someone to help you work through the stages. My door is always—"

"What stages, Tony?" I cut him off with a scathing glare. "There are no stages. There's nothing but a hole in my heart the size of the

SEIZE ME

universe. There's not a damn thing you can do or say to wake me up from this nightmare."

He cast a sideways glance and pressed his lips in a narrow line while waves of tension rolled off his body, filling the scant distance between us. No doubt, he was pissed at my snippy reply. Good. Maybe he'd shut up and drive and stop making me feel like one of his patients.

"The stages of grief, Leagh," he replied, dashing my dreams of a silent trip home. "You're not ready to move past denial and anger yet. I get that. I'm simply extending the offer. When the time comes and you're ready to start healing again, I'm here if you need to talk."

"Healing?" A humorless laugh escaped my lips. "I'm trying to survive ten seconds at a time without falling apart at the seams. I haven't even started thinking about healing."

"There's nothing wrong with falling apart. It takes time, but it will get better."

"I'm not sure I want it to," I murmured as he turned onto the long driveway.

It was my first trip back to the house since George died. Julianna and Mika had whisked me away to stay with them after Master's body had been taken to the mortuary. I didn't want to stay there alone. At the time, the thought of roaming from room to room, assaulted by his memories, seemed painfully masochistic. But now, I yearned to wrap the precious times we'd shared around me, savor them, and mourn the loss of my best friend, alone.

When Tony parked in front of the red brick and mortar steps, I turned to face him. "Thanks for the ride and, um, for the offer to pick my brain. I'm going to pass for now, but I'll see you around."

Cold rain pelted my face as I hurried from the vehicle. Aware of Tony waiting for me to get inside safely, I dug out the keys from the bottom of my purse. Glancing up, I noticed an envelope taped to the front door with my name scrolled in feminine penmanship.

I slid my key into the lock, but it wouldn't turn. When I tried a second time, my heart sank. No doubt Hayden had done her worst. Tearing the note from the door, I pulled out the pages from within and began to read.

Ms. Bennett,

5

Please find enclosed a Restraining Order forbidding you from this property. There will be no other form of communication to you from either of us. My mother and I refuse to acknowledge your disgusting association with my father. Be advised that his upstanding reputation in the community, and courts, shall remain unblemished. Should you make any slanderous remarks hinting otherwise, we will file suit against you for defamation of character.

Your personal property is exactly where it belongs—on the side of the house—in the trash. Take what you can salvage and leave. You will be arrested for trespassing if you set foot on these premises ever again.

Good riddance. May you rot in hell!

Hayden Marston

As I stepped back from the door, the rain dripped from my hair and slithered like cold fingers down my spine. Stunned by the note's contents, I forced myself to re-read it once, then twice, while my guts turned to liquid. A tingling wave of panic spread through my limbs, and the tears I'd courageously fought for days filled my eyes and spilled down my cheeks.

"Leagh? Is everything okay? What's that letter say?"

Turning toward the sound of Tony's voice, I saw his torso poised between the partially opened car door and the frame. I knew he was watching me, even though his face had blurred from my tears.

Realizing that all my belongings were shoved into the trash, I dropped the papers, my keys, and my purse and sprinted toward the side of the house. A desolate cry, like a wounded animal, tore from my throat and echoed in my ears.

Panting and crying, I flipped the lid of the garbage receptacle open. The scent of feces and decay permeated my senses. Stumbling back, I gagged and sucked in a breath of fresh air before peering inside. Paper plates filled with dog excrement had been placed on top of open and leaking cans of pungent tuna fish and tomato paste, while raw and broken eggs jiggled as drops of rain landed upon the slippery membranes. A bottle of Italian salad dressing lay on its side, dripping oil and vinegar, mixing in with the sludge. Gazing at the putrid concoction, I spied some of the expensive clothing Master had given me as gifts saturated in the pungent muck.

Rage roared through me. Staring into the slurry, I remembered how George would pull packages with big red bows from behind his back. *"I like to spoil you with pretty things, my wild little tiger."*

Anguish stabbed, slicing deep. Turning, I spotted a long branch that had fallen from the bare oak tree. Plucking it from the ground, I carefully slid the forked bough beneath the plates of dog poop and tossed them onto the grass. Spearing the sleeve of my favorite Chanel blouse, I lifted it from beneath the slimy mixture. The dusty pink silk had been completely shredded. It was totally ruined.

Rooting around the amalgam, I shoved my wet hair from my face, desperate to find one piece of salvageable clothing. But every item had been obliterated by Sloane and Hayden's savagery. Why had they done such a vile thing? It wasn't as if I'd stolen the man away from either of them. It was my understanding that Sloane had wanted out of the marriage. At least that's how George had explained it. He'd been relieved to be rid of the shrew. The bitch's venomous cruelty made no sense whatsoever.

When I spied the handcrafted wooden box that stored my collar, hope soared. Using the branch, I lifted it from the barrel and carefully lowered it to the ground. Easing open the lid, I gasped. My treasured leather collar had been cut to bits, mingled among slivers of mutilated photographs. Every treasured snapshot of me and George had been reduced to confetti. My whole world tilted on its axis.

Dropping the lid down, I threw my head back. An inhuman cry of anguish erupted from deep in my belly, and fury exploded outward. Seeing red, I shoved the receptacle onto its side and fell to my knees. Tears streamed down my face as I poked through the slop, cursing and screaming, in search of one minuscule memento of my life with George that the malicious bitches hadn't destroyed.

"Hey. Stop, Leagh. Stop!" Tony commanded, wrapping me in a bear hug from behind and strangling my hot rage. Pinning my arms against my sides, he rendered me immobile. I shrieked and struggled, resenting the hell out of his interference.

"Calm down. There's nothing left for you here."

"I know that, dammit! Do you think I'm blind? Those whores

destroyed it all. They took every piece of him away from me. I have nothing. Nothing!" I screamed.

"Come on. Let's get you out of here."

"No!" I snapped. "There's got to be something in there. Something they haven't ruined. Let me go. I need to find it. I need to find...*something*."

"Don't do this, sweetheart. Don't let them wreck your soul. Come on. We need to get out of the rain."

"Fuck you! Fuck them! Fuck the rain! Fuck everything!" Ranting, I tossed the stick aside and clawed from Tony's grasp. Scooting away, tears flowed as Sloane and Hayden's malice shredded what was left of my heart.

Tony crouched, staring at me, as rain dripped down his face. His wet, dark hair was plastered against his head. And his dark tailored suit had grown wrinkled and soggy. Gazing into his eyes, I watched his concerned expression transform into a sympathetic frown. My blood boiled.

"I don't need you or your damn pity. Go away. Just leave me alone."

"Pity?" Tony shook his head. "It's definitely not pity, and there's no way in hell I'm leaving you here. Not like this."

"You have to. Get out. It's for your own good. You can't be here if they come back."

Narrowing his eyes in suspicion, he tilted his head. "Why not?"

"Because I'm going to kill them. I'm going to take the knife or scissors or whatever they used to shred everything I owned and I'm going to slice their fucking throats. That's why!"

Tony's eyes widened for a fraction of a second before he eased toward me. "You can't do that, Leagh. You'd spend the rest of your life in jail. George wouldn't want that."

"I don't care. Don't you get it?" I sobbed. "I don't care about anything anymore."

My shoulders slumped, and every cell in my body succumbed to the piercing shards of grief. Wilted and sobbing, I gazed into Tony's chocolate eyes, feeling more alone than I ever had in my life.

"But I do, angel," Tony whispered in a soft plea as he pulled me to his chest. I clung to him as if he were a lifeline, one I wasn't sure I deserved but was grateful for, nonetheless. "I'm taking you home with me. We'll figure out the rest later."

I wanted to fight him...kick and scream until he left me to wallow in my misery. But most of all, I wanted to howl at George for leaving me alone, scared, and unprotected. Yet, I couldn't find the strength. I was exhausted and suffocating beneath the injustice of it all. Without challenge, Tony plucked me off the ground, cradled me in his arms, and carried me back to his car.

Easing me onto the soft leather seat, Tony clicked the safety belt at my hip. Hayden's wretched letter sat on the dashboard next to my purse and keys. My stomach swirled as her threats gnawed at me. Tony glanced at the envelope with a sour expression, and I was certain he'd read its contents. The fact that he'd meddled in my private business would have normally stung my pride, but at the moment, I didn't have the energy to give a damn.

He opened up the glove box and handed me a package of wet towelettes. Wiping my hands as he pulled away from the house, I didn't look back...I couldn't. Tony was right; there was nothing left for me there. All tangible reminders of my life with George were gone. Destroyed. Those vile bitches had taken everything but my memories. I worried even those wouldn't be enough to soothe this unrelenting pain.

Hayden's frightening threats spooled in my head; no matter how hard I tried, I couldn't push them away. If a whisper of George's association with Genesis got out, I'd be the one she and Sloane would come after. I needed to ask Mika to talk to the members and ask them not to breathe a word. Both he and Julianna had extended their home and hearts over the past four days, and I hated asking them for more favors. Needing help from others made me feel inadequate and incapable of taking care of myself. Hell, it took me months before I relied on George.

Squeezing my eyes tight, memories of the horrific night he died flooded my brain.

George and I had spent a lovely Sunday snuggled by the fire. I remember thinking how much I treasured our weekends when he was more relaxed and playful and not distracted by his busy docket schedule. We'd talked about taking a vacation to Taos, New Mexico in the spring. George loved the desert, but his passion was perusing the numerous art galleries. He had an amazing eye for contemporary art.

In hindsight, I should have known something more sinister than heartburn was at play when a pained expression settled over his face and he rubbed his chest.

"Are you all right?" I'd asked him.

"Yes, girl. I'm fine. Just a bit of indigestion is all. Come; let's go to bed. I'll take some antacid after I'm done teasing and tormenting you. But right now, I want to hear you moan and scream my name." A wolfish grin had spread across George's lips as he'd stood and offered me his hand. I took it, marveling at the soft velvet skin of his fingers.

I remember staring at the salt and pepper scruff shading his chin as he tied me to the bed and placed the quick release line in my palm. Every time George tied me up, he insisted I had an escape, in case of an emergency. Not often did I fixate on our forty-three-year age difference—except during bondage play. George's zest for life had always made him seem younger than his sixty-nine years. And with my fist squeezed around the safety loop, I sent up a silent prayer that I wouldn't have to use it.

I should have prayed harder.

Guilt washed over me, filling my veins with icy regret. Sitting in Tony's car, my life tattered and torn, I'd have given anything to hear George's voice...just once more. Swallowed up by a surge of anguish, I had no idea how I was going to survive without him. He'd been the center of my whole world.

From day one, the distinguished judge had made me—a below minimum wage waitress at a popular café near the courthouse—feel special. Each morning he walked through the door, I found myself pausing to admire the aura of command that rolled off him. George had been impressed that by my third day on the job, I'd met him at his regular booth with his usual order of coffee and danish. By the fifth day, Friday, he thanked me for his breakfast and invited me to sit with him for a few minutes.

Conversations with George were never brief; the man loved to talk. A bittersweet smile tugged the corner of my mouth. More than once, my boss threatened to fire me for neglecting my other customers, but I didn't care. Every second I spent with George was like Christmas morning. I found myself going to bed, looking forward to the next day and his visit.

He was sweet and kind and larger than life. His quick wit and carefree mien only intensified his intelligence and compassion. Sometimes, he'd stay after the breakfast crowd had thinned. He'd ask me questions with such genuine concern that I'd spilled my shameful secrets and lofty dreams... things I'd never told another living soul.

George never judged or condemned the choices I'd made, the ones that caused me to flee Atlanta in the middle of the night. He simply listened with a benevolent heart, lending sage advice on ways for me to live a happy life and remain safe.

From the very start, he'd wrapped me in his protection, even filing a restraining order on my behalf. It was his nature. He was forever asking if I had enough money to pay my bills or buy groceries. Even when I assured him I was managing just fine, he would fold a generous tip into my palm with explicit instructions.

"Go buy yourself something lacy and naughty. And when I come in tomorrow, you're going to tell me if you're wearing it under your uniform." His words teemed with innuendo, and he'd flash me a wolfish grin that always set me ablaze. His command was intoxicating and arousing, and like a drug, I was hooked.

Before long, George asked me to jot down my weekly schedule for him. Popping by on the nights I worked the late shift, when the café was quiet, we'd sit and chat over a piece of pie or an ice cream sundae. He made me laugh, and for the first time in a long time, the darkness gave way and light filtered through my life. He'd given me a priceless gift.

Although George could never be termed drop dead gorgeous, his charismatic soul stole my breath. He was my knight in shining armor and before I knew it, I'd fallen head over heels for the man.

As if on auto-pilot, my thoughts circled back to the fateful night he'd tied me to our bed. The pleasure he induced was euphoric, but even when the wave crested, I was hauntingly aware something was terribly wrong.

Fear, white and hot, sliced through my bliss. I raised my head and peered down between my legs. George's head lolled onto the mattress; his body deathly still.

"Master?" I shrieked.

He didn't answer.

Didn't move.

Didn't flinch.

"George!" I screamed. Adrenaline thundered through me.

Nothing.

"Oh, no. No! No!" I wailed.

An inky surge of panic consumed me. Fighting the restraints, I tugged and yanked, desperate to break free. Remembering the quick release line clutched in my palm, I yanked hard, but nothing happened. The ropes remained firmly cinched. Terror seized me as I thrashed against the bindings. Pulling and tugging the rope in my palm, it finally loosened. With a shout of relief, I clawed the cords off my wrists. Rising up on my elbows, I dug my heels into the mattress, scooted backward, then leapt to my hands and knees. Scampering to the end of the bed, I discovered George wasn't breathing.

I reached beneath his jaw but couldn't feel a pulse. My heart pounded in my ears, and tears stung my eyes. Wrestling against his substantial weight, I managed to roll him onto his side, but momentum carried him onto his back, and I was helpless to keep him from sliding to the floor. His eyes were open, staring straight through me. His glistening mouth was slack and agape.

"No! No!" I cried. Bounding off the bed, I crouched next to his motionless body and screamed his name. There was no response.

I pressed my ear to his chest, hearing nothing but deafening silence. Terror spread through my limbs in tingling pinpricks. Jumping from his lifeless body, I raced to the phone. I had no memory of what I'd said to the emergency operator. I only remembered that her litany of questions drove my panic level higher. I didn't want to talk; I wanted help for George.

"Just send a fucking ambulance!" I screamed and hung up. Racing to the foyer, I disengaged the security system and unlocked the front door.

Sprinting back to our bedroom, I heard the phone ring. Ignoring the incessant sound, I straddled his soft belly. Tears spilled to the silvery hairs on his chest, and the sound of my screams echoed off the walls. Flattening my palm against his sternum, I pressed my other hand over it and began CPR compressions to his heart.

"Come back to life... back to me. Don't leave me. Please don't leave me, Master," I wailed. "I need you. No one can keep me safe but you. Please. Please. Don't leave me. I'm so scared."

Pinching his nose closed with my fingers, I pressed my mouth to his. A sob tore from my throat as his lips fluttered lifelessly beneath mine.

"Breathe, George. Please...Breathe," I begged as I repeated the steps over and over. But it was no use I couldn't revive him.

With a mournful roar, I fell to his chest. Nuzzling my face against his neck, I howled as all my dreams disintegrated.

"No!" I barked. Sitting up, I started administering CPR once again. "You're going to live, dammit! I won't let you leave me like this. I'm not going to let you give up on us."

Time seemed to have stopped, trapping me in a never-ending loop of compressions and exhales into his sagging lips. Sobbing and counting, I stared at George's pallid face as I continued to pump on his chest, unwilling—unable—unready to give up.

"I knew you'd have to leave me someday, but not yet. Please, not yet. I'm not ready to lose you. I need you. Come back to me, George. Come back and love me and keep me safe. Please. Please, George. We're going to Taos. Remember? We'll make love under the stars. I'll buy some silky red garters and model them for you. You love it when I do that. Breathe for me, baby. Please. Just one breath. Please! Please!" Tears spilled down my cheeks, snot dripped from my nose, but I refused to stop bargaining him back to life. "You can take me to Brisbane's for dinner tomorrow night. You love their grilled salmon. I'll order it, too, and you know how I hate salmon. Come on, George. Wake up for me. Please. Please!"

The sound of sirens grew near, and I longed to tug the sheet off the bed, drape it over his naked body, and grant him a sliver of dignity. But

I couldn't stop giving him CPR...Couldn't let go of the hope that he would draw in a gasp of breath and come back to me.

Within seconds, our bedroom was choked with EMTs and police. The chaos and their thunderous voices made me dizzy. Someone wrapped strong arms around my waist and plucked me off George's body, as others swarmed in around him. A uniformed officer helped me into my robe while two somber-faced paramedics quickly opened bags and set up equipment. As the EMTs attached two rectangular white pads to George's chest, the room fell eerily quiet.

"Please, don't hurt him."

My bleak cry of torment pierced the silence as I clutched my waist.

"I've got her," another officer announced, stepping through the doorway.

Gently clasping his hand around my elbow, he led me out of the room and down the hall. He sat on the couch and pulled me next to him, placing his warm hand over mine.

"They'll do everything they can for him, Leagh. Tell me what happened, sweetheart."

Leagh? Sweetheart? I frowned and, for the first time, looked at the officer's face. Staring back at me were familiar hazel eyes. *James.* The young man was a member and Dungeon Monitor at Genesis. Until that moment, I'd forgotten he was on the police force.

"Oh, James," I choked. "Please tell me he's going to be okay. I'm scared."

"They'll do all they can, honey. I know you're scared, but hang in there. We can't give up hope," he said, hugging me to his chest and strumming a hand over my hair.

His kindness was intended to be reassuring, but being away from George, confined to another room, had me crawling out of my skin.

Peeling out of James' embrace, I bolted off the couch.

"What are you doing?" he asked, standing and latching onto my elbow once more.

"I have to get back in there. What if George wakes up and I'm not there? He'll be scared with so many strangers in our room. I need to be there when they bring him back to life."

James gripped my arm with firmness. Compassion swam in his eyes. Holding me tight, he eased me back onto the couch with him.

"The EMTs are doing everything they can. Mika and Julianna will be here in a minute. I phoned them when the call came in and I realized it was George." James' words were measured in a firm but gentle tone. "I need you to stay with me so the medical team can do their job. Okay?"

"Yes, Sir," I responded automatically. James was a switch, which meant he was both a Dominant and a submissive. He fashioned as either a Top or bottom, depending on the type of fulfillment he desired. I'd addressed him as Sir, because George had insisted I view James as a Dominant.

A slight smile tugged his lips, and he nodded. "Good girl. Now take a deep breath and tell me what happened."

I broke down several times as I relived the horrific details to James. He both soothed and coaxed answers from me as he jotted notes in a small spiral notebook. He was a trusted friend and understood the dynamics of my relationship with George. While it gave me a small sense of comfort, it was still hard as hell to speak the words.

Moments later, Mika and Julianna rushed through the door, worry lining their faces. Julianna raced to the couch and kissed the side of my head. Nervously sliding her hand up and down my back as Mika paced, looking as if he'd been kicked in the gut. I fought to keep myself together as James helped me explain to them all that had transpired.

The EMTs had been in the bedroom a long time, and when they finally made their way into the living room, working on George laying on a gurney, their bleak expressions confirmed my biggest fear; my Master was gone...and he wasn't coming back.

A cry of anguish tore from my throat. I felt my heart burst apart and shatter as I sagged against Julianna and sobbed.

Chapter Two

"Leagh?" Tony's deep, velvet voice ripped through the haze of agonizing memories.

"Huh?" I jerked my head in his direction as I swiped away my tears.

He nodded toward a large French Colonial home. "I said, we're here."

Tony pulled the car into the garage after he pressed a button on the visor.

"Come on. We'll get you into a hot shower, and I'll find you some dry clothes. You've been shivering for the past ten miles."

"Okay." I nodded numbly before stepping out of his car.

Once inside, I followed behind him as he weaved his way through a spotless kitchen, past a cozy and inviting family room, and around the corner to a wide-open staircase. His home held an air of comfort and sophistication, which surprised me. I wasn't sure why, but I'd envisioned his bachelor pad looking totally different.

Without a word, I followed him up the stairs, down a long hall, and into a large masculine bedroom.

"I've got a tub and shower in here." Extending his arm toward the spacious bathroom, I stepped in past him and caught his scent. Summer grass, sea air, and erotic spices filled my senses. The walls of my pussy clutched, and my clit tingled. I bit back the gasp rolling in the back of my throat. *What the hell was that?* My cheeks grew hot, and I was caught off guard by my visceral response. *Oh, you did not just go there! You have absolutely no business thinking with your pussy. Especially not with him!*

Many subs at Genesis fell, or dreamed of falling, at Tony's feet. He brought available subs out of the woodwork at the club with his sculpted body, gorgeous face, whiskey brown eyes, thick dark hair, olive skin, and commanding dominance. The man was more than drool-worthy. Hell, he'd even starred in *my* masturbation fantasies— secretly, of course—a time or two. But it was only in my dreams. Never once did I attempt to make them come true.

*Yeah, yeah—he's easy on the eyes. Big deal. This is not the time...*definitely *not the place to let your libido overrule common sense. You're mourning George, for fuck's sake. This is wrong on so many levels.*

I clutched the doorknob with a death-grip as the little voice in my head railed. The bathroom was huge, but with Tony standing so close and smelling so damn enticing, arousal burned low in my belly. Craving him was wrong, but I couldn't rein in my inappropriate reactions. What the hell was wrong with me? I'd just left my Master's gravesite. Waves of shame and guilt sluiced through my veins as I inwardly cursed my heartless hormones.

"Are you hungry?" Tony asked, lagging in the doorway.

Food was out of the question, especially now. My stomach pitched in dishonor and longing. "No," I replied quickly as I raised my head to meet his stare.

His gaze, like hot fingers, scraped over my flesh, sending a shiver rippling through me. Looking as if he'd just climbed out of the shower with his wet, disheveled hair I couldn't keep from gazing at his captivating body... or picturing him naked. The man was incredibly built, but his ruthless Dominant appetite scared the beejeebers out of me.

My stomach growled at the mention of food, calling me out as a liar.

One dark brow arched as he leveled a skeptic look. "When was the last time you ate, Leagh?"

"Um…I don't know. The thought of food makes me…" I wrinkled my nose and placed a palm on my still swirling stomach.

His expression softened, and he stepped closer. The heat of his body spilled over me like a seductive blanket. Reaching up, he brushed a broad finger over my cheek before tucking a strand of wet hair behind my ear. My mouth went dry, and my heart slammed against my ribs.

"You've been through a lot, angel, but you have to take care of yourself. You can't go without eating, or sleeping, or doing things to stay healthy."

I closed my eyes as Tony's finger lingered on my flesh. Memories of George's gentle hands rolled through me on a bittersweet wave. And for a few glorious seconds, I was no longer breathing in the scent of a sadist, who viewed me as an inadequate submissive, but basking beneath the tender touch of my Master back at the house on the shore of Lake Michigan. But when I opened my eyes, Tony speared me with his usual critical gaze, crushing my short reprieve from reality.

It was no secret that he, and others at Genesis, viewed me as a tumultuous *brat*. I tried to turn a blind eye to the looks of disapproval Tony flashed my way. But his annoyance always seemed to pour off him and singe my skin; making it impossible to ignore. I never sought Tony's approval. The only person I needed to please was George. If he was happy with my submission, Tony and the rest of the members could kiss off.

But George was gone. And as Tony leaned closer, the warmth of his fingers upon my cheek, coupled with his damp breath wafting over my lips, perversely turned me on.

I had to be certifiably insane.

The sexual ache mounting within confused the hell out of me. In order to keep my sanity, I reminded myself that Tony's lifestyle tastes required a specific type of sub. I wasn't even in the same ballpark with his passions. I was bunny floggers, clothespins, and bondage—the soft stuff. He was whips, quirts, and blood—a pure sadist. We were on opposite ends of the BDSM spectrum, making my sexual attraction to him even more perplexing, and absurdly ridiculous.

"Did you hear me?" he asked in a whiskey smooth voice.

Holding me with a prickly, piercing gaze, he feathered his finger down my cheek before settling beneath my chin. His subtle claim of control lit me up like a firecracker.

"Yes, Sir. Take care of myself. I will." I cast my eyes to the floor to escape the intensity of his stare.

The room felt like a sauna. The air was thick and electrified. My nipples pebbled, and slick juices oozed between my folds. Why was my body responding to him like this? I hadn't had an orgasm in days, but surely, I could go a few weeks without my hormones going completely off the charts...except obviously not.

George had seen to my needs, almost daily, whether he achieved completion or not. I brutally missed him—not only sexually—but the safety and security he provided. My throat constricted with emotion, and a fat tear rolled down my cheek.

"Awww, Leagh," Tony groaned. Stepping forward, he pulled me against his rugged chest.

The wet heat pouring off his frame, coupled with his potent, manly fragrance, vanished all rational thought from my brain. I pawed at his suit, nuzzled his neck, and writhed against his steely body like a cat in heat. Pressing my mouth against his throat, I felt his pulse hammering beneath my lips while I inhaled deeply...filling my lungs with his masculine scent.

As if possessed by a brazen nymphomaniac, I peeled his jacket over his rugged shoulders. As it fell to the floor, even more inviting heat spilled from beneath his damp cotton dress shirt. Desperate to feel his flesh, I loosened his tie before fumbling with the buttons at his collar. My fingers tangled in the fabric, revealing a tempting glimpse of his tawny flesh. I clung to him, breathless and impatient.

"Fuck, Leagh." he choked out gruffly. "What the hell are you doing, sweetheart?"

"Make love to me, Tony. Please," I implored. Pulling apart the gap in his shirt, I dragged my tongue over his hot, sculpted chest. "I'm so dead inside. Please. Make me feel alive, one more time."

"Leagh," he growled, low and hungry, as he pried me off him.

Staring down at me, Tony's eyes bore the all-familiar look of disdain. I shrunk beneath the crushing weight of my embarrassment. *George.* My wonderful Master hadn't even been in the cold, hard earth an hour and already I was begging another man to fuck me. Guilt slammed in from all directions, obliterating my insane lust.

"Just leave, please," I begged, choking on tears of humiliation.

Tony cupped my chin and tilted my head, forcing me to reveal my shame. "No. You need to know the truth, angel. I've waited forever to hold you...to touch you. If you need me to make you feel alive, I'll gladly do that for you."

I felt my eyes grow wide. "You've wanted *me*? I don't understand what you're talking—"

He pressed a gentle finger to my lips. "Shhh. Not another word. Relax. Let me help you through this."

Tony yanked his tie free, tossing it onto his jacket as he held me with a hypnotic stare. My breath caught in my lungs, and icy waves of panic filled my veins. Animalistic passion reflected in his dark, hooded eyes, and when he peeled away his dampened shirt, I couldn't keep my gaze from sliding over his chiseled body. I studied every inch of him, as if he were a work of art. Longing to reach out and rake my nails through the dark patch of hair between his flat, brown nipples, I could only lick my lips at the tapering trail of dark hair disappearing beneath the waistband of his tented trousers. His erection strained against the zipper, and I swallowed tightly as the air in the room grew even thicker...burning my lungs.

"I've dreamed about you, Leagh. You've been the center of my fantasies since the first night I saw you. I can't get you out of my head. Everything about you drives me wild."

I froze. A million questions sat poised on the tip of my tongue, yet I couldn't string a single word together. It was as if I'd been launched from one disintegrating universe into another.

Without a word, Tony devoured me in a silent, predatory stare. Unable to stop myself, I trailed my fingers over each ridge and plane of his defined shoulders. My fingers tingled as I absorbed the heat of his hard flesh. Leaning in, I nuzzled my nose and lips over the dark, coarse hair on his chest as he slid his hand into my mane and gently massaged my scalp. His hot breath slid over the shell of my ear, rendering me speechless as I trembled beneath his touch.

Taking a step back, he gazed into my eyes and began unbuttoning my blouse. Steady and sure, his strong, dominant touch helped still the chaos in my brain. Closing my eyes, I gave in to the comfort he offered and savored the brush of his fingers over my skin as he slowly stripped me bare.

"Look at me, Leagh," he ordered in a raspy command.

My lids fluttered open. His predatory gaze was imposing... stripping my body and my soul. It was too much. Too possessive. Too overwhelming, and I dropped my gaze.

"Don't touch me with your eyes," I whispered.

Tony sidled in closer, his breath skimmed over my neck. "What do you want me to touch you with, angel?"

Everything. Desperate to feel—something—anything except the ground crumbling beneath my feet, I sucked in a ragged breath. "Your hands. Just your hands. Nothing else."

"But my lips will get jealous," he replied in a provocative drawl.

I gasped as Tony eased back, trailing his fingertips from my collar bone, down both arms. His decadent beauty made my heart flutter and my libido rage. He was stealing pieces of my broken heart, and I did nothing to stop him. I didn't want to. His compassion brought something more than grief to stir inside me; it brought a flicker of life. Whether it was right or wrong, I ached for more—if only for a little while.

Leaning in, he lowered his mouth. My lips parted, welcoming, needing, wanting. The brush of his kiss was gentle, but the feel of his hot flesh sent a jolt straight to my core. Yielding beneath him, I skimmed my fingers over the stubble darkening his jaw.

Tony swallowed my tiny whimper; then his kiss turned urgent. Blistering me with demand, a deep groan rumbled low in his chest. His hands roved over my naked flesh as our tongues tangled in a torrid dance. The air grew thick in anticipation, and when his palms grazed over my rigid nipples, I moaned. The walls of my weeping pussy fluttered hungrily.

Gripping the cheeks of my ass, he pulled me flush against his generous erection. His cock jerked and nudged my belly while blistering heat penetrated his trousers.

Trying to compartmentalize my madness, I pretended it was George's desperate kiss stealing my breath, his hot body controlling my weakness. But he'd never kissed me like *this*. I couldn't hold on to the elusive fantasy, and the cold hard truth slammed through me like a blast of arctic wind.

Tearing from Tony's lips, I issued a mournful wail. Tears filled my eyes and spilled down my cheeks as I backed away. Shame, guilt, and embarrassment collided with remorse. Its ugly bite was vicious.

"I'm a... I... I'm a terrible person. How can I do something like this to George?" I sobbed. Wrapping my arms around myself, I curled my shoulders in, trying to hide my shame.

"You're not a terrible person, Leagh," Tony whispered as he cupped my chin, forcing me to meet his gaze. "You're human. You're not betraying George, your relationship with him, or his memory. Don't start beating yourself up for what you're feeling. It's a defense mechanism. It's very common. When people lose a loved one, they sometimes feel an overwhelming need for physical contact. It's perfectly normal. Your psyche is seeking validation that you're still alive...still breathing. Physical contact with another person is your subconscious confirming that you're still here. Trust me, angel. Everything you're feeling is normal."

"There is nothing *normal* about this," I hissed. Taking another step back, I glared at him. "I just left the gravesite of my Master... my best friend. I've dishonored everything about him... about us. It isn't right being here...naked and kissing a man that hates me. Please, Tony. Please, just...leave."

"Hate you?" he blinked. A stunned expression lined his face. "What the hell? I don't hate you, Leagh. I just told you I've struggled with the fact that I've wanted you for years. What in the world have I ever done to make you think I hate you?"

"Maybe hate is too strong a word. You always look at me like I'm a piece of dog shit stuck to your shoe. You call me brat every chance you get. I know you think I'm worthless as a submissive. I may not be a rocket scientist or college educated, like you and George, but I know when someone is looking down their nose at me. I'm not stupid."

"What the fuck are you talking about?" Tony asked incredulously. "I've never looked down on you, Leagh. You *are* a brat, but in a spunky, fun way. You top from the bottom constantly, but you don't do it maliciously, and you're certainly not a damn drama queen like some of the other subs. Who the hell do you think I am to judge you, anyway? I'm not Dom of the Universe, nor do I want to be." His expression softened as he stepped closer. "Sweetheart, I never meant to offend you. I'm sorry; I was only teasing. I thought you knew that. I'd never purposefully hurt your feelings."

"You didn't," I lied.

"Yes, I did," Tony corrected with a frown. "Listen. You're feisty and unpredictable, and you don't conform to traditional submissive ways. But guess what? That's exactly how George wanted and needed you. He thrived as your Dominant. The day he found you, he turned into a whole new man. You brought joy to his life. You may not have been his soulmate, but he cared deeply about you."

His words cut like a knife. I knew from the beginning George was a protector. It didn't matter to me that the fireworks were missing in our relationship. I'd wanted stability, safety, compassion. He'd given me all that and more... and I'd loved him for it.

"I cared about him, too," I sobbed. "That's why it's so wrong for me to be with you like this."

"I've already explained that to you, sweetheart. There's nothing to be ashamed of. Feelings aren't right or wrong; they're just feelings."

"No. What I'm feeling is wrong. *Way* wrong," I choked.

Tony's expression took on that familiar icy edge. His eyes narrowed, and a ripple of fear mixed with arousal swept down my spine.

"What did I do now?" I cried in exasperation.

A deprecating smile tugged on one side of his mouth. His condescending expression vanished. "You didn't do anything. It's me."

"I don't understand. That look you just had on your face, it's the same angry look you give me at the club."

"That's why you thought I hated you?" He shook his head. "No,

Leagh. I don't hate you. I never have. I spent every night watching you, despising myself for wanting what I couldn't have. You've always turned me inside out, angel. I was angry with me, because I ached for you so fucking bad."

I swallowed tightly. No matter how I tried to deny it, I'd always been keenly aware of Tony. He drew me to him like a magnet... calling to me in some strange primitive way. But instead of analyzing the prickly sensation his gaze induced, I had simply convinced myself he was disgusted by my lack of submission.

The puzzle pieces quickly fell into place. I never understood why I had to look away when he scened with Destiny, Naughty, Silver-Sin, or other pain sluts. Watching him smooth his hand over the sub's skin or sink his teeth into her flesh, I had wondered what it would feel like to be so completely claimed.

Even though Tony's need for pain scared me, his dominance was so commanding, I secretly dreamed of sampling a taste. George would have been crushed if he'd ever suspected I harbored such ridiculous fantasies, especially at the hands of another man. One of George's biggest fears was that I'd someday ache for the affection of someone younger. He never outright confessed it, but he hinted from time to time. Likewise, George worried about our age difference, but I always reassured him that I was happy and content having him as my Master and lover.

Suddenly, it made sense in a bizarre and fucked up way. I'd been secretly attracted to Tony the whole time I was with George. I tensed, fearing I'd never really loved George as much as I claimed. *Don't be an idiot. Of course you loved George. You lusted after Tony just like every other sub at the club. Don't make a mountain out of a molehill. Your heart always belonged to George.*

"Oh. I didn't know that you..."

"No. Evidently not." He leaned in close to my ear. "What if I told you that I dream about slamming you up against the wall and driving my cock into your sweet, soft body until my legs turn to rubber?"

My heart hammered against my ribs. His words ignited a scorching visual that excited and scared me half to death. I bristled, pulling back in confusion, and tried to extinguish the flames licking my core.

25

"Why are you telling me all this *now*? Why didn't you ever—"

"Say something to you? I couldn't." A melancholy smile curled his sensual mouth. "You belonged to another. I abide by the code of conduct. I might be a sadist, but I'm an ethical one."

My throat was dry. My body trembled. His words turned me inside out. "I'm flattered, but this... it's pointless. You already know I don't do pain. And I'm not mentally equipped for anything right now, much less this conversation. So, if you'll just leave, I'll get cleaned up."

Tony tensed, straightened, and issued a sharp nod. Stepping around me, he leaned in and turned on the shower, taking his time to adjust the water temperature.

I stared at his muscles as they bunched and flexed, wondering if I possessed the power to resist the temptation of his words, his body, or the gnawing need to feel whole again. I closed my eyes and sucked in a ragged breath, welcoming the chilling grief of losing George to fill me once again. It was daunting and painful but so much safer than craving something I had no business wanting...Tony.

Jerking my eyes open as his fingertips skimmed along my shoulder, he smiled and extended his hand. My fingers entwined with his, and once again, my emotions unfurled like a flag in a hurricane. For one brief moment, I ignored the pendulum of doubt swinging inside me and took refuge in his rugged arms.

"Whatever you need, Leagh, tell me. I'll give it to you."

Sadly, the one thing I needed, Tony could never give me; George. "If only it were that simple. There's nothing you can do for me, Tony. What I need, no one can give."

"What is it you need, Leagh? I'll find a way to make it happen."

"George alive, to keep me safe."

"Awww, sweetheart. I can't replace George, but you'll always be safe with me," Tony murmured against my ear. "Come on. Let's get you in the shower. You're shivering again."

Tony meant well, but he didn't know a thing about my past or how to protect me...let alone who I needed protection from. That was a whole other nightmare I had no desire to revisit.

Steam billowed over the glass enclosure like a fog machine.

"I think I can take it from here, thanks."

"Right," Tony nodded, grimly. "I'll go find you some clothes. Take some time and relax. You'll have plenty of hot water."

I watched as he left, closing the door behind him.

Stepping beneath the spray of the shower, I closed my eyes and let the soothing heat melt the tension from my shoulders and neck.

I thought about all the reasons I shouldn't let my guard down around Tony. Oil and water didn't mix, no matter how fiercely you shook them up. I thought about Hayden and her disgusting threats, wondering what George would think of his darling daughter now. If he were still alive, she never would have done any of those things. Hayden would paint on her plastic smile and wrap him around her little finger, like she always did.

"Oh, George, if only you could have seen through her façade."

The weight of the world lay heavy on my shoulders, and my insecure tears mingled with the water. Being alone again was scary, but not nearly as daunting as the loss of safety George had provided.

Without warning, the shower door opened, and Tony stepped inside. Naked. Erect. Gorgeous. I couldn't help but stare at his chiseled body and turgid cock.

"What are you doing?" I squeaked, trying not to choke on the bubbling anxiety and hunger pumping through my veins.

"I'm going to take care of you, like I promised. Turn around. Let me wash your back," Tony instructed as he reached for the shower gel and a loofah ball.

Unable to peel my gaze from his thick erection, I clenched my fists, fighting the urge to slide my palm around his swollen shaft. The distended veins and weeping broad crest were disturbingly inviting. My mouth watered, and I yearned to drop to my knees and taste the pearls of pre-come glistening on the tip. His cock jerked, as if reading my mind.

"We shouldn't be doing this," I protested as I struggled to suck the humid air into my lungs.

"We're not doing anything, angel. I'm only here to shower you... take care of you. I'm not going to damage your fragile heart." He bent forward and placed a sweet kiss on my forehead.

"Stop doing this to me," I gasped.

"Doing what?"

"You can't come in here, all hard and tempting, and tell me you're only going to wash my back. I haven't had an orgasm for four damn days. You being in here looking all good and shit...I don't need this kind of torture."

"Watch your language, sweetheart," he warned. "If you need an orgasm, Leagh, I'll give you one. But it won't be with my cock. Do you understand?"

"Oh, I understand perfectly. Thanks, but no thanks. I'll let my fingers do the walking when I get settled into a hotel. But right now, I need you to get out of here, so I can shower without having to stare at that." I jerked my head toward his cock. "I'm capable of washing my back, my hair, and...everything in between. I've been doing it for years."

"Turn around, Leagh. Now."

His tone demanded that my body obey even as my head screamed, *"No!"* Stealing one more glance at his engorged cock, I exhaled a heavy sigh, turned, and placed my palms upon the cool marble tile. The water sprayed over my face, and I closed my eyes, hoping it would wash away my embarrassment. Raw and on edge, I started as Tony's soap slick hands and scratchy loofah caressed my skin. His very touch set my skin ablaze. So many emotions overran my senses. I was helpless to capture a single one.

"Just relax, sweetheart. That's all I want you to do. Nothing else," he whispered in a silky-smooth timbre.

Focused on the slow glide of Tony's slippery fingers, my jagged nerves seemed to smooth beneath his languid touch. When he cupped the cheeks of my ass, I instinctively arched back and filled his palms.

"Behave," he warned with a chuckle. "This isn't exactly easy for me. I'm trying to be a gentleman, and that's difficult enough without you adding to it, sweetheart."

"I'm sorry," I whispered, feeling the burn of embarrassment rise on my cheeks.

"Don't be. I can handle it. I want this to be all about you, so just focus on relaxing for me, angel."

I closed my eyes and did as he requested. A soft flicker of warmth began to replace the cold void inside. I drank in the feel of his strong fingers massaging my scalp as he worked in an earthy-scented shampoo. His deep voice, full of praise, felt like a blanket of peace, one I longed to gather in tight and cling to until the turbulent sea of emotions inside me calmed.

"Spin back around, Leagh," he murmured as he gently cupped my shoulder.

Facing him again, I wasn't prepared to see the depth of desire reflecting in his eyes. Before I could second-guess my actions, I slanted my lips over his. The connection overwhelmed me, and with it, a level of peace I hadn't expected. I was ravenous for more. My kiss grew more insistent, and he met my demand with his own. Sinking his tongue deep inside my mouth, Tony tightened a fist in my hair, gripping until my scalp stung.

Leaning his solid body against mine, he pressed my back against the cool tiles as his soapy fingers toyed and teased my nipples. Plucking and pinching, he tugged on each elongated peak. Need bubbled and burned beneath my clit, and I rolled my hips, desperate to feel his glorious cock drive deep inside me. Tony issued a rumbling growl and pivoted until his hard length lay throbbing upon my thigh. I felt him smile against my mouth as he swallowed my whimpers of frustration.

Gliding his slick fingers down my belly, his palm came to rest above my mound. Easing back, he peppered kisses over my jaw, down my throat and collarbone, until he captured a tight nipple between his teeth. When he nipped at the sensitized nub, my blood surged and every nerve ending sang in demand. I closed my eyes as he tugged first one nipple then the other, before laving his tongue over each aching peak. Dancing his fingertips over my swollen folds, he teased and tempted before his hand vanished entirely. I writhed and cried out in aggravation.

"Open your eyes, Leagh," Tony commanded. "Look at me."

Lifting my heavy lids, I gazed at him as he studied me intently. A wary expression lined his face.

"I'll take you where you need to go, sweetheart. But you're with me. I want your eyes open and staring into mine." His raspy voice was like a match setting fire to an already smoldering blaze. The flames licked so hot and bright, they nearly consumed me. "This is between me and you. I won't be a substitute for George. Do you understand?"

Tony's words pierced deep. His image blurred as tears stung my eyes and memories of George flooded in a deluge of pain.

Tony grimaced. "I know you're fragile right now, and I don't want to add to your pain."

I wanted to laugh at the irony—a sadist promising not to hurt me. Tony pulled me to his chest. His engorged cock scorched and throbbed upon my stomach.

"No matter how badly I want to make you feel better, I know you're not ready. But damn, baby, you're so perfect," he murmured.

"*You're so perfect.*" George had uttered those same words right before he died. Tensing as if I'd been immersed in a pool of ice, remorse and guilt suffused every cell, imploding in a rush of unholy sorrow.

Struggling from Tony's arms, I shook my head. "You're right. I'm not ready for any of this. It would be best if you just got out." Wrapping my arms around myself, I held in the ugly sludge of disgust bleeding within.

"Leagh, you've done nothing—"

"Wrong?" I mocked. "Oh, I've done plenty wrong. But I don't blame you. I blame myself."

"No," Tony challenged, wrapping his broad hands around my cheeks. "I won't allow you to punish yourself because I touched you."

"That's not what I'm beating myself up for," I sniffed. Shaking my head, I backed away from him. "It's not because you touched me…it's because I liked it."

His brown eyes shimmered in understanding, and he let out a heavy sigh. "You're alive, Leagh. And whether you believe me or not, you needed that reminder. We've done nothing for you to be ashamed of. George wouldn't want you to slip away into the dark abyss. He'd want you to go on and be happy."

"I appreciate what you're saying. Really, I do. There's no way I can forgive myself." Tears slid down my cheeks as my stomach pitched.

"Leagh, he's dead and gone."

30

Tony's words awakened a volcano of anger inside me. As it erupted, I drew back my hand and slapped his face. "Don't say that!"

He gaped at me. Surprise, mixed with anger, gleamed in his eyes before he closed them and clenched his jaw. As if trying to calm a raging thunderstorm within, Tony exhaled a deep breath before looking down at me.

"I'm sorry, Leagh. He's gone, but you're still here. You can't stop living, angel."

"Why are you doing this to me?"

"Doing what?"

"Making me feel things I don't want to feel. Shoving things in my face that I don't want to deal with."

"To prove you can't pull down the shutters and hide from life."

"Maybe I want to."

"I'm not going to let you."

Great. "I know what you're doing, Tony."

"Yeah, what's that?"

"You're trying to crawl inside my head and fix me. But unlike your patients, *I* didn't make an appointment."

"Look, all I'm trying to do is help you start healing in healthy ways."

A bitter laugh seeped from my throat. "Healthy? You've got to be kidding. I have to find a new place to live and get a job. Hell, I don't know if I can put one foot in front of the other. Not to mention, I have no clue how I'm supposed to sail through this bitter sea of despair churning inside me. And you've got the gall to stand there and tell me my guilt isn't healthy? I've got news for you, Tony. My mental health is the last damn thing on my list right now."

"Then let me help you," he implored.

"How? Do you want to lay me on your couch and let you delve into my head? No, wait. I know. You want to cuff me to a cross and spank my ass, right?"

A slow wicked smile tugged at his lips. "I have no doubt a spanking would probably do you a world of good. And if I laid you out on a couch, it would be to have you beneath me."

Even as anger blazed in my veins, a hotter flame coiled in my womb and spread through me at the visual his words conjured in my brain.

"Stop. Please, Tony. Just stop."

"Dammit, Leagh. I want to help you through this."

"I didn't ask for—"

"No. And you never will. You're too damn stubborn." A wry grin tugged at his lips. "Finish up your shower and stop drowning in your damn guilt. Understood?"

"Yes, Sir," I snipped, plastering a sarcastic smile on my lips.

"Oh yeah, you're in serious need of a spanking." He grinned. "Your clothes are on the chaise. I'll meet you downstairs." Tony leaned into the droning water and kissed my forehead before he stepped out of the shower.

I exhaled a sigh fraught with anguish, sexual frustration, guilt, and doubt. Each emotion swirled like an F5 tornado. Oz had nothing on my surreal life.

With a huff, I smoothed a handful of conditioner over my hair. Tony wasn't going to give up or go away. It both rankled and, oddly, pacified my ragged nerves. I had to find a way to deal with him. No doubt, my head and heart would soon become mortal enemies.

The image of Tony naked was one I couldn't erase. Dark erotic eyes. Defined bronze body, wet and slick. His massive cock stood at attention like a well-trained soldier, with its swollen crest stretched tight, all but screaming for relief. I'd no more licked my lips imagining the taste of him before images of George shoved their way into my brain.

A gritty sludge of contrition enveloped me. Easing onto the shower floor, I tucked my knees up to my chin and cried.

Chapter Three

Emerging from the shower after a lengthy semi-therapeutic cry, I spied the pile of clothes waiting for me on the chaise. If I let him, Tony would take care of me, at least for a while. But I was a smart girl and knew tending to an emotional cripple took a staggering toll. Not only was it taxing, but it drained you and claimed a piece of your soul. There was no way I'd put Tony through that shit.

Dragging the towel through my hair, I pulled on the clothes he'd left me. Staring at the socks on my feet, they reminded me of clown shoes. Glancing up in the mirror, I shook my head. I looked like a poster child for a thrift store.

The doorbell rang as I hung up my wet clothes. *Wonderful.* It was probably Tony's girlfriend or a pain slut looking for relief. "Just my luck," I grumbled under my breath. The thought of him explaining to anyone why he was babysitting an emotional wreck made my skin crawl. Why did I let him bring me to his house in the first place?

"Because the bitches of Rockford Estates changed the fucking locks," I murmured in disgust.

"Enough is enough," I scolded as I started digging through my purse. I needed to call Julianna and ask if she and Mika could pick me up or drop off my car. The need to get out from under Tony's roof pressed in heavily. Plucking out my phone, I punched in Julianna's number. Raising the device to my ear, I expected to hear her sweet hello. What I heard instead was a computerized message.

"We're sorry, but your account is no longer in service. Please contact our billing department if you have questions regarding your contract. Goodbye."

"What the hell? Who turned off my phone?" As the words spilled from my lips, anger began to pump through me. Sloane or Hayden. They'd been a couple of busy bitches while I was at Mika and Julianna's crying my eyes out.

"Motherfucking whores," I hissed, and I threw my phone back inside my purse. "Those motherfuck—"

"Leagh?" Tony tapped on the open door, interrupting my litany of un-ladylike curses.

"What?" I snapped.

"What's wrong?"

"Hayden or Sloane cancelled the service on my cell phone."

His expression of worry morphed into disgust. "Don't worry about it. I'll take you out so you can buy another."

"No. I'll do it," I replied curtly. Closing my eyes, I exhaled. "I'm sorry, Tony. I know you're trying to help, but I just need my car, so I can get out of your hair."

"You're welcome to stay with—"

"No. Don't even say it." I raised my hand and cut him off. "I'm not staying here. I appreciate the offer and the help you've given me today, but I can't stay."

Even as the words rolled off my tongue, I thought how easy it would be to let Tony take care of me. But I'd be a fool to ignore what the constant power struggle between us would entail. Me, needing time to heal and start a new life; him, exerting his dominance and taking control over every aspect of it. Not to mention the sexual temptation I'd be faced with day in and day out. It was a no-win situation.

"You could; you just don't want to." Tony smirked. His sexy brown eyes twinkled, and a shiver skittered through me. Yeah, it was much safer for me if I left. "We'll discuss that later, but right now, you've got some visitors downstairs."

"Who?"

"The gang from the club. Mika called to see if you got home okay. I explained what happened and told him I'd brought you here. So, he spread the word, and they came by here to see you. Come on." With a nod toward the door, Tony extended his hand. I didn't accept, for fear his touch would set off my precarious libido again. I needed to cling to what little sanity I had left.

As I followed him down the stairs, the familiar timbre of Drake's and Mika's voices hummed through the air. I imagined the two bantering, like always, and a roar of laughter all but confirmed my suspicions. The two Doms had been friends for years and loved to swap stories from their past.

I forced a smile before rounding the corner and spied Mika, Julianna, Drake, Trevor, Nick, Dylan, and Savannah, all seated in Tony's cozy family room. Drake and Mika held everyone's rapt attention.

"And I'd just finished uncuffing Trevor when Drake leaned in on the cross." Mika's eyes danced in delight as he recounted his story. "There was this loud crack of splintering wood, and the next thing we know, Drake is face-first on the floor, still gripping the top of the cross. I nearly pissed myself laughing once I made sure he was okay."

"Hey," Drake barked with a grin. "At least I didn't enroll in a macrame class just to learn how to tie knots."

"No, you enlisted in the Navy," Mika jabbed. "Tell me something, bro. Was it for the seamen or the semen?"

"Both, fucker!" Drake beamed with a huge smile.

Laughter filled the room once again, and Trevor issued a forlorn pout.

"Awww, Trevor, don't go getting your feelings hurt. It was long before he met you, boy." Mika gave a gentle nudge to the blond man sitting between him and Drake.

"Here she is," Tony announced as he slid his arm around my waist. All heads turned my way, and I felt like a mannequin on display at Macy's.

"Oh, my gawd, Leagh! What in the world did you do? Roll a wino? Girl, we have got to take you shopping," Trevor gasped as he jumped up from between the two big Doms and rushed toward me. Squeezing me tightly, he lowered his mouth to my ear. "I love you, sister, but you need some concealer for those swollen eyes."

Trevor released me and issued a playful wink.

I looked down at my sloppy ensemble and groaned. "You don't know the half of it, Trev. On a scale from one to ten, it's been a billion point five on the craptastic meter."

"We know, pet. Tony told us what happened over at George's house." Mika's tone reflected his disdain. "Don't you worry about a thing. I've put a call into Judge Landes. We'll get Sloane and Hayden out of that house as soon as possible."

"Please don't," I begged Mika. "As soon as George's estate is settled, I was going to have to move out, anyway. I'm sure that's only going to take a few weeks, maybe less. Thank you, but...it's not worth anyone's time or trouble."

"You're welcome to stay with us as long as you'd like," Julianna offered as she stood and moved in alongside Trevor.

"Thank you, but I'll be just fine," I replied as she bumped a hip against Trevor, jostling him out of the way before swooping in for a tight hug.

"Hey!" Trevor complained in mock anger, unable to hide his grin. "That baby belly of yours could be considered a lethal weap—"

"Trevor!" Drake interrupted with a roar. "Watch yourself, boy. Pregnant women have been known to kill for comments less sympathetic than yours. You might wind up gutted by a Prada stiletto."

"She would never," Trevor gasped.

"You're awfully sure of yourself, boy," Drake admonished with a raised brow.

"Yes, I am, because she'd have to find another babysitter if she did bodily harm to me."

"That's right," Julianna giggled. Her smile faded as she stared into my eyes. "Are you doing okay, honey? You look...like a hot mess, and rightfully so."

Oh, I'm a hot mess all right, but not like you think. I just need to find a quiet place where I can curl up and die. "I'm doing okay," I lied with a sharp nod.

"Sure, you are. If you find yourself climbing the walls, you call me. I'll be there to help get you back down. You got it?"

No problem. You wouldn't happen to have a spare cell phone tucked in your Louis Vuitton bag, would you? Smiling through my anger, I nodded. "Of course. You know I will."

Mika stepped in, smoothing his hand up my arm before wrapping me in a reassuring hug. "If you need a place to stay, we'd love to have you. Understood?"

"Thank you, Sir. But all I really need is my car, so I can start getting my life back on track."

"It's right outside, pet. Julianna and I stopped by the house after the luncheon, and I drove it over here for you," Mika explained as he dug the key I'd given him out of his pocket. It was hard to believe it had been only four days since I'd given him my spare key. It had been kind for Reed to handle all the funeral arrangements so quickly. Still, it felt like four years since George had died.

"Thank you both very much."

"No thanks needed, pet," Mika assured as he and Julianna moved aside.

"Sammie sends her love, Leagh." Drake pouted as he all but swallowed me beneath his beefy arms. "We're here, too, if you need us."

"Thank you, Sir. Where is Mistress Sammie?"

"She went home to take a nap. She's going to open the club for Mika tonight," he explained. "It's still your home. Don't forget that, okay?"

"Yes, Sir. I know." I nodded to Drake as I tucked my car key into the pocket of Tony's sweatpants.

I'd no longer have to impose on any of our friends—especially Tony. For the first time in days, a sense of peace settled over me. After receiving hugs and offers to move in from all the friends assembled, I forced myself to take a seat next to Mika. These people were among some of George's most valued friends. Their love was testament to how deeply he had touched their lives. Losing him had left a void in others' hearts as well. I owed it to him to sit and visit with the group. It would be rude for me to dash out the door like I wanted to. I had to bide my time, then I'd make a quick escape.

As if reading my mind, Tony flashed me a wry smile that washed me full of guilt again. I quickly glanced away.

"So, how did the luncheon go?" I asked, needing to focus on something other than Tony's shrewd gaze pinning me from across the room.

"B-R-U-T-A-L," Trevor said with a dramatic flip of his wrist. "It was like having a root canal while passing a ten-pound kidney stone out the end of your dick!"

"Boy," Drake chastised in a gruff bark that easily drowned out everyone's laughter.

Leave it to Trevor to bring a smile to my face. I loved that sweet boy. Not that I cared less for the others gathered, but I felt more of a kindred spirit with Trevor. He'd been born and raised in the south, like me... and he'd been dirt poor, like me. But he outshined me in strength and perseverance. Growing up outwardly gay, he'd been forced to take a lot of shit from narrow-minded rednecks. Yet, he'd survived it all and come out on the other side with a gentle, loving soul intact. Trevor was a strong princess, far more resilient than he probably even realized.

"Well. it *was*, Daddy, and we all know it," he sighed.

"What happened?" I asked as I glanced around the room. I couldn't miss the way Savannah rolled her eyes or the collective expressions of disdain on the others' faces, like something sour lay on their tongues. It led me to believe that the luncheon had been ripe with drama.

"Sloane and Hayden were in rare form. Mostly Sloane," Trevor began. "We were standing in the food line behind the gruesome twosome and their hoity-toity prune faced friends. I heard one of the old cows ask Hayden, '*Who are all these strange people, dear?*'." Trevor's voice raised a couple of octaves, and he pinched his lips and scrunched up his nose as he mimicked the woman.

"And without missing a beat, that snag-nasty slug Hayden replied, '*They're petty thieves that my father exonerated. He had such a warm heart. He gave these riff-raffs a second chance.*'" Trevor tossed his nose in the air as he impersonated Hayden's voice, which sounded more like a snooty drag queen. I couldn't help but giggle. "I was so pissed I wanted to knock her off her Manolo Blahniks and right onto her sorry ass. But why ruin a good pair of designer shoes, right?"

"She actually said that?" I gasped.

"Yes, and oh, if I didn't want to bitch slap her into the next millennium. So, I did the next best thing." Trevor's eyes danced in delight, and a mischievous grin lit up his adorable face. "As soon as Hayden started talking to someone else, I dusted off my thickest Alabama accent."

As he was doing at that moment.

"And I leaned up close to the nosy woman's ear and whispered, 'All except us. Me and Daddy here, we shared a cell in Leavenworth Federal Prison. It was a scary place for a delicate queen like me. But that very first night I was incarcerated, they locked me in a cell with this big ol' bear. He made me his butt-bitch within thirty seconds. Why, I got to where I loved taking it up the ass for him so much, I just couldn't let him go when they finally released us on good behavior. And oh, sugar, that big ol' love muffin was better than good, he was *fabulous*.'"

Howling laughter filled the room. Poor Trevor couldn't even continue his story; we were all laughing so loud.

"So *that's* what made all the blood drain from that woman's face," Savannah chortled. "I saw you talking to her, Trevor. Next thing I knew, she looked like she was going to faint."

"Oh, I wish she would have. That would have been priceless." Trevor laughed. "No, she just looked at me and flashed a fake smile so tight I was afraid her facelift scars were going to split wide open. Of course, the devil in me could not resist rattling her cage just a tiny bit more. So, I turned around and slid my tongue straight into Daddy's mouth. I thought the old bag's chin was going to drop right into the potato salad."

"Trevor, you're awful. But oh, how I love you." I laughed.

"Oh, that's not even the best part, sister."

"You mean you tortured that poor woman more?" I blinked.

Drake chuckled. "Oh yes, my little hellion was in rare form today."

Trevor blew Drake a kiss before inhaling a deep breath. "So, we're still in the food line, and she's trying to scoot as far away from me as she can get."

"Hell, I can't imagine why," Nick interjected with a laugh.

"Me neither," Trevor gasped in feigned innocence. "So I wiggled up close behind her as she was checking out the desserts, and told her that my lesbian friends made the brownies. She flashed that plastic smile and said, '*That's nice*' in a snotty, condescending voice. So, I decided to warn her that she should be careful 'cuz a lesbian bug might have accidentally landed in the batter. She looked at me like I was on crack. It was hard, but I kept a straight face. Finally, she asked me what a lesbian bug was, and I told her…"

Trevor lost it to a fit of giggles. He laughed so hard we couldn't do anything but join in with him. A long time passed before he gained control, wiped his eyes, and continued.

"I told her a lesbian bug was an organism that worms its way out of the belly and into the walls of her cooch. It would turn her from a straight-shootin' heterosexual woman to a drooling, wanton lesbian. And once it worked its way into her brain, she'd spend the rest of her natural born days begging to munch on Sloane's muff."

"Trevor! You did *not!*" I gasped as howls of laughter erupted in the room.

"Oh yes, he did." Drake shook his head in displeasure, but I could see the pride dancing in the burly Dom's eyes. "And that's when I grabbed a handful of my mouthy boy's hair and shoved him in line behind me."

"I didn't mean to embarrass you, Daddy, but rude, ignorant people just piss me off." Trevor pouted.

"You didn't embarrass me, boy. I found it very… entertaining," Drake chuckled as he threaded his thick fingers through Trevor's blond hair. A prick of jealousy stung as Trevor's eyes glazed in contentment and he leaned into his Master's touch. I desperately missed that feeling of absolute security.

"I liked the way Sloane nearly choked when you gave her your evil Daddy-eye," Trevor preened, gazing up at Drake.

"She's a waste of good air," the big Dom replied dryly.

"Drake, Sir?" I murmured timidly. "Can I ask what you said to Sloane outside the church when I arrived?"

Drake flashed me a roguish grin. "You mean when she was acting like the raging bitch she is?"

My face warmed, remembering how utterly humiliated I'd felt. "Yes, Sir."

"I told her that Mika had hundreds of hours of video tape depicting George in assorted and extremely compromising positions with you. And if she didn't shut her ugly cakehole and pretend like you weren't there, I'd make sure every television affiliate got copies of the films."

"Are you serious?" My mouth fell open as I turned and looked at Mika in shock.

"Of course," Drake chuckled.

"Well, I wouldn't say hundreds of hours, but I've got a few tapes that would grab plenty of unwanted media attention." Mika winked.

"It shut her up, that's for sure," Drake chuckled. "She might be totally fucked in the head, but she knows better than to play hard ball with us. We'd slam her right out of the park."

I couldn't help but smile. George's friends would go to any lengths to protect not only his memory but what he'd left behind as well…me.

"I'm almost afraid to ask, but did anything else happen?" I arched my brows, staring pointedly at Trevor.

"I didn't get to have any more fun." He stuck out a mock pout as he peered up at Drake. "I would have liked to, but Daddy put the kibosh on all my plans. Did anyone else get a dig in?"

From across the room, Dylan cleared his throat. A sheepish grin adorned his handsome face, and the dimple on the side of his cheek indented deeply. "I, ahh, ran into Judge Bernard in the men's room."

"Oh shit, this ought to be good." Tony beamed.

I had no idea who Judge Bernard was or why he was important to the shit stirring Dylan had done. So I sat quietly and listened hoping to find out.

"Yeah, it was pretty funny. Of course, he had no idea who the hell I was, which made it all the riper. You know how Sloane was crying buckets of tears at the gravesite and again at the luncheon?" Nearly everyone's heads bobbed affirmatively. "Well, I ended up washing hands next to the honorable judge."

"Honorable? That's a lie," Mika scoffed.

"No shit," Nick replied, wearing a cynical frown.

"Anyway, I happened to mention that poor Sloane wasn't taking George's death very well. He agreed and flashed me a ridiculous look of sympathy. What a tool. So, I just had to add that it was such a shame to see Sloane so distraught and that she still must have been head over heels in love with him."

"Damn, Dylan," Mika laughed. "You're almost as bad as Trevor."

"Thank you, Mika, Sir," Trevor piped up, flashing a lopsided grin.

"What the hell did he say to that?" Tony asked. His dark, hypnotic eyes had grown wide.

"Not a damn thing. He turned a little pale and gave a sharp nod before he ran out of the bathroom. It was a damn good thing I'd already emptied my bladder, or I'd have pissed myself laughing."

I couldn't stand being left in the dark another minute.

"Who is Judge Bernard?" I asked Mika.

"You don't know who Bernard is, Leagh?" The dungeon owner quickly sobered.

"I don't know who he is either," Savannah interjected. Grateful for her act of valor, I gave her a soft smile as the awkward attention was drawn off me and onto her for a brief moment.

"What did George tell you about his divorce, angel?" Tony looked at me, and I could tell the smile he wore was a mask meant to put me at ease. Unfortunately, it had the opposite effect.

"Umm, just that Sloane wanted out of the marriage and that he was happy to oblige. He said he'd grown tired of living with a shrew."

Mika stared at me for a long moment, as if trying to decide what to say next. "Sloanc is a shrew of biblical proportions, but she's also calculating, manipulative, and probably one of the vilest women on the planet. Money was her husband. George was simply the machine that dispensed it. Years ago, one of the most newsworthy murder cases ended up on his docket. He worked the case for months, putting in twelve to sixteen hour days. Then, out of the clear blue, the suspect plea bargained, and George headed home."

I looked around the room as Mika told the story. Savannah and I were the only ones clinging to his words. The rest were staring off into space or gazing at the ground, their faces lined with something more than sadness. Anger maybe?

"Sloane hadn't expected George home for hours. And when he walked into the bedroom, he found his wife and Judge Bernard fucking like bunnies. Evidently, they'd been having an affair for years, and George never suspected a thing."

Mika's words slammed into me like a plow. George had never told me the details of his divorce. I had no inkling that Sloane had been unfaithful to him. I lowered my head and rubbed a finger and thumb over my forehead. For all the time I'd known him, George had kept the humiliating secret to himself. I felt slighted that his friends assembled in Tony's living room knew more about my Master than I did. He'd kept me in the dark, while almost everyone around me was privy to his secret. It stung like a slap to the face.

Anger quickly rushed in. I'd revealed every horrific detail of my life in Atlanta to him, but he'd never reciprocated his darkest secrets to me. Why? Why had he shut me out? Was he afraid I'd think him weak or, God forbid, love him less? I wanted to scream and throw things. I felt betrayed that our vow of honesty meant nothing to him. Fighting back my tears, I knew this wasn't the time or the place to come unhinged. I inhaled a deep breath and wiped my eyes before raising my head.

"He didn't want you to know, Leagh," Mika replied softly.

"Evidently not." I forced a weak smile.

"He'd confided in a few of us years ago. He didn't want his past to influence any part of his relationship with you. He was a prideful man," Drake explained.

"That's what kept him from telling you, Leagh," Nick leaned forward, resting his elbows on his knees as he pinned me with a serious stare. "He made a deal with Sloane that if she kept the affair with Bernard quiet, he'd grant her a divorce. All the other judges were good friends of George's. If they'd found out what Bernard had done, George knew it would cause a lot of bad blood amongst them all. He didn't want their sympathy, but most of all, he didn't want to taint the courts with backbiting or animosity."

"He was honorable, Leagh, but you already knew that," Dylan added with a reassuring nod.

"Yes," I agreed. George was honorable, but he wasn't honest, at least, not with me. The revelation hurt. Suspicions, like spots of tarnish on silver, plagued me. What other secrets had George kept from me? What other skeletons lingered in his closet that he didn't want me to see? I felt cheated, but there was nothing I could do with my anger. Sucking in a shaky breath, I turned to look at Mika. "So what did Sloane do?"

"She raped him financially, of course," he replied in a bleak tone. "But she kept her mouth shut, for once."

"What about Reed? Does he know?" I asked, casting a glance at all the Doms.

"No clue," Drake replied with a frown.

"Reed was like a brother to him," I murmured.

"He's a judge, pet. I'm not sure if George told him or not," Mika added.

Maybe I wasn't the only one George had kept in the dark. It still hurt.

"Don't go there, Leagh," Tony scolded from across the room. "He did it to protect himself."

"I get that," I replied, trying hard not to sound sarcastic.

The earlier lighthearted mood had shifted to an awkward silence.

"I think it's time we headed out," Mika announced as he turned to kiss my cheek. "If you need anything, I expect you to call. I mean, *anything*. From a toothpick to a Rolls Royce, you got it?"

As Mika rose from the couch, so did my stubborn pride.

His offer was generous, but I had no intention of asking Mika or anyone else for anything. I'd find my way alone. I'd done it before, and I could damn well do it again.

"Yes, Sir, I will," I lied convincingly. "Thank you both for everything. You've kept me sane through these horrible days."

Minutes lagged before everyone had said their goodbyes and driven away. Tony and I were alone again. Anxiety sprouted like a spring flower in the pit of my belly. It was time for me to leave as well. Get far away from the temptation of him. My self-control around him was shaky at best.

Dashing up the stairs, I retrieved my wet clothes. When I returned, Tony stood in the foyer. He didn't say a word, just stared at me.

"What?" I asked, unnerved by his silent scrutiny.

"You know they're going to be pissed, right?"

"Pissed about what?" I asked, anxious and ready to leave.

He grunted. "Pull that innocent act on someone who hasn't spent the last three years studying you like a damn book. I know every nuance about you, angel, and it won't fly with me. Don't think for one minute your friends won't be ticked off when they find out you needed something and never called."

"I don't need any help. There's nothing I can't do for myself," I huffed.

"Stubborn, minx. Come on. Let me take you out to get a phone and some clothes that fit." Tony extended his hand. I took a step back, adamantly shaking my head. "Oh, I get it. I suppose my offer falls under the category of things you can do for yourself, right, sweetheart?"

His sarcasm felt like a steel brush up my spine.

"Exactly," I snapped with a tight, irritated smile.

"Fine." His Dominant tone rolled over me in a hot, silky swell. "Look at me. Look into my eyes. *Promise* that you'll call me if you need *anything*."

"Tony...I..."

"Promise me, angel."

"Okay, I promise." I rolled my eyes. "Happy now?"

"Not even close." He issued a low growl that sent a rush of heat straight south.

"Tony," I exhaled on a deep sigh. "I'm not a child. I have a plan. I have money. I have a car. I definitely won't be living under a bridge or digging through dumpsters. I'll be fine. You've gone above and beyond the call of duty, and I thank you, but I need to go."

"No, you're not a child, and I have no doubt that eventually you'll land on your feet. But I also know you've been through a hell of an emotional shock. You are going to crash, eventually. I don't want you to be alone when you do."

"If and when I crash, believe me, it will be much easier if I am alone. Honestly, I don't want an audience when it comes time for me to bawl my eyes out. You've already seen enough of my tears."

"You haven't even tapped the surface yet, sweetheart," Tony replied in a grim tone.

"Maybe not, but I'll deal with it, okay?" He wore an expression of doubt. "Please, try to understand. It would be easy to use you…use all of my friends as crutches, but that would only prolong the inevitable. I want to deal with my grief in my own way."

"I understand your need for independence, but before you go, we need to discuss what happened upstairs."

"There's nothing to talk about." I swallowed tightly, wishing he'd leave the whole sordid episode alone. There was no way I was going to stand there and dissect what had happened in the bathroom. "Like you said, it's all normal stuff."

"Yes, the need for comfort is, but I lost my head." He scrubbed a hand over his face. "I've wanted you for so damn long, and there you were—in my house—naked and in my shower. I should have left you alone, but I couldn't. It was either join you and try to give you the comfort you needed or put my fist through the wall. I never meant for my actions to add guilt to your grief. I'm sorry, angel."

Stunned by his apology, I didn't know what to say. Leaning in, I gave Tony an awkward hug before I tugged off his socks and tucked them into his hand.

"It's okay. Look, I'll call you when I'm settled," I mumbled before dashing out the door and into the pouring rain.

He stood on the porch watching me. I heard him issue a curse as I slammed the driver's side door. Thankful I had one piece of property Sloane and Hayden couldn't take from me. George had registered the little red sports car in my name. Shoving my key into the ignition, the Mazda Miata purred to life, and I backed out of Tony's driveway.

Headed toward George's neighborhood, I intended to stop at the bank. He kept a healthy amount of cash available, and luckily, neither Sloane nor Hayden knew I had a debit card and full access to his account. That should have given me a sense of comfort, but unfortunately, I hadn't relaxed a stitch since leaving Tony's.

His masculine scent clung to the clothes he'd let me borrow. Images of his hard body and nimble fingers rolled in an endless loop through my brain. I needed to buy some new clothes... ones that didn't induce 3-D color, Dolby surround sound visuals of Tony's tantalizing dominance, his warm lips, insightful gaze, and thick, hard... *dammit!* I had to focus on something other than that man.

Pulling beneath the awning of the bank's drive-thru, I waited for the automatic teller machine to process my transaction. My behavior with Tony had been appalling, yet I couldn't erase one spectacular second I'd shared with him. Turning back to the teller machine, the simple withdraw was taking an unreasonably long time. I blinked at the message on the display.

Your transaction cannot be completed. The account is closed. Please select another option.

My heart thundered in my ears as my guts churned. "No!" I screamed. White hot rage surged. "I should have killed those fucking bitches when I had the chance."

The ramifications of not having a dime to my name crashed through me like a

sledgehammer. With a piercing squeal of tires, I jettisoned from the bank, leaving a trail of smoking rubber in my wake. The road before me blurred as tears filled my eyes. Blinking, I eased off the accelerator and glanced at the parking lot of a strip mall, adjacent to the bank. Coming to a stop in a vacant corner of the lot, I shoved the gear shift into park as tears dripped from my cheeks.

Vacillating between rage, fear, and grief, a string of obscenities tore from my lips. And as my body shook with sobs, I leaned my head on the steering wheel and cried.

Misery over Sloane's and Hayden's cruel deeds morphed into anger at George for leaving me, that slid into guilt for my actions with Tony. It all eventually dipped into despair. I was destitute.

I sat in my car feeling sorry for myself and cried a long time. Spilling more tears than I imagined possible. The dark skies rolled overhead, matching my mood. Wiping my face on the sleeve of Tony's shirt, it was pointless to sit there bawling like a child. I needed to get my shit together and figure out a plan of action.

Exiting the parking lot, I drove the city streets, unsure of a destination. Stubborn pride kept me from going back to Mika and Julianna's house, and self-preservation stopped me from returning to Tony's. Driving aimlessly for hours, I was lost in a daze of indecision. No money, no phone, no clothes, no home. Foolishly, I'd boasted to Tony I wouldn't wind up under an overpass, scrounging through dumpsters. It seemed my words had come to bite me in the ass.

Sitting at a stop light, I glanced at my surroundings. Ironically, I was a few short blocks from Genesis, and I hadn't a clue how I'd gotten there. Alarmed that I'd been so mentally out of it, I realized something must have drawn me to the club. Gazing down the street, the massive courthouse with its bronzed dome loomed in the distance. I wasn't masochistic enough to drive past it, and when the light turned green, I pressed on the gas, ready to make my way into the turning lane and flee that part of town. Suddenly, my car began to chug and lurch. Looking down at the gas gauge, I cried out in panic. The tank was on empty.

"Can't I get a break? Please? All I need is just one motherfucking break," I screeched, limping my vehicle to the curb. Too pissed to cry, I wiggled my feet into the cold, damp heels I'd worn to George's funeral. When I stepped out of the car and slammed the door, I snorted at my reflection in the window of a dry cleaner. Trevor would have a hay-day if he saw my current fashion statement: thermal shirt, baggy sweatpants, and black high heels. "Penthouse centerfold, here I come," I hissed as I stomped down the sidewalk.

The cold rain burned my face, and the clothes Tony lent me were soaked in minutes. Tired, angry, cold, and numb, I made my way to the entrance of Genesis. When I tried turning the knob, I shook my head. It was locked.

"Of course, it's fucking locked! Why would it be open? Oh, that would be too damn easy, wouldn't it? Being locked out of my house, every fucking dime yanked from my fingertips, a car without any gas, ruined leather shoes, freezing my ass off in this son of a bitching rain! Why on earth did I even hope that the fucking door would be open?"

Screaming at the portal, I gave it a swift kick that sent a ribbon of pain straight up my shin.

With a heavy sigh, I trudged around the side of the building toward the back parking lot. The wind and rain pierced my flesh like a thousand tiny needles. Gazing over the gravel strewn lot, there wasn't a car in sight. I exhaled a heavy sigh before climbing the stairs to the back entrance. I didn't know the code to unlock the door, so I curled up in the tiny alcove, attempting to shield myself from the blustery cold wind.

I knew Sammie would arrive soon and open the club, so I waited and shivered, praying she wouldn't be long. The petite Domme was a fiery little thing, but she held a world of compassion in her soft heart. She'd let me inside so I could crash in the private room George and I once shared. I'd be able to take another hot shower, and hopefully, find some dry, warm clothes that Master and I kept stored in our dresser there.

My chest tightened at the thought of stepping inside those four walls without him. We'd spent so many nights lost in our own little world. Misery had me in a stranglehold, and I couldn't seem to pry its wicked hands from my throat. For the first time in my life, I wondered if I was going to survive the pain.

Looking up at the sound of crunching gravel and the soft hum of an engine, I watched Tony pull into the lot. *Great. Just fucking great. It had to be him, didn't it?* "Shit," I cursed under my breath as he jumped out of his car, hunched his shoulders against the windswept rain, and hurried toward me.

"Leagh? What are you doing here? Why are you sitting outside?"

"Can you please just let me in?" I asked, trying hard not to whine.

"Of course, angel, but *why* are you sitting out here?"

Fighting the urge to fall against his chest, surround myself in his heat and strength and cry, I clenched my fists so I wouldn't touch him and explained the craptastic chain of events. Ending my tale of woe with my abandoned car down the street.

When he opened his mouth to speak, another vehicle pulled into the lot. Tony cursed, and a look of worry settled over his face.

"Hold on. I'll be right back."

He bounded down the stairs as the car pulled to a stop beside him. Peering into the vehicle, I recognized Destiny, a massive pain slut and one of Tony's regular bottoms, sitting behind the wheel.

"Hey, Des. Sorry, but something's come up. I need to reschedule," Tony explained.

"But you said to meet you now 'cuz you wanted to use me hard. I changed all my plans for this. And now you want to reschedule? You're joking, right?"

I couldn't miss the bitterness in her voice.

"I know exactly what I said, girl." Tony's tone held a sharp edge, heavy with dominance. It made me quiver. "I didn't purposefully mess up your plans, Destiny. But Dahlia needs my help right now, so you and I will have to wait."

"No, I don't," I called from behind him. "Just open the door, and let me in. Then beat her ass and fuck her or do whatever it is you need to."

Tony turned, pinning me with a stony glare.

"I don't follow orders from a sub, Dahlia," he growled before spinning back toward Destiny. "We'll do this another time."

Great! I'd gone and pissed him off. A proper submissive would never tell a Dom what to do; it was known as topping from the bottom. But at that particular moment, I was fed up, knocked down, and freezing my ass off. There wasn't a submissive bone in my body. There was no reason Tony had to rearrange his plans of a little spank-n-fuck, at least, not for me.

"Fine. Dahlia needs all the help she can get anyway," Destiny sneered, her words dripping with sarcasm as she flashed a hateful glare my way. "You two have tons of fun. Try not to break her, Sir."

Everything about the girl screamed of jealousy, and I wanted to laugh. What the hell was going on in her peroxide saturated brain? Did she honestly think I'd allow Tony to vent his 'frustrations' on *my* ass? Not in this lifetime... or the next.

Destiny sped out of the parking lot, sending gravel spewing in all directions. Tony turned back to me. His eyes narrowed; his face lined in an angry frown as he stormed back up the stairs.

"Don't be pissy with me. I told you to take her inside. You're the one that sent her away." I huffed as Tony punched in a complex set of numbers on the security pad.

"You don't dictate what I do, brat," he scolded as he jerked the heavy door open.

"Stop calling me that!" I bristled as I rushed past him and marched down the long hall.

"Why? It's the truth. You undermined my dominance in front of another sub. I don't care how shitty your day has been." His tone was downright caustic. "I've given you a lot of passes over the past few hours, princess, but no more, and especially, not here. You'll show proper respect, or else."

"Or else what, Tony?" I snorted and rolled my eyes. "You think for one second I'd ever let you beat *my* ass? Get real. We both know that'll never happen. You're not going to lay a hand on me, so stop with the idle threats. Got it?"

I folded my arms over my chest in defiance, shivering as the cold, soggy clothes pressed against my flesh.

"Oh, I got it. I've got a hell of a lot more than you give me credit for, angel." He stepped in closer, his warm breath fluttering over my ear. "Stop pushing me, Leagh. I'm not going to tell you again."

The harsh tone of his whisper left no doubt, Tony's patience had run out.

Raising my chin mulishly, I gave a curt nod. "Fine. You're a DM, so I assume you have a master key that will unlock George's door, correct?"

"I do."

"Then would you please let me in the room, *Sir?*"

"Only because you asked so nicely," Tony smirked as he slid the key into the lock. Pausing, his shoulders stiffened. He turned, and his dark eyes softened. "Are you sure you're ready to do this?"

"No. I'm not ready at all. But frankly, I'm out of options." I choked back a sob, quickly swallowing it down. "Please. Just open the damn door."

"No, angel, you're not out of options," Tony sighed, tipping my chin up with his fingers. "We can leave here. I'll take you shopping, get you a phone, whatever you need. We can grab some dinner. Then,

Jenna Jacob

I'll take you home and get you settled into one of my guest rooms. You don't have to stay here and put yourself through this. There *are* other options, Leagh."

It would be so easy to take him up on his offer and walk away from the painful ghosts waiting on the other side of the door. But I couldn't remain suspended in the murky limbo I'd been trapped in for the past four days. I had to find a way to work past my grief and carry on, even though I was scared senseless.

"Please, Tony. Don't make me beg; just unlock the door."

"Christ, Leagh. Do you always have to be so fucking stubborn?"

"Yes. If I'm going to survive this, stubborn is the only way I'll make it through," I whispered.

With a heavy sigh, Tony swung the door open.

Chapter Four

The spicy scent of George's cologne as it wafted from the room was a kick in the gut. Swallowing back a cry, I fingered the switch on the wall and flipped on the lights. Nothing prepared me for the barrage of memories that inundated me. Safety, comfort—hollow. Laughter, love—empty. Yearning, need—anguish.

Tony clasped my shoulder and gave a tender squeeze. "I'm here if you need me."

Without looking back, I nodded and stepped through the door, closing it behind me. Two steps into the room I closed my eyes and inhaled a deep breath. Sandalwood and spice filled my senses. In the silence of the room, I felt my heart reach out to George, craving to give him my surrender one last time. The harsh reality that he'd never again fulfill my submission was a tight fist gripping my heart.

Stripping away my wet clothes where I stood, I decided to forego the shower and crawled onto the bed, snuggling beneath the clean sheets. The blanket still held his scent, and I gathered it to my face, breathing him in as bittersweet memories crowded my mind.

"I miss you so much, Master. I've been numb since you left me. I'm sorry for letting Tony touch me, but for the first time since you left me, I felt alive. It felt like I'd finally taken a breath again, but I'm so sorry." Tears dampened the blanket. "My whole world has been yanked out from beneath me. Why did you have to die? I miss you so much."

Sobs cracked my voice as I curled into a tight ball and savored his fragrance.

"I'm so lost without you. I don't know what to do. I'd give anything to spend one more day with you, surrounded by you, wrapped in your arms. Please. Help me find a way to go on without you."

More pain bubbled to the surface as memories bombarded me. I was helpless to do anything but let the crushing grief consume me.

"Nothing's ever going to be the same," I sobbed. "I need to touch you, hold you, feel your calming caress. I'm so fucking scared, George. All those times you whispered in my ear, telling me it was going to be all right... it's never going to be alright, again. Is it? Who is going to hold me when the nightmares come? Who is going to talk me off the ledge when the fears swallow me up? I can't do this without you. I don't know how to go on, George. I'm terrified. I don't know what to do." Screaming the words, my throat burned, and my head pounded.

"Help me, George! I can't survive this. It hurts too much. Why did you have to go?"

I remained coiled in the covers for hours, pleading with him to find a way back to me—to ease my grief, my agony, my fears. Even after my tears refused to fall, sobs scraped the back of my throat. Exhausted and fragmented, I hugged his pillow to my chest. Closing my eyes, I prayed sleep would save me from the agony that pumped through my veins.

Slumber evaded, and eventually, my keening cries subsided. A strange noise emanating from the bookcase, against the wall near the door, captured my attention. My brows furrowed as I strained, listening to the soft buzz.

My guts seized. So swamped with grief, I'd failed to remember the hidden cameras and microphones fitted in the private rooms. I was being observed. Since no one else was in the club except for Tony and me, I knew he'd watched me fall apart.

Anger spiked as I envisioned him in Mika's office, leaning forward in the soft leather chair, staring into the monitor with a notepad and pen in hand, frantically scribbling down every word of my insane pleas to George. Tony had overstepped his authority as Dungeon Monitor. He had no reason to eavesdrop on me. I hadn't been engaging in a scene that required scrutiny for safety's sake. As if it were his right to spy on me, Tony had taken it upon himself to dissect my grief. *Prying son of a bitch.*

As the soft sound of angry bees emanated from the shelves, I bolted out of bed and raced to the bookcase. Peering into the camera lens, I narrowed my eyes.

"You're an asshole, Tony!" I spat before raising my middle finger to flip him off. "Leave me the fuck alone. You don't have permission to slice open my psyche, you got it? Go to hell!"

I slammed a book over the lens, blocking his view, and stomped to bathroom. Splashing cold water on my face, I cursed Tony. When Mika arrived at the club later, he was going to get an earful. I had every intention of demanding that he strip the surveillance equipment from George's room.

Fueled by my fury, I angrily wiped a towel over my face before storming back toward the room. With a mighty crash, the door burst open. Spinning toward the commotion, I yelped and impulsively tried to cover my naked body with my hands.

Tony's broad frame filled the portal. Anger seared his dark, narrow eyes, and his nostrils flared like a charging bull. His brawny chest heaved up and down in labored breaths. His fist clenched. The veins in his neck bulged, and damn if he didn't look like sin on a stick. For one minuscule second, I ached to melt on the ground at his feet.

Sanity slammed me back to reality, warning me to tread carefully with the pissed off sadist. Yet, in the back of my mind, I knew Tony would never truly hurt me.

Unfortunately, the smart ass within took control of my mouth.

"Did you enjoy the show?" I asked with a flippant jerk of my head toward the camera. "I would have thought by now you'd had your fill of watching me bawl and blubber like a baby. Tell me, Tony, were you taking professional notes? Or do you have some kinky crying fetish?"

A wicked grin slashed his lips, and his eyes danced in fiendish delight. His cold, calculating demeanor should have caused a wimpy sub like me to run from the room screaming in panic. But I was too pissed for self-preservation.

Without a word, he stepped inside and closed the door. With a quiet snick, he engaged the lock.

"What do you think you're doing in here? Get out!" I demanded.

He didn't say a word as he stalked closer. His methodical movements revealed his intent, and like a runaway freight train slamming into me, I knew I'd crossed the line. Crossed it? Hell, I'd obliterated it.

Glancing past his broad shoulders, the distance to the door seemed the length of a couple football fields. Tony would tackle me long before I reached it. My heart pounded against my ribs as he continued to prowl toward me... like a panther stalking its prey.

Even as my body trembled, I raised my chin in defiance. No way was I going to show him the least bit of fear.

Silently, Tony clasped my wrist and pulled me behind him as he stalked toward the bed. Plopping down on the edge of the mattress, he gazed up at me...assessing.

"I asked what you're doing in my room uninvited?" I demanded, mustering as much courage as I could.

"You're out of free passes, angel." His smile was dangerous, his eyes stormy. If he was trying to intimidate me—give that man a prize! —it worked.

"Why are you in such a...aahh," I cried out in surprise as he yanked me over his knees before steeling a sturdy arm around my waist and anchoring me to his lap.

"Get your hands off me! What in the hell do you think you're doing?" I shrieked.

Angry and frightened, I kicked and screamed as I tried to wriggle free.

Without warning, Tony landed a fierce slap across my bare ass cheeks.

"Oh, you did not just do that!" I growled indignantly. "Stop this shit. Right now! I am *not* one of your little pain sluts; you let me go!" I demanded as the fiery burn spread over my orbs. Crying out again as he leveled another sharp slap, I seethed with rage. "How dare you spank me like a child?"

"Oh, I dare, sweetheart, because you've all but begged for it. And I have no qualms about setting your ass on fire each and every time you want to pull the brat card on me," Tony chuckled. He spanked me again, unmercifully, emphasizing the gravity of my disrespect. "By the way, angel, your safeword is *protocol*."

I issued a howl as his hand smacked my flesh, over and over. I screamed and bucked with all my might against his ruthless hold. Tears spilled down my cheeks, and my ass felt as if a blowtorch had been set to it. But it didn't stop me from calling him every vulgar name I could think of.

"All you have to do is say the word, angel," Tony teased.

"Fuck you!"

"Hmmm. Nope. That's not the safeword I gave you, sweetheart." His condescending tone and taunting chuckle launched a more potent wave of anger within. "Did you forget your safeword?"

"No, asshole, I didn't forget!" I hissed as he brought his hand down with a sizzling whack. It would be a cold day in hell before I let Tony break me down.

"Asshole? That's not how you talk to a Dominant, angel." He all but purred his reprimand.

"You're not a Dominant. You're a fucking sadist. Let me go, or I'll report you to Mika."

Tony snorted, sending me into a caustic rage. Leaning in, I opened my mouth wide and sunk my teeth into his jeans. Tony's thunderous laugh vibrated over my entire body. He was having one hell of a good time at my expense.

"I'll stick a ball gag in your mouth if you try to bite me again, Leagh, and as for Mika? Well, he'd probably give me a pat on the back for spanking your ass. Trust me. You've more than earned it over the years."

And didn't that make me feel like a total failure? Tony's reminder that he and everyone else in the club thought my submission substandard was just one more crushing blow I didn't want or need.

"Let *him* spank me, because you don't have *my* permission," I screeched.

"Just say the word and it all stops."

"I will not safeword out. Not to you, or anyone else, so let me go!"

"Somehow I knew you were going to say that, my stubborn little minx" Tony smirked as he landed another brutal slap.

Boiling with rage, I fought to get free, but he was too strong, too capable, too...everything. Dammit, he was going to win. I stopped struggling, hoping Tony would end this embarrassing lesson and leave, but he didn't.

I slumped across his steely legs, resigned to endure his humiliation, as he continued to light my ass up. The heat sank deep into the tissue as it rolled up my spine and melted down my legs. The burn wasn't unbearable; in fact, it felt calming, in a bizarre way. And as the sting began to fuse with my bones, my thoughts grew thick like honey. As if by magic, the scattered, broken chaos swirling in my head...stilled. All that remained was a pinpoint of light in the center of my brain, pulsing in time with the echo of slapping flesh upon flesh.

Floating away to a quiet, peaceful place, I couldn't equate the sensation to any past experience or emotion. I thought it strange that I wasn't attempting to compartmentalize my response to what Tony was doing to me. Escaping my sorrow was such blessed relief, I simply let go and sailed away.

Having lost all sense of time, when I finally forced my heavy eyelids open, I found myself lying in bed surrounded by Tony's warm body. He held me close against his soft cotton shirt, and I breathed in his familiar scent as he lazily drew his fingers through my hair. I felt small and boneless. My brain sloughed in a heavy fuzziness, but I could feel the icy hot blaze throbbing on my ass cheeks. And the memory of his spanking swamped me in shame.

Even as I tensed, Tony continued threading his fingers through my mane. Gathering up my courage, I peeked up at him beneath my heavy lashes. He stared down at me as a placid smile curled the corners of his mouth.

"Welcome back, angel." His voice poured over me, deep and smooth, like brandy.

"What happened? What did you do to me?" My question came out a shy whisper. Still confused by the gossamer sensations swirling inside me, I struggled to clear the fog enveloping my brain.

"You took off on me for a bit."

"Took off? To where?" A slight slur clung to my words.

"Subspace, angel. Haven't you ever been there before?"

I shook my head. Tony frowned and pressed a sweet kiss to my forehead.

"How did you like it?"

How *did* I like it? I wasn't sure. A part of me felt off-kilter…but in a good way. While another part of me felt relaxed, as if I'd taken a soothing vacation. The mud miring my brain made processing my thoughts much slower than normal. And while I was stone cold sober, I felt drunk off my butt.

"I'm not sure. I don't think I've landed yet," I murmured, burrowing deeper against his chest, gazing up at him.

Other subs had talked about subspace, but I'd always thought it was a bunch of BS. Having finally experienced it, I understood now when they said it was mind-blowing.

He stared into my eyes, looking pleased. I wasn't sure if it was with me or himself. The longer he gazed at me, the more uncomfortable I became. Was there a proper 'after subspace' etiquette I didn't know about? What was I supposed to say? *"Thank you, Sir; may I have another?"* *"Was it good for you?"* The few un-mangled thoughts I could string together seemed superficial and utterly ridiculous to say aloud. Unsure what to do or say, I tried to pull away, but Tony held tight. Truth be told, cocooned in his strong arms, his masculine scent filling my senses, and surrounded in the decadent heat of his hard body felt…perfect.

My lids slid shut. Keeping them open took more effort than I could manage. It was easy to imagine languishing in this splendor for days, weeks, hell, even months. But the longer I lay with him, the more defined reality became. The fog in my brain began to lift. Soon, Tony would have to leave and make his appearance in the dungeon. His throng of pain sluts waited for the taste of agony Tony commanded from the end of his whip.

I couldn't afford naïve fantasies about him floating through my head. The slice of peace he'd given me wouldn't last. And even though his arms felt heavenly, offering him an easy out was for the best. Forcing my eyes open, I inhaled a deep breath.

"You don't have to stay. I'm better now. Besides, I'm sure you have asses to beat and nipples to torture."

I felt his body shake with silent laughter. Though, I had no reason to hope, I prayed he would stay a little longer. I'd yearned for the type of comfort he was providing for four long days. I didn't want to give it up. As soon as the thought crossed my mind, guilt began slithering in. Was it so wrong for me to take what I needed from another man? Wrong for me to let a sadist launch me into subspace? That fact alone blew my mind. *Me*, bunny flogger-bondage girl accepted every whack of Tony's righteous spanking and jettisoned off to oblivion. The sense of serenity he'd provided on my maiden voyage had been so surreal and calming. So much so, I wanted to go there again. My cravings were bewildering. *What was wrong with me?*

Confused and muddled seemed to be a natural state for me over the past four days. Being with Tony exacerbated my discombobulated feelings. The logical parts of me wanted to shoo him out of my room, but the selfish, empty parts of me ached for him to stay.

"I can hang out with you a little longer. Close your eyes, and get some rest. I'll keep you safe."

"Safe from what?" I mumbled against his steely chest as my eyelids drifted shut.

"Safe from sub-drop, sweetheart," he whispered.

"Mmm," I purred. I'd seen subs break down after intense sessions. George had explained that sub-drop played havoc with emotions. I'd never experienced it, but I didn't want to chance fate. Why had Tony given me such a spectacular gift, one that brought me such peace? I decided *don't ask-don't tell* might be safer. Sometimes, ignorance *was* bliss.

"Go on. Ride those endorphins a little longer, angel. It will do you some good."

As if Tony had been a hypnotist and snapped his fingers, sleep pulled me under. It was a hard, heavy slumber, free of my usual nightmares.

When I woke, the room, the bed, and my arms were empty. The lack of Tony's refuge was unsettling. Why was I missing the man? Obsessing over a sadist/shrink, who played games with my head wasn't a merry-go-round ride I needed to take, yet I couldn't seem to get off the damn thing. Why the attraction to Tony? How had he crawled inside my head so damn fast? I was supposed to be in mourning. If I'd truly loved George, I wouldn't be thinking about any other man.

Climbing out from beneath the warm sheets, I padded to the bathroom. Once done with my business, I washed my hands and stared at my reflection in the mirror.

I'd never studied Psychology 101, but it didn't take a genius to connect the dots. On some psychological level, I was substituting Tony for George. Instead of allowing the sadist to sail me off to subspace, I should have made an appointment with him on a professional level. Maybe he could prescribe a pill that would help me pull my head out of my ass.

"You're an idiot," I scolded my reflection before I turned and walked away.

I didn't want to analyze Tony's easy invasion of my psyche or my attraction to him. I'd deal with that craptastic ball of confusion... later.

Rummaging through my dresser, the only clothes I could find aside from skimpy fetish wear was a pair of black sweatpants and a pink T-shirt. My feet were still freezing, but I couldn't find a pair of socks in any of my drawers. My fingers trembled and a pang of sorrow sliced when I gripped the knobs on George's side of the dresser. I thought it ironic that only hours earlier I had been hell-bent on going back to the house we'd shared to confront his ghost. After the horrid day I'd had, the rawness kept me from pulling the damn drawer open. Just the thought of seeing his belongings sent my heart racing.

The walls felt like they were closing in. A cold sweat broke out over my forehead and upper lip. I'd been such a fool to think I could surround myself in memories of George without them sending me into

Jenna Jacob

a tailspin. Consumed by a rush of panic, I turned and raced out of the room.

Standing in the hallway, I bent at the waist, gasping for breath, as the sounds of painful pleasures echoed from the entrance of the dungeon. The scent of leather and sex hung heavy in the air. Rising upright, I glanced up and down the long corridor. There wasn't another soul in sight. It was another brutal reminder that I was utterly alone.

"Oh, George," I whispered. "I want you back so badly."

Standing in the hall, there was no place to run and escape my broken heart. I couldn't find the willpower to enter the dungeon. I would only fall apart again watching our friends engaging in their power exchanges. The toll Master's memories took in our room paled in comparison to the thought of watching happy BDSM couples fulfilling their desires. Yes, it was much safer in my room. Spinning around, I grabbed the knob as a wave of regret poured through me. It was locked, and I didn't have a key.

I closed my eyes and swore under my breath. Mistress Sammie was the keeper of the private room keys. She was, no doubt, dominating the bar, serving drinks and smiles to the members. While she wouldn't hesitate to give me an extra key to our room, I had to enter the dungeon to get the damn thing.

"Suck it up, buttercup. They're not going to stone you to death," I murmured as I forced myself to step toward the dungeon. "No, just smother you in pity."

I wrinkled my nose and hurried toward the archway. Tucking myself behind the slight recess of the wall, I peered into the dungeon. The place was in full swing. Nearly every station was in use, and most of the tables were filled with members watching and quietly talking. I was relieved that no one seemed to notice me peeking out from behind my hiding place. And like a masochistic voyeur, I scanned the stations, watching the scenes. Wrapping my arms around my middle, I tried to hold in the ache as I wistfully watched my friends.

Dylan and Nick brushed the tails of thick floggers across Savannah's shoulders, back, and butt. Her arms cuffed to a cross high above her head. The two Doms were focused on their sub, conveying with words and touches how precious she was to each of them.

Though I shouldn't, I envied her. Savannah was the center of their worlds, and Dylan and Nick made sure she knew it.

George had made it clear to me, too, but in different ways. He wasn't as generous with public displays of affection, but he spoiled me with trinkets and clothes and trips. When I would reach down and hold his hand, he would give it a little squeeze, pull away, and drape his arm over my shoulder in a less romantic attachment. I suspected he was trying to save me the embarrassment of condescending or judgmental stares. While I didn't give a rat's ass what others thought, I always had the impression that he did. George had made sure I had everything tangible that I longed for, but the one thing I ached for the most was his outward sign of our bond.

I watched as Dylan and Nick each lowered their floggers and approached Savannah. In unison, they caressed her reddened flesh with their hands as they reassured and praised her with kisses and whispers only she could hear.

I had to look away.

A bittersweet smile tugged my lips when I spied Trevor, bound in ropes, lying supine on a padded table. Drake's busy hands toyed with his sub's cock. Bright red rope had been tied tight around each of Trevor's bluish testicles, bisecting them. And as Drake stroked Trevor's long, turgid shaft, the big Dom warned him not to come. Trevor sent him a mournful plea before Drake landed his fingers in a brutal slap over Trevor's strangled scrotum. The younger man's cries of pain echoed through the room, and I cringed just a little.

The recoil of a whip sent a shiver up my spine. Glancing toward the sound, I instantly wished that I hadn't. The powerfully built Dom had his back to me, but it made no difference. I knew by the decadent muscles and colorful tattoos it was Tony. He stood behind a sub secured to a spanking bench, gripping a black and red plaited whip in his wide fist. Shirtless, his black leather pants hugged his tight ass and sturdy legs. His defined shoulders bunched and flexed beneath his bronzed flesh, and his colorful tattoos rippled. I clenched my hands, itching to feel his tempting hard flesh again. I licked my lips and remembered the taste of his kiss.

As if sensing my presence, Tony turned. As his gaze locked with mine, I could almost feel him caress my skin. Feel the same stirring heat his fingers evoked as they plucked and pinched my nipples. The buds drew tight against my tee and tingled with the memory.

His mouth fluttered with a slight smile as my cheeks grew hot. Severing the connection, he turned his attention back to the sub bent over the spanking bench. Tony smoothed one broad hand over her pale skin. Jealousy pricked my heart. Glancing at the long blond tresses shrouding the sub's face, I knew Destiny—the lucky little bitch—had finally arranged her session with Tony. As he stepped back, I couldn't take my eyes off him… couldn't force myself to look away, even as envy coursed angrily through my veins.

I stared in fascination as his whip found its mark, time and again. Commanding and confident, Tony worked the sub. His shoulders widened; his chest expanded. I watched him drink in her cries of pain as if they were welcome nourishment. Red angry welts crisscrossed Destiny's backside. Still, Tony didn't stop. He landed the single tail's popper with succinct and measured lashes. I cringed and searched deep for a sliver of any untapped longings that called to his type of extreme play. No matter how hard I searched my fantasies, I couldn't find a hint of desire close to the level he required. And still, I stood mesmerized, watching.

The sensual sway of his body, the honed roll of his shoulder, and the quick flick of his wrist was an art form all its own. His focus, keen on the sub, never wavered. It was clear to see. His whip was an extension of his heart... his soul. The sadist's pleasure was a sharp, wicked blade, and Tony walked the narrow edge with relentless precision. The intensity of his desire was a formidable mountain. Each lash commanded the girl to climb higher as he guided her through angry welts and imposing pain—persuading her ascent to the peak, absorbing her tears and screams, he fed his dominance.

Tony was poetry in motion, his command powerful and unyielding. Compared to Destiny, my submission was useless…weak. My heart grew heavy realizing that if given a chance to submit to Tony, I had nothing substantial to offer. I would simply slide through his sturdy fingers like sand.

Tony set the whip down, squatted next to Destiny, and gently brushed the hair from her face. Tears streamed from beneath her closed eyelids. Tony leaned in and sipped the moisture from her cheeks between his lips with tender reverence. The comfort he now showed Destiny wasn't at all different from what he'd granted me. The realization I was just another sub in need of Tony's compassion sucked the air from my lungs. I was nothing more than a Dominant obligation to him. And while I shouldn't have allowed it to hurt…it did.

Hot tears slid down my face, yet I couldn't stop watching his every move. Tony released the sub from the bench, wrapped her in a blanket, and lifted her into his arms. Lowering his mouth to her ear, he whispered, probably in the same whiskey smooth voice that made my pussy weep.

Betrayal stabbed deep. A voice screamed inside my head that my behavior with Tony had come full circle, and this was my comeuppance. Karma was indeed a hateful bitch.

Tony pressed a kiss to the sub's forehead, awarding the same affection he'd given me. The tender act set my stomach swirling and my body quaking. Somehow, I'd twisted myself into believing I was someone special in his eyes. How could I have been so damn naïve?

With Destiny's limp body clutched to his chest, Tony turned toward me. Spying my tears, his brows furrowed as a puzzled look lined his features. And when he began walking toward me, I realized he would have to pass by me to take Destiny to his private room. He'd lay her in his bed and climb in next to her and drown the woman in sublime aftercare…maybe even make love to her. Tony would willingly give her all the things I'd stupidly let swim in my head and touch my heart.

I didn't want to pass him and head to the bar, so I turned away as he approached, swiping off my tears before casting my gaze to the floor. I didn't want Tony to see the sophomoric hurt I'd inflicted upon myself. When I felt his presence behind me, it was like a fucking disturbance in the force. I closed my eyes for a half second, calling myself a zillion kinds of fool as Tony stopped alongside me.

"What's wrong, angel?"

What's wrong? You. Her. My whole fucking life!

"Nothing," I mumbled.

I felt his stare bore into the side of my face, like a damn laser beam.

I kept my gaze pinned to the floor and slid my trembling hands behind my back.

"Why are you standing in the hall crying, sweetheart?"

Sweetheart? I'm not your sweetheart... I'm the brat! Remember?

"I accidentally locked myself out. I was on my way to get a key from Sammie."

"Mistress Sammie, you mean."

"Yes, Sir." And, dammit, why was I allowing *him* to correct me? He wasn't my Dom. He wasn't my mentor. He meant nothing to me, and I damn well didn't matter to him. A fact I needed to start hammering into my head then and there. "Have a good night, Sir," I replied in a curt and icy tone. Turning on my heel, I marched to the bar.

I didn't know what was worse, mooning over a playboy sadist like a love-sick puppy or the expressions of sympathy from the members seated at the bar.

"Hey, baby." Sammie's loving smile was like a balm. "I heard you were here. I was going to pop in and check on you when I got a lull, but so far, it's been crazy busy."

"It's okay. I'm fine," I lied.

Sammie studied my face before her lips turned down in a sad smile. "No, you're not. Not yet, but you will be. You're a strong woman, and you'll get past this."

I answered with a quick nod. "I need to ask a favor."

"Anything."

"Can I have the key to George's room? I accidentally locked myself out."

"Sure." Sammie grinned as she reached for the key.

A couple of the members seated at the bar issued hushed sympathies. Thanking them, I reassured them that I was fine while trying not to climb out of my skin. Sammie laid the key upon the polished mahogany surface, and I snatched it up, quickly.

"Can I get you something to drink?"

"No, thank you, Mistress. I'm going to go to my room and go to bed."

"If you need anything else, you just let me know, okay?"

Bristling, I wanted to scream. I'd been offered help for the umpteenth time. I was sick to death of everyone treating me like I was a damn invalid.

"Yes, Ma'am. Thank you." I forced a smile before scurrying back toward the hallway.

Rounding the corner, I saw Tony standing next to his room, digging into his pocket. Destiny was upright and slumped against his imposing body. He turned his head and stared at me before sliding his key into the lock.

A cold sweat broke out over my forehead, and the walls seemed to breathe as I tried to align the key with my own lock. The doorknob began to blur. Behind my eyes, silvery lights flashed within a smoky black haze. My ears filled with a droning hum, muffling the noise coming from the dungeon. My knees began to buckle as darkness swallowed me up.

A deep, masculine voice kept calling my name. There was something cold and wet across my forehead. I opened my eyes and found I was in bed, back in my room. Mika was seated on the edge of the bed next to me. Worry lined his face.

"That a girl." Mika smiled tightly.

"What are you doing here?" I swallowed, spying a crowd of faces peering in through the open door behind his left shoulder.

"You passed out, pet. Have you eaten today? You promised me this morning you'd eat after the funeral."

Shit. Busted. "I…Um." My stutter drew Mika's infamous Dom glare. And he leveled that damn intimidating thing at me with maximum effect. "After everything that happened today, I never got around to it."

"I see," he replied with a disgruntled sigh.

"Dammit, Leagh," Tony hissed.

Snapping my head to the left, I saw that Mr. Whip-That-Ass himself stood on the opposite side of the bed near the nightstand. Arms crossed over his beefy chest, his dark eyes blazed in a mixture of anger and concern. And strangely, his face looked ashen and unusually pale.

"Look, I'm sorry. I didn't mean to forget. Okay?"

Their displeasure was a double shot of guilt that burned like cheap whiskey.

"Don't start with the attitude, angel. I'll make sure you get a red ass, and this time, you won't like it."

"What are you doing here, anyway?" I snapped. "Don't you have a sub to take care of? I'm fine. You can leave."

Tony's jaw clenched as his eyes narrowed. "You don't listen worth a shit, you know that?"

"Yeah, yeah. I know. Proper submissives don't..."

"Leagh," Mika growled in warning.

I exhaled a heavy sigh then turned my attention back to Mika. "I'm sorry, Sir. I had every intention of eating today. I swear."

"Well, you're going to now, little one," Master Stephen announced as he stepped up to the foot of my bed, wearing the requisite Dom scowl.

What was it with Doms? Did they have to pass Intimidation 101 before they could pick up a flogger? And just how many pissed off Doms were in here, for crying out loud? I glanced around. *Three. Three against one.* The odds were definitely not in my favor. Drake shouldered his way through the throng gathered at the mouth of my door, his expression tense. *Four. Great.* Now I was up to four angry Doms. It was a banner night for me.

Sitting up, I glanced at the furious but concerned faces and tossed my hands in the air.

"Fine. I'll eat! But somebody's going to have to give me a ride to a burger joint, because my car's down the street with an empty gas tank. Who's got a pair of tennis shoes in a size five, because my favorite Jimmy Choos are ruined from the fucking rain? Oh! And I'll need to bum a few bucks because Hayden and Sloane have taken every penny I own." My voice cracked as fat tears spilled from my eyes. "And while you're at it, can somebody please bring my Master back, because I can't do this anymore? I just can't."

Disgusted and utterly pathetic, I drew the blanket over my face and sobbed.

Mika leaned in and pulled me to his chest as I silently cursed myself for not being stronger.

"I'll be back in a few minutes," Stephen announced. "I'm going to run out and get the girl some food. If Carnation finishes comforting Destiny before I get back, please let her know that I'll return shortly."

"Will do," Tony replied. "Thank you for allowing your girl to stay with Destiny."

"I'm happy to help," Stephen replied. "When I get back, I'll help you get Leagh's car, too."

Sobbing against Mika, I listened as Tony and Stephen arranged their plans. A small part of me wanted to pull back and demand they stay out of my life, but a bigger, more grateful part of me felt nothing but relief. The bed dipped behind me as Tony's rugged body covered me from behind. His hot breath danced over the shell of my ear, and I trembled at the tangled rush of emotions crashing through me.

"Shhh. It's going to be all right, Leagh," he whispered. "We'll get you through this."

"Tony's right, pet," Mika soothed, brushing a hand over my hair. "You've had one hell of a bad day. But it's behind you now. We're going to get you back on your feet. No matter how long it takes."

Long minutes passed before I was able to pull myself together and stop the tears. Mika and Tony continued to hold and reassure me while I felt like a hundred different ways of humiliated over my meltdown.

Only when Stephen returned with a fast-food sack and a thick chocolate shake did Tony and Mika ease back. Immediately missing Tony, I sucked down my disappointment and sat up in bed, still unsure if I could gag the burger down. But with Tony, Mika, Drake, and Stephen watching me like a damn science experiment, I managed to eat half of it, and thankfully, it was enough to appease them.

The crowd outside the door had moved on, and one by one, the intimidating Doms left my room...all except Tony.

"Don't do this to yourself again, young lady, or else," Tony lectured as he sat in the spot Mika had vacated.

I pursed my lips in a frown. "It's not like I planned to pass out. It's been a bad day; that's all."

"Bad day or not, you'll start taking care of yourself, or I'll cuff you to this bed and do it for you. Are we clear?"

"Yes, boss," I huffed.

Tony bristled. "I have no idea how you've managed to go through life without a blistered ass twenty-four, seven."

I shrugged. "I guess nobody wanted to waste their energy."

"Until now," he quipped with a mischievous smirk as he stood. "Get some rest. I'll be back to check on you in a little bit. Stephen and I are going to go rescue your car."

Before he could step away, I reached out and clutched his hand. "I know I've said this already, but thank you. I really do appreciate what you've done for me."

Tony's expression softened as he leaned in low and pressed a soft kiss to my cheek. "I've only just begun, sweetheart. Get some sleep."

Chapter Five

A loud knock on my door, accompanied by the sound of giggles, woke me from my dreams. The clock on the nightstand displayed one, but my sleep fogged brain wasn't sure if it was morning or afternoon.

"Come on, sleepy head, open up. Pregnant woman needs to take a load off out here."

Julianna. With a small grin, I flipped on the bedside lamp, jumped out of bed, and raced to the door. When I pulled it open, not only was I met with her big, round baby belly, but Savannah and Trevor's smiling faces as well. My brows furrowed in confusion as I glanced at their arms brimming with shopping bags.

"What is all this?" I asked as Julianna pushed past me, dropped her packages on the floor, and climbed onto my bed. Stacking the pillows against the headboard, she leaned back on them and stretched out her legs.

"We went shoppinnggg," Trevor sang out with a laugh.

"For what?" I asked, motioning both him and Savannah in before closing the door behind them.

"For you." Savannah grinned. "After you crashed out last night,

Jenna Jacob

Tony snatched your clothes and shoes and gave Mika the sizes who then called Julianna—".

"Who called Savannah and me this morning, and voilà, you now have clothes!" Trevor added gleefully.

"Tony came to my room last night?" I gasped.

"Yeah. You didn't see him?" Trevor asked.

"Um, no."

Glancing over at Julianna, I watched Savannah's smile fade as she stared at the pregnant woman. "Hey, are you all right? Do I need to get Mika or something?"

"No!" Julianna barked, gripping the other woman's wrist in desperation. "It's only Braxton-Hicks contractions. If you tell him they've started up again, he'll come down here and carry my ass back home. I needed this. He's been on me like a mother hen. I'm *not* going to let the warden drag me back until I'm good and ready to go…which might be never. Spending the day shopping with you guys was the first productive thing I've done in weeks."

Savannah and Trevor unloaded the packages along with the ones Julianna had left on the floor before climbing onto the bed. We all sat watching Julianna who'd tossed her head back, closed her eyes, and gently strummed her belly. She exhaled long, slow breaths in a steady, rhythmic pattern.

"Stop that! I don't know nothin' about birthin' no babies, Miss Julianna," Trevor screeched, imitating Prissy from "Gone with the Wind." We all laughed as a goofy grin curled on his lips.

"How long have you been having the contractions?" I asked.

"A couple of weeks. Mika's about to have a heart attack…*if* I don't kill him first. You have *no* idea how hard I had to beg before he'd let me out of the house, even with Savannah and Trevor vowing to watch over me."

"Okay, but if you need Mika and you're not telling, I'll be the one who ends up with a red ass," Savannah warned. "I learned my lesson about helping you keep secrets from your Master, Julianna. The last time I tried to help you hide the fact that you were preg—"

"You ended up finding your submission *and* your happily ever after, so don't go there, Vanna," Julianna countered with a grin. "I just

72

need to rest for a bit. If they don't go away, one of you can race up to his office and get the prison ward, okay?"

The buzzing sound of the hidden camera snagged my attention. "Um, sis?" I gulped and pointed toward the bookcase. "I think you're already busted."

Julianna's eyes grew wide as she squinted at the shelves. "For Pete's sake, I'm fine, Master!" she called out toward the device in exasperation.

"Ten, nine, eight,"

"Trevor, what are you doing?" Savannah asked, wrinkling her brow at the grinning blond man.

"Seven, six," he continued as he started to laugh.

"Five, four," I chimed in with a giggle, helping Trevor count down the seconds until Mika stormed the room.

"Awww, shit," Julianna groaned as she struggled to sit up. Her gaze locked on the door and worry creased her forehead. "Leagh, while I still have a chance to tell you, I hope the clothes fit. If they don't, Savannah and Trevor can help you exchange them, since I probably won't see the light of day until this baby is born. There's a new cell phone in one of the bags. I added it to Mika's account. Don't worry about the bill or any—"

Suddenly, the door burst open. Mika stood, filling the frame as a menacing growl bubbled from deep in his chest. My eyes grew wide. Julianna simply whined, sending him a pitiful pout before she stretched her arms out to him.

"I know the drill, Master," she mumbled.

"After this baby is born, I'm going to spend weeks...no, months, spanking your ass," Mika fumed between clenched teeth.

"I know, I know. You tell me that every day." An impish grin replaced her dramatic pout. "Can I just say that I'm really looking forward to it?"

"What makes you think I'll let you enjoy it, precious?" Mika snarled as he leaned low. Julianna looped her outstretched arms around his shoulders and threaded her fingers around his neck. Mika plucked her from the bed and nestled her against his chest.

Julianna nuzzled his neck, trailing kisses up his throat and over his jaw. "Because you always do, Master. And because you love me so much."

A slight smile tugged his lips as he shook his head. "You naughty little minx. If you don't stop hiding the truth from me, I'll make sure you don't enjoy them, my love."

Julianna groaned. Mika turned his attention to the three of us left sitting on the bed. I felt Savannah's body tense.

"I hope you're happy with the clothes, Leagh." Mika smiled, then quickly sobered. "And next time you're in a bind and don't contact me, I'll let every Dom in the club redden your ass. Do I make myself clear, little one?"

I swallowed tightly. Not for one second did I think Mika was bluffing. "Yes, Sir. Crystal."

"Good. Come to my office tomorrow. I want to discuss something with you. By the way, I've asked Tony to keep an eye on you. I expect you to give him the same respect you show me, understood?"

Tony? He'd asked Tony? Was Mika fucking insane? Anxiety crashed through me like a wrecking ball. I wanted to beg him to let Sammie do it, or Drake. Hell, anyone but Tony. But nobody argued with Mika. Nobody. His club... his rules. "Yes, Sir. I promise."

"Good girl. And you two," Mika peered sternly between Savannah and Trevor before giving a little wink. "Thank you for keeping an eye on Julianna, who I'm taking home now. Enjoy the rest of your day, pets."

"See you guys soon," Julianna called out as he carted her out the door.

"You hope." Mika's warning echoed in the hallway as the door shut behind them.

"Every time Mika puts on his badass Dom hat, he scares the beejeebers out of me," Savannah whispered.

"Oh, like your two Masters are total teddy bears? Right!" I giggled.

"Not on a good day." A broad smile lit up her face, and her pretty brown eyes sparkled with absolute love.

It felt good to laugh. I tried to keep my guilt at bay as Trevor opened the numerous packages, laying the clothes out on the foot of my bed. I had no idea how I was going to repay Mika and Julianna, but I would find a way.

"It's time to start modeling, sis." Trevor beamed as he pulled me from the bed and shoved a stack of clothes into my arms.

After an impromptu fashion show that lasted a solid hour, I donned a pair of skinny jeans and a sinfully soft Angora sweater. Slipping into a pair of sexy Jimmy Choo ankle boots, I felt more alive than I had in days.

"Now that you're all dressed up and looking sexy, let's go grab a late lunch," Trevor urged, tugging me toward the door.

It really didn't take much coaxing before the three of us piled into my car and headed to Maurizio's. As we walked inside the restaurant, memories of George stole my breath. A ball of anguish clogged my throat as I blinked back tears.

"Oh, baby, I'm sorry," Trevor whispered. Pain wracked his face as he stared at me. "Let's go to Los Pueblo instead."

I shook my head and sucked in a ragged breath. "No. I want to stay here. Just no booths today, okay?"

I would be fine as long as we didn't sit in one of the secluded booths where George enjoyed doing all sorts of taboo things to me in public. Of course, no one could see, but it turned him on knowing we could be discovered easily.

"Hey," Scotty, the bartender/manager, called out with a wave of his hand. "Take a seat anywhere."

"Here's a table," Savannah announced as she rushed to set her purse down on an empty four top.

"Perfect. Thank you." I forced a smile. "Let's have some drinks."

"It's like, three in the afternoon," Savannah blinked as she gaped at me.

"You make it sound like it's a bad thing," I chuckled.

"Hell no!" Trevor shot us both a conspiratory grin. "It's five o'clock somewhere."

"I don't drink very much," Savannah confessed. "Someone has to stay sober to drive us back to Genesis."

"No problem," I assured. "I can drink like a sailor on leave."

Well, I usually could. Having skipped breakfast and lunch, the four sweet, woody bottles of wine proved a bad call of judgment...Really bad.

Savannah suggested food might sober us up a bit, so we ordered a couple of appetizers, most of which went uneaten. We were too busy laughing and drinking and drinking even more.

"We need more wine," Trevor announced. Standing he wobbled to the bar for another bottle. When he returned, he wore a frown.

"Whass wrong?" Savannah slurred.

"Snotty...umm, I mean, Scotty." Trevor nearly fell to the floor in a fit of giggles.

Tears leaked from Savannah's eyes, as well as my own. I patted the chair next to me, and Trevor slunk down onto the seat, still laughing hysterically as I wrapped him in a hug.

"What did Snotty say?" I asked, then snorted, and our laughter grew thunderous once again.

"This is the last bottle for us," Trevor pouted, holding up the half empty carafe.

"Slotty's a dirty rotten sloundrel," Savannah sulked.

Trevor and I weaved to the bar and tried to wheedle shots of vodka, but Scotty was adamant. Once our last bottle of wine was empty, our beverage choices were limited to coffee, tea, or soda. He'd cut us off. It was probably a good thing too, because the three of us were so blasted we had to make trips to the bathroom using the buddy system.

Raising our glasses with the last of the wine, Savannah's cell phone rang, and rang, and rang. Carefully placing her wine glass on the table, she pawed at her purse but couldn't find the right compartment that held the ringing device.

"Awww, just fnuck it," she groused as she held her purse to her face and spoke loudly into the leather bag. "Leave me a massage...err, I mean, a message at the beep. Beep!"

Trevor and I howled. That's about the time Scotty sauntered up to our table.

"You three seem to be having a fine time this evening," he announced with an arch of his brow. "Whoever is driving, I'll take your keys now."

"Are you a donnannit too?" I asked. "You sure give orders like one."

"No, Leagh, I'm not. But I am curious. Do your Dominants know where the three of you are right now?" Scotty asked with a suspicious glare.

His question hit me like a Mack truck.

Looking at Trevor first, then Savannah, when Scotty's gaze landed on me, his face fell. "Oh shit, Leagh. I'm sorry, baby. I didn't mean…"

"Oh honey, shhh. No. No, don't cry," Savannah commiserated as she plucked the napkin from her lap and wiped my face.

I hadn't even realized that tears streamed down my cheeks.

"It's okay, Snotty. Just can you call Dadd…Drake for us, please," Trevor whispered as he wrapped his arm around my shoulder and squeezed me tight.

I held the stiff cotton linen to my face and sobbed. Scotty's innocuous question knocked the foundation out from under me. And once I'd turned on the water works, I couldn't seem to find a way to shut them off.

Trevor and Savannah led me to the ladies' room and set me on a red velvet chaise. They held me as I bawled and bawled.

"I juss wanted to have a regular day, you know?" I sniffed. "And poor Slotty, he's prolly feeling like a hot plate of shit but isss not his fault. Isss really not. Isss mine."

"Noooo. Nobody's fault, L," Trevor soothed. "It'ss not fair, that's all. George loved you and you loved him. It's gonna hurt for more than a day."

"You're doing real good, Leagh," Savannah encouraged. "You're a strong lady. You're gonna—*hiccup*—gonna get through this. We're all gonna h—*hiccup*—help."

Trevor started to giggle.

"Sh—*hiccup*—it," Savannah giggled before starting to laugh. Hard.

And like a chain reaction, my sobs turned to snorts, and my tears of sadness turned into tears of laughter. Even in my drunken stupor, I realized how blessed I was to have such loving and supportive friends. When the bathroom door opened, the three of us looked up. Our laughter died instantly when four very unamused Doms—Drake,

Jenna Jacob

Dylan, Nick, and Tony—stepped in. Standing shoulder-to-shoulder, they looked down at three guilty and extremely inebriated subs.

"Don't put on your frownie face, Drake. We just had a little wine, that's all," Trevor explained as he held up his finger and thumb, measuring a one inch gap.

"You address me as Drake, now. boy?"

"Um, Dadddy, I'm s-ssorry," Trevor stuttered.

"You're sitting in the ladies' room for fuck's sake. You're telling me you only had a little bit to drink?" Drake snorted.

"Well, you're *standing* in the ladies' room, Master. How much have you had to drink?" Trevor giggled.

"Shhh, Trev—*hiccup*—vor," Savannah warned.

"Not near enough to keep me from whipping your ass bloody, you mouthy little shit," Drake thundered.

"Oh," the young man replied sheepishly. "Gotcha."

"Kitten?" Dylan slashed a brow at Savannah as she slunk down a little lower on the chaise.

"Yes, Mass—*hiccup*—ter? Dammit, I can't st—*hiccup*—stop these fucking things."

"Oh, precious. You're not allowed to use that kind of language, no matter how drunk you are," Nick reprimanded.

"Sorry, Sir," she whispered and hiccupped again.

"Leagh, what's going on here, sweetheart?" Tony asked as he crouched in front of me. Taking the soggy napkin from my fingers, he patted it against my cheeks.

His brown eyes sparkled with compassion and understanding. I desperately wanted to wrap my arms around his neck and hold on to him, forever.

"We came here for lun.. lun... food. But the wine was so nummy. I mean yummy. I dunno. Did we eat?" I asked, leaning forward, looking between the blurry images of Savannah and Trevor. She frowned and shook her head.

"Oh, I guess we forgotted to eat. I think wewere gonna do that, but I nn...needed a drink. Did chew know... George's is...his ghost is everywhere I go. So, we had some drinks, and I fin'lly got to laugh. So, we had a wholeeee bunch more of both and..."

Through my wine induced fog, I realized that I'd probably gotten Savannah and Trevor into a world of trouble with their Masters.

I looked up at Dylan and Nick and Drake. "Isss not their fault. Don't be mad at S'vanna and Trev 'cause of me, Sirs. I just wanted a day where my heart wasn't being ripped apart. And they didid that for me. I love them. I really love them." I turned back to Savannah and Trevor. "I really love you guys."

"We love you, too, Leagh," Trevor choked, blinking back tears.

Savannah nodded and gave my leg a tiny squeeze. "Yes, we do."

"I wasn't sure I could make it through all this ssshit, you know?" I explained to the Doms staring at me as their images blurred. "But S'vannah and Trev took the hurt away for a few hours. Don't punish them for that."

I begged the other Doms to be lenient on my behalf. "If it hadn't been for me, they'd have... never have... dis'ppointed you guys. They love you."

With the realization that I was the only sub in the room that didn't have a Dom to atone to, another wave of anguish caught me unprepared.

The four Doms exchanged a glance. Without a word, Drake bent and cupped his massive hands around Trevor's cheeks. Bending down, he slanted his lips over the young man's mouth, lifted him to his feet, and wrapped his burly arms around the thin man in a passionate embrace.

Nick cupped Savannah's chin as another hiccup split the silence. He couldn't help but grin at her. "You've had a *whole lot* to drink, haven't you, precious?"

"Uh-huh." She nodded with a goofy grin.

"I'm going out on a limb here, kitten, but I suspect you'll feel like homegrown hell in the morning. What do you say we take you home and tuck you into bed? It's late," Dylan coaxed as he and Nick each took an arm and helped Savannah stand.

"Okay," she exhaled on a wistful sigh before she melted against her two Doms, kissing them as if she'd not seen them in months.

I was left sitting alone, Tony's erotic eyes gazing into mine. I'd have given anything for him to lean in and kiss me and let me drown in his affections one more time.

"Come on, Leagh. I'll drive you back to Genesis and get you tucked into bed as well," Tony urged as he reached out and took my hand.

"I love you, Daddy," Trevor murmured as Drake led him out the door.

"I love you, too, boy. Let's go home."

We filed out of the ladies' room, clinging to the strong arms of sober and generously understanding Dominants. And as I waved goodbye to my partners in crime, I felt a goofy smile crawl across my lips.

"Thank you, guys, I had a won'erful time," I called out as Tony helped me into his car.

The night was cold, and when he climbed in and started the ignition, I released my seatbelt and slid across the seat, snuggling against Tony's hot body.

"What are you doing, angel?"

"Trying to get warm," I replied as I closed my eyes and drank in his blessed heat.

Slinking down further in the buttery soft seat, I rested my head in his lap as he silently drove down the street. The fever emanating from beneath his zipper called to the woman in me. I nuzzled my head into his lap. His thick erection pressed against my ear.

"Why do you have a hard-on?"

Tony chuckled. "Why is your head on my cock?"

"I asked you first."

"Because you're near me," Tony replied as he lowered his hand and threaded his fingers through my hair.

I closed my eyes and purred. His touch was sublime. Still high on wine, I trailed my fingertips along the inside of his thigh.

"Leagh," he said in warning. "What do you think you're doing?"

"You're touching me. I'm touching you. Iss all good."

"It's too good. And that's what I'm afraid of."

"When we get back to Genesis, will you make love to me?"

"What?" he gasped.

"Make love to me."

"No."

"Why not? Your cock is hard. It wants to. And you've told me that you want me."

"You're drunk, sweetheart."

"So?"

"Baby, when we make love you'll be stone cold sober. There won't be any regrets."

"Are you just saying that to me, or do you say that to all the girls?"

"What girls?"

"Your harem of pain sluts. When they get drunk, are you so chivalr...chirivlous..."

"Chivalrous?"

"Yeah, are you that with them?"

"I don't have sex with subs from the club."

Rising up, I gaped at him—both images of him—and blinked. "You're bullshitting me, right?"

"No, I'm not. And stop cussing."

"So, you whip 'em and you take 'em to your room, but you don't fuck 'em. Is that what you're telling me?"

"Language," Tony scolded.

I sighed. "In'ercourse. You don't have intracourse with them?"

"No," he chuckled again. "Why is that so surprising to you?"

"I thought BDSM was a bunch of kinky sex."

"Oh, angel. You've got a lot to learn." I frowned, and Tony laughed. "I enjoy the power exchange. It's not about the sex for me."

"So, who...you know, who cleans out your pipes?"

Tony laughed. "I have a friend with benefits, but we're not in a relationship."

"Oh." Mulling his words over, I settled my head back down on his lap and closed my eyes. His erection felt as if it had grown even larger, and I wanted desperately to ease his zipper down and taste his rigid cock. Instead, we rode in silence with his fingers massaging my scalp as darkness pulled me under.

The next thing I knew, Tony was rousting me awake before he led me up the back stairs of the club. I couldn't focus on much of anything, because the hall was spinning like a carnival ride. My stomach pitched, and my mouth watered.

"Hurry. I don't feel so good," I confessed. Tony looked down at me and cocked a brow.

"You're turning green, Leagh. Keep that shit down until we get inside your room, or we'll both be decorating the carpet," he warned as he jammed the master key into the lock.

As soon as the door opened, I raced to the bathroom and fell to my knees in front of the toilet. Tony stepped behind me and gathered the hair from my face in his fist. I retched until there was nothing left, then slumped over the commode. I wanted to curl up into a ball and cry. Limp and exhausted, I felt like the biggest idiot on the planet.

Spitting the acrid taste from my mouth, I rested my forehead in my palms. "You can go now. Show's over," I mumbled.

"Not on your life, angel," Tony whispered as he lifted me from the floor and carried me to the edge of the bed. Once seated, he crouched low and removed my boots. "Do you want me to set the trash can next to the bed?"

"No," I groaned as he tugged my sweater over my head and released my bra.

Lowering me onto the mattress, he removed my jeans. Staring down at me, Tony's hungry gaze lingered on my hard nipples before burning a path down my belly, pausing at the hot pink thong covering my pussy.

"Fuck me," he mumbled under his breath. He closed his eyes and shook his head, dragging himself from the trance. Yanking the covers over me with a heavy sigh, Tony stalked to the bathroom and returned with a large glass of water and three pain relievers.

"Take these and get some sleep," he barked.

I frowned at his tone and the angry expression lining his face, but sat up and followed his instructions. The beginnings of a headache throbbed behind my eyes.

"I didn't mean to piss you off. You didn't have to come save me, you know?"

"I'm not pissed, Leagh," he growled. "Someone has to keep a

damn eye on you. Now, go to sleep," he ordered as he turned on his heel and stormed out of the room.

"If you're not pissed, I'm a freaking virgin," I murmured before snuggling deep beneath the covers and closing my eyes.

≈

I woke the next morning feeling as if a cotton factory had taken up residence inside my mouth. My head pounded with every beat of my heart, and even the soft light emanating from the bathroom had me squinting. Oh, it was going to be a banner day all right, but I had no one to blame for it but myself. Sitting up, my stomach swirled. I held my palm against my forehead and groaned. Sliding into a pair of fuzzy, pink slippers, I pulled on my robe, intending to head to the bar and get something to wash down the sand coating my tongue.

I dropped the room key into my pocket before stepping into the hallway. Glancing up and down the corridor, I was grateful no one was around. Making my way toward the bar, the sound of a door closing behind me caused me to pause and turn. Looking over my shoulder, I watched Master Stephen and his submissive, Carnation, share a soulful kiss near his private room.

As if sensing my presence, the Dom opened his eyes and raised his head. With a broad smile, Stephen turned and strode toward me, leaving Carnation alone. Startled, her mouth fell agape as she slung a hateful glare my way before hurrying to follow behind her Dom.

"Dahlia." Addressing me by my club name, Stephen clutched me to his chest in a tight hug. When he pulled away, his green eyes sparkled as a smirk spread over his lips. "You don't look so good this morning, Dahlia. Feeling a little hung over?"

"Ah, yes, Sir. How did you know?" I asked shyly, wondering if everyone at the club knew I'd tied one on the night before.

No doubt, Carnation would have everyone convinced I was a raging alcoholic before the damn doors even opened. Nearly every shred of gossip that floated through Genesis originated with Carnation. She had a nasty habit of judging and insulting her fellow subs, and unfortunately, I'd been on the receiving end of her callous remarks more than once. Her eyes narrowed, jealousy written all over her face. I tried to ignore her, as I often did, and focused on Stephen instead.

"Tony and I picked your car up from Maurizio's after you'd gone to bed."

"Oh," I groaned. "I'm so sorry about that, Sir. Thank you for helping out with my car. I never meant to be a bother to you or Tony, Sir."

"It was no trouble at all. I was more than happy to help out any way I can. You're going through a difficult time. It will get better. Just take it one day at a time, okay?"

"I'll do my best, Sir. Thank you," I softly replied.

Stephen was a gentleman in every sense of the word, from his gentle smile to his understanding seafoam eyes. What the man saw in Carnation was beyond me. The girl was a self-absorbed trainwreck.

Sidling up against Stephen, Carnation flashed me a tight, condescending smile. "Master always helps out, even when it screws up our plans. We got here early last night to be the first to play on my favorite cross."

Of course, she did. If Carnation wasn't on display, she wasn't happy.

"But Sir Tony asked for Master's help, and by the time he got back, the equipment I wanted to scene on was in use. So, we had to play in our private room. At the end of our session, Master was so exhausted, he suggested we spend the night. Now I'm going to be late for work, but that's how it goes."

Accusation came through loud and clear. It was *my* fault she didn't get her spank and tickle in front of an audience. Most subs tuned into the sensations their Dominants gave them during a scene, but not her. She'd twist and turn on the cross, scanning the crowd to see who was watching before she'd start to wiggle, moan, and scream as if auditioning for the lead role in a kink film. The bitch had player written all over her. Stephen needed to open his eyes...and quickly.

"I'm so sorry. I didn't mean to inconvenience you, Master Stephen." I directed my apology straight to his face, ignoring Carnation altogether.

"It wasn't an inconvenience at all," he replied with a wave of his hand. Turning an unhappy expression on Carnation, he scrubbed a hand through his thick golden hair. "You got your reward. Stop complaining."

"Oh, I wasn't complaining at all, Master. You took very good care of me," Carnation replied in a sickening, sultry tone, fluttering her lashes in an attempt to look innocent.

Gag me.

"Of course, you weren't," Stephen replied with a sour expression.

"I just wanted to scene in the dungeon, Master. Is that a crime?" she asked, pawing at his dress shirt and all but humping his leg.

"Yes, I know you did. But you still haven't grasped the concept that submission isn't about getting your way. You need to stop topping from the bottom, my pet," Stephen chastised. His expression conveyed his displeasure with her antics.

What she needs is a ball gag shoved in her big fat mouth, Stephen, I thought to myself as I bit the insides of my cheeks to keep from smiling.

"If there's anything you need, Dahlia, please don't hesitate to ask." Stephen brimmed with such genuine kindness, I wondered why he kept a collar around Carnation's neck. He outclassed her...in every way. The man deserved a submissive who represented him in a positive light. Someone far better suited for his sophistication and compassion than that wretched twit.

Shame washed over me for thinking such ugly thoughts. I had no right to judge their happiness. I'd been on the receiving end of the same unflattering sentiments I felt toward the two of them. My less than stellar reputation was the reason a few of the members outwardly questioned my commitment to the lifestyle. If they were happy with their relationship, I had no business criticizing it.

"Yes, Sir. I understand, and I appreciate your generous offer."

"Master has a heart of gold for those who don't take it for granted," Carnation slammed with a sickening grin.

As if on cue, Tony shoved open the back door with his shoulder as he juggled a tray of Styrofoam cups in one hand and a white paper bag in the other.

Coffee! Now there's a real Saint.

"Excuse me, but I think Tony, Sir, could use some help." I flashed Stephen a soft smile as I scurried down the hall.

"Good morning, angel. How's the head?" Tony grinned. The anger he'd directed toward me the night before had vanished.

"Pounding like a construction crew working overtime, Sir. Here, let me help." I rescued the wobbling tray of coffees from his hand as I studied his eyes. Not a hint of irritation lingered. Perplexed but not willing to look a gift horse in the mouth, I didn't question his mood. "Now, if you'll kindly pull the knives out of my back?"

"What happened? Carnation?" He frowned, casting a glance toward the end of the hall.

"It's nothing. She isn't happy that Stephen helped you bring my car back to the club last night. Thank you, by the way."

"Of course, she's not. The limelight wasn't shining on her," Tony muttered under his breath before raising a hand to give a wave. "Stephen. Didn't realize you'd stayed overnight. Good to see you both."

"Please don't get her started again," I whispered sarcastically.

Tony flashed a mischievous grin and slipped his arm around my waist as we walked toward the other pair, stopping as we four met in the middle of the corridor.

"I was so disappointed we didn't get to watch you and Destiny scene last night, Master Tony," Carnation gushed before sticking out her bottom lip in an exaggerated pout. Her dark eyes roamed over his rugged body, all but undressing him in front of her equally attractive and muscular Master.

"I was busy elsewhere," Tony replied in a cold but polite tone.

"We're heading out. I need to get some work done today, and Carnation is late to her job. You two have a good one," Stephen announced, extending his hand.

Tony shook it and smiled. "You, too, man. See you tonight."

I followed Tony to the bar, placing the coffees on the smooth mahogany surface. When the back door slammed shut, I exhaled a sigh of relief before hopping onto one of the barstools. Tony sat next to me, watching me with a sideways glance.

"So, what did she do?"

"What she does best, insult and belittle. I don't get it. She's the second sub in two days who's given me shit," I groused. "Carnation can kiss my happy ass. She's a waste of good air. But what the hell have I ever done to Destiny to piss her off?"

"You're a free sub again, angel. Some women are territorial, because they're insecure. Don't give them the power to hurt you. And I'm not going to tell you again to watch your mouth. They're just extending their claws, insecure that you might steal their Dom." Tony shrugged as he wiggled the cups out of the cardboard tray.

"So, you're Destiny's Dominant?"

"Me? Oh hell, no. She's a free sub, too."

"Not in her mind," I whispered before sipping the dark brew. "Why would they consider me a threat in the first place? I'm the club brat, remember?" I smirked.

"You are a brat, but I can fix that." Tony arched his brows. "Don't you remember when Savannah first came here with Nick and Dylan? Some of the subs were horribly rude to her."

"Are you serious? I never knew that." I blew into the cup before taking another sip.

"Of course, you didn't. She wasn't a threat, because George was committed to you."

Was. The reminder forced a pang of sorrow deep in my bones.

"I still don't get it. We're not in high school anymore. They need to grow up and get over themselves. I have no intention of hustling Doms. And I'm certainly not going to eat sh...poop from insecure subs, either."

"Talk to Savannah; she survived it. Maybe she'll have a few pointers for you. Just be respectful and you'll be fine."

"I give respect, when it's given to me," I challenged, eyeing the white sacks on the counter.

"Don't lie to me, Leagh, or I'll take you over my knee again, here, and now." Tony warned with a sly grin. "But you enjoyed that, didn't you?"

"We're not going there," I rebuffed as I ripped open the paper bag and plucked out a fat blueberry muffin. My mouth watered as I peeled the paper away. "You got this from Marcie's Bakery down the street, didn't you?"

Tony nodded, pulled his muffin from the bag, and took a big bite. "I love these things," he mumbled with a mouthful.

"Me, too." I closed my eyes and bit into the buttery goodness. The plump, tart fruit exploded over my taste buds, and I moaned in delight.

"Don't do that," Tony growled as he took another bite.

"Do what?"

"Moan like that. It turns me on." He smirked.

"Shut up and eat," I scoffed, rolling my eyes.

Tony took a sip of coffee, set his cup down, and turned to face me. "You sure enjoy giving orders, angel. I think you might have a streak of Domme in you."

"Eat," I giggled with exasperation.

"Keep it up, Leagh. I'd love to see how high I could make you fly," Tony needled as a gleeful twinkle danced in his eyes.

I sobered and swallowed tightly. "I don't want to talk about that yet...or about what happened in your bathroom between us, okay? It's confusing. I'm trying to dissect it all, but I need more time. Hell, I don't even know if I *can*."

"When you're ready, I'm here." He nodded, placing his broad hand over mine. "There's no rush, angel. Take all the time you need."

"Thank you," I whispered and took another bite of the muffin.

"So, tell me, what do you have planned to do today?" he asked, reaching up to brush a crumb from my lips. His thumb lingered, and I fought the urge to slide my tongue from between my lips and suck it inside my mouth.

Something wicked flickered in his eyes, as if he'd read my mind. When he abruptly moved his hand away, I grabbed my coffee and took a sip, washing down the lump of desire lodged in my throat.

"I'm supposed to meet with Mika this morning. He wanted to talk to me about something. After I think I'll walk down the street and get a newspaper. I've got to find a job."

"Oh, that reminds me. Last night, Mika asked if I would talk to you. He's staying home to keep an eye on Julianna. Evidently, she's having some issues with her pregnancy."

I nodded. "Braxton-Hicks contractions."

"They're freaking him out." Tony grinned.

"Oh yes, I know," I laughed. "Poor man. What did he want you to talk to me about?"

"He's offering you a place to stay, here at the club, for as long as you'd like. Rent free, so you don't need to worry about paying him a dime. Trust me, he wouldn't take it, anyway. But he's concerned that staying in the room you shared with George is going to be too hard on you... emotionally. He'd like to modify one of the empty private rooms into a studio apartment."

"I can't do that." I frowned. "I need to get out on my own."

"He knows that, but until you're on your feet again, he needs to do this for George. We both think it would be healthier for you if you started fresh in a new room, though." He held up his hand as I opened my mouth to speak. "Just listen. Living at the club with the constant reminder of George is going to be hard enough. You don't need to surround yourself in the space you shared with him, day in and day out."

"Maybe I don't want to throw my memories of him away," I argued. George's scent was getting harder to detect in the blanket, but I still felt his presence in the room. I didn't know if I was brave enough to close the door on all we'd shared so soon.

"Why?" he asked, arching a brow.

"Because," I snipped, jutting out my chin.

"That's a child's answer, Leagh. Give me a reason why."

"Ah, so we're playing doctor-patient now?" I quipped. "Because I'm not ready to let him go, that's why."

"Angel, he's already gone," Tony acknowledged as he cupped one hand around my cheek. "I know you miss him. I know you feel lost. But we're your safety net now. All of us will do whatever it takes to help you get back on your feet. You have a lot of life ahead of you. Mika is only trying to help guide you through your grief as easily as possible."

"No, he's trying to push me through it," I countered with a huff.

"He and Julianna care very much about you. Mika doesn't expect you to make a decision today. Just think about it. But don't cut off your nose to spite your face," Tony replied. Sliding his hand away, he reached into his shirt pocket. Damn me for wanting to savor his touch a few minutes more. Handing me a business card, Tony stood. "I need to get ready for work. If you decide you don't want to change rooms, text me, and I'll let Mika know. But think long and hard before you make a decision. Will you do that for me?"

"All right," I sighed.

"Good girl," he whispered. Leaning down, he kissed my cheek.

Tony's praise warmed me like the summer sun, but the touch of his lips set me on fire. He felt good...too damn good. Inwardly chastising myself for how easily he charmed my arousal, I quickly focused on all the reasons Tony was bad for me.

"I'm going to hit the shower and head to work. I won't be around much the next couple of days, so stay out of trouble," he warned. "I'll be here at night, but I don't want other Doms coming to me with complaints."

"Wow. That hurt." I grimaced as I slid from the barstool.

"You know what I mean. Sit down." Tony scowled.

"No." I shook my head and stared into his eyes. "I should be grateful that you didn't call me brat, but honestly, your expectation that I'm going to disgrace you while your back is turned hurts a lot worse. Don't worry, Tony. You won't get any reports about bad behavior."

I turned and stormed back to my room as an avalanche of ineptness thundered through me.

I don't want other Doms coming to me with complaints. "Bastard!" I hissed as I stripped and started the shower.

Standing beneath the hot spray, I scrubbed away the oily film Tony's insult left behind. I may never win a "Submissive of the Year" award, but I didn't purposefully go out of my way to be disrespectful, either. The man was a callous and insensitive prick. I'd wanted to rail at him so badly, but I'd kept my cool and walked away. That, in itself, was progress. Could he not see that? *Probably not.* His stinging condemnation was another glaring reminder that entertaining fantasies about the man was foolish and a waste of my time.

Chapter Six

The next few weeks crawled by. I spent too much time sleeping and weeping. Surrounded by the memories of George wasn't helping. After serious consideration, I agreed to move into a new room. Mika pulled out all the stops, transforming a private play room into a cozy living space. The new apartment was much smaller than the one I'd rented before moving in with George, but at least my new furnishings far surpassed the hodge-podge I'd scrounged from the thrift store eons ago.

Ironically, my new digs were flanked by Tony's room on one side and Master Stephen's on the other. The walls were thick, and I usually heard little to nothing. But a few times I'd been awakened by the sound of raised voices as Stephen and Carnation argued. Thankfully, I'd not been exposed to a whisper as Tony cared for his throng of pain sluts.

After a few weeks in my new place, I found myself growing stronger. I spent less time crying and more time focused on getting on with my life. While I slid back into the depths of depression, I didn't allow myself to linger there for long. I mentally yanked up my big girl panties and started back on the road without George.

After my spat with Tony in the bar that morning, I tried to distance myself from the man. But he wasn't easily dissuaded. He visited often, usually with breakfast or dinner in hand, and offered up suggestions on ways to help me cope with my grief. While the loss of George was becoming easier to manage, I still wasn't healed.

Plagued by the thought I might possibly be using Tony as a form of super glue to mend my broken heart, his daily visits weren't helping me figure that emotional mess out.

I couldn't help but notice it was a struggle for the normally controlled Dom to keep his hands off me. Every time he reached out to caress me, he pulled his hand back as if he'd been burned. And the times he lost his head and kissed me, I felt the earth shift beneath my feet.

For the most part, we just talked. Tony shared stories of his family. The man had more brothers and sisters than I could keep straight. But he spoke of them with such devotion, I knew the love he felt for his family was unconditional. Thankfully, he never pressed for information about mine.

I spent my days looking for a job like I had at the café, one that would pay me in cash under the table, without having to fill out an employment application. It limited my options, but I continued to scour the want ads in hopes of being able to support myself once again.

I carried a copy of the restraining order George had executed inside my purse, but it did little to alleviate my worries. Matt would someday find me. I managed to keep a lid on my fears, staying diligent of my surroundings, and carried on one day at a time.

Nights at Genesis were the loneliest, but that was my own doing. I chose to isolate myself inside my room and read while I fought the urge to seek out Tony.

Fantasizing more and more about the man only added to the rollercoaster of longing and self-restraint raging within me. He filled my nightly dreams with animalistic sex and control, and it was becoming increasingly hard to shove my tangled emotions for him aside. My ridiculous jealousies had grown stronger, as well. The thought of watching him working the subs, fulfilling their needs, played havoc with my sanity. So, I hid from him, like a child. It was gutless but emotionally safer for me.

Mika stopped by the club a few nights a week, but for the most part, he stayed by Julianna's side. Trevor, Savannah, and I visited her several times a week, but the poor thing was climbing the walls. With four weeks to go until her April thirteenth due date, I worried she'd go nuts before the baby arrived.

Dressed in Burberry skinny jeans and a grey Akris cashmere sweater, I stared at the clock on the wall; it was ten-twenty-five. Mika had phoned a few hours earlier and asked that I meet him in his office at ten-thirty. Just as I reached for the knob on my door, there came a knock.

Pulling it open, I found Tony dressed in a sleek, tailored Italian suit, looking decadently drool-worthy. His deep bronze skin, peeking beneath the unbuttoned collar of the white oxford shirt, beckoned my tongue. His tie hung loose beneath the crisp collar. A panty-melting, nipple hardening smile curled his lips as his gaze roamed up and down my body in hungry approval.

"You look gorgeous, angel," he said in a smooth seductive voice as he sidled in close to me.

"Thank you. You look extremely handsome yourself," I whispered as a rush of heat ignited within. "What's with the suit?"

"I'm giving a lecture today at the university."

"Ah, I see. Arming all those young minds with scalpels and probes to dissect and analyze people's deepest secrets?" I smirked.

"Why, Miss Bennett, I believe you're purposefully maligning the science of psychology."

"You think?" I giggled.

"Hmm, if I didn't know better, I'd say you were begging for a red ass," Tony growled as a lurid grin crawled across his lips.

"No, Sir. As you can plainly see, I'm *not* on my knees," I said with a sassy smirk. "What are you doing here?"

He moved in close behind me, pressing his hard body against my back. "I can order you to your knees if you'd like, sweetheart," he growled in my ear. "We both know you'd enjoy the hell out of it."

His erection was hot and hard and wedged between the cheeks of my ass. My nipples drew up tight, and a rush of cream oozed onto my already wet thong. Unable to hide my thundering arousal, I gasped then sucked in a quivering breath.

Jenna Jacob

Yes, I *would* enjoy the hell out of being naked, on my knees at Tony's feet. It was how my nightly dreams with him began before morphing into sizzling sexual escapades that always ended with thundering orgasms. It felt pathetic that my sex life had been reduced to vivid, wet dreams.

"I stopped by to escort you up to Mika's office."

I tamped down my arousal, turned, and took a few steps back to put some much needed distance between us.

"Why? What's the meeting about? What have you two cooked up for my life *this* time?"

Tony leaned in closer, reaching around me, landing a hard swat on my ass. I jumped and yelped in surprise.

"What was that for?" I demanded. The sting spread down my legs and made my knees quiver. I placed my hand on his shoulder to steady myself, fighting the urge to close my eyes and savor the dull throb.

"Your smart mouth," he growled, a glint of mischief dancing in his eyes.

"I didn't say anything that wasn't true."

"Leagh, when people are trying to help you, it's polite to say thank you, not ask why or lash out with flippant remarks."

"It wasn't flippant, it was true. Besides, I didn't ask for help."

Tony chuckled softly. His hypnotic eyes held me prisoner. "No, you didn't. You never do. And that's the problem. You need to realize that just because you don't ask for it doesn't mean we're not going to give it."

"Yes, I get that, doc," I replied, flashing him a sarcastic smile and peeling myself away from his gaze. "I just don't want people feeling obligated. I'm better every day. I'm still having a little trouble finding a job, but that will eventually work out, too. I'm sure."

"Do you honestly think we feel obligated to help you?"

I shrugged. "I don't know. I've certainly done nothing to deserve it."

"You think that you have to earn our support?"

"It would make me feel less guilty."

"You have nothing to feel guilty about. You were George's sub. He touched the lives of a lot of people here. If we ignored the needs of the

94

sub he left behind, it would be as heartless as spitting on his grave. Stop getting your hackles up every time we try to help you, okay? You're part of our family here, like it or not."

"Okay," I whispered.

"Good girl. Now, let's go."

"Yes, Sir." I nodded.

Tony's eyes flared as another devastating smile spread across his mouth. My traitorous pussy fluttered. *Focus,* I chided inwardly.

Climbing the back staircase, Tony pressed his wide palm against the small of my back. While the heat of his skin made my body ache, the closer we got to the top of the stairs the more tension I felt rolling off him. What did *he* have to be nervous about? Something was wrong. I stopped and turned around. A grim expression lined his face.

"What does Mika want to talk to me about?" I demanded, searching for clues in his dark eyes.

"Reed's coming to see you," Tony replied, brows drawing together ever so slightly.

"Okay. So, explain why that makes you nervous. What does he want?"

"I'm worried he might upset you. I'm sure his visit has something to do with George. You've been making great strides over these past few weeks. I don't want anything to cause a setback."

"You're right. I am getting stronger. Whatever Reed has to say, I'll handle it. I'll be okay."

Tony's nod was less than reassuring, but I didn't want him delving into my psyche any further in the stairwell. Turning back around, I climbed the last few stairs, my mind whirling with questions that would hopefully be answered soon. I sucked in a deep breath and fortified myself for what lay ahead.

Tony reached around me and knocked on Mika's door. Julianna opened it. Her round belly looked bigger than it did the day before. The petite woman looked miserable, as if someone had stuck an olive on a toothpick. The makeup trying to conceal the dark circles under her eyes couldn't hide the fact she'd not been sleeping. Seeing her bright and cheerful smile helped ease my worries for her and the baby.

"What are you doing here?" I exclaimed as I reached out for a hug. "Better yet, how did you manage to break out of prison?"

She giggled as she bent at the waist to deflect her enormous belly and hugged me tight. "I bribed the warden with a blow job, of course."

"So, you made him an offer he couldn't refuse. That a girl," I giggled. "Lord, you look like you're ready to pop. Are you sure you're going to make it four more weeks?"

"I hope not. I feel like the Hindenburg. My feet are swollen, and I can't get these stupid contractions to stop. Thankfully, the doctor thinks I might deliver early, which would be a blessing."

"You will not deliver my son until he's done cooking, is that clear, pet?" Mika barked, wearing his most intimidating Dom scowl.

"It's a boy?" I grinned.

"Master thinks so." Julianna rolled her eyes. "I think it's a girl. He deserves a girl that will have all the boys drooling after her someday, don't you think?"

"You're so bad," I laughed.

"Behave, pet!" Mika warned.

"Oh, Master. I am behaving. How much trouble can I get into like this?" Julianna patted her baby belly and grinned.

"With you, my love, anything is possible." Mika shook his head before gathering me into a tight hug. "Thanks for coming up, Leagh."

"You're welcome, Sir." He released me and extended his hand, inviting me to sit on the long leather couch. I eased onto the cushion as Tony took a seat next to me. I couldn't help but grin as Julianna plopped into Mika's office chair with a groan.

"I received a call from Reed Landes yesterday morning. He wants to speak with you, so I invited him to come here."

"Do you know what he wants, Sir?" I asked, poised on the edge of a soft, buttery couch.

There was a loud knock at the door before Mika could reply. When he opened the door, Reed stepped through wearing a broad smile. It was almost too wide, and I could see the underlying tension in his eyes.

"How are you holding up, Leagh?" he asked as he bent and kissed my cheek.

"I'm doing pretty good...finally. How about you?" I asked,

studying the defined lines around his eyes that I'd never noticed before.

"It's different around the courthouse. But we're adjusting. Listen, I'm sorry I didn't contact you earlier about what happened with Sloane and Hayden and the house. George wouldn't have wanted it that way, but Hayden filed a repossession claim, declaring you a squatter. She'd altered the verbiage of the customary order, exempting you from due process. If I had appealed, George's estate would have been tied up in legalese for months. As it stood, Hayden was going to inherit the house regardless, but it pissed me off that she'd used Bernard to file, sign, and expedite the order." Reed shook his head in disgust.

"It's not a problem. I knew I wouldn't be able to stay there." The pain I thought I'd managed to put to rest came rushing back. I shoved a tight smile past the surging rawness.

"Bernard's involvement is a blatant conflict of interest," Mika growled.

"No doubt about that, but to prove it, I'd wind up having to drag Sloane's affair and George's reputation through the mud." Reed looked at me, his eyes filled with regret. "I'm sorry, Leagh. I know you lost everything, but I couldn't in good conscience do that to him."

"No." I shook my head. "I wouldn't have let you. Hayden did it to spite me. She always hated the fact I was younger than her. She thought my relationship with George was disgusting. Besides, the threats she and Sloane have leveled against me have me gagged and bound. If word about George's association with Genesis got out, they promised to sue me for defamation of character. That's a can of worms I'd rather leave unopened."

"The truth isn't defamation, darlin', but I get your drift. They skirted the law when they froze George's checking account and turned off your cell phone. But even without Bernard's interference, an honest judge would have had to side with Hayden, since she's next of kin."

"Don't worry about it. I'm looking for work, and I'll be back on my feet soon." At least I hoped so.

"We'll make sure she gets everything she needs, Reed," Mika announced. His amber eyes reflected a wealth of compassion.

"I know you're in good hands here, Leagh, but if something major comes up, call me. You still have the restraining order, right?"

My body tensed. I felt Tony, Mika, and Julianna's gazes all but sear my flesh. I issued a curt nod.

"Good. I made a vow to George. If anything happened and you needed to get out of town, I would arrange it all and get you to a safe location."

Tony bristled and slung his arm over my shoulder protectively. The minute we were alone, his interrogation would begin. What on earth was I going to tell him? Anxiety spiked, but I focused on Reed.

"Thank you," I whispered. "I appreciate knowing you're here if I need you."

"It's the least I can do for George." Reed's smile was bittersweet as he stepped toward me and squeezed my shoulder. "You were very important to him, Leagh. He loved you very much."

Emotion clogged my throat, and I swallowed tightly.

"I know the friendship you two shared meant the world to him, Reed. It will be a long time before the void he left in our hearts heals."

Reed stood, straightened his shoulders, and sucked in a ragged breath. "Indeed. The reason I came here today is to let you know that tomorrow morning at ten o'clock, I'll be reading George's will. He made some arrangements for you, Leagh. I'm sorry I haven't had a chance to wrap this up sooner, but my docket was booked."

My heart squeezed, and bittersweet warmth filtered within. Not only had he given me a safety line through Reed, but I knew George too well; *arrangements* meant money. He'd gone to his grave still yearning to provide for me.

"You don't have to be present at the reading, Leagh. Hayden will be there, and I know there is a wealth of bad blood between the—"

"I'll be there," I interrupted with a confident nod.

The false self-assurance I projected did little to mask the fear of Hayden's threats singing through my brain. Knowing I'd be face to face with the atrocious bitch sent a shiver down my spine. If I failed to show up at Reed's office, it would be the same as crowning her queen of intimidation. I refused to wilt away or cow down to the skanky whore. I'd made a vow, long ago, that I would never let another soul steal my strength.

Still, I held no illusions. Hayden would be royally pissed if George left me a ball of lint. Especially after she and Sloane went to so much trouble destroying all the treasured gifts he'd given me. But I wasn't a fool, either. The pretentious princess would soon have more money than Midas, and with it, the power to make my life a living hell. I'd have to watch my temper and my tongue—two things I wasn't very good at—or pay a huge price.

My fear amplified. My stomach swirled, and I wiped away the beads of sweat forming above my lip. Tony slid his broad hand to my nape and gently massaged the tense muscles. His reassurance did little to appease the icy swell of fear swallowing me up.

"Honestly, Leagh, you don't have to attend," Reed repeated as his gaze dipped to my trembling fingers. "I can come by here after the meeting and give you the details."

"No. I want to be there." *Liar* "The words will be coming from your lips, Reed, but they're the last connection I have to George. Don't deny me that, please." Tears stung my eyes as my stomach continued to pitch and yaw.

"Of course not, sweetheart," Reed sighed in resignation.

"Thank you," I replied with a weak smile. "I'll see you in the morning."

Without waiting for him to reply, I bolted upright from the couch and raced out of Mika's office. Taking the stairs two at a time, I dug the key to my room from my pocket.

The air around me seemed heavy and thick, as if a plastic bag had been placed over my head. I struggled to fill my lungs before suffocating on anxiety and fear. The thought of slicing open the fresh scars of George's death, in front of Hayden, had me in a nosedive to hell.

Heavy footsteps echoed behind me as I rushed into the hallway. The scent of leather poured over me, and with it, a barrage of memories clawed my heart. Tears blurred my vision as I raced inside my room and lunged toward the bathroom.

Bending over the sink, I splashed cold water on my face as I gasped for air. Sobs wracked my body. I fell apart at the seams. Stupidly, I thought I'd worked past my stage of fear. But it was back, choking the life out of me.

"Deep breaths, Leagh. You're having a panic attack," Tony explained, rubbing a comforting hand over my back. "Relax, and take long, deep breaths."

Gripping tight to the handles of the faucet, I did as he instructed. Water dripped from my face as I fought to fill my lungs with air.

"Don't let Hayden do this to you, sweetheart. She's not worth it."

"I know," I gasped. "But she scares me. I don't know how to fight her."

"You don't have to. She can't do a damn thing to you unless you let her," Tony whispered in a calm, reassuring whisper. Tucking a strand of hair behind my ear, he pressed a kiss to my temple. It felt heavenly. "You're a strong woman, much stronger than Hayden will ever be. You walk into that meeting tomorrow with your head held high. There's nothing she can do or say that will strip away your power."

"I know. But the fears are back, like before. I don't want to feel this vulnerable anymore. It's too overwhelming."

Tony wrapped me in his arms and held me close. "What do you need me to do for you, angel?"

"Take it away. I don't know how, but please. Just take it away."

"I do," Tony assured. "Do you want to make you fly again, sweetheart? I can take it away for a little while."

Yes. Oh, yes! I needed that pristine silence…that place where the black oily sludge congealing inside me couldn't touch me.

"No." I shook my head. "I can't run away from my feelings, Tony. If I give into them, they'll drag me under. I have to plow straight through them and put the pieces back in place."

"I understand, angel. But if it's too much, I'll take it away…Calm the chaos and give you a bit of mental peace."

"Thank you," I sniffed, wishing it wasn't so easy to feel safe with him.

"What do you need right now, Leagh?"

I clung to his body and sobbed, missing George and needing his reassurance now more than ever. Vanquishing my fears wasn't Tony's responsibility, but the tattered pieces of my heart needed mending, and I couldn't find enough thread in my soul to do the job alone.

"I need you to talk to me," I sniffed. "I can't sort my feelings out. They're too jumbled, and I don't know where to start."

"We can get them organized. Come on." Tony snagged a towel off the rack and patted my face dry. With a firm but gentle hand clasped around my elbow, he led me to the bed. "Lie down and scoot over a little bit."

I scooched to the center of the bed, and Tony climbed in next to me. Wrapping me in his arms, he rolled me to my side, and hugged me tight against him. Lying in his arms, I silently damned the weak, frightened woman inside me, while cursing the unrelenting attraction I felt toward him. Still, I took what he offered without apology. I needed his strength.

"I want you to close your eyes and take some deep breaths. Focus on the sound of my voice and clear your mind. Do you understand?"

"Yes, Sir." Meshed against his strong body, I closed my eyes and absorbed his surging warmth as I tried to quell the fears of what tomorrow might bring.

"Good girl. You're doing wonderfully. I want all your focus on my voice as you let your body go lax. Release all the tension in your muscles." I exhaled a deep sigh as I softened against his steely frame. "Very nice, sweetheart. You're doing fine. Keep your breathing slow and find a comfortable rhythm. Don't tense a single muscle. I'm going to ask you some questions, and I want you to say the first thing that pops into your mind. Don't analyze it. Just respond, understood?"

"Yes," I whispered.

"What scares you most about your meeting with Hayden?"

"That she'll have me arrested."

"Have you done something illegal?"

"No."

"Then, she has no cause to have you arrested. Right?"

"Unless someone says something bad about George."

"Do you have control over what others say about him?"

"No."

"Are you going to speak ill of George or tell anyone that he was a member of the club?"

"No. Never." I shook my head.

"Then her threat is an idle one, angel. She can't do anything to you. It's a smoke screen to provoke fear. She's trying to hold you hostage to other people's actions. Are you going to give her the power to scare or hurt you?"

"No. I won't give her a damn thing," I protested.

"Relax. Breathe. Release your tension again, angel. Good."

One by one, Tony plucked my fears, held them up for me to inspect before crinkling each one in his fist and tossing it aside. Methodically, he conquered my fears and insecurities with patience, logic, and understanding.

"Do you feel better now?" he asked as his fingers fluttered against my cheek.

"Yes. Thank you. I'm sorry I lost it like that. It crested like a giant wave and pulled me under. I couldn't stop it."

"No need to be sorry. The minute you start to feel overwhelmed, do exactly what we did here. Breathe, relax, and take each worry, one by one. And if it's not working for you, call me, come get me in the dungeon, or text me. I'm here for you, angel, if you'll let me."

"I appreciate what you're doing for me. But I really need to try to do this by myself."

"One day, you will. But cut yourself some slack, Leagh. Your life has been turned topsy-turvy, and now you have to dredge up feelings you've struggled to put behind you. It's hard to have to dig up sad and hurtful emotions. It's a lot for anyone to handle."

I nodded as Tony's cell phone buzzed. He tossed a glance toward the clock as he squirmed, fishing his phone out of his pants pocket. "Shit. I'm going to be late."

"Go," I urged as I rolled away and sat up in the middle of the bed.

"Hello." Pausing, he listened, then sat up, and nodded. "I'm on my way. Thanks, Trish. Can you reschedule my four o'clock? I need to take care of some things after the lecture. Thanks. See you tomorrow."

Tony ended the call and turned to me with a smile. "Be ready at four-thirty. We're going out for dinner."

"Okay," I replied on a wary tone. "Why?"

He started to laugh. "I'm going to break your habit of asking why, Leagh, even if I have to do it over my knee. Say, okay, Sir."

"Okay, Sir. Now why are you taking me to dinner?" I smirked.

"You know what? You're not a brat. Not at all. You're a minx." He grinned. Leaning in, he brushed a whisper of a kiss across my lips. "Because I want to, that's why. I need to run. I'll see you this afternoon."

"Enjoy your lecture, and try not to corrupt those young minds too horribly." I grinned.

"The only mind I'm going to corrupt is yours, sweetheart. Only I'm not going to stop there. I intend on corrupting your body, too." Flashing me that stunning smile, the one that made it hard for me to breathe, Tony stood and hurried out the door.

"I sure hope so," I sighed, flopping back on the bed.

Tony had planned a romantic dinner for two, complete with candle light, champagne, and a roving violinist. It was the best night I'd had in forever. While George and I had frequented plenty of expensive restaurants, the one Tony had chosen beat the rest, hands down. He was making it damn hard to keep him from seeping into my heart. And still wearing the same suit he'd had on this morning, he looked like every woman's fantasy.

He knew all the right words to say. And every time he pressed for me to open up, he led me through another door that erased my grief. Being away from the club, talking to him about my relationship with George was neither difficult nor painful. Tony had a way of making me feel as if I was adding another healing layer to the scars that remained. All night, the carefree way Tony cupped the small of my back, caressed my cheek, or held my hand, fanned the flames smoldering inside me. There were times I almost felt whole.

Once back at the club, Tony walked me to my room. Standing outside my door, I felt as nervous as a teenager on my first date. Filled with a sudden shyness, I didn't know what to say or do. When he brushed his fingers through my hair, the tingles colliding inside me left no doubt; I was a woman, fully grown.

"I had a wonderful time tonight, angel." Tony's voice was deep and smooth, practically melting me from the inside out.

"I did, too," I murmured shyly, wondering if he had any clue how hot he made me.

"We'll have to do it again, sometime…soon." His voice dipped to an even lower seductive cadence.

"I'd like that." I nodded ever so slightly.

The tension was thick, and I found it hard to breathe, even more so when Tony leaned in and slanted his lips over mine. I'd spent weeks, days, hours dreaming of tasting his fiery passion again. But nothing prepared me for the conflagration of hunger twisting inside me.

Gliding his tongue over the seam of my lips, I opened my mouth, inviting him in. The electrifying invasion of his tongue had me gripping the sleeves of his suit coat. I held tight as Tony ate at me with devastating precision.

Pushing me up against the door, he gripped my wrists, pinning them above my head as he ground his thick erection against my belly; sucking in my mewling cries of delight. Stripping me of all inhibitions, I arched my pussy against his driving shaft, silently cursing the clothing barring him from being inside me.

And just as quickly as he'd seized my passion, Tony pulled back. A look of alarm blazed in his hungry eyes.

"Fuck," he muttered. "I'm sorry, Leagh. I shouldn't have done that."

"No…it was…"

Tony shook his head and took a step back, leaving me wet and aching for his warmth. "I'm not going to make the same mistake twice, sweetheart. When you're ready, let me know."

Clenching his jaw, he turned and stormed down the hall. In stunned silence, I stood watching as he jammed his key into the lock of his door and disappeared into his room.

I bit back a growl of frustration, went inside my room, and crawled into bed.

～

S eated in Reed's office the next morning, waiting for Hayden to arrive, all the reassurance and comfort Tony had showered upon me the night before was but a foggy memory. Attempting to calm myself, as he had taught me was like trying to piss up a rope. It was not happening.

Tense and on alert, I was desperate for Tony's soothing magic. Why hadn't I let him come with me when he'd all but demanded at dinner the night before?

Because you're a stubborn, idiot. My inner voice of reason mocked.

Reed sat at the head of the long conference table to my right. Tapping my toe nervously, I watched as he opened a large manila folder, then reached inside and pulled out a small white envelope before handing it to me.

"It's a private message George left for you, Leagh. You can read it now if you'd like. Or wait until you're somewhere private. It's yours to keep."

My fingers trembled, and my throat constricted. Staring at the familiar scrawl, I smiled. George swore his writing was legible, but it wasn't. Tears stung the backs of my eyes as memories filled my mind.

George had brought a card to the café one night. He'd handed it to me with a broad smile.

"Card," I'd said.

"Yes. It's a card. For you," he'd confirmed, as a confused frown lined his face.

"What's does this say?" I'd asked. Pointing to the word he'd written on the front, I'd thought he was playing a game.

"What do you mean, what does it say? It says Leagh!"

"Oh. I thought it said guess, so that's what I did," I'd laughed.

The envelope I now held in my hand bore the word, 'Guess,' which was, of course, 'Leagh' in George's horrific penmanship.

I brushed my fingers along the indentation of my name as if were a lost treasure. This was the only tangible piece of George that Hayden and Sloane hadn't destroyed. The conference room door swung open, and I quickly slid the priceless note inside my purse.

Reed's secretary stepped inside the room as Hayden *and* Sloane waltzed in. The poor man didn't bother masking his surprise.

"What the hell is she doing here?" Sloane thundered. Her expression looked damn near demonic as she slashed a cold stare at me.

"Please, take a seat, Sloane. I should ask the same of you." Reed arched his brows, awaiting the woman's reply as his secretary quickly vacated the room.

"Surely, you haven't forgotten the terms of my divorce, have you, Reed?" Sloane purred as she and Hayden moved to the other side of the table. Their identical feline-like movements unnerved me.

Reed's lips drew together in a tight, angry line as his jaw ticked. "No, I've not forgotten a damn thing. And neither did George. But he was a cautious man, so if you're thinking about contesting a single word of his will, you're wasting your brain cells, dear."

"There is no stipulation about contesting, Reed. I would never have agreed, otherwise. Surely, you don't take me for a fool." Her tone was unmistakably condescending.

"You're a lot of things, but a fool isn't one of them. However, George ensured there was a loophole," Reed replied with a satisfied smile.

"I doubt that highly. But we'll see, won't we?" Sloane sneered.

I had no idea the meaning behind their tense volley, but I had a sneaking suspicion I would soon find out.

"Can we get on with this charade?" Hayden interrupted as her arrogant gaze homed in on me. "I have decorators to meet. I need to gut every room in *my* house and dispose of all the sleazy, disgusting shit left behind by a certain squatter."

Hayden's insults stung, but imagining the look on her face when she discovered the toy bag under our bed or the cross and spanking bench in the guest room had me howling—on the inside. Somehow, I managed to keep my mouth shut and not ask if she was sure she didn't want to keep them in case she wanted to get her kink on.

Reed cleared his throat and withdrew several sheets of paper from the folder in front of him. Pages that held my Master's last wishes…his last words. It seemed paltry in comparison to the abundance of light he'd brought to my life.

As the legal jargon rolled off Reed's tongue, I focused on thoughts of George and ignored the two venomous women seated across from me. Anger and resentment rolled off them in a choking wave, but I was there for my Master, not them.

"As per my divorce decree dated the sixteenth of May, two thousand and one," Reed recited, "My ex-wife, Sloane Ingram Marston, and Hayden Ingram Marston, will share equally the remaining assets of my estate.

Reed's words wrapped around my brain, sending a shock wave clear to my toes. I couldn't imagine George leaving Sloane a steaming dog turd, let alone half of his estate. Why on earth would he do such a thing? I was beyond flabbergasted. It obviously had something to do with divorcing the shrew, but half his damn estate? That had to be in the millions. Why the hell didn't he throw both her and Bernard under the bus when he discovered their affair? The whole thing made absolutely no sense.

"If any beneficiary," Reed continued, "directly or indirectly, contests any provisions set forth designed to thwart my wishes, the contesting beneficiary provisions shall be revoked and all provisions shall be disposed of under the terms set forth in the sealed addendum to my Will."

Reed lifted another document and began speaking again as I tried to silence the questions racing through brain. "With the exception of separate trust established November 16, 1978 in the sole name of Paula Willhite-Harrington, shall be—"

"That wretched whore," Sloane spat in disgust.

I had no idea who this Paula woman was, but she was not a friend to Sloane, that much was obvious. Did George have another daughter? Another ex-wife perhaps? Questions continued bombarding me. Reed ignored the blast of contempt pouring off Sloane and kept right on reading. Once this was over, I planned to ask him about the mystery woman, Paula.

"And one million dollars," Reed announced, "already established in an account at the Federal Community Bank in the name of Leagh Marie Bennett."

My heart thundered in my chest as his words echoed in my ears. Stunned by George's generosity, relief slowly seeped through me. I could buy a new identity, enroll in college, and get my degree in advertising. Best of all, I could pay back my friends. The amount of money George had set aside for me was staggering. What touched me most—more priceless than the amount of money—was George's need to keep me protected and safe. It was the one thing I loved the most about him.

"Over my dead body," Sloane screamed as she leapt from her chair. Her face twisted in rage as she glared at me and slammed her fist on the table. "You're not going to touch one red cent of *my* money. Do you hear me, bitch?"

Her venomous outburst jolted me from my daydreams and filled me with fear. Snapping my head in Reed's direction, the man looked as if he was struggling to control his own anger. Gripping the hinge on his glasses, Reed tore them from his face and slashed the evil bitch a scowl.

"Sit down, Sloane. George's directives are not up for debate. You will refrain from your snide commentary until the will has been read, or I'll have you escorted from my office." Sloane huffed and issued a curt nod. "George had every legal right to name Leagh as a benefactor. Need I remind you that George inherited his fortune? You simply married into it, Sloane. The exterior of your grief-stricken ex-wife persona is showing cracks."

"How dare you sling insults at me?" she fumed. Her face darkened to a deep crimson.

"It's not an insult, Sloane, it's the truth," Reed dryly replied.

I bit the inside of my cheeks to keep from laughing.

"If I were you," he warned. "I'd count my blessings George didn't liquidate every penny and give it to Paula ten years ago."

"Our divorce decree supersedes his will, Reed. Don't think I haven't done my homework. You biased prick."

"I'm sure you've received a plethora of legal advice from Judge Bernard, both in and out of bed, Sloane," Reed drawled with an exaggerated roll of the eyes. "But you're entitled to what is left of George's estate. You don't get to dictate who he bequeaths a fucking dime to. If Bernard, your all-knowing legal advisor, was here he'd inform you the same."

"Oh, he'll be hearing from me. In fact...Immediately," Sloane hissed turning her hateful gaze toward me. "You won't touch of dime of my money, you white trash gold-digger. I'll have your account frozen while your bony whore ass still sits in that chair. Don't think I won't."

"For heaven's sake, Sloane. You can't do that, and we both know it. Stop being so damn dramatic." Reed's tone teemed with exasperation.

Sloane flashed him an icy smile as she pulled out her phone and began texting. My heart was in my throat. She obviously carried tremendous power as Judge Bernard's personal fuck-toy, and I was convinced this was just one of many tricks up her sleeve. Giving a cursory glance at Hayden, I discovered a smarmy smirk poised on her lips. My blood pressure spiked. I wanted so badly to lean over the table and bitch slap both her and Sloane for attempting to thwart George's wishes.

Sloane slid her phone back into her purse, leveling an arctic glare Reed's way. "Let it be noted that I'm contesting George's will, and paperwork on my behalf is being filed as we speak." She and Hayden stood in unison, tossing their noses in the air, as if they'd practiced the move for years.

"You're actually going to throw away thirty million dollars because your panties are in a twist that you violated your prenup, Sloane?" Reed chuckled.

She stopped and turned toward Reed. "Don't think, for one second, you'll be presiding over this case. Need I remind you it would be a gross conflict of interest? And if you stick your nose into any of this, I'll have you disbarred."

"Suffice it to say, Bernard won't be presiding over or actively engaged in the process either. I'll make certain he suffers the same fate. I don't have a single qualm about revealing your little secret or having that son of a bitch disbarred. Are you certain you want to play hard ball with me, Sloane?" Reed smirked, arching a brow.

109

Jenna Jacob

I couldn't help myself. I laughed. It was empowering to watch Reed stick up for all the shit George had to swallow in order to live in peace from his hateful ex. The haughty hag had that and more coming to her.

"I don't know what you think you're laughing at, you kinky little bitch," Hayden screeched as she rushed around the table, looking like she was ready for a throw down. I lurched from my seat and curled my fists. Lunging forward, I baited her to take a swing. I wanted nothing more than to knock her flat on her arrogant ass.

When Hayden recoiled in fear, I smirked. "Sticks and stones may break my bones, but whips and chains turned your Daddy on like a fucking light bulb. I made his dick so hard a cat couldn't scratch it," I taunted in fiendish glee.

Chapter Seven

Reed grabbed my arm and pulled me back, just as Hayden lurched toward me with a feral scream. Simultaneously, Sloane grabbed a fistful of her daughter's hair and hauled her back.

"I'm going to kill you. You fucking bitch! Then every penny of Daddy's money will be mine!" Hayden spat as her eyes bulged, and her face blazed bright red.

"Wrong, princess. It's not yours and never will be. You have to share it with Mommy dearest. You want to tangle with me? Bring it, you repulsive, pampered bitch," I hissed. "I'm not afraid of you or your childish threats."

As the words tumbled off my tongue, my body trembled. Not in anger, but in a mixture of self-preservation and adrenaline. I could tell she was ready to scratch my eyes out—not because of the money—for pure spite

"Did you just threaten Leagh in my presence, Hayden?" Reed barked as he stepped in front of me and blocked both women from my view.

"Of course, she's not, Reed," Sloane quickly assured as her voice quivered. The woman was clearly shaken by her daughter's behavior and back-peddling to smooth Reed's retribution. "Hayden is despondent over the loss of her father. She has no idea what she's saying."

"Blow those lies up someone else's ass. If anything happens to Leagh, if she breaks so much as a fingernail, I'm pressing charges. Do you understand?" Reed bellowed. His body taut, and his hands clenched at his sides. "I can't stand the sight of either one of you. George was a good man. This meeting is over. Get the hell out of my office. Now!" Reed growled as he pointed at the door.

Peering over his wide shoulder, I watched as Sloane yanked the door open before shoving Hayden out. As soon as it closed behind them, Reed turned and leveled me a gaze brimming with anger.

"What the hell possessed you to bait Hayden like that?" he spat.

I blinked in confusion. "What did you expect me to do? Stand there and take her death threat without trying to defend myself?"

"Yes!" he yelled.

"You're insane," I countered. The worry in his eyes doubled my own fear. "Why are you so upset, Reed? What do you know that you're not telling me?"

"Fuck," he sighed and scrubbed a hand through his thinning dark hair and paced for a long minute. "The college kid that was found dead in his car about eight years ago, do you remember that?"

"I wasn't living here then. What does some dead college kid have to do with Hayden?"

"A twenty-two-year-old Loyola University student was found inside his brand new Camry. He was parked outside his apartment complex with an EpiPen pen shoved in his chest. Inside the vehicle was a swarm of bees. The kid was highly allergic to bees."

"Okay. I still don't know what this—"

"Let me finish, Leagh," Reed scolded as he held up his hand. "The locks on his brand new car had been tampered with. He'd been unable to get out of a car filled with bees. The coroner's report estimated he'd been stung over three thousand times."

"You're telling me this...because?" I had no idea where Reed was going with his story.

"His name was Ethan Breuer. He was Hayden's boyfriend."

My mouth fell open. Time seemed to freeze as Reed's words knocked the air from my lungs.

"Are you trying to tell me that Hayden killed him?"

"I never said that. But possibly, like me, you find the details surrounding the young man's death a bit more than coincidental. I have no proof Hayden killed him, and I don't have proof Sloane didn't do it, either. I'm simply saying I wouldn't put it past either one of them. They're both cut from the same cloth and crazier than a couple of shithouse rats."

My mouth went dry, and the room began to spin. I gripped the back of the leather chair I'd been sitting in to support my trembling legs. "Why would either of them want this kid dead? What did he do?"

"Hayden had made up her mind that she was going to marry Ethan. In fact, at the time of his death, she and Sloane were shopping for bridal dresses. Both had ironclad alibis. Ironically, they went shopping the day *after* Hayden caught Ethan and another girl in bed together. Tell me, do you get the impression Hayden is the forgiving type? That she'd find the man of her dreams in bed with another woman and race right out to the bridal boutique the very next day?"

"Not in this lifetime." My head swam. "So, Hayden got a taste of what George felt when he found Sloane and Bernard in bed that day."

"Oh, Hayden doesn't know a damn thing about Sloane's affair."

"Right, because Sloane would run the risk of Hayden being crushed and hating the nasty heifer. And she's invested way too much time and energy grooming Hayden to be a perfect little mini-me," I scoffed with a brittle smile.

Frazzled by the fear that Hayden would actually make good on her threat, I began to panic. It had been a long time since I'd felt death loom so close. It was as immobilizing as it had been in the past. Then, something strange began to happen. Anger began to bubble over and consume my fear.

"Why didn't you tell me any of this before the meeting, Reed? I've just signed my name to the top of Hayden or Sloane's hit list."

"I didn't think things were going to go to hell in a hand basket, but the minute I saw Sloane walk through the door, I knew it was going to get ugly. I wish I'd never asked you to come today, Leagh."

"That would have pissed me off even more," I hissed.

I was lashing out at George's best friend, trying to blame him for my own mistakes. If I hadn't run off at the mouth and had kept a lid on my anger, I wouldn't be choking on a mountain of fear. Their animosity I could live with; the prospect of being at the top of their hit list—not so much.

"Look, I'm sorry, Reed. I'm really not blaming you. I'm mad at myself and…shit. Hindsight is a steaming pile of crap, isn't it?" I sighed. "Did George know about Ethan's death?"

"He shared his suspicions with me, and we discussed the possibility of Hayden's involvement. But all we had was speculation. The official police report concluded that a queen had built a nest in the wheel well of Ethan's car, and the bees migrated through the ventilation system."

"You've got to be kidding me." I snorted in disbelief. "Was there a hive anywhere in Ethan's car?"

"No." Reed pursed his lips and shook his head.

"I didn't think so either. And that piss-poor excuse was the best the cops could come up with? Who the hell was heading up the investigation…Bernard's friends?" I was furious.

"George and I suspected that Bernard put pressure on the police chief. They're hunting buddies."

My mouth gaped. "You're telling me that George, *my* George, had an inkling his daughter or maybe his ex-wife committed murder, and he did nothing about it?"

I couldn't comprehend any part of Reed's story. George, the man I *thought* I knew, would never have ignored either woman's involvement in a petty shoplifting, let alone murder.

Reed held up his hands, deflecting my anger. "He considered the possibility, but again, he had no proof. He certainly never confronted Hayden or Sloane. But after Ethan died, George became extremely cautious. He would only visit Hayden in a public place. He was tenacious about staying safe when he had to deal with either woman."

"I can't imagine him living like that." I shook my head, wondering if I ever really knew George at all.

It was unfathomable for me to imagine the man I'd spent three years with living in fear of his own daughter and ex-wife. And silly me had assumed the reason he met with Hayden away from the house was to shield me from her caustic tongue. But knowing now he'd done it to protect himself from potential harm sent a chill down my spine.

"But all this happened after their divorce."

"Yes, a couple of years later. Why do you ask?" Reed's brows furrowed.

"I'm trying to figure out why George agreed to leave Sloane half of everything. I mean, I know he wanted to keep peace among the judges and all that, but there had to be something more. Why did he do it, Reed? Why did he leave Sloane half of his estate? You knew him longer and better than I did. What was she holding over his head? And who is this Paula person? Why did George start a trust fund for her some thirty odd years ago? Is she his daughter?"

Reed clenched his jaw. Inhaling a deep breath, he stared at me but didn't speak for a long moment. "Leave it alone, Leagh. It has nothing to do with you, okay?"

"I need to know, Reed. Even if it has nothing to do with me, it has something to do with George, and I need to know."

"No, you don't." He shook his head.

"Tell me, Reed. I have to know," I begged. My stomach twisted.

"Nothing good can come of it, Leagh. Just let it go," Reed pleaded.

"Tell me, dammit," I screamed as I stalked toward him, standing toe-to-toe with the tall man. Anguish flashed in his eyes, and sorrow lined his face. My heart thundered in my chest as I tried to prepare myself for the bombshell I knew he was about to drop.

"Paula was George's mistress," Reed whispered.

"You mean, before me, right?" My fingers tingled, and my mouth grew dry.

"I mean, for the past thirty-eight years, up until he died."

Time stopped. Air seized in my lungs. My heart clutched. My body began to tremble, and my stomach lurched to the back of my throat.

Blindsided, no amount of preparation could have ever equipped me for Reed's confession.

"That's impossible," I shrieked. "I *lived* with him! Why are you lying to me?

"I'm sorry, Leagh. It's not a lie. When George married Sloane, she signed a prenup that she would take no other lovers. George was already in love with Paula at the time, but her husband—

"Stop! Not another fucking word. I don't want to hear this," I cried as I slung my purse over my shoulder, then turned and ran.

"Leagh. Wait!" Reed called out as I yanked the door open and raced down the hall.

Unwilling to wait for the elevator, I found the door to the stairwell, tore it open, and ran down the stairs. Tears streamed down my face as I gripped the railing. Propelling myself down, flight after flight, taking the steps as fast as my feet could carry me.

A mistress! For thirty-eight years, George had a fucking mistress? Where? When? Was he spending time with her when he was supposed to be at work? All those times he went out of town for research? Had he really been gone or simply shacking up with her? Did he love her more than me? Why did he want another woman? Wasn't I good enough? "How, George…how could you do this to me?" I sobbed.

Sliding off the last step, I gripped the railing tight as forward motion flung me headlong. Wobbling backward, my ass bounced on the last step. Panting and gasping, I couldn't stop shaking. The life I'd shared with George had been nothing but a well-choreographed lie.

"Leagh?" Reed's deep voice echoed down the stairwell as the sound of footsteps from above reverberated in my ears.

"No," I whispered as I stood and forced myself to pull back the door leading to the elegant lobby of the office building. As it slammed behind me, people glanced my way, stared for an uninvolved second, and turned away. Digging through my purse, I clasped my keys and made my way out the revolving door.

The sidewalk teemed with businessmen and women, all scurrying about their busy day. The sunlight blinded me. I raised a hand to shield the glare as I stepped off the curb, wanting only to find refuge in my car and cry.

Reed's deep voice screaming my name was cut short by a horn blaring. The deafening squeal of tires, a thunderous boom, and pain exploding through my body were my only warning before blackness devoured me in one horrific bite.

~

D eep, familiar voices tugged me from the darkness, urging me to
float above the inky abyss.

"Any change yet?"

"No."

"You look like shit, Tony. When was the last time you slept, man?"

"A couple days ago."

"Go home. Get some rest. I'll stay with her."

"I'm not leaving her, Mika. What if she wakes up?"

I tried to call out to them, but my throat was blocked. My eyes
were so heavy I didn't have the strength to lift my lids. And though I
tried to stop myself, I couldn't keep from sinking back into the empty
void.

The nightmares came fragmented and real. Matt's snarling voice...
the gun. The dead baby boy, Nathan, still and peaceful in my arms.
Tears and lullabies. Hospitals and blood. My father's angry face. My
mother's laughter morphing into silent screams. When the blessed
peace settled in my head, the pain throbbed sharp beneath my flesh.
Sounds melted into an irritating cacophony before falling silence and
still. I floated between heaven and hell. Unsure when or which realm I
would finally awaken.

Beep

Beep

Beep

The incessant alarm buoyed me to reality. I opened my eyes. The
room was dark, except for a soft glow leaking beneath the foot of a
door. Looking around, I saw machines and tubes. The pungent smell of
alcohol and flowers assaulted my senses in an unsettling combination.
Rolling through thoughts in my brain, I had no idea what had brought
me to this strange place. As I tried to sit up, pain sliced deep in my
head, and a muffled moan rumbled in my chest and reverberated
against a blockage in my throat.

Sudden movement drew my attention, and as I lolled my head to
the right, Tony's head lifted from the mattress as his body shifted in the

chair beside me. His soft brown eyes, heavy with sleep, opened and began to fill with tears as his chin quivered.

"Oh, baby," he whispered. "Thank fuck, you're back."

Standing, he leaned over and gazed into my eyes. Two tears spilled over his lashes and glided into the stubble covering his face. Dark circles ringed his leaking eyes. I tried to talk, but my throat was clogged with something more than emotion. Tony pressed his warm lips against my forehead, and my heart dissolved beneath his tender kiss.

"I've been so scared, Leagh. So fucking scared." Tony spoke against my skin as his tears spilled onto the pale blue cotton gown draped upon my shoulders.

Tears slid down my cheeks; still, his lips huddled against my forehead as he murmured his relief that I'd opened my eyes.

I wanted to tell him not to cry, but the best I could conjure was a groan.

Tony slowly eased back, wiping his cheeks before he softly blotted mine away with the pads of his thumb.

"Shhh, don't try to talk, sweetheart. There's a tube in your throat to help you breathe. You're in the hospital." He sniffed and swallowed tightly as fresh tears streaked his handsome face.

His overwhelming emotions frightened me, but his glowing smile settled me. I raised my weighted right arm and cupped his cheek.

"Oh, sweetheart," Tony choked as he enveloped my hand with his and closed his eyes. "Your touch feels like heaven."

Peeling my hand from his face, he placed a reverent kiss in my palm. "I want you to blink one time for yes and two times for no. Can you do that for me, angel?"

I blinked once, and Tony smiled.

"Excellent. Do you remember the accident?"

Accident? What accident? My heart thundered in my ears, and I felt my eyes grow wide before I blinked twice.

"Thank fuck," Tony exhaled. "When you left Reed's office, you got hit by a car."

I squeezed Tony's hand as I felt my brows furrow in confusion. I didn't remember a damn thing. How could I not remember something as horrific as being hit by a car?

"Don't panic, sweetheart. You're going to be fine. I know you're scared and have a million questions. I can see it your eyes, but relax for me. Take some deep breaths. Okay? I'm right here, and I'm not going anywhere. I promise."

I blinked once and tried to relax, but my mind wouldn't stop spooling through the fog that wouldn't seem to clear.

"It was a hit and run. Some of the witnesses got the license number of the car, but it came back stolen. The cops are anxious to talk to you, but so far, they haven't found the person who hit you. You've got a couple cracked ribs. One of them punctured your lung. That's why they have you on the ventilator. I'm sure it'll be coming out soon, now that you're awake. It won't be long until you can ask all the questions racing through that gorgeous head of yours."

I blinked once and squeezed his hand. Glancing down, I began to take inventory of my injuries. My left arm was encased in a thick white cast from below my elbow to my hand. Only the tips of my fingers were visible. I could see my toes peeking from beneath another cast covering my leg from my knee to my ankle.

"It looks a lot worse than it actually is, angel. I'm sure if you could talk, you'd argue with me," Tony replied with a strained chuckle. "You have a fractured ankle and wrist, and your knee was dislocated, but they fixed that in the emergency room when you were brought in. Other than a ton of scrapes and bruises, and the doctor wanting you to be sedated for the past few days to let your lung heal, you're a hell of a lucky woman.

My heart bounced off my ribs as Tony listed off the injuries I'd sustained. More worrisome than a few broken bones was the fact that I couldn't remember a damn thing about the accident.

"You also have a mild concussion. Things might be a little fuzzy, and you might experience some heightened anxiety, but resting your brain will help it heal."

Anxiety? Everything coming out of Tony's mouth filled me with anxiety. Maybe the concussion kept me from remembering the

119

accident? My head throbbed like a bitch when I tried to focus too keenly.

"I've got to tell you, angel, I've been out of my mind sitting here, watching you and worrying. I don't know what I would have done if…" Tony exhaled a deep sigh. I could see he was struggling to maintain his composure. "When I first got here, they wouldn't let me see you. I was climbing the fucking walls. Reed faxed over some paperwork, listing me, Mika, and Drake as your next of kin. I'm sorry, but none of us knew how to contact your family."

No. No. You can't ever contact them. I screamed inwardly. Gripping his hand tight, I squeezed my eyes closed twice.

"Sweetheart, I'm not stupid." Tony leaned low. "I know there's a reason you carry a restraining order, I just don't know who you're hiding from. Trust me. We'd never do anything to put you in harm's way. We're here to keep you safe, I promise."

Hoping that the gratitude filling my heart might somehow be conveyed, I blinked once, very slowly.

"You're welcome, angel." Tony smoothed a knuckle over my cheek. His dark expressive eyes were filled with compassion and something else. Something I couldn't quite put my finger on. "It's so good to see your beautiful eyes again. I can't tell you how many hours I've waited for you to look up at me like you're doing right now. And just as soon as that tube comes out, I'll get to see you smile for me again."

Tony bent low and nuzzled his nose against my cheek. I savored his familiar rugged scent. Drank in the heat of his body, and basked beneath his gentle touch.

Easing back, his compassionate brows furrowed. "Are you in pain, sweetheart?"

I blinked twice.

Holding onto my good hand, Tony settled back in the chair next to the bed. "Doctor Coleman, the orthopedic surgeon who's been looking after you, has assured me that you should heal up just fine. You're going to need some physical therapy, but don't worry. You *are* going to be okay."

Again, I blinked once, but even as Tony told me not to worry, fear blossomed in my stomach. I wanted to remember the accident, but my brain felt as if it were wrapped in gauze. *"When you left Reed's office, you got hit by a car."* Focusing on Reed as a starting point, flashes of images began to appear. Sloane. Hayden. Running down the fire exit as Reed called my name. George. His mistress. His lies. A low groan rumbled in my chest.

"What is it, sweetheart? Where does it hurt?"

My heart? While the dull throb of my body wasn't pleasant, it paled in comparison to the agony in my soul. I blinked twice and gently shook my head. Staring up at Tony, tears clouded my vision before leaking out the corners of my eyes.

"Things are coming back now, aren't they?"

I nodded.

"I'm so sorry you had to learn about George like that. Reed was on the sidewalk and saw it all happen. He called Mika right away and rode in the ambulance with you. Reed's a mess, angel. He's blaming himself for telling you about Paula…"

I closed my eyes and turned my head the other way. I didn't want to hear her name again. I didn't want to know anything about her. I wanted her to stay an apparition. It would be easier for me to hate a ghost than an actual human being.

"Listen to me, Leagh. Don't jump to conclusions. You don't know the whole story. There's more to this than you think."

Jerking my head in his direction, pain erupted in my head like a sledgehammer. My eyes flew open, and I pinned Tony with a hateful glare. *Jump to conclusions?* The man I loved, and thought loved me, had another woman on the side. A woman he made love to, laughed with, and shared parts of himself that I thought were mine. I didn't want to hear the *whole story*. The bits and pieces that had already been revealed to me were quite enough.

"Let me explain it to you," Tony sighed.

Blinking twice, I shook my head and closed my eyes, shutting Tony out.

"Okay, my little hardheaded minx, I'll let it rest for now. But we will talk about it later."

I slowly shook my head. *No, we won't,.* I vowed. Keeping my eyes closed, I escaped back into the darkness.

Even when the disturbing nightmares returned, they were far easier to cope with than my fucked-up reality. In my dream, I heard the gunshot, smelled the bitter scent of copper pennies, and saw the blood on my hands. The sound of someone calling my name saved me from reliving the horrific events again. When I opened my eyes, a sandy haired man with twinkling blue eyes stood by my bed.

"Hello, Leagh. It's nice to finally meet you. My name is Dr. Coleman. I've been taking care of you for the past two days.

Two days. It didn't seem possible I'd lost two *whole* days. Looking around the room, a dark-haired nurse stood at the foot of my bed, wearing a reassuring smile. On my left, Tony stood, gazing down at me. The stubble on his face was thicker than normal. He looked as if he hadn't left my side. Tony hadn't been taking care of himself, and I worried as I gazed at the even darker circles that resembled bruises around his tired eyes. But the level of comfort from just having him near made me realize Tony was my beacon of calmness.

He stepped up alongside the bed and cupped my cheek. "Everything is going to be okay, sweetheart."

I gave him a quick nod, and that breathtaking smile of his spread across his lips.

"You'll be back on your feet in no time, Leagh. Both of them," the doctor chuckled. "I think you'll feel a lot better once we got this vent off you. We'll let you suck on some ice chips and maybe say a few words. Does that sound like a good idea?"

I nodded, anxious to get the damn tube out of my throat and feel human again.

Dr. Coleman and the nurse hovered over me as Tony stepped away. Following the doctor's instructions after he lowered the bed, I coughed as the tube scraped free of my esophagus. It hurt to swallow, but it was a blessed relief not having that nasty thing blocking my airway.

"All done. Does that feel better?" Dr. Coleman asked with a smile.

"Yes." My voice sounded brittle and raspy, but I didn't care. I could finally talk.

"I'll be back later to check in on you," the doctor announced with a reassuring smile.

"Thank you," I whispered, wincing as I swallowed again.

"Don't let her talk too much," he said to Tony. "Ice chips will help her sore throat."

"I'll take good care of her. Thank you," he smiled, shaking the doctor's hand.

After they left the room, Tony turned his attention toward me. Doting on me like a mother hen, he spoon-fed me crushed ice, shushing me each time I tried to talk. I couldn't have asked for a better nurse, or a more infuriating one. I wanted to talk!

The next day, a steady stream of visitors started bringing flowers, and food, and smiles. Reed was the first to come, full of apologies and burdened with remorse. I did my best to assure him the accident wasn't his fault. Worried he would start discussing Paula again, I was grateful he didn't and neither did Tony. It was only a matter of time before the good doctor gathered up his figurative scalpel to probe and start digging deep into my psyche, but Tony seemed content letting me gain back my strength and start physically healing. Besides, I wasn't mentally ready to tackle the anger or pain I felt toward George.

The day I got released from the hospital, the whole gang showed up to whisk me back to my little room at Genesis. Mika looked haggard and tried his best to be patient and understanding with Julianna's snippy, miserable mood. I wanted to tell her she'd be back to her happy-go-lucky self soon, and that I remembered how I'd once felt as big as a house with legs. But that was from another lifetime none of them knew about. So, I simply lent support to her as best I could with a bittersweet smile.

Drake and Tony began to argue about which one of them was going to lift me from the bed into the wheelchair. Evidently, the nurse filling out my paperwork had dealt with overbearing, testosterone-laced men before. With a heavy sigh, she shoved them out of the way before helping me out of bed. It was a good thing she'd had her back to the fuming Doms, because the caustic scowls that lined their faces frightened even me.

Dylan, Nick, and Savannah had loaded up the numerous vases of flowers onto a push cart. Trevor held all the balloons. With my belongings stowed in a white plastic bag, we paraded out of the hospital. En mass, we loaded into the bevy of vehicles parked at the hospital entrance and headed home. Stretched out in the back of Mika's Escalade, I leaned against Tony's wide chest. Tilting my head, I smiled up at him.

"Thank you for…everything."

"You don't need to thank me, angel. I'm going to take good care of you." He leaned down and pressed a kiss on the top of my head.

By the second day home at Genesis, Tony had moved in with me. And over the weeks that passed not only did he manage to juggle work and fulfill his duties at the club, but he cooked my meals, gave me sponge baths—which were so awkward for me, I sent him to the drug store to buy adult bath wipes. He washed my hair, dressed me, and taxied me to every doctor appointment. Tony even took me out to lunch a couple times a week. The man was a saint. Even when I'd become grouchy and snarly for not being able to care for myself, he ignored my crabby moods, only threatening to spank me half a dozen times.

I couldn't help but admire the man, not only for his compassion and constant care, the way Tony seemed to always put my needs above his own; but also, for his strength. The man was a damn Boy Scout. He slept alongside me every night, and except for a chaste kiss on my cheek or forehead, he didn't once touch me in a sexual way. The nightly ache for more was a frustration all its own.

He coddled me to the point of madness, and every time I tried to reject his care, he'd caress my cheek, my arm, or my hand and remind me, *"It's a Dom's job to care for a sub."* Tony had taken root in my heart. No matter how much I wanted to distance myself from the emotions he roused, I couldn't stop itching to wrap myself around him and never let go.

While my road to recovery was long and bumpy, Doctor Coleman seemed pleased with my progress. After being fitted with a shorter cast, I was given the green light to start putting weight on my ankle, but I still had to use a crutch. My mobility improved, but my anger and resentment that George had kept a secret mistress remained a constant, stabbing sting. The letter Reed had given me, the day of the accident, had stayed inside my purse...unopened. Convincing myself that the note was filled with bullshit lies, I couldn't find the wherewithal to read the damn thing. I wasn't ready to forgive him.

Several times, Tony tried broaching the subject of both the restraining order and George and Paula, but every time, I cut him off, refusing to open the box of my stormy emotions. Tony never forced the issue. He'd simply suggest that I think of ways to come to terms with my resentment toward George. I knew Tony was right, because ignoring my unresolved anger kept making the elephant in the room grow larger and larger.

I sat in bed watching him straighten his tie as he dressed for work. The man was captivating in his dark suits. I imagined his female patients had a hard time focusing on their issues as they stared into his piercing dark eyes and perused his scrumptious hard body. A sophomoric surge of jealousy swept through me.

Tony stepped to the edge of the bed and cupped my chin in his palm, forcing my gaze to his. A flutter of excitement swirled in my stomach.

"I have a pretty light schedule today, but if you need something before I get back, call Trevor or Savannah, okay?"

"I'll be fine. I've got books to read, and there's always five hundred channels of nothing to watch on TV if I get desperate." I smirked.

"Maybe you should keep the television off, and the books closed today, and focus on forgiving George," Tony replied, arching his brows.

And there was that damn elephant, sitting right in the middle of my chest. I swallowed tightly and issued a slight nod. "Soon, when I'm ready."

"You can't move forward, Leagh, if you allow yourself to be chained to the past."

"I know. I know," I huffed.

"Good. Now do something about it," Tony instructed with a gentle smile. Bending low, he placed a soft kiss on my forehead. "I'll be back as soon as I can."

"Have a good day, doc," I called to him as he turned and opened the door.

"You, too. We'll talk when I get back."

As the door closed, a sense of dread settled over me. His parting shot left no doubt. Either I dissected my tumultuous emotions or Tony *would*. And dammit, I hated that he was right. If I didn't put the past behind me, I'd stay stuck in this rut of anger and resentment. Truth be told, I'd grown weary of coping with the constant struggle of George's betrayal. I just didn't know how to sort it all out.

It took several long hours before I finally worked up the courage to open my purse. Pinching his letter between my fingers, no melancholy smile tugged my lips as I stared at his sloppy writing. Indecision clawed deep. Turning the envelope over in my hands several times, I finally tore it open and pulled out the pages of George's handwritten note. Inhaling a fortifying breath, I began to read.

My beautiful Leagh,

If you're reading this, then I am gone. I'm no longer your Master, and with a heavy heart, I release you, sweet girl. Be brave and strong, and hold your head high as you find another to nurture, care, and protect you. It won't be hard. You're an alluring woman, with a stunning exuberance for life. You brought light to my dark and empty world. I'm forever grateful for all the times we shared.

I'm sorry I'm not with you now, to hold you close and reassure you. But trust and believe in yourself. You're a resilient young woman. Don't allow my death to set you back. The account I've set up will hopefully keep you in comfort for many years to come. Should you need for anything more, Reed will be there for you. I've asked him to intervene in the event that Matt should ever find you.

I only ask one thing of you—don't ever live in fear again, pet. Carry on with your life, and be happy. That's all I've ever wanted for you, and I hope I succeeded in bringing you joy. Thank you for the special times we shared, and do not mourn me.

If there is a heaven and a way to watch over you, I'll be with you, pet...Always.

Goodbye, my wild little tiger.

George

Tears streamed down my cheeks, and guilt weighed heavy in my heart. None of his words felt ingenuous. In fact, I could almost hear the warmth of his voice echoing in my ears. And for a brief moment, I remembered the soft touch of his caress.

Yet something niggled in the back of my brain. Scanning his words over again, I realized not once did his message contain the word 'love.' Nowhere in the note did he confess or confirm that he loved me. I felt my brows furrow as I wracked my brain, trying to remember if he'd ever said '*I love you*' out loud. I couldn't pluck a single instance. Had I imagined—through his overwhelming kindness—that he loved me? Again, I shuffled through the special times we shared, but it seemed that no matter how many memories I conjured, there was not one single recollection of him *ever* saying the words. And while I vividly recalled the countless times I'd told him I loved him, not once did he return the sentiment.

How could I have ignored something so blatantly obvious?

Because you didn't want to.

A cold disconnect seeped through my bones, and an urgent need to find the answer to one *very* important question consumed me. Snatching up my cell phone, I placed a call to Reed. Fifteen minutes later, the phone trembled in my hand as I held it to my ear. Beads of sweat dotted my forehead, and my throat grew dry.

"Hello," the soft voice of an older woman resonated through the device. I swallowed down my angst.

"Hello, Paula?"

"Yes. Who is this?"

"My name is Leagh Bennett. I believe we had a mutual friend, George Marston."

"Oh," she gasped in startled surprise. "Y…yes, hello, Leagh."

"I'm sorry to intrude, but I need a moment of your time, please? It's a question, really… just one. Then I'll never bother you again."

"All right." Paula sounded nervous. She wasn't the only one.

It was the moment of truth. I sucked in a deep breath, already steeling myself for her answer.

"Did George ever tell you that he loved you?"

"Wh…what?" she stammered.

"Did he tell you that he loved you? Please. I need to know."

"I…don't…my relationship with George was quite complicated. You see, my husband, Terrance, suffered a stroke in his late forties. He's been in a vegetative state at a nearby nursing home for the past forty years."

"I'm sorry, Paula. Please don't think me rude, but could you please just answer my question?"

I didn't want to know about her life or the circumstances that had knitted her and George. And I certainly didn't want to hear the details of their affair. I simply needed to know if he'd ever said the three little words to her that he'd never said to me.

"Well, yes…All the time, in fact. Why do you ask?"

"It's not important," I assured her, forcing an impassive tone. "Thank you. I appreciate your candidness, and I'm sorry that he's no longer in your life."

"My goodness," she exclaimed, obviously surprised by my condolence. "And if I may, the same to you, dear."

"Thank you. I appreciate that. Goodbye."

After ending the call, I sat on my bed, numb and empty. I may as well have been floating in space. A cold void sluiced through my veins, permeated my soul, and siphoned off any remaining devotion I felt for George.

Lost in a fog of thought, I didn't hear Tony come into the room. It wasn't until he climbed onto the bed and cupped my face in his hands that I realized he was back. Wearing a worried expression, he picked up the pages of George's note, still lying in my lap, and began to read.

Without a word, he joined me on the bed, draped his arm around my shoulder, and tucked me against his chest. I clung to him and breathed in his manly scent, amazed Tony knew exactly what I needed. And even as I drank in his silent reassurance, I worried I was setting myself up for another brutal fall. But I couldn't fight the feelings he fostered in me.

"I phoned Paula a little while ago," I whispered.

"You called her? Why?" Tony asked in disbelief.

"After I read George's note, I realized that never once did he tell me that he loved me.

He enjoyed my company, in bed and other ways. And on some

level, I think he cared about me a great deal, but I realize now he was never *in love* with me. Paula owned his heart. I was just...I don't know...someone to fill in the gaps, I suppose. I tried to convince myself that our relationship had been a charade, but that's a lie. He cared about me on a surface level; we simply lacked depth. I don't know how else to explain it."

"You're not upset that George wasn't in love with you, angel? You're not crying or cursing. Aren't you angry about that?"

"Every day since I woke up in the hospital, I've been angry with him. It's not solved anything, only made me bitter. It wasn't his fault that he didn't love me. I was a fool to imagine he did. But kicking my own ass or wallowing in pity isn't going to resolve a thing. If I'm going to pity anyone, it's George. I feel sorry for him. I mean, think about it. He spent nearly his whole life wanting a woman he couldn't have. He married Sloane knowing he'd never have Paula and ended up spending the last years of his life with another woman he didn't truly love, me. It was like the gods had played some kind of cruel cosmic joke with his life. I never knew how cheated and empty he must have felt."

"But you filled some of that emptiness, Leagh. I know that for a fact. And yes, it's not easy aching day in, day out, wanting someone you can't have."

My body tensed, and I wondered if his comment was aimed at me.

Tony let out a soft chuckle before clearing his throat. "Paula's married."

"I know; she told me about her husband."

"Then you know he's been incapable of loving her for a long time. I'm sure she struggled with her own demons before having an affair with George."

"Maybe. I don't know. I honestly don't care." I shrugged. "I've spent as many days being jealous of her as I have being pissed off at George. But the bottom line is neither of them had much happiness. I think if things had been different, the two of them would have shared something uniquely profound."

"I think they did, in their own way, at least, as best they could. So have you worked through your anger at George?"

"Not by a long shot. I'm still livid with him. Trouble is, staying angry with him makes me feel like a victim. I don't like it. Allowing George to make me feel like a victim is ten times uglier than him keeping his affair with Paula a secret. Like I said, I just feel pity for him. He spent years a hostage to Sloane's greed. And when the poor bastard finally got free, she blackmailed him. With so many odds stacked against him, the man never stood a chance."

"I think you're right. I also think you have a wealth of compassion inside that bruised and battered heart of yours. Life's not always fair. But I have a sneaking suspicion you know that first hand. Don't you?"

Tony was digging for clues about my past, but I wasn't ready to unload that steaming pile of shit yet. My trust issues had taken a massive hit with George's affair. I wasn't ready to stick my neck back on the chopping block quite yet.

"Yes. But we're not discussing the skeletons in my closet," I whispered.

"I realize that. But long before Reed mentioned a restraining order, my hand's been on the knob of your closet, just itching to open it."

"I'm sure it has been." I issued a wary glance at Tony.

"Good. You won't be surprised when I finally pick the lock on it, will you?" A devilish grin crawled across his face. "But I digress. You've told me how you feel about Paula and George. Now, tell me how Leagh feels."

I scoffed. "You'd make a great shrink, you know that?" I grinned as Tony threw his head back and laughed.

"So I've been told. Stop evading my question, angel."

"I'm not. I was just making an observation. Besides, you'll think I'm crazy."

"I deal with crazy people all day. You won't shock me. Now go on," Tony prompted.

"Mixed in with all the anger and pity, there's this bizarre sense of satisfaction. I know I brought a little ray of light into George's unhappy life. And while it would be easy to sit here and feel like he played me, the truth is he made me feel more accepted and cared for than any man in my life ever has. And for that, I'm grateful. Sounds crazy, right?"

"No, it doesn't sound crazy. It sounds like you've been let down by a shit load of unworthy men all your life, sweetheart," Tony replied with a sad frown.

"Don't. I can't stand to be pitied." I shook my head. "Remember in Mika's office when Reed told me that George loved me very much?"

"Yes."

"I think he did...in his own way. But the love I want in a relationship is the forever after kind. I didn't want to see it before now, but George and I never had that kind of depth. I just needed to believe that we did."

"And?" Tony prompted.

I pondered silently, trying to figure out if there was more to say. I remembered when Tony had calmed me and showed me how to pluck each emotion as it whizzed by.

"I don't want to waste time beating myself up for something that wasn't real. I want to learn from my gigantic mistake and never give myself to a man who doesn't love me back with his whole heart. I know that might be nothing more than a pipe dream, but I'm not going to settle for less than a man whose heart I can own." I softly laughed and shook my head.

"What was that chuckle for?"

"Owning a man's heart doesn't sound very submissive, does it?"

"It's not about submission, Leagh. It's about finding the yin to your yang. There's not a thing wrong with wanting to own a man's heart and soul. Just make sure the next man who owns yours treasures and protects it as if it were his own."

"Yeah, well, I doubt Prince Charming is going to come galloping down the halls of the club on a white stallion," I replied with a hint of sarcasm.

"You never know. He might be here already," Tony cryptically offered.

Was he referring to himself? Was there a possibility that the sultry fantasies I'd dreamt of might come true? Hope fluttered, and right on its heels, a tiny voice inside my head pelted it away. *Tony's wired for a woman more intense than you could ever dream of being.* Mentally shaking the lofty fantasy from my brain, reality left me irritated with myself for harboring such ridiculous notions.

Jenna Jacob

"I think you've dissected all of this in a very healthy way, Leagh. I'm proud of you."

Tony leaned down and pressed a sweet kiss on the top of my head. Neither of us said anything for a long time. Wrapped in his warmth, I closed my eyes and internally said goodbye to George once and for all.

~

Several days later, I sat propped up in bed reading a romance novel. Boredom had taken a heavy toll. I was antsy to get out of my small room and do *something*. Glancing at the clock, I sighed, discovering it was only two in the afternoon. Tony wouldn't be back for hours. My cell phone rang as if someone knew I needed a lifeline to the outside world.

I smiled as I checked the caller ID. "Hello, Trevor."

"She's on her way to the hospital," Trevor squealed. "It's baby time!"

"Really?" I screamed. "How long ago did they leave?"

"Mika just called Daddy from his car as they were heading to the hospital. Daddy was at the bank and called me," Trevor giggled. "Between the two of them, I'm not sure which one is spazzing out more. I think they're both ready for a guest shot on 'Wild Kingdom.' Anyway, I told him I was gonna call Savannah, and that I'd get a ride with her. We're all going to meet up at the hospital. If Daddy and Mika don't stroke out before they get there."

"Call me as soon as you hear something!" I demanded with a wide grin.

"I will. Savannah's on her way over to pick me up now. Hey, do you want to go to the hospital with us? She's got Nick's monster truck. We'll hoist your ass up into the backseat?"

"Damn, Trev, I'm not a fucking cow. You don't have to hoist me anywhere, just help me into the truck. But hey, thanks for the warm and fuzzy love, you little shit," I laughed. "If you're sure she won't mind stopping by to pick me up. I'm going stark raving mad here today."

132

"Not one bit, and you are not a cow. Why didn't you call me earlier? I would have come over and hung out with you."

"I didn't want to be a bother."

"Shut the front door, sister, or I'll tell Tony you need a spanking," Trevor teased. "Okay, we'll be by to pick you up real soon. Byeeeeeee."

Trevor hung up, and I grinned. Julianna was in labor. Soon, she'd know the joy of being a mother. Tears pricked my eyes as memories of my sweet little Nathan came flooding back. I shook them away and sucked in a deep breath.

"Hell, I've got to get dressed!"

Snagging the lone crutch next to my bed, I pressed the rubber tip into the carpet and swung my good leg from the mattress. Tucking the padded support beneath my arm, I slid my heavy casted leg off the bed. I'd made the move a hundred times, but as I stood, the crutch slipped out from under my arm, and I landed with a jarring thud onto the floor.

"Ahhhhh!" I screamed. Rolling to my right side, I tried to push myself into a seated position. The weight of both casts pinned me to the carpet like a bug. I squirmed like a naked turtle on its back, cursing a blue streak.

"Dahlia? Are you all right?" A man's voice seeped through the dark wooden door.

"Yes. I think so. Maybe? Hell, I don't know. Who's out there?" I called back.

"It's me, Stephen. What's wrong?"

"I fell down, and I'm trying to get the hell up," I grunted, trying to lever myself onto my good arm and leg to no avail. "Shit!"

"Hang on. Let me get a master key from the bar."

I closed my eyes and huffed. "Great. Stephen's going to come save your ass, then nark you out to Tony for trying to get dressed on your own. Dammit. He'll have my ass for not waiting for Savannah and Trevor's help."

Seconds later, the door swung open. Both Stephen and Carnation rushed into the room.

"Oh hell... Are you all right?" Stephen asked, his deep voice thick with worry.

Carnation's eyes grew wide, as well, before she started laughing.

"Shut up," I hissed. "You think this is funny? Maybe you should give it a shot." Anger bubbled in my veins.

"You laugh at her?" Stephen barked at his sub. "What the fuck is wrong with you?"

Sliding an arm beneath my legs and the other beneath my arms, he gently lifted me from the floor.

"I'm sorry, Master, but she's so pathetically obvious," Carnation ridiculed, looking at me with a scowl. "Tell me, Dahlia, how long did you wait for some unsuspecting Dom to walk down the hall before you started screaming for help?"

"What?" I gasped. "Are you on crack? I didn't scream for help."

Stephen's whole body tensed as he turned, slashing Carnation with an angry scowl. "Go to the bar and wait for me. I'll deal with you shortly."

"Are you kidding?" she screeched. "Don't tell me you actually fell for her stupid act. Are you blind? First, she pretends to pass out in the hall, and now falling down, claiming she can't get back up. Oh, and she just happened to be naked on top of it. She probably laid there for hours waiting for a man to come by that she could show off her tits. You can't see the game she's playing? Seriously? She's nothing but an attention whore now that her old fart of a Master died."

"Not another word," Stephen thundered.

Pinning me with a seething glare, Carnation's lips peeled back. "Don't even think about sinking your claws into my Master, or I'll bitch slap you into next week!"

"To the bar. Now!" Stephen roared. Veins protruded from his neck. His entire face turned crimson.

Rolling her eyes, Carnation stomped out of the room.

He exhaled a deep breath. "I'm sorry about that, Leagh. That girl has a laundry list of issues. I've tried to help her work them out, but I think she's beyond redemption."

"It's okay, Sir. She's never liked me, anyway," I explained as Stephen seated me on the side of the bed. "I'm sorry I've inconvenienced you and caused trouble between you both."

"Nonsense. You're not an inconvenience." Stephen shook his head.

"How did you fall down in the first place?" His brows arched with dominant censure. I suddenly wondered if every Dom practiced such an intimidating look in the mirror until they got it right.

"Mika and Julianna are on their way to the hospital. She's in labor. Trevor and Savannah are coming here to pick me up. We're going to be there when the baby arrives, and I accidentally fell when I got out of bed to get dressed. I wanted to be ready so we could leave for the hospital right away."

A huge grin lit his face, and his green eyes sparkled. He was handsome and urbane.

"That's great news. I should head over there myself and lend Mika some moral support. He's been a mess for weeks. I've never seen him so stressed." I laughed in agreement before Stephen suddenly sobered. Scrubbing a hand through his thick, wheat colored hair, his lips tightened. "But first, let's get you dressed. Where are your clothes?

I blinked up at him. "You don't have to help me, Sir. I can wait for Trevor and Savannah."

"Obviously, you can't, or I wouldn't have found you on the floor. Now, tell me what you want to wear and where to find it."

It was pointless to argue with the man, especially when he was in full Dom mode. Pointing to the closet first, I directed him to the dresser next. Stephen plucked up the articles and returned to the bed. My wardrobe was limited to clothing that would fit over the ugly, thick casts. Grateful that Julianna had purchased a butt-load of stretchy, soft cotton sets from Soma. They were sold as loungewear, but their collections could easily pass for street clothes.

Swallowing my pride and embarrassment, I couldn't help but flinch when Stephen cupped my breasts and tucked them into my bra before fastening the front clasp. Kneeling on the floor in front of me, he slid the thong up my legs. It bothered me when Tony dressed me, and with Stephen's head virtually between my knees, the whole event pegged the needle on the humiliation scale.

Just as Stephen leaned in closer, the door swung open and in walked Tony. Stopping dead in his tracks, his eyes grew wide, his nostrils flared, and his mouth dropped open.

Chapter Eight

"Stephen?" Tony's tone dripped with accusation.

"Tony!" Stephen exclaimed as he jerked his hands from my panties and bolted upright. "I was… Leagh took a bit of a fall."

In the blink of an eye, the shock on Tony's face turned to fury, and every ounce of it was directed straight toward me. "How did you fall out of bed?"

"I didn't, Sir," I whispered, regarding the discarded crutch, wishing I'd thought to hide the evidence of my stubbornness.

Tony's gaze traveled the same path as mine, and without a word, he studied the placement of the walking aid. Then, like a raging bull, he charged the bed.

"Roll over," he demanded. A fire of retribution blazed in his eyes.

"Why?" I asked, frantically glancing between him and Stephen.

"I said, roll over!"

"Ah, I think it's time for me to leave," Stephen replied with a hint of laughter. "I have a little punishment of my own to dispense."

"Wait," I cried to Stephen. "Tell him that you were just helping me get dressed and not…"

Stephen chuckled. "Tony knows I'd never lay a finger on another Dom's sub. Besides, I don't think he's angry with me for trying to get you dressed. He's obviously not happy that you fell getting out of bed and didn't wait for help."

"But I'm not his sub, I'm..."

Before I could finish my sentence, Tony shoved me onto my stomach, pinning my arms beneath my belly, before aligning a sharp, bare-handed slap across my ass.

"Your stubborn pigheadedness stops now!" Tony barked as he landed another stinging blow. "George may have allowed you to set your own limits, but I won't tolerate it. Do you understand me?"

Pissed was an understatement for the both of us. Before I could string together a list of obscenities, the door opened again. Straining my neck, Savannah and Trevor stood in the portal. Identical expressions of shock were poised on their faces. An indignant growl rolled from the back of my throat.

"Whoa, damn," Trevor cried.

"Yikes," Savannah hissed. "Bad timing. Very bad."

"Dammit, Tony! Stop," I growled. Humiliation overrode the sting spreading through my flesh as I launched onto my back, sending a look of desperation toward my friends. "Don't just stand there. Help me, you two!"

"Uhhh, well," Savannah stuttered, her eyes still wide. "Don't take this the wrong way, Tony, Sir, but...Hell no, Leagh. He's the last Dom I'd want to piss off."

"Everyone out!" Tony bellowed as he turned and pointed toward the door.

Stephen chuckled as he ushered Trevor and Savannah out of the room.

Wiggling toward the far side of the bed, I glared at Tony as he narrowed his eyes and snarled.

"What the hell were you trying to do that made you fall?"

"What in the hell are *you* doing here in the middle of the day?"

"I'm asking the questions now," he warned, crawling onto the bed like a panther stalking its prey.

"Julianna's at the hospital. She's having the baby."

"I. Know. I cancelled the rest of my appointments to pick you up so *we* could go to the hospital."

"Oh," I frowned. "Well, that's why Trevor and Savannah are here...they're taking me."

"Really?" he challenged sarcastically. "Were you planning on telling me about this little excursion you'd arranged?"

I hadn't. Not until now. "I...guess so. I mean with the excitement of the baby coming, I would have sent you a text at some point."

"You *guess*? So, in other words, you didn't really think about letting me know, did you?"

"Well, no. You were at work. I wasn't going to bother you," I explained. "Wait a minute. Since when do I need your permission? You're not my Master. You're not my Dom. You're—"

"I'm your protector," Tony roared.

"Since when?" I barked, bristling defensively.

Tony's jaw clenched as he rose to his knees and scooted off the bed. Anger drained from his face and something more frightening took its place...hurt. He scrubbed a hand through his hair before his guarded gaze settled on me.

"Since I spent two days and nights glued to the side of your hospital bed and another four after you woke up. You can't tell me you don't feel a strong connection between us. You think I'm nothing more than a friend? Open your damn eyes. You mean a hell of a lot more to me than just a friend, Leagh. And for fuck's sake, stop topping from the bottom."

Tony drilled me with an unhappy stare. Guilt for disregarding his feelings—obviously, the same ones I'd tried to ignore since the day of George's funeral—and rebuffing Tony's claim as protector crushed me. Not only had I spent weeks trying to deny my attraction to him, I'd gone so far as to invent excuses—some valid, but most not—why anything more than friendship with the man was destined to fail.

As if the reality fairy hadn't smacked the wand of clarity upside my head enough, I realized if I wanted a relationship with Tony bad enough I'd stop trying to hide and put forth some effort. He'd been under no obligation to care for me, yet he rearranged his entire life to do just that. And he'd never so much as asked for a thank-you in return. I could no longer ignore the fact that Tony had situated himself smack dab in the middle of my heart and my life. It was time for me to take off the blinders and roll the dice.

"Tony, I'm—"

"Let's finish getting your clothes on and head to the hospital," he instructed as he forced a tight smile. As if sensing my unease, he winked. "We don't want to be the last to hear how Mika passed out during delivery now, do we?"

A palpable tension hung in the air as we rode in silence. No matter how hard I arranged an apology in my head, it fell short of erasing the callous way I'd challenged him. With his attention focused on the road, Tony wordlessly slid his hand into mine. A tiny smile curled on the corners of his mouth.

"Stop fretting. There's no pressure or time limit for us to figure this out, sweetheart. Day at a time, remember?"

A lump formed in my throat as my gaze dropped to our entwined fingers. I marveled at the easy way his thumb strummed the inside of my wrist. Tony had a way of calming me and lifting my burdens. He made me feel like a joy in his life and not an obligation.

"I'm sorry." The two words paled to what I felt inside, but it was the best I could do.

"I don't want you to be sorry, angel. What I want is for you to let me in."

"I just need a little more time."

"I know. It's just...I've been waiting for you a long time now." Tony quickly glanced at me and gently squeezed my fingers before turning his attention back to the traffic on the road. "But lucky for you, I'm a very patient man."

I swallowed tightly as I stared at his profile. *Why are you asking him for more time? Haven't you wasted enough time? Tony's the first man to offer you a healthy relationship. What in the hell are you waiting for?* My inner voice urged me to take the plunge, but a part of me wondered if I was truly ready. Suddenly, Tony's words echoed in my brain. *"There's no pressure or time limit for us to figure this out. Day at a time, remember?"* Deciding that's what I needed to do, I exhaled a soft little sigh, ready to let it play out and see where it took us.

Once at the hospital, Tony snagged a wheelchair. He zigzagged down the halls like a maniac, popping wheelies as I held on for dear life, laughing like a loon. Turning the corner to the labor and delivery waiting room, Tony slid the wheelchair sideways, aligning me next to an empty chair. Our friends from the club watched his zany antics with wide eyes and broad smiles.

"When is that baby going to get here?" Tony grinned.

"Still waiting, Sir," Trevor grumbled. "Honestly, how long does it take to pop one of those little suckers out?"

I laughed. "Twice as long as you think it should, and a thousand times more painful."

"And how do you know that, Miss Thing?" Trevor teased.

Melting back in the wheelchair, I opened my mouth and quickly closed it. Suddenly all eyes were on me. I glanced at Tony's expectant expression. If I intended to let him in, I knew I'd have to unlock my past. I figured tossing out a few secrets versus bombarding him with the whole ugly truth might not make it so overwhelming.

I turned to face Trevor. Revealing what I had to say would be a lot easier than explaining it to Tony.

"I had a baby once," I softly confessed. "He was stillborn."

"Oh, Leagh," Trevor gaped. "I'm so sorry. I didn't mean to pry."

Bless Trevor. He knew I'd left a horrible past, but the sweet man never once tried to pry out the details of my former life. As a blush rose on his pale cheeks, I shook my head.

"It's okay, Trev. I named him Nathan. He was beautiful. He had a perfect round face..." Emotions I'd long ago folded away flowed back, unfurling the painful memories. "I don't know what color of eyes he had, but he had a full head of snow white hair. They let me rock him and sing to him and count all his fingers and toes before they took him away."

I swiped the tears from my cheeks, swallowed tightly, and forced a nod. "He's in a much better place. It was a blessing he didn't have to live..." *Through the nightmare my life turned into.* "He had a heart defect that they never detected in any of my prenatal visits. My doctor told me that Nathan most likely wouldn't have survived the delivery. But we didn't know that until after. He just stopped moving a couple weeks before my due date. That's when I knew something was wrong."

"Oh, angel. That must have been horrible for you," Tony murmured as he slipped a hand to my nape and massaged it gently.

"It was." I nodded. The whole room was somber. I flashed a smile, needing to lift everyone's spirits back up. "I didn't mean to put a black cloud over all the excitement. None of that is going to happen to Julianna. She's got a healthy baby ready to come into the world."

"Yes, she does," Savannah chimed in, giving me a supportive wink. "I was over there yesterday, and that little bug was kicking up a storm. Julianna is convinced he or she is going to be a pro soccer player."

The energy in the room was abuzz again with thoughts of our friends' impending blessing. Tony eased his hand from my nape before tangling his fingers in mine.

"You're an amazing lady," he whispered as he leaned in and kissed my cheek.

"No, just a survivor," I replied softly.

Before Tony could respond to my comment, Mika rushed through a set of double doors. Dressed in dark green scrubs, he smoothed a paper cap from his bald head.

"How is she?" Drake asked in a tone tight with worry.

"She's hanging in there, but damn, my girl is *not* happy," Mika laughed. "Nobody told me Satan was going to possess my beautiful pet during labor. She says this is all *my* fault, and damn if the little minx isn't threatening to cut me off pussy for life!"

Collective laughter filled the room as Mika cursed under his breath.

"I don't know how long this is going to take, but you all might be here a while. She's only at five and a half, whatever the fuck that means. All I know is she's got to reach a ten before we get the prize." A goofy grin spread across his full lips. "They kicked me out to give her a shot in the spine."

"It's an epidural, Sir," Savannah grinned. "She'll be more like the Julianna you know and love soon."

"I hope you're right, dear girl. I'm about ready to call for an exorcism in there." Mika grinned as he turned toward Drake. "Any word from Dad or Sarah, yet?"

"Emile said they would try to be on the next flight out. They're on standby, but if I know your dad, he's not only secured the last two seats, he's upgraded to first class." Drake beamed.

"No shit," Mika laughed. "Okay, when they get here, will you send them back to suite 304, please?"

"Will do, brother." Drake nodded as he stood. "Suite, huh? You got a penthouse view in there?

Mika flashed him a sly grin. "It's got the view I've always dreamed about...my Julianna bringing my child into this world. It's amazing, man. Fucking amazing."

The two men wrapped each other in a tight hug. "Give her a kiss for me, brother, and tell her I love her," Drake instructed, choking with emotion.

Mika nodded with a reassuring smile, then issued a quick wave before he turned and left the waiting room without a dry eye in the place.

The hours ticked by slowly, but the atmosphere remained electrified. Anticipation hummed even as Drake made several calls lining up members to help work the club. Dylan and Nick texted away, stopping to exchange information about zoning laws as they tried to resolve an issue on one of their construction sites. But by four-thirty, the energy began to wane.

Emile and Sarah rushed into the room, and a flurry of hugs and laughter ensued. The older couple was animated in their excitement. Mika and his father bore an uncanny resemblance. Even the tone of their deep, rich laughter sounded the same. Sarah, Emile's sub, wore a diamond studded collar around her slender neck. The woman oozed submission, graceful and acquiescent. Together, she and Emile painted the perfect portrait of a happy lifestyle couple. I found it somewhat startling when I realized I ached to be in her shoes. I glanced at Tony beside me, wondering if destiny might hold a sliver of mercy for us someday.

"We'll be out to give you an update as soon as we find out what's going on." Emile smiled as Drake ushered the pair through a set of double doors.

A half hour later, Sarah rushed back into the room.

"It's a boy!" she exclaimed on a breathless sigh. "Tristan Emile LaBrache has arrived. He's chubby and pink and, oh my! He's just perfect. The little slugger tipped the scales at eight pounds, six ounces, and has a set of lungs that rival Emile's most thunderous orders."

She giggled as tears filled her shimmering blue eyes. A roar of cheers erupted through the waiting room, and Trevor wiped a tear as it slid down his cheek.

"Is Julianna okay?" Drake asked expectantly.

Anything concerning Julianna turned the big Daddy Dom into a giant marshmallow. Before she and Mika had found one another and fallen in love, Drake had been her protector.

"Yes, Sir," Sarah assured. "She did wonderfully. Neither she nor Mika can stop grinning through their tears of joy. I can't begin to explain the wonder of it all, watching that little boy come into the world…well…it was like I just witnessed a miracle."

"Thank heavens," Drake replied on a mighty exhale. His broad shoulders slumped with relief.

Sarah swiped away her happy tears. "As soon as mom and baby are cleaned up, they'll let you go back, a few at a time, to meet Tristan." Sarah beamed as she hurried out of the room once again.

"They have a boy," I sighed wistfully.

Tony squeezed my hand and drew it to his lips. "I'm sorry you lost Nathan."

Leaning to the side, I rested my head on his shoulder. "So am I. He would have been nine years old now."

"Nine?" Tony asked in a shocked whisper.

"Yes, I got pregnant when I was seventeen, and no…he wasn't planned," I explained with a weak smile.

"And the father?"

A wave of dread swamped me. Peeking up at Tony, I shook my head. "I paid a terrible price getting involved with Nathan's father. And while I'll probably always feel regret, surviving all that came from it changed me. I don't want to talk about that today. It's a day for happiness, Tony. Can we leave it alone for now?"

"Every day should be a happy day for you, sweetheart."

Lifting my head, I boldly gazed into his eyes. "Every day I spend with you…is."

That broad smile of his, the one that melted me every time, blossomed over his mouth. Sliding his hand into my hair, Tony drew me in close. The intensity of his kiss spoke volumes, far more than words could convey. I tasted his passion and adoration. And for the first time, there was no guilt over George or fear I was making another stupid mistake, just an overwhelming rightness I couldn't deny.

Sinking deeper into his kiss, my lips parted in welcome. Needing and wanting, I accepted his tongue. And he explored each soft crevice of my mouth as I drowned in his heady scent, his intoxicating taste. And his persuasive demand. The world around us ceased to exist. Fire spread from deep in my womb, stretching out through my limbs, and I whimpered as Tony slowly eased away.

"Leagh," he murmured in a deep and ragged timbre.

Lifting my right hand, I tangled my fingers in his shirt as I stared at his wet, swollen lips. Tony leaned in again. The soft stroke of his tongue along the seam of my lips—his question silent but demanding —did I want more? Want his passion and control, his pleasure and guidance, his power and contentment? Little did he know, I'd lost the battle to resist him. Tony had crawled inside my soul deeper and more thoroughly than any man had before. Touching me on such a primal level, I couldn't turn back now if I wanted to. And heaven help me, I didn't want to.

On a ragged moan, I surrendered to his kiss. Opened and gave him the power to strip my defenses. Seize my vulnerabilities. And claim my wounded soul.

"Ah-hemm," The comedic sound of someone clearing their throat interrupted our heated kiss.

Tony hesitantly pulled away, and as his focus settled past the top of my head, one side of his erotic mouth curled in a smile. Twisting in the wheelchair, I spied Mika's father standing behind me.

"You two keep that up, and I predict you'll be back here in nine months," Emile laughed as he leaned in and slapped Tony on the back.

Tony snorted. "I think Tristan would love a little brother or sister, but you might check with Mika and Julianna to see if they're up for it that soon."

"Smart ass, I was talking about you and Leagh," Emile chuckled with a shake of his head.

"Yeah, I don't think Mika's ready to re-live these last couple months anytime soon," Nick chortled.

"Hell, I doubt *we* could survive dealing with him like that again," Drake drawled with a huge grin.

"Mika wanted to know if you and Leagh could come back first. He has a favor to ask you," Emile announced, looking at Tony.

"Sure."

Before I could blink, Tony leapt from his chair and wheeled me toward the double doors.

"We won't stay long," I promised our anxious friends as Tony sped me away.

Tristan was as beautiful and as precious as Sarah had boasted. Julianna looked exhausted, but she glowed with that new mother joy, and Mika was nearly bursting with pride.

"Do you want to hold him?" the proud daddy asked Tony.

"Who? Me?" The color drained from his face. "No, man. I'll break him or something."

I laughed and shook my head. "I'd love to hold him, if that's okay, Sir."

"Of course, Leagh," Julianna smiled. "He doesn't feel nearly as heavy now as he did inside my belly."

I giggled as Mika arranged the little bundle into the crook of my arm. Tony crouched beside me. A sparkle of wonderment flickered in his dark eyes as he stared at the tiny baby.

"Can you help me support his little butt?" I asked, trying to take down the fear factor Tristan spiked in Tony. I felt him reach beneath the baby and softly begin to rub his back.

"Oh, wow. He's so small," Tony marveled.

"He's so beautiful," I cooed, leaning in close to inhale the sweet scent of baby lotion.

Holding the little boy, memories came flooding back. A whirlpool of emotion threatened to pull me under. His perfect round face and

146

dark lashes resting on his cheeks reminded me of my Nathan. *No mourning allowed. Those days are done.* The gentle mental prod, coupled with the tuft of dark, curly hair on Tristan's head, kept me from spiraling into the murky depths of sadness. But it didn't stop the tears from spilling past my eyes.

"That's exactly what happened when I looked at him," Julianna sniffed. "He's so…beautiful."

"He's more than that," Tony whispered. "He's a precious gift from God."

Nuzzling Tristan close to my face one last time, I sucked in a shaky breath and smiled. With a tiny nod, Mika lifted him from my arms.

"I should have these stupid casts off in about two more weeks if you need a babysitter."

"We'll take you up on that," Mika grinned as he settled Tristan back in Julianna's arms. "By then, we should have the green light to try for another."

A low growl rumbled in Julianna's throat as she sliced Mika with an evil glare. "Not likely, Sir. Your toy box is off-limits for at least six weeks."

"Six weeks?" Mika choked. Seconds later, a wicked grin curled his mouth. "That's okay. We can improvise."

"And on that note," Tony laughed, "we should head out so the others can come back." Bending to give Julianna a kiss, he smiled. "You did damn good, momma."

Mika looked down on his family; joy, pride, contentment, and love swam in his eyes. My heart warmed with happiness for both him and Julianna.

"Don't worry about a thing at the club," Tony assured. "I'll snag James, and we'll appoint some DMs until Drake makes it in."

"Thanks, man. I was going to ask if you might handle that for me."

"I'd be happy to. Give me a shout if you need anything else," Tony offered as the two men hugged, slapping each other in manly fashion. "Congratulations, bro, or should I say Dad? Tristan's an awesome little dude."

"Yeah, he is at that." Mika beamed.

The minute we returned to the waiting room, Drake and Trevor bolted past us impatiently. After saying our goodbyes, Tony and I headed back to the club. Our conversation was light, focused mostly on the new baby. I worried that since I'd opened the door to my past, Tony would take the opportunity to shove a shoulder against the thing and splinter it to smithereens. But, thankfully, he didn't.

Swinging by a fast food drive-thru, we grabbed some burgers before hurrying back to my room. Tony wolfed his dinner down, and I sat nibbling on mine, watching him get ready. When he peeled off his dress shirt and donned the requisite black, *Genesis Security* T-shirt, I couldn't keep my gaze from his rippling muscles. My mouth watered, and I wanted to moan. My attraction to the man had grown at a steady pace, but over the past few days, it seemed to have taken off like a rocket ship. The nights were becoming more frustrating, and I found myself lying awake with a constant burning ache as I listened to him snore. Fighting the urge, more than once, to wiggle my way beneath the covers and wake him with my mouth. I was unsure how much longer I could behave.

As if sensing my stare, Tony turned and flashed a seductive smile. The eager arousal in his eyes dismantled my control. Setting my burger aside, I met his carnal stare with a seductive gaze of my own. It was like waving a red flag in front of a bull. Tony ate up the distance between us in three long strides. Cupping my chin, he forced my eyes to meet his while the muscles in his jaw ticked.

"I'm trying to be an honorable Dominant here, but you're making that extremely difficult, angel."

"Who said you needed to be, *Sir?*" Staring at his full lips, my voice dipped to an intimate whisper. Having already memorized his taste, I craved to gorge myself on his heated breath, soft lips, and slick tongue.

His chest expanded in quick, labored movements. His nostrils flared. "You've not given me the green light yet. It's up to you to decide if and when you're ready."

Suffused in the untamed hunger vibrating off his rigid body, I slid my tongue over my bottom lip with a slow, sensual glide. "Green," I replied in a kitten-like whisper.

"Fuck," he whispered. Bending low, Tony gripped a fist in my hair and slammed his mouth against mine.

There was no hint of finesse in his kiss, just raw, animalistic entitlement, jolting me straight to the core. Wired and more alive than I'd ever felt before, I arched up to him.

Without breaking the kiss, Tony released my hair and knelt down in front of me. The soft stroke of his tongue on mine nearly had me coming undone. Sliding his hands beneath my cotton top, he framed my waist before skimming his palms up my torso to cup my throbbing breasts. The air froze in my lungs as he dragged his thumbs across my nipples. The tingling buds drew even tighter, stinging with an ache to be tasted, toyed with, and teased. My tunnel clenched in demand, while Tony swallowed my desperate whimper. Sliding my shirt up, he exposed my lacy peach bra.

Breaking the kiss, he eased back. His red, swollen lips glistened. And his hooded gaze left a searing trail of heat as it drifted across my flesh in a languid glide of approval. With nimble fingers, he released the clasp of my demi-bra. Brushing it aside, he palmed my breasts as they spilled into his hands.

A tortured growl rumbled in his chest as he bent and flicked his slick tongue over each taut bud. I cried out as a surge of electricity shot south, but Tony didn't relent. He opened his mouth and sucked in deep, first one breast, then the other, before dancing his talented tongue in tormenting circles around the tightly drawn crests.

"Yes," I moaned on a raspy sigh.

Deliberately avoiding the sensitive tips, he stirred the dizzying current through me. The pulsating torture was maddening. Need swelled and pounded incessantly beneath my clit. Tangling the fingers of my uncast hand in his hair, I coaxed his hot mouth back to the aching tight tip of my breast once again.

"Tony," I breathlessly called out. "Please."

Writhing on the chair, mindless by his visceral hunger, hot nectar spilled from inside me.

"Please what, pet?" he murmured against my flesh.

"More. I need more. Stop teasing me. I can't stand this game anymore."

Slowly easing back, his teeth scraped along the glistening tissue until he held my nipple between his teeth. With a sharp bite, he released it as I cried out on a whimper.

A feral glint danced across his eyes. "Tell me what you need, angel."

"I need you to fuck me, Tony. Please. I need to come," I panted. "Christ, it's been weeks. I can't take this anymore."

The glimmer of sadistic delight vanished from his eyes, and an almost arctic expression lined his face. It was as if he'd suddenly closed the shutters and barred the door to lock me out.

"What? What's wrong?" I gasped.

"Sorry, doll, but I have no interest in being a convenient fuck buddy. If all you need is to have the edge taken off, well, you'll have to do that yourself."

His scathing words sliced deep. My mouth gaped in utter astonishment as Tony slid my shirt back in place, stood, and slowly backed away.

"What the fuck?"

"Language," he barked.

"You rev me up only to shut me down like I'm a fucking car. What kind of sick, sadistic games are you trying to play here?"

"One more curse word and I'll wash your mouth out with soap," Tony threatened in a low, controlled tone. Stepping closer, he leaned in, hovering over me. "Tell me, Leagh, what exactly is it you want from me besides an orgasm? Do you even know?"

I swallowed tightly. *I want you to love me. Protect me. Own and train me to be the kind of submissive you want. But most of all, I don't want you to shut me out or fucking die on me!* The truth sizzled on the tip of my tongue.

Pinching my lips together in a tight, angry line, I had no desire to eat a bar of soap or gamble on Tony's rejection when he discovered the weak, scared woman inside me.

"I asked you a question. What do you want from me, deep down inside, Leagh, besides an orgasm? You were quite clear that you needed relief. But what about trust? Control? The things that go deeper than a few minutes of mindless pleasure?"

Tony gripped the erection straining beneath his jeans. "Every inch of my body screams for you, from my throbbing dick, all the way to my greedy soul. I have no intention of simply scratching your itch. When I decide to make love to you, I'm going to sear myself into every cell of your body…thoroughly and completely. When I slide into your hot, little cunt, it's going to be for all the *right* reasons. The ones that leave no doubt how absolute and unconditionally I own you!"

His fervent pledge and the ferocity blazing in his chocolate eyes slammed through me…all the way to my toes. Yes, I wanted an orgasm —not simply for the sake of relief—but to strengthen our connection. How could he not see that? Every hour I spent with him, I longed for a hundred more.

"But before I begin to possess you, you're going to show me every damn skeleton you've got locked inside your well-guarded closet."

Even when peeling back my layers with his emotional scalpel, as he did now, Tony had the uncanny ability to free the chains inside me. The dream of opening up to him both thrilled and terrified me. I had two choices. I could sit suffocating on my own stubborn pride or I could start being honest with him. Was I ready—would I ever be—to rip open the scabs of my past and make them bleed?

"Why do you have such a hard-on to dig up my dirt? It's over and done with," I snapped, trying to stall for time and come up with a way to wriggle out of responding.

"My hard-on has nothing to do with your past and everything to do with the sweet taste of your lips…your sinful soft breasts, and candy-hard nipples. Now, start talking."

He backed me into a corner, and even though my body responded to his erotic words, my mind rebelled at his demand. I raised my chin defiantly.

"I don't want to. But if and when I change my mind, you'll be the first to know. Go work the dungeon. I'm done."

A sarcastic smirk played on his lips. "There you go again, topping from the bottom. George may have let you get away with that shit, but I won't! And just so you know, this conversation is far from over, little one."

"Not if I refuse to play your little power game. What are you going to do about it, Tony…Spank my ass?" I hissed. Hating that I sounded like a spoiled child. It pissed me off even more that Tony knew how to push my buttons so damn easily. "Go ahead. Spank me. I'll just fly into subspace. Oh, but that's not what you want, is it? No, you want to slice and dice me open, so you can read the puddles of blood like some flippin' Rorschach test. Let me tell you something, mister. That's not going to happen."

"I don't put much stock in a Rorschach. However, you might as well get real comfortable in that chair, sweetheart. I have a feeling this could take all night."

"Oh, that's right. You're the big bad Dom, and I'm just a meek, little sub. Go right ahead. Ask all the questions you want. It doesn't mean I'll answer a single one of them."

Tony threw back his head and laughed. My anger surged, and my blood pressure spiked. I clenched my fist into a ball, wanting nothing more than to punch him in the jaw.

"Leagh, you're not equipped to play these kinds of games with me." His smile vanished, and his eyes narrowed. "Let me warn you now before you get in over your head. Reverse psychology won't work on me. I'll chew you up one side, and spit you out the other. You're way the fuck out of your league, angel."

I bristled. His condescending tone scraped up my spine. Anger and sass weren't going to deflect Tony's mission. He had the upper hand when it came to mind fucks, and we both knew it. The tenacious bastard wasn't going to stop until he clawed me open. A fat tear slid down my cheek as Tony continued to hold me in his unyielding gaze.

"You're some piece of work, you know that?" he chided. "I'm sure this little trick of yours worked on George, but it won't on me, sweetheart."

"What trick?" I spat, angrily wiping my cheeks.

"Turning on the water works and trying to gain his sympathy with those big ol' crocodile tears. They're not going to work on me, sweetheart." Tony flashed a mock smile.

"You bastard. I hate you!" I screamed as I raised my right knee, aiming to launch my foot into his balls.

Tony sidestepped to the left, and my foot glanced off his thigh. "I wouldn't be here if I thought you hated me, Leagh. Oh, and trying to kick me in the nuts is going to cost you…big."

Before I could toss back a verbal barb, Tony swooped in and wrapped his hands around my waist. He plucked me out of the chair like a ragdoll. I yelped and tried to smack him upside the head with my cast.

"You hit me, and so help me…I'll haul you to the dungeon, chain you to the cross, and fire up your sexy ass with my whip."

Incongruent to the fury rolling off him, he gently eased me onto the bed. Yanking my cotton pants off, he tossed them to the floor.

"Spread your legs for me, angel," Tony instructed in a husky voice. His slow, seductive stare raked over my legs, zeroing in on the scant peach thong covering my sweltering mound.

"In your wildest, wettest dreams," I spat, squeezing my knees together. Pushing off from the mattress, I sat up. "Give me back my pants and get the hell out of my room."

Tony sucked in a deep breath before he turned and walked toward the door.

Thank goodness. Finally, he's going to leave me in peace! My inner voice cheered.

Pausing near the dresser, Tony bent and lifted his black toy bag off the floor before returning to the side of the bed.

"What do you think you're doing?" I demanded.

"Reminding you that I'm the Dom and you're the sub," he replied with an evil grin.

Tossing the over-sized duffle onto the bed, he plucked his cell phone from his pocket, fired off a text to someone, and pocketed the device. Slowly, Tony pulled back the heavy zipper. Reaching in, Tony pulled out a bundle of white cotton rope

"You are *not* tying me up. You can't."

"I am. And I can. It might take a little creativity with your casts and all, but I'll manage."

"I don't doubt your abilities, Tony, but I didn't give you permission to touch me."

"Really? I haven't heard you use your safeword, sweetheart. You're not going to be stubborn and refuse to say it again, are you?"

I wanted to slap the cocky smirk off his lips. *Stubborn? Oh, you son of a bitch. You haven't seen stubborn yet.*

"I will *never* safeword to you." Not while my pride was at stake.

"Is that so?" A sparkle of challenge danced in Tony's dark eyes. "We'll just have to see about that, won't we? In case you change your mind, your word is still *protocol*."

As he peeled off my shirt and bra, I gritted my teeth. The lesson Tony intended to teach was nothing more than a test of wills. Did he honestly have such little faith in mine? Things were about to get ugly, real fast.

Peeking out from beneath my lashes, the lethal calmness of his stare terrified me beyond words. Still, I wasn't about to clue him in on how thoroughly he unnerved me. When his attention settled on my lips, I flashed a condescending smirk to which he replied with a surly snarl. A part of me wanted to laugh. For a man who made his living helping others unravel their inner feelings, Tony was woven tighter than an Oriental rug.

I'd never seen him so out of sorts. He was always calm and in control until now. He obviously had no trouble doling out his tender aftercare to the throng of pain sluts that fell at his feet, but when it came to me, he hitched up his bad-ass Dom boots. It chaffed, but, at the same time, fed some twisted, impatient part of me that ached to yield to his command. Emotions swirled inside me like a springtime cyclone as Tony unleashed his *creativity*, binding me to the bed. In short order, he had my legs spread wide and one wrist tethered to my casted arm, strung up nice and tight to the headboard.

"Okay. You've tied me up. Are you happy now?"

"Sweetheart, the only happy bone in my body is my hard dick. Trust me. It'd be a whole lot happier if it was balls deep in your sweltering cunt. But I'm content having you all splayed out nice and pretty for me."

Desire slammed down my spine, exploding into the fray of anger and wounded pride. Come hell or high water, there was no way I was going to let my frustrated libido win.

"You obviously aren't going to spank me, or fuck me, so give me a hint here, Tony. Just what do you have in mind?"

He stroked a broad finger along my cheek. "I hope your tongue's as wicked wrapped around my cock as it is testing my patience, angel."

I laughed to hide the shiver of arousal that skittered through me. "You've made it quite clear that options off the table. Guess you're never going to find out, are you? And since you won't fuck me, do you mind telling me why I'm naked?"

"Stripping away your barriers, sweetheart." A satisfied grin crawled across his face as Tony pulled a set of clover clamps from his bag. "The real question you need to ask is whether or not you're going to leave claw marks all over that stubborn pride you're clinging to, or are you going to do what you really want to and submit?"

"Why ask? It's obvious what I want doesn't matter. You're going to take it whether I give it or not," I snapped.

"It definitely matters," Tony declared. "I'm not forcing you to do anything. You're the one who holds the power, angel. I'm not the enemy. That tenacious pride of yours is."

He circled one taut nipple with the pad of his finger, then the other. I sucked in a quivering breath as the outer muscles of my stomach rippled. Inside, they swirled, wild with nerves.

"Relax, angel. I haven't even started yet."

That's what worried me the most. Tied to the bed with my nipples hard as cherry pits, cream spilling from my folds, and his dark hypnotic eyes piercing all the way to my soul. Tony was on crack if he thought I held an ounce of control. He *owned* my control, and he damn well knew it.

"Okay, Tony. You've proven your point. You can untie me now," I replied, holding tight to the threads of anxiety unraveling inside me.

"What point is that, pet?" Tony asked, sitting on the mattress, still toying with my nipples.

Unable to stop the tremors that shook me, I issued a heavy sigh of resignation. "That you're the alpha Dom and I'm nothing but a helpless, hopeless brat. There. I said it. Now let me out of these stupid ropes."

Solemnly, he stared at me. Dominance oozed from his pores. And damn, if every cell in my body didn't shriek to give in and allow him full reign over me—all except my head.

"You misunderstand my intentions, sweetheart," he murmured, plucking and pinching my sensitized nipples.

As he rolled the tightly drawn tips between his fingers and thumbs, pulses of electricity multiplied beneath my clit. Damn my betraying body.

"This lesson slash punishment isn't about humiliation. And it certainly isn't about crushing you beneath my boot. I have no desire to break your spirit, sweetheart. This is about boundaries, trust, honesty, and communication, the foundations of a healthy relationship."

It sounded as though he sought a role far deeper than that of my protector. The idea both excited and frightened me. I didn't know if I could I give him the level of trust he demanded. Hell, I wasn't even sure I could share the details of my fucked-up life with him. Yes, I'd confessed my past to George, not because he expected me to but because his protective mien gave me hope that he'd keep me safe. But after learning about dominance and submission, if I truly wanted Tony to guide me, I had to reveal every disgusting scar that scored my heart. This "lesson/punishment" he aimed to hand down served to reinforce how truly vulnerable I'd become beneath his hands.

"And control," I replied on a nervous whisper.

"Yes, I ache for your control, sweetheart." Tony bent low, hovering a hairsbreadth from my lips. "And you want to know a little secret? Deep down, you ache to give it to me, but you're holding back. You're dying to tear down those walls and open up to me, but you're afraid. Trust me, Leagh, there's nothing you can say that will change how I feel about you. Whatever you're trying to hide isn't hurting anyone but you. Don't give it the power to hold you back from living. I'll never be able to reach you, not the way I want to…not the way I burn to, until you knock down those walls and let me in. Trust me, angel, once I crawl inside your head and your body, you'll know what it means to be whole."

My pulse pounded, and my pussy clenched. The hunger in his voice set my skin ablaze.

"I will open your eyes to what submission really means. You'll fight me, just like you are now. You'll balk at my rules and protocols. But just remember, every time you push back, it's because you're secretly begging for me to launch you higher and harder than you've ever gone before."

Like the way you tossed me into subspace so damn easily.

"Make no mistake, angel, I don't intend to stop pushing until you blossom for me like a rose"

If Tony was trying to frighten me out of accepting the submissive fantasy he offered, he was doing a damn good job. The idea of letting him climb that deep inside my head and heart scared the crap out me.

"But I promise you this, no man, Dominant, or Master will treasure your gifts more than I. All you have to do is open the door and let me in. Trust that I'll cherish everything you give me."

The passion of his declaration took the starch out of my anger and dissolved the fears dancing in my brain. I desperately wanted to believe his promises, more than I wanted my next breath. He was offering me the moon and the stars, still I worried he may not feel the same once he discovered the quantity of excess baggage I carried.

A part of me ached to tell him about Matt, but I knew what Tony's reaction would be. He'd thump that captivating chest of his and lock me away in an ivory tower. I had no doubt Tony wanted to take on the role as my protector and mentor, but how on earth was I supposed to give my power to such a strong Dominant?

I'd been George's collared sub, but his expectations paled in comparison to Tony's. The few rituals George required had never been truly submissive, not really. They'd been sexual in nature and more of a role-play between us. Tony would require a hell of a lot more than a handful of half-assed rituals. He'd want to take over every aspect of my life. And once he'd gleaned the details of my past, he'd want to isolate me to the point of madness. Just knowing that should have sealed the deal. It was a no brainer. But the conviction in his voice, and the sincerity twinkling in his eyes, held the promise that he'd show me a world—up until now—I'd simply dreamed about.

Tony continued to torment my nipples with his enticing fingers. After tweaking each peak, he grasped the metal clamps and pinned me with his erotic eyes.

"Do you trust me, angel?"

Unable to speak, I nodded as he readied the clamps.

Jenna Jacob

"Say it aloud. Feed my dominance with your surrender."

"I trust you, Sir."

His eyes narrowed. His nostrils flared, and he inhaled a ragged breath. I thought he was going to roar like an animal, but instead, a slow smile of absolute satisfaction spread over his lips. Tugging one nipple, he rolled the aching tissue and aligned the metal clamp over the swollen, red tip.

Chapter Nine

Pain like liquid silver spread from the center of my breast and exploded along an invisible fiber linked to my clit. Sucking in a hiss, I writhed and moaned as Tony attached the second clamp.

"Ahhh," I cried, arching my back off the bed as lightning seared an identical path to my core.

"Breathe the sting away, angel. You'll take this pain for me, won't you?" Tony's beguiling tone pummeled the last of my defenses.

Feathering his fingertips along the swell of each breast, he trailed the broad pads down my ribcage. My abdomen quivered as his digits danced a deviant waltz toward the apex of my bare mound...then stopped.

As pleasure mixed with pain pulsed through my raw, awakened nerve endings I sucked in one trembling breath after another

"Is this too much for you? Can you take this, Leagh?" Tony demanded in a bellicose tone.

Swallowing tightly, I nodded.

"Answer me, angel. I need to hear your voice."

"Yes, I can take it," I replied in a raspy whisper.

Rocking my hips in silent appeal, I longed for his fingers to continue their quest. The walls of my pussy constricted, and the thin membrane surrounding my swollen clit constricted. The accidental massage brought a sliver of relief. I closed my eyes and repeated the process, savoring the building arousal as arcs of pain seared beneath my nipples.

"Look at me, Leagh," Tony instructed before driving his finger deep into my cunt.

Gasping, my eyes flew open wide. My walls squeezed around his digit, sucking, milking, and pulling him in.

Gliding fast and deep into my slickness, I knew he could feel how aroused he'd made me. The earthy scent of my essence hung heavy in the air, spicy and pungent. Sparks of delight detonated deep in my womb, ignited through my veins, and escaped the back of my throat as a mournful whimper.

"So hot. So slick. Fuck, Leagh, your cunt feels like silk and lava. I'd love to dive into your hot little pussy, slide my tongue between your thick folds, and drown in your juices."

"Tony!"

"Tell me what you want, sweetheart."

"Your mouth. Your tongue. Your fingers…anything…just make me come!" I cried.

"You need more than an orgasm, angel."

"No, I don't, dammit," I cried. "I just need to come! Please touch my clit."

I writhed on his hand, searching for a knuckle or thumb…any fragment of skin I could rub against my clit. The absence of stimulation was maddening. With his free hand, Tony rolled the metal chain beneath his palm. The slight jostle of the clamps sent an eruption of pain sputtering up my spine.

"I'm the one in control here, little one. This exercise is to impress upon you the importance of what topping from the bottom gets you. Insolence guarantees frustration and pain."

"I get it," I gasped as he flicked his thumb across my clit. "Please. I need to come."

"No." Shaking his head, Tony arched his brows in warning. "You don't have permission, Leagh. You'll take everything I give you without coming, unless you safeword out. Do you understand?"

"Yes, but seriously. You've got to let me come, Tony," I panted and prayed he was only fucking with my head.

But his nimble fingers drove me to the edge faster and harder than I'd known possible. If he intended for me to hold back my release much longer, it wouldn't matter if I had his permission or not—I was close to going off like a stick of dynamite—and soon. I'd never been denied orgasm. How the hell was I supposed to stop the tsunami once it peaked?

"No, angel, I don't," he softly chuckled. "This lesson is for you, even if I'm the one reaping the benefit. Do you grasp the purpose of this exercise?"

"No," I wailed. "I can't think about anything except coming. Please. Tony."

"Maybe I need to show you, instead of trying to explain it."

A mischievous glint darted across his eyes as he wedged another finger inside me. Stretching and filling the wet walls of my cunt, he wiggled in deeper until he hit upon the sweet spot. Crying out, I rocked against his embedded hand as his fingertips burnished my electrified bundle of nerves. And when he pressed his thumb against my clit, locking his determined gaze with mine, a sadistic smile curled his lips.

"Don't come, angel," he warned.

Strumming an incessant rhythm, both inside and out, his blissful torture escalated to blinding demand. Panting and grinding upon his masterful hand, my release quickened. The urgency thundering through my veins all but swallowed me whole. Ecstasy swelled, exquisite and hot. My whimpering moans merged into breathless screams as I started tumbling over the edge.

Tony tugged the chain and simultaneously yanked his fingers from my pussy. My climax evaporated like dust in the wind. A howl of frustration-laced pain tore from my throat as tears slid past my temples and spilled into my hair.

"You can't do this to me," I wailed. "Please!"

"I can and I did. You're paying this price for me. It's not for you. Do you understand the meaning of this punishment, now, angel?"

"Yes! You're forcing me to submit," I sobbed.

Tony frowned. "No, that's not what I'm doing, sweetheart. I'm giving you a taste of submission. Hopefully, you'll look inside yourself and see if giving up control is what you truly want. I won't ever force it from you, Leagh. So, set aside your sexual frustration and tell me what you're feeling."

Smoothing a palm over my face, Tony calmed the chaotic storm rolling through me. Sucking in a deep breath, I tried to gather my thoughts.

"Ever since George introduced me to the lifestyle, I wanted to learn more," I sniffed. "But he never wanted to go any deeper than bedroom dominance. He never expected me to submit like you and the other Doms do."

"Keep going," Tony encouraged as he wiped my tears with the pads of his thumbs.

"I don't want to be a 'Stepford sub.' The thought of losing my identity scares the hell out of me." I sucked in a breath of courage. "That day you took me to subspace shocked the hell out of me. I've thought about it a lot, but I still don't think I'll ever be a pain slut. If that's what you expect from me, then all this needs to end now. I can't change who I am for you or anyone else."

Finally, giving voice to the fear our needs would never mesh, I closed my eyes. I couldn't bear to see the confirmation on Tony's face.

"I never said I wanted you to change, angel. If anyone needs to adjust, it's me."

"But I don't want you to. You'll end up hating me, and there's more...I need to tell you more," I implored.

Tony gave a thoughtful nod. "Go ahead."

"I can't lie. I thoroughly enjoyed sailing off that day, but I realized I never would have achieved subspace if I hadn't been vulnerable and weak. I'm not normally a weak woman, and I keep wondering if maybe I'm not a submissive after all."

"First of all, I know what I want. I want you. I don't want a robot sub or a total pain slut." Tony shook his head. "Not once have I ever thought you weak, Leagh. Submission takes a hell of a lot of strength and control. You've never had the chance to experience it...not fully. My goal isn't to mold you into something you're not. It's to mold you into something more than you are already. Your spirit is like a breath of fresh air. All I want to do is give you wings to fly higher than you ever dreamed possible."

"By not letting me orgasm? That's not making me fly. It's just pissing me off," I mumbled begrudgingly.

Tony smirked. "It's a lesson and a punishment, Leagh. You won't always like what I do to you. But if I only give you what you want, you're not really submitting to me. You're only submitting to yourself."

I'd never thought of it quite that way before, but I still wanted the damn orgasm.

His demeanor took on a righteous edge. "And don't you ever try to kick or hit me again."

I frowned and nodded.

"Every time you try to top from the bottom, I'm going to make you pay the price. There's no way in hell I'm going to allow you to toss out smart-ass insults and condescending remarks toward me, or any other Dominant here."

"Why does my behavior matter to you?"

"Because *you* matter to me. If I'm going to take on the role of protector and mentor, you have to know what I expect from you."

"But why me? Why do you want to train me?"

"You mean, besides the fact that you need it?" He arched a brow.

"That's not funny," I grumbled.

"No, but it's the truth," Tony pressed. "I've been honest with you from the start, Leagh. And I've been attracted to you for a long time. You're still in a vulnerable place. I care deeply about you, and I refuse to sit idly by while Doms stream out of the woodwork trying to lure your submission. The thought of you giving your power to anyone but me makes me crazy. If you accept me as your protector and mentor, you'll have to abide by my rules. But I'll make damn sure you reap the rewards, if that's what you want."

"I have to decide right *now*?" I blinked.

"No. We've got a ton of groundwork that needs to be laid before I put a training collar on you." He dipped his head, leveling a serious stare. "You'll have to open that closet, Leagh, and trust me. Whatever is inside isn't going to scare me away."

"You say that now," I scoffed. "But what if it does?"

"Are you a mass murderer?" He grinned, and dammit, if I didn't melt all over again.

"Of course, not," I replied incredulously.

"Then you have nothing to worry about." His playful expression sobered before he rose from the bed. Checking the circulation in my limbs clearly indicated Tony's lesson was far from over. "Are your arms and legs doing okay?"

"Yes, they're fine." I nodded.

The weight of Tony's expectations sent an unnerving itch crawling beneath my skin. And the fear of spilling the secrets of my past wasn't only dangerous for me. The minute Tony found out about my involvement with Matt, he would be at risk, too. George had wheedled out my history with the assurance that he had money and friends in high places. With George, I had a guarantee if push came to shove, he'd find a way to keep me alive. But I'd never felt the riotous attraction to him that I did Tony, and my fears began to manifest into monsters. Tony didn't have the type of network available to him that George did. And I wasn't one hundred percent sure Tony would understand why I chose to stay with Matt for as long as I did. There was no guarantee Tony wouldn't think me as guilty as Matt when the truth was told.

Uncertainty filled me with anxieties and insecurities. I wanted out of the ropes, to sit up and clear my head, sort out my doubts and desires. Clutching a fist, I felt for the quick release line in my palm, but it wasn't there. A rolling wave of panic washed through me as memories of my last night with George crashed down upon me. Tugging at my bindings, fear—thick and oily—tightened in my throat, squeezing the air from my lungs as sweat erupted over my body. I was trapped.

"Protocol!" I choked on a frightened cry, jerking and thrashing against the bindings. The clamps bit hard, but the panic flooding my veins dulled the biting pain to a bothersome throb.

"Fuck!" The color drained from Tony's face as he reached up and gave a hard yank on the rope. Instantly, my hands were free "I'm sorry, baby…this is going to sting."

Deftly releasing the metal pinchers from my nipples, I cried out as the blood raced back into the tips with a caustic bite. Gathering me into his arms, Tony crushed my throbbing buds against his chest so tight I could barely breathe. "I've got you, sweetheart. I'm right here."

Ruthless tremors wracked my body as I clung to him, desperate to absorb his reassurance and strength. Ambushed by the deluge of emotions, I was powerless to reel them in. Sucking in great gulps of air, I wrestled to calm myself.

"It's okay, angel. You're safe. I'm not going to let anything happen to you. I promise."

"I'm sorry," I whispered.

"No, shhhh. You've nothing to be sorry about."

"Yes, I do. I freaked out. I just don't know what set me off like that," I confessed against his soft cotton shirt.

"I do. I hit a trigger. I suspect we'll discover a few more landmines as we go along. Don't be surprised if you get blindsided again, angel."

"But I don't want anymore. I've tried so hard to shove the night George died aside."

Tony leisurely threaded his fingers through my hair. "So, this trigger I hit, did it have something to do with George?"

"Yes."

"We'll talk about the details later. But I think you trying to ignore, rather than deal with, the memories is why you reacted the way you did."

"I don't want to dwell on it. I've got so many conflicted emotions when it comes to him. I don't know if I can sort it all out." Admitting my failure felt easy, tucked in his steely arms.

"Don't let it overwhelm you. We'll work through them together. I'm not going to leave you like George did."

"You can't promise that," I refuted on a shaky breath. "No one gets out alive."

"That's true, but I plan on being around for a long, long time," Tony assured. Easing back slightly, a sly grin lit up his face. "Someone's got to keep you in line."

Interrupted by the muffled ring of Tony's cell phone, he slowly released me and stood.

"What's up?" he asked into the device as he stepped toward the foot of the bed. Resting the phone against his shoulder, he untied my feet. "Hang on, let me ask her."

Sliding my legs together, I felt my brows wrinkle in question.

"James is on the phone. He's running the camera board in Mika's office. Did you call an on-site mechanic to work on your car?"

"A what?" I blinked. "No. Is someone messing with my car?"

"No. She didn't," Tony barked into the phone. His body tensed. "Call it in. Let me get someone to stay with Leagh, and I'll meet you at the back door. You're armed, right? Good. See you in a few."

Ending the call, Tony shoved the phone into his jeans pocket. Worry lined his face as he scrubbed a hand through his ebony hair.

"What's going on?" I demanded, fear rising inside.

"James said a tow truck pulled into the back lot a few minutes ago. Some guy is working under the hood of your car with a flashlight. We're going to go see what that clown's up to, but I want you to stay here."

A different sort of panic stormed through me. Had Matt finally found me, or was Hayden attempting to make good on her threat? Neither scenario made sense. It had been weeks since our clash in Reed's office. Surely Hayden had cooled off by now. And Matt wouldn't dick with my car. He'd just put a bullet in my head, quick and clean. My imagination ran wild. Maybe it was just a mix-up, and the guy was working on the wrong car. If not, Matt or Hayden had orchestrated some nefarious plot, and Tony would be in danger.

"No!" I cried, fearing for his safety. "Don't go out there. Let the police handle it."

Tony plucked my robe from the chair and helped me slip it on. "Sweetheart, that guy might be long gone before the police arrive. James is just going to flash his badge, and we're going to ask some questions. That's all that's going to happen. Relax." Cupping my chin, he raised my head, bestowing a reassuring gaze. "Don't worry. I'll be right back."

Before I could open my mouth to argue, Tony stepped to the door. When he jerked it open, Drake's big body stood in the portal, concern lined the big man's face.

"Need some help?" the big Dom offered.

"Thanks. Hell, I'm not even sure what we're walking into. But I need someone to guard Leagh's door until we find out what that fuck-knuckle's up to." Tony's voice resonated with an icy edge.

"You got it. Nick and Dylan just walked in. I'll get them back here and up to speed."

"Thanks, man. See if Savannah can come inside and stay with Leagh."

"Will do." Drake nodded before he dashed down the hall.

"Tony?" My voice quivered.

As he turned, I could see anger clouding his coffee-colored eyes. The reassuring smile he flashed my way failed miserably. "You'll be safe and sound. Just sit tight until I come back. Okay?"

"Wait. Don't you think you big, bad Doms are overreacting a little?"

"You tell me. I'm in the dark here," he quipped sharply. "Until I find out who you're hiding from and why, I'm not taking any chances with your safety."

Guilt and fear left an acrid taste in my mouth. Tony deserved the truth, and I knew it. But it wasn't the time or the place. A flurry of commotion outside my door drew my attention. Savannah rushed in, her brown doe eyes wide with concern. Climbing onto the bed, she hugged me tight.

"We'll be right outside the door if you need us, kitten," Dylan vowed. There was no hint of his dashing dimple, but a reassuring promise laced his voice.

"Don't worry, precious, no one's going to get past us. You two kick back and try to relax," Nick pledged.

"We will, Sirs." Savannah forced a smile.

"Thanks, guys." Tony issued a grim nod. Glancing over his shoulder, he issued me a look of warning. "Don't leave this room."

The door closed behind him with an eerie click.

"Leagh, what the hell is going on?" Savannah gasped before nibbling her bottom lip.

"I don't know. Obviously, the guy out there's made a mistake." It's what I wanted to believe.

"For his sake, let's hope so," Savannah replied. "Poor guy's probably going to crap his pants when Tony, James, and Drake confront him. I sure wouldn't want to be in his shoes."

I managed a tight smile as I tried to convince myself it was an innocent blunder. But my woman's intuition screamed otherwise.

"Why would someone want to mess with your car? You know, don't you?" Savannah's keen gaze drilled into me. "I won't breathe a word. If my sister Mellie was here, she'd tell you…I keep secrets like Fort Knox."

I couldn't tell her about Matt, so I took a deep breath and relayed my suspicions about Hayden. Savannah took it all in stride, but I could see in her eyes she was doubly worried.

"I hate having to sit here and wait. I should be out there asking him questions, but I'm too scared. Dammit, why do I have to be such a wimp?"

"Wimp?" She snorted. "Leagh, you're one of the strongest women I know. You're a damn rock in comparison to me and every other sub in this place. Hell, you've got more backbone than that big ol' T-Rex at the Field Museum."

Her scolding brought a smile to my face. I hugged her tight. "You do wonders for my self-esteem, sis. Thank you."

"I'm not saying that to pump you up, Leagh. It's the truth." She nodded with conviction after pulling back. "Everyone here loves you. No way Hayden will ever lay a finger on you, not with us around."

Long minutes later, the door opened, and Tony stepped inside. His expression was grim and his eyes were wild.

"What happened?" I swallowed tight and held my breath.

"As soon as we ran out the back door, he dropped a screwdriver and took off in his truck. He got away, but not before James got a license number. The cops just got here. They're tracing the plates, and James is running interference for you and answering their questions." I could feel a tremendous rage pouring off Tony.

Undaunted by his intimidating anger, I had to know if it was Matt. "What did he look like?"

"Short, about five foot-five. Black hair. Beady little eyes. A couple day's growth on his face. He looked dirty and mangy. Who the fuck was he, Leagh? And what's he holding over your head?"

I blinked as my mouth gaped open. I had no clue who Tony was talking about. Matt was tall with thinning blond hair and blue eyes, the polar opposite of the man Tony had described.

"I…I don't know," I stammered.

"Dammit, Leagh, tell me the truth," Tony bellowed.

Raising my chin, I squared my shoulders. Just because I was at a postural disadvantage, I wasn't going to give him the upper hand, especially when I was being honest.

"I *am* telling the truth," I hissed. "I don't know a man by that description. And I have no idea why someone would be messing with my car."

"Let's try this again," Tony snarled as he prowled toward the bed. "You weren't born and raised in Chicago. You've probably spent hours trying to get rid of that southern accent, but it's still there…in your voice. Where are you from originally?"

"Atlanta."

"Why did you come to Chicago?"

"I like the snow," I quipped sarcastically.

"Oh boy, I think it's time for me to leave," Savannah squeaked, casting a wary glance my way.

Tony exhaled a deep sigh and closed his eyes. Nodding, he sucked in a ragged breath before escorting Savannah out the door to the waiting arms of her Masters.

Lucky girl. She gets to escape.

"Thanks all for your help," Tony conveyed before he closed the door.

"Are you going to continue this little inquisition?"

"Indeed, I am, unless you want to safeword out. In which case, I'll gather my stuff and go back to my room." Stalking back to the bed, he cupped my face in his hands. "Open up and trust me. Just once, take a fucking chance. How much longer do I need to prove myself to you? Maybe if you told me why it's so hard for you to trust, I might understand why you're deaf, dumb, and blind to the fact that I love you."

Tony spat the words as if they'd been laced with poison. But that didn't stop my world from tilting on its axis. *He loved me? How? When? Why?*

"You can't love me," I choked in disbelief. "You don't even know me."

Tony launched a humorless laugh. "I know you better than you know yourself, angel. Nearly everyone in this club knows how I feel about you...everyone, *except* you. Tell me what I want to know. We're not leaving this room until I have some answers."

It had been much easier side-stepping Savannah's questions. He already knew about Hayden's threats. No way would I be able to pacify him with half truths about Matt. But telling Tony the whole story...he might easily change his mind about me. On one hand, it might be a good thing. We were worlds apart in regard to the lifestyle. But on the other, it would be devastating. I didn't want to lose him.

Tony studied me for a long moment then sat on the bed beside me. "You really don't know who that dude was, do you?"

"No!" I replied adamantly.

"Why do I get the feeling you were expecting me to describe someone else? You were, weren't you?"

"Yes," I mumbled with a heavy sigh.

"Who is it, Leagh? Who are you hiding from?"

"A man named Matthew Price." Pausing, I sucked in a deep breath and closed my eyes. "I think he wants me dead."

Cringing, I readied myself for Tony's explosion or implosion, or some other combustible caveman reaction. After deathly quiet moments passed, I gathered my courage and peeked up beneath my lashes. The expression on his face was a combination of disbelief, confusion, and indisputable rage.

"Who is he, and why does he want you dead?"

Oh, how was I going to explain all this to him? "He and my dad grew up together. They were like brothers. He was like an uncle to me. I trusted him."

"Matt is the reason for the restraining order?"

"Yes."

"Does he know where you are?" Tony asked. I could almost see the wheels turning in his head.

"No. George had the papers drawn up as a safety precaution," I explained.

"Help me out here, angel. A trusted family friend wants to kill you? Why?"

"I can't tell you," I mumbled, casting my eyes to the silk fabric of my robe.

"Can't or won't?"

"Both. If he finds me, he'll find any and everyone who knows his secret. I won't have your blood on my hands, Tony."

"You think Matt is going to kill me if I know his secret?"

"He will," I declared.

"Start at the beginning and tell me the whole fucking story." Tony's icy edict chilled me to the bone. "If and when the time comes, I'll deal with the prick. Tell me what happened in Atlanta, angel?"

I closed my eyes. I couldn't bear to see Tony's reaction when I revealed my ugly sins. Suddenly, it all came rushing back in a huge wave of regret.

"I was seventeen, three months until I graduated high school. I went to a party with a girlfriend at some guy's house. I didn't know him, but her older brother did. Anyway, there was alcohol and pot and tons of people. I wanted to act like I was all grown up, so I had some drinks, smoked some weed, and got pretty wasted. This really hot guy had been watching me all night. He had stunning blue eyes and a sexy, lazy smile. He waited until I was blasted before he introduced himself. His name was Craig Walters. He was twenty-six, and a broker for a big investment firm in Atlanta. He got me another drink and invited me outside to look at the stars. He led me to the side of the house where it was nice and dark. I remember it was really quiet out there. I couldn't even hear the music from inside."

I swallowed the lump in my throat as a tear slipped down my cheek.

"He raped you," Tony whispered softly as he swiped the tear away.

I nodded, thankful I didn't have to utter the vile word. "He didn't use a condom, and I got pregnant."

"Nathan?"

A mournful sob slid from my throat, and more tears spilled over my cheeks. I nodded once again, and Tony wrapped me in his arms, holding me tight until I could go on.

"My folks were devout Southern Baptist. My mom taught Sunday school, sang in the choir, and led prayer groups three times a week. My dad was a Deacon and mentored disadvantaged kids. When they found out, they went ballistic. I thought my dad was going to stroke out. He was so pissed. My mom just cried...cried so hard. My dad called me horrible names. He was more worried about being shunned by people at the church than he was about me. Both my parents decided they weren't going to let a whore and her bastard child live under their roof, so my dad hauled me to my room, packed a bag, and tossed it out on the lawn before shoving me out the door."

"Aww, baby," Tony groaned. "Where did you go?"

"I called Matt from a gas station down the street. I wanted him to talk to my dad and try to reason with him. But he said no. He told me that once my dad made up his mind, there was no way to change it. So, he picked me up and took me to his house. He took care of me."

"He supported you, financially?"

"Yes. After Nathan was delivered, Matt paid for a burial plot and made the arrangements for me."

"What did you do for him?"

The innuendo in Tony's question wounded. I raised my head and stared at him. "I can't believe you just asked that."

"I'm sorry, angel, but...you seem to have a penchant for older men."

"It wasn't like that." I scowled. "I never slept with him. For crying out loud, he was my father's best friend...well, the was before I fucked it up. When my dad found out that Matt had taken me in, they never talked again."

"I'm sorry, sweetheart. Please go on."

"Matt had money. Lots and lots of money, but I never knew what he did for a living. I was young and naïve, and growing up in such a sheltered environment, I just assumed he was the CEO of some conglomerate. He dressed impeccably and always looked like the quintessential businessman. After Nathan was laid to rest, Matt took me to dinner and asked what I planned to do with my life. When I confessed I had no clue, he offered me an enormous salary and asked if I wanted to work for him. I was so stupid. I didn't even ask what the job was. I just leapt at the obscene amount of money he'd offered, which of course, I didn't actually receive, because he insisted on investing it for me." A bitter chuckle escaped my throat. "At first, he taught me a bunch of different computer programs and eventually introduced me to the wonderful world of offshore banking and how to transfer money to his accounts all over the world. The man had billions of dollars."

"Let me guess, not a single penny of it was legal?"

"No."

"How did you find out?" Tony asked.

"I'd been working for him for about two years when something happened in the Caymans. I'm not entirely sure what, but it caused a ripple effect through the Caribbean, South America, all the way to Russia. From bits and pieces of conversations I'd overheard, I suspected he was in involved with guns and drug cartels, maybe more."

"Are you sure he's even still alive? People in those circles don't usually have a very long lifespan."

"I don't know. I've never tried to find out. I didn't want to raise any flags."

"Smart move, sweetheart," Tony agreed. "You told George about this?"

"Yes."

"Didn't he try to have Matt arrested?"

"He wanted to, but I begged him not to. George assured me he had friends in high places, but I feared Matt's power and influence was much greater than George's. Matt often boasted about the friends he had in our government. I didn't want George to scratch even the surface of that hornet's nest."

"Okay, couple of questions. How did George file the restraining order with Matt's name on it without raising a flag, as you call it?"

"He told me he had it sealed. Reed's the only other person, besides you, that knows whose name is on it."

"Okay. So, Matt's hooked up with bad guys. What happened that made him turn on you?"

"I figured he was involved in drugs and guns, but I didn't think he was dangerous. On a phone call, I overheard Matt saying that the guy who'd screwed things up in the Caymans was dead. But I didn't want to think he had anything to do with it. I wanted to believe he was innocent. Anyway, a few days later, a man from the Justice Department came to the house. Matt sent me upstairs to my room, but I sat on the landing, listening. He tried to bribe the guy, but he wouldn't bite. He threatened to freeze all of Matt's assets and bring in the FBI to confiscate his computers, bank records, the whole nine yards. I heard the man mention subpoenas, and I think he started to make a phone call. That's when I heard a gunshot. Matt killed the guy. Killed him dead, on the entryway carpet."

"Son of a bitch," Tony murmured. "What the hell did you do? You must have been terrified."

"I was. At first, I fought the urge to throw up. I wanted to run out the front door and get away from him, but I was scared he'd put a bullet in my back if he even suspected I wanted to leave. So, I went downstairs and grabbed a bucket and bleach. I walked into the foyer. I'd never seen a dead body before. Matt was on the phone ordering someone to come get the body. He took one look at me with the bucket and smiled. My blood turned to ice, but I got down on my hands and knees and started cleaning the guy's brains off the floor. At that exact moment, I started making plans to get the hell out before Matt killed me next."

Tony didn't say a word. He simply clutched me to his chest even tighter, anchoring me to the present, to him. I could feel the tension coiling inside him.

"The next morning, Matt called me into his room. He was packing a suitcase and told me I was to pack one as well. He said he was taking me to Tahiti for a few days to show his appreciation for my loyalty to him. There was no way in hell I was going to leave the country with that man. So, I convinced him it would look like he was fleeing if I went with him. I'd never accompanied him on any of his trips out of the country. And if anyone came snooping around, I promised to tell them that he'd left for China instead of the islands. He agreed it was a good idea, thanked me and walked out the door. I sat in that house all day and half the night plotting. Knowing he kept a close eye on his personal checking account, I couldn't risk withdrawing anything from the ATM and tipping my hand. So. I scrounged up what money I could find. It was only a hundred and thirty-seven dollars."

A cynical smile tugged my lips. Talking about Matt resurrected vulnerabilities I hadn't given thought to in years. But Tony's fingertips fluttering up and down my arm served to contain my emotions before they had a chance to swamp me under.

"I couldn't fail to see the irony. There I was, surrounded by opulence, yet I could only manage to get my hands on a hundred and thirty-seven dollars. At one o'clock in the morning, I threw two outfits into a plastic bag, disengaged the alarm system, and snuck out the back door."

Tony released me and gazed into my eyes. "And came here...to Chicago."

"Yes," I nodded. "I didn't have enough money for a plane ticket, so I figured I'd catch a bus. I needed to find a city big enough that he couldn't easily find me. Small towns were out of the question. Hopping the rail train from the suburbs, I finally made my way downtown to the bus terminal. I didn't have enough money for New York or L.A., but I did for Chicago, and the bus was leaving in a matter of minutes. It seemed the safest place for me to go. Matt knew I hated snow. Chicago would be the last place he'd look for me. So, I bought a ticket and got on the bus."

"Have you ever talked to your parents about his illegal activities?"

"No. I haven't talked to my dad since the day he kicked me out. My mom came to see me in the hospital after I'd lost Nathan. She told me the reason my baby died was because it was an abomination, and God was punishing for me being a whore."

"Your own mother said that to you?" Tony gaped.

"Yeah," I nodded sadly. "I looked her straight in the eye and told her to leave. Matt was there. He escorted her out of my hospital room, and I never saw her again. I remembered thinking he was my savior. I can't believe I was so damn stupid."

"Don't do that to yourself, sweetheart. He was a family friend. You were young. There was no reason to doubt he was a good guy. It takes life experience to realize that some people are trustworthy and others aren't. They don't walk around wearing a sign stating they're good or evil. You were just an unlucky victim."

"No, I'll be unlucky if he ever finds me."

"Where did you go…how did you survive once you got here?"

"I was petrified. I didn't know where to go, who to trust, or what to do. So, I hopped a city bus and got off at the first church I saw. I went inside and talked to the preacher. I told him I needed help, but I couldn't go to the police. He said not to worry, then called a woman named Hilary, who came to the church. She was in her early eighties, but she was so spry and full of life. Anyway, she picked me up and took me to her little house. She fed me, showed me to a guest room, and let me take a shower. Hilary didn't ask any questions, she just opened her heart and gave me a safe place to spend the night."

Tony slid his fingers into my hand and gave a little squeeze.

"The next morning, I woke up and fixed breakfast for us. We sat at her kitchen table eating and talking about survival. She told me that when she was just a baby, her mother held her against her chest, hiding under the stairs of their house in London, during the blitz. Her older brother, father, and grandfather had been killed in separate blasts. She and her mom escaped to America, arriving with twenty-two dollars in her pocket. A family took them in until her mom found work and was able to get on her feet."

"So, the woman spent her life paying it forward?"

"Yes. She was an amazing person. We hit it off, and she invited me to stay. I lived with her for a couple of years, helping out with the laundry, cleaning, and cooking, and she helped me in ways I'll never forget. Even after I moved out and got an apartment, we stayed in touch. When her son sold her house and put her in a nursing home, I visited her four times a week. And when she died two years ago, I was with her, holding her hand. I miss her every day."

"Aww, angel. I'm sorry. The world needs more people like Hilary," Tony smiled.

"Yes, it does."

176

"I get it now, sweetheart," he said softly as he placed a tender kiss on my forehead.

"Get what?"

"Why it's so hard for you to trust. Everyone you've ever loved has either disowned you, turned out to be a wolf in sheep's clothing, or died on you. I understand why you guard your heart. I do. I see you now in a different light. It makes sense why you fight so hard to present a tough exterior. You're a strong, resilient, and amazing woman. Even when you try to hide those parts, they still shine through. But you're also delicate and fragile, like a baby bird, and can be broken so easily."

Tony brushed his palm over my cheek. Embarrassed by his praise, I shrugged.

"Opening up and revealing that to me took guts, Leagh. Thank you for trusting me enough to share your secrets. I'll keep you safe, sweetheart. If Matt ever tracks you down, I'll make certain he doesn't lay a finger on you. And one more thing, I'll *never* turn my back on you, love."

The conviction in Tony's deep voice surrounded me like a suit of armor.

"Thank you. I know I don't act like it, but I *do* trust you, Tony. I think you're the first person who's ever truly deserved it. But giving up my power and letting someone take over is hard for me." A beleaguered smile tugged one corner of his mouth. "I know. I know... I'm not the poster child for submission. Honestly, if it hadn't been for George, I wouldn't have even known the lifestyle existed."

"How so?"

I scoffed and shook my head. "He came into the café one night, nervous as a cat in a dog pound. He started telling me about a friend who owned an adult club and asked if I'd go with him to check it out. I was shocked and scared I'd end up in the middle of some kind of kinky orgy or something. But it was the first time he'd asked me out, and I wasn't going to turn him down."

Tony sat listening patiently as I rambled on.

"He confessed that he'd actually been to Genesis a few times and was intrigued by what he saw. After he assured me it wasn't an orgy and asked if I could keep an open mind, I was so curious I said 'yes.'"

"I'll never forget the first night you came to the club," Tony whispered as if he were reliving it right along with me. "Your eyes were so wide, and innocence poured off you like summer rain. My dick got hard just looking at you, and I remember hoping you were George's daughter."

"Oh my," I chuckled.

"Yeah, when I found out otherwise, I was devastated. A better man would have turned the other way, but I couldn't keep from watching you. Fantasizing about all the wicked things I wanted to do to you...all the things I still want to do to you, angel."

Yes, now...do them now, Tony. Please!

I knew he'd read my mind when he chuckled. "Go on, tell me the rest."

"After he'd showed me around the club, we went up to Mika's office and watched through the mirror. Mika explained about Doms, Masters, Tops, subs, slaves, bottoms, switches, and the whole nine yards. Told me what every piece of equipment was called and how it was used. Watching it all got me so turned on, it was hard not to sit there and squirm on the couch."

Tony laughed. "I like to make you squirm."

I made a face and continued. "They explained the dynamics of the power exchange and what people gained from it. I guess you could say they gave me a crash course in BDSM," I chuckled softly, remembering how my mind was spinning that first night.

"I realized how George seemed to be into it, and even though I had a long list of things I wouldn't do, I agreed to be his submissive."

Tony grinned. "For someone who didn't know whit about the lifestyle, you were smart to set limits from the start."

"Yeah, well, I didn't know that's what I was doing. I just knew that the thought of being cuffed to a cross or tied down in any way freaked me the hell out. I was scared to be in such a vulnerable position."

"It takes a tremendous amount of trust." Tony brushed his lips over mine. "I know you trust me, Leagh. You never would have let me tie you up if you didn't. You may not realize it, but you're a very special treasure to me, sweetheart."

Tony's words made my heart swell and a lump form in my throat. I'd been afraid he would reject me for my involvement with Matt, but he vanquished those fears with his gentle understanding. I had no idea what my tomorrows would bring, but for the first time since George had died, a sense of peace settled over me thanks to Tony.

The bubble of serenity surrounding me didn't last long. Tony's cell phone rang once again. And as he silently listened, I watched the color drain from his face.

"I'm going to put you on speaker, James. Leagh needs to hear this, too."

After pushing a button, Tony laid the phone on the bed. At the sight of his trembling hand, I tensed.

"Leagh, honey, we've got a little problem with your vehicle out here."

"Problem? What kind of problem?" I asked, not bothering to hide the fear in my voice.

"That dude dickin' with your car wired a nasty little brick of C-4 to your spark plug. The Chief just got here and called for the bomb squad to come take a look at it."

Chapter Ten

A rush of adrenaline shot through me, hot and buzzing. Shadowy black spots gathered behind my eyes. I sucked in several deep breaths as my heart pounded in my ears. *C-4. Bomb squad.* This couldn't be happening...this had to be a nightmare.

"Before you freak out, Leagh, listen to me. We don't know for sure that this has anything to do with you. The guy may have had a beef with Mika, or the club, and just happened to pick your car."

"He wired it with explosives?" The visual of shoving my key into the ignition, turning the engine over, and a deadly ball of fire exploding into the night sky filled my brain. If James hadn't been paying attention to the security feed in Mika's office, I'd be dead.

Tony wrapped his arms around me and pulled me in close.

"I said don't freak out, Leagh. We'll find this nut-sack and get some answers," James assured.

"Did you get any leads from the license plate?" Tony asked. His tone weighed with anxiety.

"Yep. A half dozen officers are headed to the address pulled from the registration as we speak. Chief sidelined me, said it was a conflict of interest for me to work on this. I told him I just wanted five minutes alone with the prick when they brought him in. But he wouldn't go for that, either."

"If this was meant for Leagh, I'll be at the head of the line, regardless what your chief says," Tony growled.

Listening to the men posture, I didn't give a rat's ass who beat the crap out of the bad guy first. I just needed to know which evil was after me: Matt or Hayden. Dread, thick and dark, thundered through my veins along with the urge to run. Glancing at the casts weighing on my arm and leg, I knew my options were limited. Tinges of hopelessness joined in the swirling fray, and trying to keep a lid on the panic swelling inside grew more difficult by the second.

"I've asked a couple my detective friends to pay Hayden and Sloane a visit to see if they might have had a hand in this. I'm going to ride over with them, but I'll have to wait in the fucking car. I'll call you back as soon as I have more news."

"Thanks for keeping us in the loop, man," Tony replied before ending the call.

As he moved away and pocketed his phone, I reached for the crutch by the side of the bed.

"Where do you think you're going?" he asked, gripping my wrist.

"I have to get out of here." Fear coated my words. "Someone is trying to kill me. If that blast had gone off, it would have destroyed Genesis. I can't stay here if it's going to put all your lives at risk. I have to find somewhere safe to go...and I need to do it now!"

"Easy, baby," Tony soothed, releasing my hand. "We'll get some answers soon. But until we know what's going on, you've got to try to stay calm. You'll drive yourself crazy with what ifs. I won't let anyone hurt you. Come on, sweetheart, try to pull yourself together."

"I can't!" I gasped. Panic took over, and I shoved him away. "You've got to help get me out of here. Please."

With single-minded purpose, Tony crawled onto the bed. Crowding me with his chest, he pressed against me until I lay flat. Straddling my thighs with his, he gathered up my wrists and pinned them above my head. Looming over me, he lowered his body on top of mine.

Even in the throes of unmitigated fear, desire coiled like a snake low in my belly. Determination lined his face as he leaned in and captured my mouth. I didn't think anything could redirect my terror, but his potent kiss did just that. Cocooned in his strength and swayed by his lips, I found my salvation.

He tasted like a lifeline of sanity.

Absorbing the heat of his hulking body, I sipped on his slick tongue. Every humid breath Tony exhaled became a tender mercy I greedily sucked into my own lungs.

His kiss drained my fears and twisted them into desire. He imprisoned me in passion and power.

Tony claimed my mouth—owned it—owned me.

Sliding his hands beneath the edge of my robe, he pushed the silk aside. Exposed to the cool air and sensual glide of Tony's palms, my nipples pebbled. Wedging his knee between my legs, he roughly parted my thighs and swallowed my whimper of surrender. As he skimmed his fingers up my slick folds, I groaned. Driving a finger inside my wet tunnel, his thumb found my clit, and I tightened around him as he swallowed my gasp. Without a shred of modesty, my knees fell open, and I arched into his hand.

Trailing hot kisses over my jaw and down my neck, he paused, nipping at my pulse point. Squeezing a second finger alongside the other, his touch left my body quivering.

"What else do you need to tell me, sweetheart?" he growled against my throat.

"Nothing. Please. Don't stop, Tony. I don't have any more secrets. I swear."

Tony raised his head. Savage hunger, wild and ruthless, flickered across his dark, hooded eyes. Imprisoned by his ardent pull, I longed for him to unleash the beast clawing inside him and let it devour me.

"Ah, there's still one secret you're keeping from me." Tony's eyes narrowed as his jaw ticked.

Sexually saturated neurons misfired in my brain and made it hard for me to concentrate. *There is nothing left to tell him.*

"Tell me, angel. Are you ready to belong to me? To be *mine?*"

"Yes," I hissed, his masterful fingers strumming incessantly.

His nostrils flared, and a low growl of possession rumbled from his chest. I cupped the back of his neck to draw his mouth back to mine.

A slow smirk crawled across his lips. Challenging my control, the muscles in his neck and shoulders tightened and bulged. "Did you forget that I'm in charge here?"

"No," I replied with an impatient shake of my head.

"Good girl. We play by my rules today, tomorrow…forever. If I'm what you truly want, give me your power."

An arduous learning curve lay ahead, but Tony's vow echoed in my ears. *"I promise you this, no man, Dominant, or Master will treasure your gifts more than I. All you have to do is open the door and let me in. Trust that I'll cherish everything you give me."*

Finally, my heart and head aligned. Free of the fear of Tony abandoning me, I felt blanketed in faith that he would indeed never let me fall. A new road laid out before me. One that was no longer shrouded in darkness and distress, but shimmered in light and happiness, and most important of all…love.

"Take it, please. It's yours," I offered on a shaky sigh.

"What is it you want, angel? Tell me. It's as simple as that," Tony prompted, strumming his fingers in a persuading rhythm.

"I want to taste your lips, please."

"Mmm. I love the way you beg. Very nice," he murmured. Bending low, Tony brushed his mouth over mine. "Stick out your tongue. Taste me to your heart's content, angel."

Extending my tongue over his smooth lips, a tiny groan of pleasure vibrated from the back of his throat. Brazenly, I plunged deeper, tangling my tongue with his, exploring every inch of his mouth. Tony allowed me to feast on him, and I gave myself over to the smoldering heat swirling between us.

As if sensing my surrender, he suddenly pulled back. Sliding a hand into my hair, he squeezed tight in a palpable surge of dominance as he leaned in and sucked my lower lip between his teeth. Skimming his tongue over the plump flesh, he bit down hard before plunging deep inside and cutting off my cry.

His embedded fingers danced a decadent waltz over my sensitive knot of nerves. With his exacting strokes, the familiar tingle coalesced beneath my clit, spreading outward. Yet he plunged deeper still, swallowing my keening cries.

Tony peeled his lips from mine and his fingers stilled, just as I reached the peak.

"Describe how it feels, angel."

"Hot. Pulses of fire...shooting through me," I panted, rocking against his hand, desperate for more stimulation. "Building. Cresting. Higher...and higher."

"What's cresting?"

"My orgasm," I choked.

"Do you have permission to come for me yet, angel?"

"No."

"No, what?"

"No, Sir."

"Very nice," Tony cooed. "That's right. You don't have permission. And I refuse to let you fly without taking a little pain for me, my beautiful angel."

Pain? My eyes flashed wide in alarm. I swallowed tightly as he pinned me with an expectant stare. "But I don't like pain, Sir."

"So you think. But that spanking I gave you? I know deep down you crave it...ache for it. You haven't tapped into the depths you'll endure for me...At least, not yet. But you will. And I intend to teach you...everything."

Images of whips and blood, quirts and welts, paddles and bruises crowded my mind. Tony was right; I didn't know the depths of my submission. Hell, I still wasn't completely convinced I even was a submissive. The only thing I knew for sure was I didn't want to fail him. But if he incorporated sadistic pleasures into my training, I was doomed to disappoint. Our desires might mesh, but our BDSM needs never would.

My body was on fire, but my mind had turned to ice. I couldn't expect Tony to set aside his needs for me. Not on the off chance I might someday learn to crave the edgier side of BDSM. I'd done it again. I'd allowed my stupid fantasies to run roughshod over reality. Tony was, and always would be, a sadist. I opened my mouth to stop the madness just as a thunderous knock came from the other side of my door.

"Tony. Leagh. Open up," Drake bellowed.

My car. The bomb. The club.

Reality rained down in a deluge of ice-cold spikes. Dazed beneath the potent spell Tony cast upon me, he'd erased the terror with nothing more than a kiss. But it was back, bigger and badder than ever, coalescing in my veins like wet cement.

"Fuck!" Tony growled. Extracting his fingers from my pussy, he licked my juices from them, then, with a frustrated sigh, he crawled off me. Tossing the bedspread over my quivering body, he stormed to the door and jerked it open.

"We have to evacuate the club," Drake announced, his voice tight with tension.

"What?" I gasped.

"Why?" Tony asked.

"Bomb squad wants to remove the C-4 from Leagh's car. Evidently, it's a homemade device so they want us all out of here," Drake explained with a sour expression. "Oh yeah, and the cops are bringing in dogs to sniff the club for explosives."

"Shit," Tony hissed. "Mika's not going to like this."

"No, he's pissed as hell. He left Julianna and Tristan at the hospital and is on his way here now."

Guilt sluiced through me. The whole entire mess was my fault. Deep down, I knew the C-4 had been intended for me. Mika and Genesis weren't the target. My presence at the club had brought a shitload of danger down on my friends. Either Matt or Hayden wanted me dead, and neither had any qualms about taking out innocent people in the process. Fear and remorse slammed like an injection of adrenaline. And once again, the manic need to flee punched hard.

"Okay, let me help Leagh get dressed, and we'll go to my place," Tony announced to Drake.

"No!" I cried.

Tony spun toward me confusion wrinkling his forehead.

"I've got what you asked for, Daddy," Trevor announced as he squeezed past Drake and entered the room. His blue eyes were brimmed with fear as a stack of dark-colored clothing trembled in his hands.

"What's this for?" Tony asked, looking at the young man.

"We need to get Leagh out of here. If someone's watching for her outside, it would be best if she wore a disguise," Drake replied with calm reassurance I couldn't relate to.

Nausea swirled in my stomach, and I forced down the saliva pooling in my mouth. Was someone planning on putting a bullet in my head once I stepped out the door? How was I going to get out of the club unnoticed wearing pounds of plaster? Clothes alone wouldn't be enough to disguise my broken limbs.

"Son of a bitch," Tony murmured. With a snap of his head, he looked over his shoulder at me. "Put them on. I refuse to take any chances with you, Leagh."

"Okay," I whispered with a nod.

"If we dress her like a man and get her out of here," Drake explained to Tony. "I'll take her to my place and meet up with you there."

"Why your place?" Tony asked.

"She can't go to your house, man. Obviously, someone's been watching her. They know she's here...knew her car. They've probably seen you two together. If they've done their homework, they damn well know where *you* live."

The more Drake expounded, the heavier my heart sank. It wasn't just my friends at the club that I'd put in danger. I'd painted a big, fat bullseye on Tony's back.

"I know someplace she'll be safe," he assured Drake. "We'll meet up at your place, and I'll take her from there. Let's do this."

"Wait!" I cried out. "Where do you plan on taking me after Drake's?"

"To my parent's house."

"No way," I snapped. "You're crazy if you think I'm putting your family in the middle of my shit."

"Stop, Leagh," Tony instructed with a sympathetic smile. "This isn't up for discussion. Besides, there's no place on the planet safer. Trust me."

"Come on, sis, don't fight him," Trevor begged as he plopped down next to me. His pale face seemed even whiter. "If Tony says you'll be safe there, you can bet your ass you will be. Please go to his folk's house for me?"

"Evidently I don't have another choice, do I?" I asked, glaring at Tony.

With a challenging smirk, Tony edged in closer. "No. You don't."

"Trevor, help Tony," Drake directed. "I need to get the dungeon cleared."

As soon as Drake left, Trevor laid out the clothing on the bed.

"Come on. Let's get these on you," Trevor cajoled. Flashing an impish grin, he winked. "I'll finally get to make a man out of you, sister."

His attempt at humor did nothing to erase the aura of anxiety rolling off him. As my mind raced, Tony and Trevor stripped me down and dressed me up. After pulling a dark hoodie over my head, they tucked my hair up under a ball cap.

Every time I opened my mouth to speak, Tony shushed me with a censuring glower. Sitting on the bed, I watched Trevor run out the door to find Drake. Determined to get some answers, I narrowed my eyes at Tony.

"Would you please explain to me *why* you think I'll be safe at your parents?"

"Sweetheart, I don't *think* you'll be safe. I *know* you will."

Tony's vague answer only pissed me off more. "And how are you so sure? Wait, the more important question is *why* would you put your family in jeopardy because of me?"

A sly grin tugged one side of his mouth. "They're not going to be in any danger, and it's quite obvious you *still* don't trust me. Don't go taking back your control now, just because things are getting dicey."

"Dicey? You call this dicey? You're out of your mind. This is life and death, Tony. Mine, yours, and your family's. I do trust you, and I'm not taking back my control. I just want some damn answers." The smile on his face grew wider. "I don't find the least bit of humor in any of this."

I was shocked by his total lack of concern for the family I knew he loved so much.

"You're not listening to me, angel." He frowned. "My family is going to be perfectly safe. They have…connections. I can guarantee my dad has the ability to find out faster than the cops if someone is truly trying to kill you."

"Your dad? What? Is he in the mafia or something?" I choked in alarm.

Tony's eyes grew wide. "Oh, so since I'm Italian, you automatically jump to the conclusion that my family is in the mafia. Stereotype much?"

"I didn't mean it like that." I pouted.

"You watch too many damn movies."

"You just said your family had connections. What the hell am I supposed to think?"

"They *do* have connections, but that doesn't mean they're involved in the mafia."

"Will you stop beating around the bush and just say whatever it is you're trying to say? With all that's going on around here, I'm not capable of playing these mind games. I'm scared half to death. And every second I stay in this room, I'm putting the people I love in danger."

I dropped my head and cradled my forehead in my palm. Tears began to swell. I closed my eyes. I was sick of crying, yet I couldn't stop the fat drops from spilling down my cheeks.

The bed dipped, and Tony wrapped me in his arms. His decadent heat seeped into my bones, while his intoxicating scent filled my nostrils. The reassuring strength he provided called to the scared child in me, like a searchlight through heavy fog. Melting against him, I clutched his rugged chest, holding on for dear life, and sobbed.

"Leagh, don't cry. I don't want you torturing yourself," he softly laughed "That's my job. Look, everything's going to be okay. I promise."

Oh, how I ached to believe him, ached for it more than anything in the world.

"First things first. I need you to stay calm, so we can get you out of here. Okay?"

"Don't make me go with Drake. I want to stay with you," I sniffed as I wiped the tears from my cheeks.

Jenna Jacob

"I'll be five minutes behind you, sweetheart. I trust Drake with my life, and I trust him with yours. Think of this as just another step on the road of your submission. Let me take all the worry and fear out of your hands. You know I'd never let anything happen to you."

"You make it sound like it should be easy," I protested.

"It is. If you let it be." Tony eased back, tilting my chin up with his fingertips. His gaze suffused with understanding, he feathered a kiss over my lips. "It's foreign and scary, and you feel like you're free falling without a net. But don't think for one second I'll ever let you fall. I'll always be there to catch you, Leagh. I promise."

The surety reflecting in his eyes made it impossible for me not to believe him.

Believe *in* him.

"I'll do my best."

"That's all I'll ever ask of you, sweetheart."

Once again, Tony pressed his lips to mine. I could taste his promise, and it filled me with a sense of determination. Fear closed in on me from every angle, yet Tony's kiss granted a shield, fortifying me against the unknown.

"Ah-hem," Drake interrupted loudly.

Startled, I jerked away from Tony and stared up at the burly Dom filling my doorway.

"I wasn't done yet, sweetheart. Get back here," Tony growled as he gripped my hair and pulled me in to finish the kiss.

"You two will have to get a room later. Right now, we've got to get out of here," Drake grinned, tossing a roll of black duct tape at Tony.

Blinking at the shiny black adhesive as it sailed through the air, I darted a worried glance between the two Doms.

"What's that for?"

"Christ, girl. Do you have to question everything?" Drake growled with a teasing grin as he swaggered toward the bed and lifted me into the air with one beefy arm. "We know what we're doing."

"Right. Um, exactly, what *are* we doing?" Tony arched a brow at the tattooed Dom.

"Taping her ankle to mine of course." Drake shot him a wide grin. Tony still looked confused. "Here's how it's going to work."

After a quick explanation, the two men taped my casted ankle to Drake's sock, before hiding the evidence beneath the cuffs of our pants. With my casted arm wrapped around the big Dom's waist, he slipped on a trench coat, concealing my bulky arm. Drake slipped his arm around my waist and lifted me a fraction of an inch off the floor. With my useless leg attached to his, he took a couple of steps. Our legs moved in tandem. Although, we were joined together as if ready for a three-legged race, to the casual observer, it appeared that our steps were simply in sync.

We strolled down the hall to the back door. "I'll see you soon," Tony whispered in my ear before he cast an uneasy glance toward Drake. "Take care of her, bro."

"You can count on it, man. We'll meet you back at my place. I've got Dylan, Nick, and Savannah lined up to drive Trevor home."

Drake gave me a nod, then pulled the heavy metal door open.

Stepping onto the landing, the back of the club looked like a carnival. The only thing missing were rides and cotton candy. Police cars and an armored vehicle choked the parking lot as strobes of red and blue danced over the brick buildings. Onlookers gathered in clusters.

"Keep your head down," Drake murmured.

Casting my eyes to the ground as members exiting the club pressed around us, Drake inched off the top step.

"When we get to the car, I'm going to drop my keys. When I bend to pick them up, I'm going to cut the tape on our ankles. Hold on to the car; I don't want you to fall. Okay?" Drake whispered as he seamlessly hauled me down the rest of the stairs.

I nodded. Focused on the ground in front of me, I tried my best to shield my face beneath the dark hood of the jacket.

"Don't look up. There's a guy way too interested in who is coming out of the club," Drake whispered just loud enough for me to hear. "Don't say a word. Just nod your head and play along."

I had no idea what he'd planned, but I'd gladly do anything he wanted as long as it kept me alive. Just the fact that someone was watching us made my heart jackhammer in my chest.

"It's a damn circus back here. Fuckin' assholes have to go and ruin our night, Trevor. What the fuck," Drake ranted in a loud angry tone. "When we get home, *boy*, I'm going to put that sweet mouth of yours to work. Understand?"

A part of me wanted to laugh at Drake's charade, but I was too damn scared to do anything more than issue a silent nod.

"That's my good boy," Drake praised in a deep booming voice as he clutched me tight against his burly frame.

As we made our way into the chaos, Drake's cell phone rang. Cursing under his breath, he picked up the pace, all but dragging me to his car. When he plucked out his phone, his keys dropped to the ground. While it wasn't exactly how we'd planned it, I leaned against his vehicle as he bent down. Within seconds, the duct tape gave way, and Drake hooked his arm around my waist to open the passenger door.

"Hello," he barked into the phone as he lowered me onto the leather seat. "We'll be pulling out of the lot in a second. Hang on."

Forcing my stare to the zipper of my hoodie, Drake closed the door before quickly climbing into the driver's seat. With the phone wedged between his shoulder and his ear, he didn't say a word, simply started the engine and wound his way through the congested parking lot.

As we pulled onto Myers Street, I glanced up to see more members spilling out from the front door. Gawkers clogged the sidewalks on both sides of the street. Peeking over at Drake, his face was lined with worry, and he quickly glanced in the rear-view mirror.

"Nothing so far. If that changes, I'll call you back. Give me the address again. North on Taylor Street and take a left on…Got it. I'll meet you there."

Drake hung up. His gaze darted back and forth from the road to the mirror, over and again. I kept my mouth shut so he could focus.

"That was Tony on the phone. James called him as we were leaving the club," Drake began, his attention nervously bouncing from the road to the mirror. "When he and the detectives started to pull into George's driveway, the damn house blew up."

"Blew up? Oh my…How? What the hell happened?" I gasped.

"No clue. The fire department is on their way, but Tony wants you at his parent's house. Now."

192

"Okay," I whispered, watching Drake cast his eyes back to the mirror. "Is someone following us?"

"No. I'm just making sure it stays that way," he replied. Tension rolled off his big frame like lava. "Listen, Leagh. You need to start trusting him. Tony's been in love with you for a long time. I know I probably shouldn't tell you that, but it's the truth. He'd lay down his life before he'd let anything happen to you, girl."

Drake glanced my way. Compassion and concern glimmered in his gray eyes. It surprised me. From the first time I'd met the big scary Dom, I'd shied away from him. Even after Trevor and I became friends, I kept my distance. Julianna swore the man was nothing but a big teddy-bear, but I never believed her. Drake always looked like he was ready to rip off the head and shit down the neck of anyone who crossed him. Hearing such poignant words from his lips, I understood what Julianna had meant.

"I don't know that I deserve him, Sir."

He flashed me a crooked smile. "Bullshit. You're exactly what he needs, girl. You're all sass and attitude. I've watched Tony for years. Watched him grow bored whipping the same asses night after night. Ever since he started taking care of you, hell, he's back to how he used to be...happy and full of life. You've done that for him, just like you did it for George. Problem is, you can't see it."

I didn't see it. Didn't understand how I could possibly have given anything to Tony. Nothing close to all the ways he'd supported me.

"Why are you telling me all this?" I asked.

Drake let out a heavy sigh. "Look, I made a lot of mistakes when I had Julianna under my care. But I learned a big lesson. Never keep your mouth shut if a sub needs help."

"I appreciate your candidness, but Tony and I...we're so—"

"Opposite?" Drake interrupted.

"Yes." I nodded.

"Haven't you ever heard the old saying, opposites attract?"

"Well, yeah, but..." I scoffed. "When it comes to the lifestyle, we're not just from different planets...we're from different solar systems."

"That doesn't mean you can't make it work. Give him a chance, Leagh. You're not meant to be alone."

"What's that supposed to mean?" I couldn't mask my indignation.

Drake shot me a scowl. "It means you need a strong Master. Don't get me wrong. I'm not criticizing George, so don't take this the wrong way. But you spiral up and fly out of control like a damn top. You need someone with enough backbone to keep you in line."

"I do not. I just don't—"

"Please. I've watched you for years, too." Drake pondered for a long moment. "Don't buy into all that gossip that floats around at the club about you, girl."

"Easy for you to say," I groused.

"Shit. People have been talking trash about me for years. I'm the evil Dom. Or haven't you heard?"

"Oh, I've heard," I chuckled with a sly grin. "But you want them to think you're a bad-ass. It gives you street cred."

Drake laughed. "That it does, girl. It also helps Mika out. So, I don't mind being viewed a prick."

Turning down a quiet, residential street, he slowed, peering up at the house numbers.

"Well, it looks like the whole family came to welcome you," Drake announced as he pulled to the curb in front of a large brick house in the middle of the block. His headlights illuminated a dozen broad-shouldered men ambling down the front steps toward the vehicle.

An older man made his way toward Drake's side of the car. He had dark skin, hair, and eyes, and his facial structure looked like an older version of Tony. The other men, the younger ones, remained on the sidewalk. Standing shoulder to shoulder, they made an intimidating fortress.

"I hope for your sake you're Drake," the older man threatened as he leaned in, eyeing the big Dom. Slowly, he cast a gaze my direction, examining me with a curious expression.

"Yes. And you're Tony's dad, right?"

"How'd you guess?" The man smiled. He was Tony's father all right. They both had the same devastating grin. "Vito Delvaggio. Come. Let's get you two inside. I'll introduce you to my wife, Alisa."

"Thanks," Drake nodded as he put the car in park and cut the engine.

Thankful he was going inside with me, I had feared he'd simply drop me off and leave. As Drake climbed from the vehicle, Vito leaned in close. The two men shared a short, private conversation. I strained to hear what they said but couldn't. A prickly sensation danced over my skin. Vito slapped Drake on the back with a nod before he hurried around the front of the car and opened my door.

"What else happened?" I asked, looking up. The street light illuminated both men's somber expressions.

"Someone is following my son. Don't worry, young lady. I've given my boy a specific route to take. I guarantee he won't be followed much longer," Vito preened, pride flickering in his dark eyes.

Tony had assured me his father wasn't in the mob. And yes, I probably *did* watch too many movies, but I couldn't shake the feeling that I'd just stepped onto the set of *The Godfather*.

Drake bent low and lifted me from the car.

"I can walk," I huffed, feeling like an invalid in his massive arms.

Hoisting me up against his chest, he grinned. "This is faster."

Drake paraded me past the line of men, and I felt their curiosity rake over me. As we started up the stairs, I heard a deep voice whisper behind me, "Tony's one lucky son of a bitch."

The man had it all wrong; *I* was the lucky one.

Upon entering the house, the aroma of cinnamon and fresh baked bread filled the air. My mouth watered, and I instantly relaxed as the cozy atmosphere surrounded me.

"Alisa," Vito bellowed in a tone identical to Tony's. I couldn't help but smile. "Leave the damn baking alone for five minutes, woman. We have company."

No doubt about it, Tony's dominance was definitely genetic. I bit back a giggle.

"Just who do you think you are, barking out orders at me like that, Vito Delvaggio? You be nice to me, or I'll shut the kitchen down and let you starve to death. You can't even open a can of soup, for the love of Pete."

A petite dark-haired woman, wearing a mock scowl, scolded

Tony's dad before turning her attention our way. Flashing a bright, happy smile, she looked every bit the loving mother Tony had described.

"You must be Leagh and Drake. Let's find you a comfortable place to sit." She motioned for us to follow before leading us into a spacious living room decorated in creams and mauves. "Would you like the couch or a recliner, dear?"

"The couch is fine Thank you, Mrs. Delvaggio."

"Call me Alisa, please," she invited as Drake lowered me onto a soft, comfy cushion. Smiling at the woman, Drake sat in the empty chair beside me. "I've got a fresh pot of coffee and warm cinnamon rolls. I'll be right back."

As Alisa darted out of the room, Drake chuckled.

"What's so funny?" I asked, yanking the ball cap off my head and fingering the tangles from my hair. I found nothing humorous, not while Tony was in danger.

"She's the quintessential Italian mother, that's all. The world could be crumbling out from under us, but she'll make sure everyone has food in their bellies."

"It *is* crumbling out from under me," I replied softly.

"No, it's not. Chin up, buttercup. If you haven't figured it out yet, you're not alone. So, stop thinking that way. Whoever is behind this shit, we'll do whatever it takes to make sure you get through it unscathed. You hear me?" Drake arched a brow. I nodded without rebuttal. Even though he'd shown me his soft underbelly, Drake still scared the beejeebers out of me.

Suddenly, the front door burst open, and Tony rushed into the foyer. Wildly searching the dining room, his head snapped in our direction. His gaze settled on me, and it felt as if we'd been apart an eternity. A rush of emotions played across his face, and I felt the same powerful wave of relief that reflected in his eyes.

Wanting nothing more than refuge in his strong arms, I reached out to him. Shucking the duffle bag off his shoulder, it fell to the floor as Tony lifted me off the couch and clutched me to his chest.

I clung to him, savoring his warm breath on my neck, the staccato beat of his heart, and the euphoria filling my soul that he'd made it safely back to me.

Neither of us said a thing. The potent connection between us conveyed more than mere words could say.

I wasn't sure when or how it had happened, but Tony had branded himself deep in my soul. The stark reality that no man had ever truly loved me until Tony came full circle. He'd changed me—changed my life—and in that single moment, I knew I was destined to be his. I couldn't hide from the truth any longer…I was in love with him.

Tony's strong fingers tangled in my hair. Tugging my head from his shoulder, he slanted his lips over mine. Rejoicing in his passionate kiss, I gave back as good as I got.

"Anthony, you're home!" Alisa exclaimed.

Tony broke the kiss. With a furtive smile, he stared into my eyes. "Yeah, Ma. I'm finally home."

His double entendre filled me with warm, fuzzy joy. While he settled me back on the couch, Alisa placed a tray laden with gooey cinnamon rolls and mugs of steaming coffee on the low table in front of me. She turned and spread her arms wide. Tony wrapped his mom in a big bear hug, lifting her straight off the floor. She gave him a quick kiss on the cheek before he set her back down. Tony clasped Drake's hand and thanked him for '*delivering my package safe and sound,*' before sliding in next to me on the couch.

As we sat and ate, Tony shared a watered-down version of the night's events with his parents. The knowing looks that Tony and Vito shared made it abundantly clear Alisa knew nothing about her son's kinky inclinations.

Tony explained how he tried to shake the man following him, but by some divine intervention the dude got pulled over by the police. Or rather, a close friend of Vito's who happened to be a cop *and* happened to be on the very same road. *Right.* I flashed Tony's father a grateful smile.

From one of the numerous calls Tony received from James, we found out the guy tailing Tony had been hauled to jail. The police discovered he was in possession of fake documentation for five different aliases.

A short time later, James called again. Only this time Tony put him on speaker phone.

"The fire department is still trying to put the fire out at George's house," James began. "Homeland Security and FBI have joined in on the investigation."

*Police. FBI. Homeland Security. If they started prying into my past...*I tensed.

"Why? Is that standard procedure or something?" Tony asked.

Even with the background noise echoing through the device, James exhaled a heavy, audible sigh. "Depends on the case, but since George was a State Supreme Court Justice and houses usually don't blow up by themselves." There was a long pause. "Fuck, you're going to hear about it in the morning anyway...Look, they've pulled two bodies out of the house, but neither has been positively identified yet."

My blood turned to ice, freezing the breath in my lungs. *Bodies?*

"Leagh, you should expect a visit from one or all three of the agencies involved. They're going to want to ask you a ton of questions, I'm sure."

It took several seconds before I could draw in a breath. "I didn't have anything to do with the fire. I'm not involved in any of this. I don't even know what the hell is going on."

The pitch of my voice increased, keeping tempo with the panic rising inside me. Tony was quick to grab my hand.

"They know that, darlin'," James sympathized. "But, unfortunately, it does involve you."

"How?" I blinked in confusion.

"The tow truck from the club was found a couple of blocks from here. There's no sign of the driver. One of the bodies they pulled from the house was male. Seems a little too coincidental, but we'll know later on tonight if it's the same guy or not."

I didn't know how I was supposed to feel. On one hand, I was relieved the threat against me might be over if one of the bodies happened to be Hayden. But on the other, wishing death upon anyone was like sending an engraved invitation to karma asking her to come back and bite me in the ass.

"Fuck me. I need to go. They just brought out another body. If I don't call you back tonight, I'll come by in the morning," James replied.

"Sure, man. See you then."

With each piece of information received, I grew more anxious. Though Tony smothered me in reassurance, he also watched me like a hawk. He was assessing and cataloguing my reactions like a culture in a Petri dish. Once he got me alone, he'd want to peel back my layers and analyze every one of my jagged emotions. In a weird way, I hoped he would as I couldn't even begin to sort out my mess of emotions alone.

Drake received a call from Mika to let him know the dogs didn't find any explosives in the club. Although the news was comforting, guilt for putting the lives of my friends in jeopardy rode me hard.

It was close to one o'clock in the morning. The cinnamon rolls were gone, and both men's phones had finally stopped ringing when Drake stood up.

"If you guys are good here, I'm going to head home and see Trevor," he announced.

"Oh, you have a son?" Alisa asked with a smile.

Drake nodded with a slight smirk. "He's my boy."

I nearly choked.

"I loved having boys. They're so much fun. How old is he?" Alisa asked.

"They sure as hell are," Drake replied with a chuckle. "He's twenty-eight."

"Really? You don't look old enough to have a son that age." Alisa blinked.

Tony coughed, and I had to bite the inside of my cheeks to keep from laughing.

"Thanks. It was a pleasure meeting you both," Drake responded with a smile to both Alisa and Vito.

"It was a pleasure meeting you, Drake." Alisa smiled warmly. "Be sure to come back and visit us again. And next time, bring your son. I'd love to meet him."

"Come on, man. We'll walk you out." Tony glanced at Vito and jerked a nod toward the front door.

Drake paused and arched a brow at me. "You do what Tony tells you to do, Leagh, and you'll be just fine."

"I intend to. Thank you for everything, Drake, Si…seriously, thank you," I stuttered, nearly calling him Sir in front of everyone.

Tony shot me a smirk, shook his head, and clapped Drake on the back. As they stepped through the portal, I heard Tony's phone ring once more. Snapping my attention toward the entryway, I barely noticed Alisa placing her hand over mine.

"Don't worry, Leagh. You're one hundred percent safe here with us. I promise."

"I'm sorry to bring my troubles into your home, Alisa."

"Nonsense," she chided with a smile. "As far as we're concerned, you're family now."

Her unconditional acceptance floored me.

"Thank you. I'm honored."

Alisa scanned the room with a conspiratory glance, then leaned in close. "And let me tell you, no one fucks with my family," she whispered with a mischievous grin.

Chuckling softly, I got the impression Alisa Delvaggio didn't drop the F-bomb often. She reminded me a lot of Hilary, except much younger. Both ladies were proper on the outside and a little untamed on the inside. It would be easy to grow close to Alisa.

"Now, this is a sight I've waited a lifetime to see," Tony announced with a broad smile as he swaggered back into the room. "The two most important women in my life smiling. Or are you two plotting something evil?"

"We would never do anything of the kind," Alisa challenged with a hint of insult.

"Uh-huh," Tony grunted in disbelief. "We need some sleep. I'm going to take Leagh up to my old room. You okay with that, Ma?"

Reservation clouded Alisa's face. "I know you want to keep Leagh safe, Tony, but…"

"I know. I know. No fun stuff until we're married. Give me a break, Ma. We're just gonna go to bed…to sleep."

She studied her son, as if weighing Tony's sincerity. Her scrutiny was fierce.

"Okay, but I trust you to keep your word, Anthony," she lectured.

"Oh, for the love of...I'm a grown man now, Ma," Tony muttered on an exasperated sigh.

"This is still our home, young man," Alisa bristled and popped up from the chair, placing her hands on her hips.

I wanted to laugh as the big, bad Dom got called down by his mommy. Instead, I kept my mouth shut and my eyes focused on the coffee table. Sex might be off limits in her house, but Tony would find a way to spank my ass if I gave him half a chance.

"Ma, I know the rules. They've been the same for the past thirty-one years. Besides, Leagh and I haven't even had sex...yet. Okay?"

A look of surprise burst over Alisa's face before her expression softened. A proud smile spread across her lips. Reaching up, she patted his cheek. "That's because you're a good boy, Anthony."

I bit my lips to stifle a giggle. Over his mother's shoulder, Tony pinned me with a glower.

I opened my mouth. I just couldn't help myself. "He's a very good boy, indeed," I razzed with a cheesy grin.

Tony cocked his head as both brows arched in disbelief. Strutting past Alisa, he rounded the coffee table and leaned in close. "Little subs who play with fire *will* get burned."

"Maybe, but I'm safe here," I taunted in his ear as he lifted me off the couch into his arms.

"Good night, Ma," Tony called over his shoulder as he snagged up the duffle and carried me up the stairs.

"Sweet dreams," Alisa hollered after us.

Once at the top of the stairs, Tony laughed. "You think just because we're not supposed to make love that I'm not going to fuck with you long and hard?" A wicked gleam flashed in his dark eyes.

I gasped, "Wha...but you can't. You just promised your mother..."

"Do you really think I follow my mother's rules, angel? Besides, I can think of a hundred different ways to fuck you with my throbbing cock safely straining against my jeans."

"You wouldn't dare," I whispered tersely as he turned the handle and kicked open a door at the end of the hall.

The evil laugh that peeled from his throat sent a ripple of nervous desire up my spine.

"Wanna bet, sweetheart?" Tony chuckled as he gently sat me on the edge of a big, soft bed.

I shook my head. Around the room, dozens of sports achievements hung on the walls. An enormous bookcase crammed with trophies stood near a polished oak desk. Awards for football, baseball, basketball, and soccer filled the shelves, while a battered Lacrosse stick stood tucked in one corner by the door.

"A bad-ass Dom and a mega jock, too?" I teased with a smirk.

"Yeah, well," he replied with a sheepish grin. "I can't talk Ma into letting me box this shit up. But don't let your surroundings fool you, I'm a bad-ass Dom in your eyes, angel."

"She won't let you box it away because she's proud of you." I smiled watching him shut the door and set the duffle bag on the bed. "I'm proud of you, too."

His head snapped up, and the look of surprise melded into a soft contented smile. Tony sat next to me and framed my face with his broad hands.

"Why are you proud of me, angel?"

"Because you're an amazing man." I longed to tell him all the ways he'd touched my heart, but I struggled to find the right words. "You didn't have to take me under your wing and haul my gimp-ass to doctor's appointments or do all the thousands of things you've done for me. But you did. And all I've done is infuriate you, well, most of the time. It's not that I mean to…it's just that I don't feel like I deserve you."

He bit back a smile and studied me for a long moment. "Continue, angel."

I sucked in a deep breath. Averting my gaze, I plucked at a piece of lint on my pants. "When I'm with you, I feel different. Whole. You stir something big inside me...not just sexually, but… oh, hell...I'm messing this up. There's this huge need inside me to make you happy."

"So, you *do* want to submit to me?"

I issued a shy nod. Tony tipped his head and brushed his lips over mine. Raising one hand to his cheek, the dark stubble tickled my fingers, and I kissed him back with tender reverence. He moved his hands and wrapped me in his steely arms, drawing me tight against his warm body. Urgent and hungry, he tangled his tongue with mine, nibbling and nipping it with his teeth.

Tony pushed me high and hard and sent my senses reeling. With frantic fingers, he freed the buttons and peeled away the fabric of my shirt as his smooth hands skimmed over my shoulders.

Reluctantly pulling back, Tony lifted me from the bed and onto his lap. Straddling him, I clearly saw the level of desire blazing in his dark eyes.

"Your kiss feels different, Leagh. I'm not sure what that means, but I like it. Kiss me again, sweetheart. I want to feel it once more."

"It means…Oh, Tony," I whispered. Unable to say the three little words aloud, I poured every ounce of love brimming inside me into that one glorious kiss. Unleashing my passion for him—to him—I held nothing back.

Melting back to the mattress, Tony took me with him. Tearing at each other's clothing, our hands caressed heated flesh until the only barrier between us was my saturated thong and Tony's tented briefs.

Rising from the bed, he stood and pulled me to the edge once again. Sitting, I gazed at his perfect body and tried to calm my ragged breaths. Drawn to his straining erection, I licked my lips, anxious and wired for a taste of his thick, hard flesh.

"Tell me what you want, Leagh." His tone was raspy with need.

I didn't hesitate to respond. "I want to taste you."

"Good girl," he groaned, peeling off the briefs. His cock jutted forth, wide and inviting. A pearl of clear pre-come lay poised on the broad crest. My mouth watered. "I've dreamed about this. About sliding past your pouty lips and sinking deep into that sassy, hot mouth of yours."

Fisting his cock as he spoke, Tony stepped closer. The bead grew larger, then slid down glistening over his fingers. My lips parted. Anticipation spiked.

"Feel me, angel," he commanded on a hoarse tone.

I wrapped my hand around him. Heat enveloped my palm, and his ragged heartbeat drummed against my fingers. I moved my fist upward in a soft stroke as Tony seized my hair and inched me toward his angry cock. Parting my lips, his command washed through me, and the submissive within roared to life.

Focused on bringing him as much pleasure as he'd allow, I slid my tongue over his hot flesh, taking time to learn every ridge and vein. When I swiped over the weeping crest and his masculine flavor exploded over my tongue, Tony exhaled a shaky sigh, and I swallowed him down with a sultry moan.

Opening wider, I engulfed him until his coarse hair tickled my nose. I slowly traced my tongue over his pulsating veins before swallowing him whole once more. Back and forth, I bathed his cock while my hand cupped his heavy balls. Tony moaned when I lightly raked my fingernails over the orbs. Smiling inwardly, I tucked that knowledge away.

He allowed me to immerse him in splendor, and the burn of submission grew into a blistering fire. The flames licked higher, and so did my craving to serve him. By accepting this tiny taste, I found my freedom.

"Just like that...slow and deep. Yesss. Christ, you feel so fucking good. So much better than I ever imagined," Tony murmured. "I've waited a lifetime to shower your throat and brand you with my come."

Gripping my hair to the point of pain, he took command of the rhythm. Starting off slow and smooth, he soon picked up the pace, thrusting fast and hard. Sexual tension pulsed in the air, electrified and hot.

"That's it, baby. You feel so hot and soft...so damn silky. I could stay here forever with your luscious lips wrapped so tight and your slick tongue teasing my dick."

His words sent a flutter of pride to mix with the blistering fire churning beneath my clit. Lashing my tongue against the sensitive underside with each urgent stab, I felt Tony's orbs draw up tight and hard. Forcing my head back, he drove in further until he prodded the back of my throat. Lust flared in his eyes, and he clenched his teeth with a visceral grimace. His steely cock swelled on my tongue. Frantic for his creamy treasure, I whimpered as a low growl vibrated deep in his chest.

"Mine!" Tony commanded in a low, gravelly roar.

Thick ropes of hot, salty come exploded over my tongue and down my throat. The need to please him rode me hard. Gulping down his seed, Tony's whole body trembled as he continued to thrust and fill my mouth, and I swallowed each burst, while I mewled like a newborn kitten.

Tony gasped, filling his lungs, as I swirled my tongue over his rigid shaft. I sucked and licked every drop clean. He trailed his knuckles down my cheek as he gazed down at me. Like a river, his affection and approval flowed over me, and my heart nearly burst with joy.

He took a step back and knelt down in front of me, unshed tears glistened in his eyes. "I've waited," he paused and cleared the emotion from his throat. "I've waited so fucking long for you...dreamed of what it would be like. But you're ten times more amazing than anything I ever fantasized about."

Slammed by the intensity of his declaration, I felt my chin quiver as I blinked back my own tears. "I love you, Tony."

Chapter Eleven

His eyes grew wide in stunned surprise. Slowly, his whole face lit up like a child on Christmas morning.

"Oh, Leagh, I love you, too."

He wrapped me in his arms and claimed my lips in an intoxicating kiss as he dragged me beneath him to the middle of the bed. Pulling back, he positioned himself above me with his neck muscles taut, his breath ragged, and looking so commanding and gorgeous I wanted to weep.

Dropping kisses over my jaw, he worked his way to my ear. Capturing the lobe between his teeth, he nipped it and issued a hungry growl. His hot breath sent goose bumps prickling over my skin. Trailing more kisses down my neck, he skimmed his teeth over my pulse point. And as I squirmed, he dipped lower still, laving his tongue over each tightly drawn nipple, and driving me out of my mind.

My wanting pussy clutched and cramped, my clit throbbed in time with my thundering heart. Enthralled with my breasts, he stayed there a long time, savoring the sensitive peaks as he amped me up with his fingers, lips, teeth, and tongue. My body blazed, but he seemed in no rush to put out my fire, even when I whimpered and begged for his mouth to settle on the place I needed it most. He simply chuckled against my pillowy flesh and kept right on tormenting and teasing.

Like a steel pipe, his hot cock lay wedged between our bellies. Rolling my hips in demand, I was sure to combust if he didn't slide inside me soon.

Tony placed his hand over my mouth. I blinked down at him, afraid I'd been too loud. With a mischievous wink, he stared at me as he sank his teeth into my areola and bit down hard. My screams vibrated against his hand as he tugged the tender tissue with an animalistic growl.

Sliding his tongue over the pulsating fire, Tony absorbed the pain as it radiated outward. And after the sting subsided, he raised his head and flashed me an impish grin.

"Keep nice and quiet, angel. We don't want Ma coming in to ruin our fun, do we? After all, I've just started to warm you up. It'd be a shame to have to stop now." The devilish glint in his eyes left no doubt; Tony had tons of torture in store for me. And damn if it didn't turn me on.

"Once again for me, sweetheart."

With his hand still cupped over my mouth, he bit down on my other nipple. I clenched my teeth and bit back my cry. Before the pain wrapped me in its icy fire, Tony laved his tongue over my tortured nub sending me soaring once again.

Feathering his fingers from my mouth, he plucked and licked, sucked and nipped on both nipples. The pebbled peaks burned with an exquisite fire that drifted along an invisible filament, charged with electricity and hard-wired to my clit.

Dragging his tongue down my stomach, Tony inched closer to my sweltering pussy.

"Yes, please," I croaked, arching my hips eagerly.

"Patience, sweetheart," Tony soothed.

"I don't have any at the moment. Please, Tony!"

"You don't have any at *any* moment, sweetheart," he chuckled and landed a quick slap upon my clit with his fingers. I jolted and sucked in a gasp of surprise. "This isn't for you. It's for me. Remember that, angel. I'm not done warming you up...not by a long shot."

208

"But I *am* warmed up. I'm so damn hot I'm going to explode soon," I mewled. "Please, Tony. I'm dying."

Supporting his upper body on solid arms, a slow smile curled his lips.

"All this time you thought a sadist only relished in the pain. Agony can be found in numerous ways, sweetheart. I'm just the man to show you."

"Y-you are?" I whispered.

Tony answered with a wolfish grin. Sliding lower, he positioned himself between my legs. Hooking a finger under my thong, he tore the delicate silk from my body. His gaze dropped to my pussy. Nostrils flaring, he licked his lips. Placing his warm, strong hands on my thighs, he bent my knees and splayed me open. Exposed and vulnerable, Tony took absolute command, and oddly, I wasn't the least bit afraid. In fact, being like this with him seemed the most natural feeling in the world.

I was safe.

I was treasured.

But most of all, I was loved.

Bending low, his hot breath flowed over my thighs. Pausing at the entrance of my aching pussy, Tony closed his eyes and drew in several deep breaths before he raised his heavy lids.

"The smell of your cunt makes my mouth water, angel. Such a heavenly aroma. You're hot and heady, sweet and spicy. I can't wait to taste you." His erotic words painted lurid images, and I could almost feel his mouth on my entrance. "Who do you belong to, Leagh?"

"You. I belong to you."

"Yes, you do, and do you trust I'll give you what you need?"

"Yes. Yes. Please," I whimpered anxiously.

"Even if it's not what you want?" Tony arched a brow. A ghost of a smile twitched the corner of his lip.

His question plowed through me like a freight train. Suddenly, the dynamics of the lifestyle he'd tried to explain became crystal clear. In giving Tony my power, my control, I would find the peace and fulfillment I'd craved. Certainty that he'd never abuse the fragile pieces of my soul, but rather nurture and treasure the submission I gave to him overwhelmed me. He'd put my needs above his own, in order to help me become the best submissive I could be.

Dominance and submission genuinely had nothing to do with kinky sex, but everything to do with trust, faith, and letting go. Without an ounce of reservation, I was ready for Tony to set me free.

"I'm yours, Sir. Take what *you* want."

His dusky eyes grew even darker. The full force of his dominance seemed to infuse his entire being as I watched his chest expanded. Kneeling between my thighs, Tony placed his thumbs on my folds, spreading me open. The cool air wafted over my aching clit, and my tunnel clutched as a shiver surged through me. Dipping his head, Tony blew a gentle breath over my fluttering center, causing a tiny squeal to sing from the back of my throat.

His shoulders shook in a silent laugh. "Keep quiet, angel. I'm so close to tasting you, I wouldn't be able to stop if I had to."

"I will," I whispered.

"That's my girl," he murmured.

Leaning forward, he flicked his tongue over my clit. My whole body jerked, and my hips arched off the bed. Tony pressed a wide palm over my abdomen, holding me in place, then swiped his slick tongue up my folds. A deep rumble of delight rolled in his chest as I gasped, and before I could draw in a ragged breath, he devoured me in a ravenous frenzy.

Leaving me moaning and writhing, white shards of light exploded behind my eyes. Thrusting his tongue deep, he burnished my clit with his nose. The inferno churning in my womb fanned through my limbs like kindling catching fire.

Over and again, he sailed me to the edge, only to pull me back down. Teasing and toying with my release, the maddening frustration of each wicked lick sharpened the sensations. He didn't build my release simply by striving for an orgasm, Tony made love to my cunt... slow and thorough. Commanding as a true Dom he persuaded me up and down...hard and fast...soft and sweet. The symphony of his tongue possessed me. And when he summoned the surge without pulling back, I panicked.

"Help... can't...stop," I cried out in a desperate whisper.

"I don't want you to stop. Come hard for me, baby," Tony insisted as he pinched my clit between his finger and thumb and surged his tongue in deep.

My casted hand gripped the bedspread while my other clutched the pillow beside me and pressed it over my face. My muffled screams echoed in my ears as I gave over to the tingling current detonating within. My stomach bunched. My body quaked. The walls of my pussy constricted around his tongue. Rapid spasms tightened and released. Still, he persisted as my pulsating heat squeezed him. Wrapping his lips around my clit, he sucked the hypersensitized pearl into his mouth, simultaneously sinking two fingers in deep. Tony had no intention of letting me glide back down.

Immersed in his command, he forced me up again—higher than before. Burnishing his fingers on the sensitive bundle of nerves, Tony scraped his teeth over my clit. Drowning in the pleasure he sought to give, I tossed the pillow aside, gasping for air. Muscles taut, I arched my hips, grinding my pussy on his mouth. I rode the wave as it crested higher and higher until I splintered into a million quivering pieces.

Panting and sweating, Tony eased back. His dark eyes shimmered with a brilliant sparkle of admiration and satisfaction. His mouth and chin, coated in my juices, glistened.

"Again," he whispered, leaning in and extending his tongue.

"No," I hissed, weaving my fingers through his black hair. I tried to tug him back from my fluttering cunt. "I can't."

"Yes, you can," he rumbled. "For me, you can."

"It's too much," I moaned.

"Is my sweet angel's swollen clit too sensitive right now?" he chided.

"Yesssss. It burns."

"It burns because that's exactly what I want it to do, sweetheart."

As if to prove his point, he swiped his tongue over my cunt again, rolling the tip atop my engorged nub.

"Tonyyy," I whimpered as bolts of lightning coalesced into blissful and excruciating agony.

Climbing to his knees, he leaned over the bed and snagged his jeans. Rifling through the pockets, he pulled out a condom.

"We can't," I gasped. "You promised your mom."

"I think you're finally figuring out that I'm not such a good boy, after all." Tearing the foil packet open with his teeth, he quickly rolled the latex into place.

Aligning his broad crest to my opening, he gripped my hips, and in one painful yet blissful thrust, he buried himself deep inside me. I gasped and sucked down a cry. Tony stilled, allowing me several moments to adjust to his considerable size. Stretched...packed to the point of discomfort, I worried I might not be able to accommodate him.

Ever so slowly, he began to move, dragging the broad crest over my electrified nerve endings. Resting his weight on his elbows, Tony gazed into my eyes before he began to rock back and forth in a slow, agonizing rhythm.

"That's it, baby. Relax and let me in. Let me all the way in...clear down to your heart and soul."

He was already so deep inside me, already owned everything about me, there was nothing left to claim. The coarse hair on his chest scraped over my tender nipples with a sinful tingle, and the blazing current of desire quickened as he bent and captured my lips. Surging my hips upward, I met his steady rhythm, riding the passion rising inside us.

Needing more, I arched up to him even higher and draped my free leg around his waist before digging my heel into the small of his back. Tony lifted from my mouth, sucked in a quivering breath, and issued a low curse before wedging a hand beneath the small of my back to drive in deeper still. As if a chain had snapped, I felt his control unfurl. The beast he'd kept guarded finally broke free.

Pounding into me with deep urgent strokes, the intensity of his passion lined his chiseled features. Focused and in command, Tony chased his pleasure, and mine. Soaring beneath his fervent rhythm, a stunning sense of helplessness filled me. Nothing had ever felt so right as his energy flowed in me...through me, surrounding me in a blissful and blistering completeness. I embraced it freely, giving him the last remaining remnants of my control.

Exquisite pressure built into a conflagration, tossing me to the four corners of the earth.

"Please, please," a desperate whisper tore from my lips.

"Not. Yet," Tony grunted, lust curling his lips. "Look at me, Leagh. I want to watch you come undone beneath me."

Fighting through the mist clouding my vision, I gazed into his smoky, carnal eyes, and as if a veil had been lifted, I could see straight into his soul. This amazing, patient, and giving man had stolen my heart, and though it should have scared the hell out of me, I never wanted him to give it back.

"Tell me, angel. Say it out loud."

"I love you," I panted. Precariously poised on the precipice, the craggy ground beneath me crumbled. "Pleaseeee."

"And I love you. Now come for me, baby. Come hard," Tony commanded in a harsh whisper.

The churning whirlpool dragged me under, pulling him right along with me. And as we fragmented together, Tony buried his face against my neck, sinking his teeth into my tender flesh. The pain heightened my orgasm, sending a kaleidoscope of colors to burst behind my eyes. And as my tunnel contracted upon his driving cock, my thin squeal of delight melded with Tony's growl of pleasure. I felt the sizzling heat of his release jettison within the condom. Time slowed as our quivering bodies shook and the echo of our panting breaths filled the room.

Tony cupped my ass with both hands and rolled to his side, taking me with him. Sated and boneless, I melted against him. Resting my cheek on the hard muscles of his chest, I purred as he stroked my sweat-soaked hair. Nuzzling his lips against my forehead our breathing slowly returned to normal.

"Wow," I murmured.

"That was…"

"Beyond amazing," I finished for him.

"And then some," he agreed.

"I've never…hmmm," I paused.

"You never what, sweetheart?" Tony coaxed.

"I've never felt anything that intense before."

"Me either, but get used to it," he chuckled softly.

Oh, I could get used to it all right, used to it every damn day of my life. After several long, silent moments, Tony shifted and tugged the covers from under me, only to draw them up over my body. Grabbing his underwear, he covered his crotch and opened the bedroom door. With a clandestine look in each direction, he turned and flashed me a smile.

"I'll be right back. I need to get rid of the evidence," he whispered, glancing down at his still hard cock covered in latex.

I couldn't help but giggle as he dashed out the door.

Returning quickly, Tony crawled into bed and re-positioned me in his arms. Pressing his lips to my head, he exhaled a sigh laced with contentment. "Get some sleep, angel. I'll be right here when you wake."

Tony didn't have to tell me twice. As soon as I closed my eyes, the darkness carried me away, and I didn't open them again until sunlight warmed my face. Blinking at the unfamiliar surroundings, a broad smile curled on my lips as the sounds of Tony's snores resonated in my ears.

I didn't want to disturb him, but I needed to use the bathroom. Slowly sliding out from under his heavy arm resting on my hip, I scooted toward the edge of the bed. Suddenly, a hand gripped my wrist, and I yelped.

"Where do you think you're going?"

"The bathroom," I scoffed with a derisive shake of my head.

Tony bounded out of bed and stormed to the other side. Cinching my hair in a painful grip, he tilted my head back and narrowed his eyes.

"Where are you going?" he repeated, with a tone teemed in irritation.

"The bathroom?" I squeaked.

"Uh-huh," he mumbled, releasing his hold. "Much better without the sarcastic attitude. We talked about that, remember?"

I cast my eyes toward the floor and nodded.

"Come on. Let me help you." Tony didn't wait for my reply. He simply lifted me off the bed. Snagging his jeans and the duffle bag from the floor, he glanced out in the hallway to make sure the coast was clear, then marched—both of us naked—down the hall and into the bathroom.

When he set me down and didn't leave, I stared at him with wide eyes. "Um, you can go now."

"Can I?" He chuckled. "How nice of you to give me permission, pet."

I exhaled a heavy sigh. "I didn't mean it like that."

"Maybe you shouldn't have said it like that, hmmm?"

I opened my mouth to argue, but closed it with a pout. Holding my bladder grew painful, but I endured as I watched Tony rummage through my clothes and toiletries. As if sensing my stare, he paused and gazed up at me. One brow raised in question.

"Ah, thank you for bringing my things, but I need to pee."

"Then go."

"I'd like a little privacy. You've never stayed to watch me pee when you've helped me to the bathroom before. I'd prefer not to have an audience. So, if you don't mind?" I made a shooing motion for him to leave.

"I do mind," he replied sternly. "Get your business done, so I can get you cleaned up." His insensitive tone chaffed. I hadn't expected it after the night we'd shared. "I wasn't sure how long we'd have to stay here, so I brought some of your things from the club."

When I failed to sit on the toilet, he looked up at me.

"I'm well aware of what it is you'd like me to do, angel," he began as he stood and stepped into his jeans. Zipping them, he left the top button unfastened. I couldn't help but stare at his stunning physique and the tapering of dark hair that disappeared below the open waistband. "I'm not here to always give you what you want. I'm here to give you what you need. So, sit on the pot, empty your bladder, and let's get your hair washed."

I felt my blood pressure rise as my lips drew into a tight, angry line. Closing my eyes, I sat on the toilet. Heat rose on my cheeks while embarrassing sounds echoed in my ears. When I finished, I shot Tony a seething glare.

"That was humiliating, thank you very much."

Flashing an evil smile, Tony shook his head. "Oh, I can think of far more humiliating tasks for you, angel. Keep pushing and you'll see."

"Aarrggh," I groaned as I finished my business as discreetly as possible before I stood and flushed. "No, thank you. I might enjoy your spankings, but degradation isn't one of my kinks. Trust me."

"Come here." Tony smiled, opening his beefy arms.

The petulant child inside me didn't want a thing to do with him, but my legs ignored my pride. I wobbled across the room. And as he pulled me to his chest, a delightful feeling of security flowed through me, banishing my rebellious urges.

"You're mine, angel. Everything from the top of your head down to your toes belongs to me. Headaches, menstrual cycles, and all bodily functions are mine. There won't be any more secrets, and you won't be allowed to hide anything from me. Do you understand?"

"Yes," I whispered with a slow nod.

"Good."

To prove his point, Tony loosened his hold, made his way to the toilet, and lifted the lid. Without a shred of modesty, as if it were the most natural thing in the world, he relieved himself. It was as if we were a married couple going through a normal morning routine. *Bizarre.*

A few minutes later, I was bent over the bathroom sink while Tony lathered my hair in shampoo. His broad fingers massaged my scalp in such a relaxing manner, I couldn't help but purr.

"How did you come up with the club name Dahlia?" he asked.

"George picked it out for me. At first, I wanted to be called 'Hell Raiser' but he said that wasn't a proper submissive name. So, he chose 'Dahlia.' In Spanish it means, Star of the Devil."

Tony laughed. "Hell Raiser suits you better."

"I know, right?" I grinned as he rinsed the suds. "So, can I ask you a question?"

"Of course," Tony replied, threading conditioner through the wet strands.

"Why do you do what you do? You know, inflict pain."

"In part, I like fulfilling the needs of subs that enjoy or crave edge play. It feeds my dominance and allows me to satisfy the hidden artist in me. I look at flesh as a canvas. The stripes…well, they're my unique works of art."

"No offense, but why don't you just go to the art store and buy some water colors and an easel?"

"I already have all that stuff. I like to paint," he chuckled.

"Can I see your works?"

"Um, no."

"Why not? I thought we weren't supposed to keep secrets," I pressed as he rinsed my hair one last time.

"Manipulative little minx," Tony growled, landing a wet hand on my bare butt cheek.

"Ouch," I protested.

Twisting my tresses into a towel atop my head, Tony led me to the edge of the tub. "I forgot to pack the adult bath wipes from the club. So, I guess I'm going to have to give you a sponge bath the old-fashioned way."

"It's okay. I'll do it myself."

Tony pinned me with a fierce scowl. Dominance rolled off him in a hot wave.

"Is this really how you want to spend the day, sweetheart? Challenging me every chance you get?" His expression softened. "Talk to me, Leagh. What's wrong?"

The minute he shifted into psychologist mode, I became nervous.

"I don't know. My life's a mess. I mean, last night was the most spectacular night of my life, but this morning, I feel like...I can't even pee or wash myself alone. It's like you're trying to take over my entire life. I just want five minutes to... I don't know, maybe breathe on my own."

"Stop." Tony knelt in front of me, capturing my gaze in a stony hold. "You're trying to take back your control. This tells me that either you're not ready to hand it over all the way, or I'm not doing my job as a Dominant. Which one is it? Or is it a little bit of both?"

Frightened by the uneasiness reflecting in his eyes, I swallowed tightly. "I'm not trying to consciously take it back, and you're an amazing Dominant. That's not it."

"Last night, I got a taste of your submission. I felt you let go. It was the most amazing experience of my entire life. I know you felt it...felt that deep-seated need to please suck in its first real breath of life. I think it scared you. So now you're trying to yank the walls around you, because it feels foreign, and you don't know how to come to terms with what you already know you are…a submissive."

"I'm not trying to shut you out, and you're right, it does feel strange. What does that have to do with you forcing me to pee in front of you? I don't know what you're trying to prove or what you want from me."

"Yes, you do." He smirked. "The reason I didn't let you pee in private was because of your snarky attitude in bed when I asked where you were going. If you'd simply said that you needed to use the restroom, I would have given you time alone. That little taste of humiliation was punishment, Leagh."

I exhaled an exasperated sigh.

"Taking care of you is my Dominant duty. And when you arbitrarily yank that away from me, I have no other choice than to correct your behavior. Socrates once said, 'Sometimes you put walls up, not to keep people out, but to see who cares enough to break them down.' I care enough, Leagh. Make no mistake, I won't allow walls between us on any level."

"I swear I'm not trying to block you out, Tony. I like the way you take care of me. I like the way you make me feel, but it's all so strange and new, and it makes me feel unsure of myself."

His warm smile instantly put me at ease. "I know it does. I told you it would, but that's when you have to reach down deep and trust me, angel. If you don't trust me, this is never going to work."

"I know that." Just thinking of Tony not being with me caused a sick, swirling sensation in the pit of my stomach.

"Honest answer, angel…do you want this to work?"

"Yes, I do," I replied, gazing boldly into his eyes.

"Good. Then stop defying me, and let's get your sponge bath started. When we're done, we'll get dressed and go downstairs. I'm sure Ma is cooking up a huge breakfast for us."

Adjusting the water temperature as it spilled into the tub, Tony washed my back and arms, gently drying each section before moving to the next. I winced as he brushed the washcloth over my nipples.

"That's the beauty of proper nipple torture, sweetheart. The next day, they're still nice and sensitive."

"I think the word you're looking for is sore," I laughed.

"I can make them ache even more," he growled in promise.

With his hips wedged between my splayed-out thighs, he gently drew the soapy cloth up my folds. I couldn't help but hiss. The lips of my pussy were also sore from all the activity the night before.

"A little tender there, too, sweetheart?" Tony asked. Bending low, he inspected my cunt as he rinsed the soap away.

Suddenly, the bathroom door swung open. Alisa stood in the portal, a look of horror blossoming over her face.

"Anthony Michael Delvaggio!" she cried. "What in the world... you promised me!"

Tony jolted and leapt to his feet as I slammed my thighs together.

"Ma!" Tony thundered. "A little privacy here?"

I felt the heat rise on my cheeks, and I wanted to climb into the tub and swirl down the drain with the running water.

"I'm very disappointed in you. You know the rules," she scolded.

"It's not what you think, Ma. I'm helping Leagh with her sponge bath. She can't very well hop into the shower now, can she?"

A look of mortification replaced the anger on Alisa's face. "Oh my, I'm...I'm sorry. Do you need any help?"

"No, Ma. We'll be done in a few minutes."

"I'm sorry, you two. I didn't mean...I heard the water running downstairs, and I came up to jiggle the handle on the...well, it's been leaking and..."

"It's okay. Don't worry about it," Tony reassured. "Just close the door when you leave. I don't want Leagh getting cold."

"Right." His mom issued a nervous nod before backing out of the room and closing the door.

Tony started to laugh. I shot him an irritated scowl and smacked him on the shoulder. "It's not funny."

"Yes, it is," he chortled.

"You're just lucky she didn't walk in on us last night. There'd been no way you could have wiggled out of that one, mister."

"That's no lie," he grinned. "I still wouldn't have stopped. If she walks in on us tonight, I'm still not stopping."

Tony's promise sent a shiver of anticipation snaking down my spine.

Thirty minutes later, we were both clean and dressed and sitting at the kitchen table. Alisa barely made eye contact with either Tony or me as she served up a scrumptious breakfast of pancakes, sausage, eggs, and toast. Tony and Vito did their best to fill the awkward silence, but I could tell Alisa was still embarrassed about walking in on us earlier.

I relaxed back in my chair, sipping my second cup of coffee, when Tony's cell phone rang. Glancing up at him, I worried it might be more bad news.

"Hey, Mika," Tony greeted. "How's that little man of yours?"

I smiled, remembering the feel of Tristan in my arms and the smell of his sweet baby fresh skin.

"No," he replied as I watched his brows furrow. "Yeah, I'll turn it on right now. Thanks."

Tony hung up, jumped from his chair, and hastily carried me into the family room. Setting me on the couch, he turned on the television and turned up the volume of a nationally syndicated morning news show. A female reporter prattled on about something, but I wasn't listening. My attention was riveted to the image of George's house, fully engulfed in flames, filling the screen. Firefighters and police officers bustled in the artificially lit background like ants.

"What the hell…" I whispered.

The next image that flashed on the screen was a professional family photograph of George, Sloane, and Hayden. As Tony sat next to me, I grabbed his hand. My heart hammered in my chest. Glancing from the TV as Vito and Alisa entered the room, I quickly turned my attention back to the anchorwoman, focusing on her words.

"Officials have still not determined the cause of the fire, but sources close to the investigation say explosives were involved. And with the blast claiming the lives of both his ex-wife, Sloane, and daughter, Hayden, questions about Judge Marston's multi-billion-dollar estate are being raised. For that, we take you live to Chicago and our on-scene reporter, Sasha Clevenger. Sasha, what can you tell us?"

The blue-eyed, blond newscaster stood in front of George's burned-out house. Black soot stained the once red brick, and the broken-out windows reminded me of a cold, dead skeleton. A handful of firefighters traipsed in and out of the opening where the front door once stood.

"Unfortunately, officials are being tightlipped about this mysterious explosion, Bianca. Through court records we've obtained, we know that Judge Marston's ex-wife, Sloane, had filed an injunction contesting his will. Some of our sources speculate it might have something to do with his longtime, live-in companion, Leagh Bennett. So far, we've been unsuccessful in reaching Ms. Bennett for comment. We do know, however, that she is not a suspect in the explosion at this time."

My stomach pitched and threatened to purge as I watched a montage of photos spool over the screen. Photos of George and me, together, at several high-dollar political dinners. Pictures I didn't even know existed were being broadcasted for the whole world to see.

"No. No. No," I repeated under my breath in horror.

Tony turned and looked at me. His dark eyes filled with fear. The same fear that was crawling through my veins and choking the air from my lungs. Suddenly, a loud knock came from the front door.

"Tony?" I cried. Fear gripped me in a chokehold as I whipped my head toward the door.

"It's okay," Vito assured, walking toward the entryway. "The boys are back out there keeping an eye on things, Leagh. They won't let anyone suspicious near the house."

"That was a *national* news channel, Tony," I murmured. "Matt's going to be able to find me now."

"Even if he does, I won't let him hurt you, I swear." Tony wrapped his arm around my shoulder as I fought the urge to vomit.

James walked into the room, looking first at me, then at the television. "Fuck," he muttered. "I wanted to get to you before you heard about all this."

"I'll make some more coffee," Alisa announced before darting toward the kitchen.

James and Vito sat across from us as Tony held me close.

"Is it true? Are Sloane and Hayden really dead?" I asked.

"Yes," James affirmed with a solemn nod. "We also positively ID'd the guy, as well. His name was Fredrick Willis. He's the same dude who was outside the club last night, and he's got a rap sheet a mile long...specializing in explosives."

"What about the guy that was following Tony last night?" Vito asked with concern.

"His name is Arthur Feeney. When he found out Willis was dead, he started singing like a canary."

"Hold that thought. I want to know who the fuck is talking to the press," Tony barked.

"That's the same thing the chief, half the damn precinct, and I want to know," James groused.

"So, what is this Feeney guy saying about Willis? Did Hayden hire them to kill me?"

"It wasn't Hayden, it was Sloane," James replied with a grim expression.

"Sloane?" I gasped.

"Yeah, she hired Willis to take you out. The story we got from Feeney is that Willis planted the C-4 in Leagh's car, but when we interrupted him, he freaked. He called Feeney and told him to watch the club while he went to George's house to get the rest of what Sloane owed him. Evidently, Willis didn't trust her. I can't imagine why," James added sarcastically. "Anyway, he'd always planned to kill her after he got his money. The fire investigator found pieces of a homemade incendiary device. He must have planted the explosive in the basement. How or why it detonated with Willis inside the house, we'll never know."

"Did this Feeney guy say why he was following me?" Tony asked.

"Sort of. He's not the sharpest crayon in the box. He was parked in back at the club and still on the phone with Willis when the cops showed up. Feeney said he was nervous and didn't want to hang around. But Willis told him to stay put to watch for the girl, Leagh and her boyfriend." James looked at Tony. "You're the boyfriend. The two men had been watching you and Leagh for days."

"Lovely," Tony groused.

"Anyway," James began again. "When they started to evacuate the club, Feeney said he tried to call Willis but couldn't get an answer. It freaked him out even more, but instead of bugging out, he did what Willis told him to do—tail Tony."

"What was he going to do to Tony after he finished following him?" Vito asked.

James shrugged. "Feeney said he didn't know what he was supposed to do, other than try to find Leagh through Tony. Trust me. Willis was the brains between those two dip shits, and he obviously wasn't very smart...dumb bastard got himself blown up."

"Okay, we've got a bigger problem here," Tony stated with a grim expression. "Leagh's been trying to hide from someone for a number of years. Someone who might want to kill her. Now that the fire and deaths have made national news, Leagh's face and location is being blasted to everyone in the country."

James snapped his head my way, concern lined his face. "Who's after you? Is it an abusive boyfriend? Ex-husband? Who?"

"No. Nothing like that. I worked for a very bad man and witnessed something I shouldn't have. There's nothing you can do, James. It's big. Bigger than any of us can handle," I explained, trying to avoid spilling the whole sordid story.

A shiver of fear rippled through me.

"Dad, we need to contact Uncle Enzo," Tony blurted with urgency.

Vito's brows furrowed. He turned a startled glare at his son. "No."

"Dad. He's the only one who can help us."

"No. He's dead to me. You know what he's involved in, Tony. I cut him out of my life twenty years ago in order to keep my family safe."

"I know, Dad. But he's the only chance I've got to keep *Leagh* safe," Tony implored. "I love her."

Vito closed his eyes and issued a heavy sigh before staring back at his son. "Not a word of this to your mother, you understand me?"

"Yeah, I hear you, Dad. I swear."

"If you're talking about what I think you are, you two need to shut the fuck up," James issued in a terse whisper. "I can't know about this shit."

"Then plug your ears," Tony replied with a humorless chuckle.

"What do you want me to ask him to do?" Vito grumbled, disregarding James' warning.

"I need him to find out all he can about a man named Matthew Price. Lives in Atlanta, or he did. A heavy hitter in drugs and guns. He could be anywhere by now. He may be outside the U.S."

"Fuck me," James whispered before slapping his hands over his ears.

"No," I cried. "Tony, you can't ask him to do that."

"Shhh, it's going to be okay. If Matt knows where to find you now, I'll be damned if I'm going to sit idly by and wait for him to start scouring Chicago. Uncle Enzo lives in L.A. If his search raises any red flags, Matt may think you've already left the city. It might buy us some much needed time."

"Time for what?" I trembled.

"Time for me to figure out what we're going to do."

"*We're* not going to do anything. *I* have to get the hell out of here and start over someplace new."

"That's never going to happen, angel." Tony shook his head. "Everyone else in your life has turned their back on you. I'm not going to be one of them, and you need to get that through your head. You're mine, sweetheart. We're in this together...for the duration."

As if he'd waved a magic wand, Tony's pledge quieted the panic snaking through me.

"Do I even want to know who Matthew Price is?" James drawled.

"No," Tony replied, his tone icy and cold. "And for fuck's sake, don't go snooping around looking for info on him either. We need that prick to think Leagh's left Chicago."

"That goes against my grain, man," James argued, running an unsettled hand through his hair. "I took an oath."

"To protect and serve," Tony interjected. "Leagh needs to be protected."

"I get it, but there's got to be something the department can do, I can do, to help her."

"There isn't," I whispered.

"What did you get yourself into, girl?" James asked, his aqua blue eyes brimmed with worry.

"A mess," I sighed.

"I'll make the call," Vito announced with a weary voice before leaving the room.

James glanced at Tony. "You guys doing okay here?"

"Yeah, we're okay. Ma's making me feel like I'm twelve again, but we're making it work."

James grinned. "Kind of puts a crimp in the sex department."

I bit my lips together and cast a guilty gaze downward.

"Having to be quiet sucks. That and not having any toys with me," Tony mumbled with a sly grin.

"Poor bastard," James commiserated with a roll of his eyes. "The reason I'm asking is I got a call from Stephen on my way over. He doesn't know anything other than what's been reported on the news, but he wanted me to let you know if you and Leagh needed someplace to stay, he's got a loft near the club."

Tony smiled. "That's generous of him, but Carnation and Leagh don't get along. I don't want to add more stress onto an already fucked-up situation."

"Oh," James made a strange noise. "He and Carnation...they're not together anymore. He uncollared her yesterday."

"What?" I gasped as my eyes grew wide.

"Really? You're actually surprised?" James chortled. "I'd have cut that bitch lose months ago."

"Good for him. He needs someone more...human," Tony replied wryly.

Vito entered the room, holding a cell phone to his chest. "How old is Matthew?"

"He's in his sixties," I stated, mentally calculating my father's age. "Sixty-one. He's about six foot three, thinning blond hair, and blue eyes. No scars or tattoos that I know of."

With a nod, Vito relayed the information with firm resolve. The thank you that rolled off his tongue was forced at best before he ended the call. Appalled that I'd put him in an uncomfortable position with his brother, I sucked in a deep breath.

"Thank you, Vito, and I'm sorry you had to—"

"It's not you, Leagh. My brother...well, he made his choices."

"Thanks, Dad," Tony offered with a sullen expression.

"Now, we wait," Vito said, sending us a ghost of a smile meant to reassure.

"I need to get back to the station," James stated, rising from the couch. "Call me if you need anything. I'll keep you guys updated if anything new happens."

After we said goodbye to James, Alisa appeared with a tray of coffee. "Oh, I guess I'm too late."

"It's okay. James had to get back to work," Tony explained.

"Oh, well, I'll take this outside and see if the boys would like some," she nodded.

Vito held the door for her and followed his wife onto the front porch.

"Who are all those guys outside?" I asked, looking up at Tony.

"Three of them are my brothers, the rest are cousins. I'll introduce you."

"And they stayed out there all night?"

"No, they camped out in the den in the basement. When I called Dad yesterday, he rallied the troops. They'll be here until the threat against you is over, sweetheart."

"Don't they have jobs? Families?"

"Yeah, they work for my dad," Tony replied with a cryptic edge.

"So, what does your dad do? He's not in the mafia. I know that."

"He owns a produce company," Tony growled. Leaning in, he nipped my earlobe. "What do you want to do today, angel?"

"Well, I don't want to watch anymore television," I replied with a dour frown.

Tony helped me into the kitchen where I sat at the table and chatted with his mom as she combined ingredients for two apple pies. The woman was a machine when it came to cooking. I suspected baking helped her cope with the drama I'd brought to her doorstep, but as the brawny men from outside trailed in and out of the kitchen, snagging pastries and sandwiches, I realized she was simply trying to keep them fed.

Alisa introduced me to Tony's brothers and cousins as they filed in, one at a time, while I helped measure ingredients for a batch of chocolate chip cookies. As the woman began rolling out dough for another pan of cinnamon rolls, Tony reappeared in the kitchen.

"Want to come with me and check out some of the books my dad has in his office?" Tony invited with a wink.

I could tell it was a ruse to get me out of the kitchen while keeping Alisa in the dark about the call Vito made on my behalf. It bothered me that the two men shielded her from what was going on around her. As Tony helped me waddle down the hallway, I issued him a sideways glance.

"Please, don't ever do to me what you do to your mom, okay?"

"What are you talking about?" Tony asked, his brow wrinkling.

"Hide things from me like you do Alisa."

"My dad is a dominant man, Leagh, but he's not a Dom. While he would never outright lie to my mom, he keeps things from her as a way to protect her. I'm not saying it's right, I'm just saying this is how their marriage works. I won't keep a damn thing from you, sweetheart. That's not the kind of relationship I want with you."

"Good. Because it'd be a deal breaker, Tony. Just so you know."

He shot me a probing gaze. "That goes both ways, angel."

"Deal."

When we entered Vito's office, he sat behind a wide wooden desk, staring at the green, spring foliage out the picture window on his right.

"Dad?"

"Come on in." Vito nodded. "And close the door."

Anxiety spiked as Tony shut the door behind us. We both took a seat as Vito opened his mouth to speak.

"Uncle Enzo called back. There's good news, Leagh. At least, I think it's good news."

I held my breath, clinging to his every word.

"Matthew Price died two and a half years ago in a parasailing accident off the coast of Belize."

Exhaling as relief flooded through me, I blinked. "Died?"

"You sure?" Tony asked.

"Yep, it says so on his death certificate." Vito grinned.

Reality slowly started to sink in. Matt was dead. Sloane and Hayden were dead. There were no more threats hanging over me. No more reasons to carry a restraining order or constantly be looking over my shoulder. A giant boulder had been lifted off me, and I began to giggle.

"I'm free. I'm finally free."

Suddenly, the sunlight seemed brighter. The air felt thinner, and life took on a whole new meaning.

"Not totally," Tony grinned with a knowing wink.

"Yeah, but with you is exactly where I want to be."

Tony leapt from his seat and pulled me into his arms, wearing a smile so bright, it almost blinded me.

"Let's go home, angel." Lust teemed in his eyes.

"Yes, please," I replied on a wistful sigh.

"Thanks, Dad. I asked a huge favor of you with Uncle Enzo, but I think you understand how fantastic this news is for Leagh, and for me."

"Of course, I do, son. It was well worth it. I'd do it again in a New York minute just to see the smiles on your faces."

"Oh, thank you, Vito. Thank you so much," I gushed.

Back in Tony's room, he packed the duffle in seconds flat. After showering Vito and Alisa with my heartfelt thanks, Tony and I were in the car, headed toward the club. Along the way, he placed a call to James and filled him in on the wonderful news. I couldn't wipe the smile from my face.

My newfound freedom tasted better than chocolate.

Chapter Twelve

I t was good to be 'home.' My pseudo apartment in Genesis, and the privacy it afforded, felt like a breath of fresh air. A new chapter of my life had begun, one as a liberated adult, and my mind raced with opportunities like a job and a real home of my own...someday.

"You haven't said much since you found out Matt was dead, angel."

"I know." I frowned. "For some strange reason, a part of me is sad. Another part of me wishes I'd paid more attention to the outside world when I was with George. I should have at least read the Atlanta newspaper online. When I think of all the years I spent hiding from Matt, so afraid he'd find me..." I shook my head. "I've wasted so much precious time."

"Don't be so hard on yourself. You did what you had to in order to stay safe and alive. I'm proud of you, sweetheart. It just goes to show how incredibly brave and strong you are."

I snorted. "I wasn't strong or brave. I hid like a big wuss."

"No, you used your head. You methodically sought a city and a job where Matt couldn't easily find you. Then, day after day, you stepped outside and kept right on living in spite of that fuck-nut. *That*, my love, takes guts."

Tony painted a picture far more courageous than I considered myself to be, but it warmed my heart that he saw me as gutsy.

"Are you excited for tomorrow?" Tony asked from the bathroom, unpacking my toiletries.

"Tomorrow? I don't even know what day it is, everything's been such a cluster. What's going on tomorrow?"

"You have an appointment with Dr. Coleman, remember?"

"Yes! I totally forgot." I blinked. "Please, please let this be the last night I have to wear these damn casts."

Tony strutted in from the bathroom, his thigh muscles rippling beneath his jeans. Every time I fixated on his mouth-watering body, my pussy wept. This was no exception. Prowling onto the bed, his body heat surrounded me before he laid down and pulled me against his hard chest.

"Think positive, angel, and we'll see what tomorrow brings."

"I will." I nodded, snuggling deeper against him. "You feel good."

"I do, huh?"

"Yes." I smiled.

"I bet I can make us both feel even better."

His innuendo sent a shiver snaking up my spine. Tony shifted above me, and the hunger dancing in his eyes almost took my breath away.

"Make me feel...everything. Please?"

A sly smile tugged his mouth. "Have I ever told you how hard I get every time you beg?"

Pressing his hips to mine, he ground his rigid erection against my pussy. I sucked in a gasp. The friction stung my sore folds.

"Maybe we should hold off another day or two."

"It's not that sore," I vowed.

A wicked chuckle vibrated the back of his throat. "I'll have to take a look and decide for myself, angel."

Kneeling up, Tony peeled off my soft cotton pants. With his hand beneath my knees, he lifted and spread my thighs wide. Leaning in low, his warm breath caressed my juncture, and I closed my eyes and moaned. He trailed soft kisses over the tops of my thighs, edging nearer to my throbbing center.

"You're driving me insane. Please," I begged impatiently.

"Oh, sweetheart, the torture I have in store for you hasn't even started yet." Tony feathered a kiss over my clit, and I cried out. "Yes, I see how swollen and red the lips of your cunt are now. We'll need to hold off until you're all healed up."

Bolting upright, I felt my eyes grow wide. "Are you out of your mind? No!"

Both his brows arched high, and he shot me a look of warning.
Shit.

"I didn't mean it that way," I stammered. "I just meant that I'm not that sore. We don't have to stop...honest."

"Is that for you to decide or me?"

"You, Sir," I mumbled, duly chastised.

"That's right. And if I think you're too sore, then you are. Understood?"

"Yes, Sir," I grumbled, feeling a pout form on my lips.

"Don't look so forlorn, angel. Do you honestly have such little faith in me?"

"I have all the faith in the world in you. I just don't know what you've got planned."

"Good, at least you realize I have the ability to improvise."

With a slight nod, I settled back down on the bed, anxious for whatever deviant trick he had up his sleeve.

"Let's talk about your limits for a minute, angel."

Narrowing my eyes, I shot him an apprehensive look. "What are you planning to do to me?"

An evil laugh rolled off his tongue before he slid one forearm beneath my knees and hoisted them to my chest. Without a word, he dipped his thumb into his mouth, coating it in saliva. I knew exactly what he intended, but before I could squeeze my butt cheeks together, he ran his slickened thumb around my puckered opening. Arousal and fear churned inside.

"Anal play, angel. How often did George play with your ass?"

"Never," I replied on a quivering moan.

"Are you a virgin here?" he asked, increasing the pressure ever so slightly.

"Yes."

A look of surprise danced over Tony's face. "Even after he collared you, he didn't claim you there?"

"No. Was he supposed to?"

"It's how a lot of Master's claim their subs. Was it his choice or a hard limit for you?"

Tony's Q&A session unnerved me. Discussing mine and George's sexual exploits felt awkward as hell. "He never tried to...he liked..."

"Don't be shy, sweetheart. I've got you as exposed as a woman can get. He liked to what?" Tony circled his thumb over my gathered ring, sending little arcs of pleasure to sizzle through me.

"He liked to go down on me."

"Ahh. He did that a lot at the club, but I assumed he took your ass at home."

I shook my head.

"Well, well. Guess I owe George a debt of gratitude. I'll be the first to claim this tiny opening of yours."

I swallowed tightly. The thought of Tony's massive cock anywhere near my virgin asshole sent panic chasing the shards of delight his thumb induced.

"You can't," I blurted, trying to scoot away from him.

Determination stamped his face as he gathered my upturned legs together with one beefy arm. Pressing them to my chest, he held me prisoner to his nefarious plans. "I most definitely can, but not today, angel, so stop fretting. But I'm going to begin your anal training here and now."

"What are you going to do to my butt?" I gasped.

"Anything I want to, sweetheart," he chuckled.

Tony bent low. Self-conscious, with his face so close to my backside, I panicked.

"Don't!" I cried out as heat rushed to my cheeks. "I'm not...it's dirty."

"You have a safeword, angel. I expect you to use it if you need to."

I cringed as Tony's thumb breeched the rim, but the second time he dragged it out and slid it back in, the sizzling current lighting up my tissues shoved all my embarrassment aside. Each gentle stroke brought with it the inevitable, and like spun sugar, I dissolved. The zapping arcs of electricity intensified, swallowing me whole in urgent demand. Each time he surged past the taut ring, pulses of pleasure ignited, hotter and brighter, until they coalesced into one euphoric explosion. Blindsided by the unexpected and intense orgasm, I screamed out loud and long as I shattered. Tony drove in deeper, adding a finger alongside his thumb while my hypersensitive opening clutched and spasmed around him. The sensations he'd evoked were mind-blowing.

Aftershocks detonated like misfiring neurons, even after Tony had slid his fingers from my quivering ass. How had he managed to make me come so fast without even touching my clit? It had been a first for me. Immersed in utter amazement, the realization that I'd not asked his permission to orgasm slammed me hard.

"I'm sorry," I panted.

"For what?" Tony asked. A knowing grin spread across his mouth. "Spontaneous explosions are allowed, pet."

"That's what happened, I swear."

"I know. I enjoyed the hell out of it, too. It gives me lots of wicked ideas. You're going to love how I torture you with ass play, sweetheart."

"Uh-huh," I replied hesitantly.

"You'll see." He winked.

Tony climbed off the bed and headed toward the bathroom, leaving me to process his threat and how easily he'd instigated my orgasm. Turning toward the sound of running water, I watched Tony at the sink. He caught my gaze and pinned me with a dissecting stare. Withering beneath his probing look, I cast my eyes down. Hiding from the intensity of his regard was akin to waving a red flag at a bull. I knew he'd come back to bed and start picking at my layers. It's what he did, and he did it well. *Dammit.*

I gazed at the bulging erection strangling beneath his jeans when he returned with a wash cloth. While he tended to my backside with the warm cloth, I began mentally preparing for Doctor Tony to make his appearance.

"Playing with your ass isn't dirty to me," he began in a serious tone. "In fact, it's a huge turn on. I'm more an ass man than a pussy man. Not to insinuate that I'm an ass instead of a pussy, or anything, I just thoroughly enjoy anal play."

"I'd never call you a pussy or an ass."

"Ah, but you've called me an asshole before, angel, twice in fact. I haven't forgotten that."

"Darn, I'd spent a lot of time hoping you had," I murmured, remembering my first journey into subspace.

"You wish," he teased. "But back to our original topic, why do you associate ass play with something dirty? You can't tell me you didn't enjoy it, sweetheart."

"No, I can't," I softly confessed. "I worry that I'm not clean there."

"But you are. I bathed you just a few hours ago. You'll be clean every time we play. It's one of the tasks I'll have designed for you to follow before we play."

"Tasks?" I asked feeling my brows arch.

"Of course. I've already started a list for you."

"When do I get to see this list?"

"When I'm good and ready, Miss Impatient." Tony smirked, rounding the bed as he unbuttoned and unzipped his jeans. "You tend to forget you're not driving this bus. *I* am."

He could have told me the club was on fire, and I wouldn't have cared less. My attention lay on the lip-smacking hard-on straining against his boxers. The desire to lean over and drag his dark briefs off with my teeth rode me hard. Shifting on the bed, I rolled to my side and sat up, watching as Tony freed his engorged cock from beneath its cotton confines.

"Going somewhere, angel?" Tony asked, arching one brow.

"No, Sir. Just getting ready."

"Ready for what?"

"Your cock. What else?"

"I see. What am I going to do with my cock, sweetheart?"

"Let me suck it, of course," I answered in a low, raspy tone.

"Did you not hear what I said a minute ago?"

"No, I just want to taste you," I replied, ignoring the icy edge in his tone.

Suddenly, Tony gripped my hair, forcing me to gaze at his blatantly annoyed face. "I'm done playing games, Leagh. I want you *and* I want your submission. Do you think trying my patience is going to get you what *you* want?"

Apprehension swept through me, followed by a surge of fear that quickly morphed into rejection.

"No, Sir," I replied with as much courage as I could muster.

"This isn't a test of wills, pet," Tony bellowed. His eyes narrowed, and his lips drew in a tight, angry line.

"I'm not trying to test you. I just...wanted to taste you." My voice trailed off, and I looked away from him.

"Eyes on me," Tony whispered, tempering his anger. "So, you want to taste me, but instead of asking, you took it upon yourself without a single direction from me."

"But I thought that's what you wanted me to do."

"But you didn't *ask* or wait for my instructions. Instead, you readied yourself and tried to coerce a desired response from me."

"That's not what I was doing," I argued.

"That might be so, but you arbitrarily assumed the role of Dominant and topped from the bottom. I want you powerless under my command, pliant and willing to submit because you *want* to...Because it feeds a fundamental fire inside you."

"That's what I want, too," I implored.

"Good. Then let me draw the light of submission from you. Sometimes, you have to close your eyes and take a leap in order to find out what's missing inside you. Find what's truly important."

"I understand what you're saying. But isn't a good submissive supposed to know the needs of her Master...err, I mean her Sir?"

Tony's eyes smoldered. "I like the way Master rolls off your tongue, angel. And yes, she conforms to the Master's needs, but unless you can read my mind this quickly in our relationship, you don't know what my wishes are until I tell you."

A frown pursed my lips. There were so many rules and regulations attached to submission; the complicated waltz of protocol seemed daunting. Aside from the phenomenal sex, I still wasn't totally convinced I had it in me to be a sub.

"We're still in the early stages of learning about one another,

Jenna Jacob

Leagh. One day, you'll know my wants and needs, but while we're getting to know each other's quirks and thrills, I'm the one who holds the map. So, unless you're unhappy with the journey, trust me to lead the way. Okay?"

Glancing up at him, I nodded.

"Use your voice, angel. I need to hear you."

"Yes, Sir."

"Very well, let's start over. Lie back down on the bed, angel."

Supine once again, Tony straddled my stomach. With long, uneven strokes, he fisted his cock close to my face. So close in fact, I could smell his musky scent, feel the heat rising off his wet crest. Watching as he unmercifully pounded his cock, I prayed he'd grant me a pass and instruct me to open my mouth and suck him down deep. Licking my lips, I waited.

"You remember how I taste, don't you, angel?"

"Yesss," I sighed in disappointment. I didn't want to remember. I wanted to experience it all over again.

"Tell me," he urged in a low husky voice.

"Hot and Slick. Thick and salty, but not bitter or overpowering. You're just right."

"So are you, princess," Tony panted, his gaze penetrating. "I've memorized your taste, and I can't wait to tie you down and drown in your sweet honey."

The thought of being bound and at his mercy made my whole body tingle.

"You like watching me stroke my cock, don't you?"

"Yes," I moaned. *But I'd much rather be sucking your cock.* Opening my mouth, I raised my head slightly off the pillow.

"Still trying to control things, I see," Tony rumbled in disapproval.

He slapped the tip of his cock against my mouth, smearing his slick pre-come over my lips and splattering some onto my tongue.

With a coy smile, I rolled my tongue over my lips, moaning as I licked his spicy flavor. "Who? Me?"

"You need a spanking, angel, and my palm is just itching to give it to you."

"In case you haven't noticed, your hand's a little occupied at the moment," I taunted.

Tony's eyes darkened. His jaw clenched. I wasn't sure if he struggled to hold back his release or would stop altogether. When he continued, I couldn't help but tease him even more.

"I bet you'd rather slide that big cock inside my mouth where it's warm and wet, instead of jacking off with your fist," I purred in a soft sex-kitten voice. "I'm more than willing to help you out with that."

"Oh, my sweet little brat, you have no idea. I'm dying to slam my cock to the back of your throat...feel your soft lips wrap around me, and growl as your slick tongue glides over my aching veins." His gravelly tone triggered a flow of heated slickness from my pussy. Writhing beneath him, I prayed he'd stop playing this stupid game and let me suck it already.

"Do it. Please!" I implored.

A beastly growl rumbled from deep in his chest. His fist a blur of brutal strokes as sweat dripped from his forehead.

"Open your mouth," he barked, his face contorting. The grimace reflected the pleasure unraveling inside him. "Stick out your tongue."

Greedily obeying his command, I panted in anticipation of his slick, hot seed. And as the first stream jettisoned from his red cock, Tony cried out in rapture as I opened wider, determined to catch each drop.

His robust flavor raced over my taste buds and pooled in my mouth. Gulping down the deluge, Tony continued to spill upon my lips and down my chin before I opened again, and he painted my tongue. I accepted it all, while the ache of disappointment throbbed in my soul.

Sweating and panting, Tony leaned over and kissed my forehead before he climbed off and headed toward the bathroom. Feeling defeated and confused, I wiped my face on the sheet and rolled to my side, away from him.

All I'd wanted to do was make love to his cock...give him the quivering pleasure he'd given me. What was so wrong with that? We both would have enjoyed it a hell of a lot more than him jacking off on my face. I couldn't deny the sensation of being branded by his seed felt incredibly erotic. What I didn't understand was why I felt so degraded and cheated.

I needed time to sort out my tumultuous emotions, but I wasn't naïve enough to think Tony would give me five minutes alone. I felt his gaze boring into the back of my body seconds before I felt the mattress dip and he joined me.

"Talk to me, angel. What's wrong?" Tony whispered in my ear as he crawled in behind me.

"Nothing," I lied.

He cleared his throat with a tone that shouted 'bullshit.' "That's not how you wanted our session to play out, was it, sweetheart?"

I pursed my lips and frowned. *Dammit, the man read me like a fucking book.*

"Not so much," I grumbled.

Tony feathered his fingertips up and down my arm in gentle reassurance. "It's not how I'd have preferred it either. But there was a lesson in it for you. Tell me what you learned."

"That it doesn't matter what I want or don't want. You're the boss. You make the rules. I'm just your come receptacle," I snapped, fighting back the tears that burned my eyes.

"Whoa." Surprised concern infused his reply.

He gripped my shoulder and flipped me onto my back. Once again, he climbed atop me, pulling my arms high above my head and pinning my elbows against the pillow, his expression a combination of disbelief and anger.

"You're not a come receptacle to me, Leagh. Fucking never! Every one of your needs, wants, and desires matters to me. Even after we'd discussed topping from the bottom, you continued to try to manipulate me, so you could get the result you wanted."

"No, I wanted to make you feel good. I wanted you inside my mouth. I wanted more."

"Yes, it's what *you* wanted that had you taking control and trying to coerce me into doing exactly what *you* wanted me to do. I'm not the submissive here, sweetheart. You should have simply asked me."

I made a noise of disbelief. "So you're telling me all I had to do was ask to suck your cock?"

"Yes!" he exclaimed on an exasperated hiss.

"Anything I want or need, I just ask, and you're going to give it to me?"

"Maybe." He smirked. "It depends on whether or not I think you've earned it, need it, or if it will enhance your submission. And no, a Ferrari won't make you a better submissive, so don't bother asking."

"Very funny," I replied with a cynical curl of my lips.

"I want you to do something for me, angel."

"What's that?" I asked as Tony dipped low and brushed his lips over mine.

I shivered as his warm breath caressed the shell of my ear. "I want you to fly for me again."

"Is that my punishment for topping from the bottom?" I asked.

"No. I'm going to spank you for the sheer pleasure of it—yours and mine."

Even as I quivered in anticipation, the worry that I wouldn't be able to find that peaceful place again lodged in my brain. What if the first time had just been a fluke? How disappointed would Tony be if I failed him?

"I don't know if I can. Hit subspace, I mean."

"You leave that to me, pet. Just let go. I'll take you there. Focus on how right it feels to give yourself completely to me, all right?"

"I'll try."

"Good girl."

Tony repositioned himself on the bed. Sliding a strong arm beneath my waist, he pulled me onto his lap, taking time to arrange my heavy casts upon the mattress. My nipples scraped over his cotton jeans, and as his broad hand caressed my orbs, I didn't bother biting back a moan of pleasure.

"That's it, baby. Relax and let me set you free."

Resting my cheek on the bed, I closed my eyes, waiting for the pain he sought to give me. A soft smile tugged my lips when Tony began lightly patting my ass. There was a huge difference between the way he spanked in punishment and how he spanked for pleasure. I never wanted to piss him off again.

Focused on the echo of flesh slapping flesh, the warmth enveloping my ass grew to a smoldering heat with slow, steady measure, sensual and erotic.

"That burn is the doorway to the stars. Float through it, sweetheart. I've got you."

"Mmm," I purred. Weightless sensations prickled through me, making my limbs lighter.

"You're a precious treasure to me, Leagh. Give me your heart, your soul, your fears, and your joys. And I promise to cherish every damn one of them."

Gray static flickered behind my eyes. In the distance, I saw it, a pinpoint of light. It called to me, beckoned for me to slide deeper, capture it, and never let go.

"All the heat that's sinking deep is the fire and passion I hold for you. Let it consume you, love. Fuse it to every cell in your body and carry me with you forever more. Now fly for me, angel. Sail far and deep. You are mine," Tony's rich voice vibrated through me.

And I surrendered to the delicate mist that suspended me in its ethereal peace.

When I opened my eyes, the room was dark except for a shaft of light emanating from behind the bathroom door. My ass cheeks throbbed with a delightful sting as Tony lay spooned behind me. The sound of his soft snores resonated in my ears, and his warm breath wafted over my shoulder. Closing my eyes again, I sighed, filled with contentment. And for the first time that I could remember, unafraid of my tomorrows.

The sound of a cell phone pulled me up from the depths of sleep. As I opened my eyes, I felt Tony roll from behind me. Turning, I watched him dig the device from the pocket of his jeans.

"Hello," he answered, his voice still thick and gruff with sleep. "Ah, yeah. What time is it?"

Sitting up, he scrubbed a hand over his face before turning to look at me. A slow smile curled on his lips, and he gave me a sexy wink.

"Let me grab a shower and get dressed. I'll be out in a few minutes." He paused for a moment, listening to the person on the other end of the line. "No problem. Thanks, man."

"You have to work the club tonight, don't you?" I asked, hoping I didn't sound as dejected as I felt.

"Yes, I do," he replied, leaning in to drop a tender kiss on my lips. "But you're going to come with me and sit at the bar. Catch up with Sammie and Trevor and Savannah. You need to get out from behind these four walls, sweetheart."

The thought of sitting and watching Tony throw his whip, dominating Destiny or any one of his other pain sluts, made my stomach roll.

"I don't mind staying in. Besides, there's a book I've wanted to finish before I need to take it back to the library. It's all good. I'll just see you when you get back," I replied in a nervous rush of words.

"Really? After all we've talked about, not to mention the lesson I taught you earlier, you're going to sit there and blow smoke up my ass? Dammit, Leagh, are we ever going to get past this?" Tony raked his hand through his hair before turning toward the bathroom.

"Wait," I cried. "I don't want to go sit in the dungeon."

He turned slowly, staring at me as if I'd grown an extra head. "Why not?"

I sucked in a deep breath. It was now or never. I had to open my soul and trust him with my all my feelings...the good, the bad, and the ugly, jealous ones.

"It kills me to watch you with other subs."

His shoulders sagged as the tension left his body. "When have you ever watched me with another sub? Now that I think about it, you've never been outside your room when the club's been open since George died."

"Once," I confessed quietly. "The night I passed out. You walked past me with—"

"With Destiny in my arms. Yes, I remember." Tony nodded in understanding. "Leagh, the subs I scene with don't hold a candle to what I feel for you. You know that, right?"

I nodded and cast my gaze toward the floor. It was stupid and childish of me to be jealous of the things he did with other subs, but I couldn't help it. The green-eyed monster inside leapt to life, and I couldn't seem to wrangle it back in. Watching him whip and soothe, spank and caress another sub while I sat and watched would be akin to shoving knives through my heart.

"I know, but I still can't watch you do it," I mumbled, still unable to look at him.

Tony didn't say a word, didn't move. The silence dragged on for an uncomfortable amount of time until I couldn't stand it. Glancing up, I found him staring down at me, grinning like an idiot.

"What's so funny?" I bristled.

"You're jealous," he replied in a sing-song voice.

"I am not!"

"Oh, you are, sweetheart," Tony laughed as he pounced onto the bed. "And I like it."

I didn't want to, but I giggled as he rolled me on top of him and squeezed me tight, still grinning like a loon.

"Well, I don't," I pouted dramatically. "It makes me feel like I'm back in high school. It's stupid."

"Aww, it's not stupid, angel. It just shows me how much you care."

"I do care about you, Tony. I love you. You know that."

"Yeah, and that makes me the luckiest bastard on the planet." He beamed. "I'll make a deal with you. I'll monitor the play stations as DM tonight if you sit at the bar and talk to your friends again."

"Okay." I nodded, inwardly relieved he wouldn't be touching the subs.

"I'll talk to Mika and Drake. I'm sure we can come up with a list of Doms who enjoy edge play who might be interested in working the subs."

"Wait. No." I held up my hand and shook my head. "You can't stop doing what you like because of my stupid jealousies."

"I can do whatever I want to. I'm the Master," Tony challenged. "Do I need to prove that to you again?"

"No. And that's not what I meant," I sighed, feeling my irritation rise from the way he twisted my words. "If you stop fulfilling your sadistic needs because of me, you'll end up resenting me, and I'll be wracked with guilt."

Tony sobered and reached up to tuck a strand of hair behind my ear. "Baby, since you've come into my life, I've had an awakening of sorts. Fulfilling the needs of pain sluts has lost its appeal. So, there's no need for you to feel an ounce of guilt over *my* choices. I'm not going to resent you coming into my life...ever. Trust me. I'm a thousand times more complete inflicting sweet agony on you, sweetheart."

Rolling me beneath him, Tony kissed me with a passion so reverent and full of promise it made my toes curl. Gliding his mouth down the column of my throat, he nipped and growled as he worked his way to my nipples. As he dragged his tongue from one beaded tip to the next, I threaded my fingers in his hair and tossed my head back. Soft moans tickled the back of my throat as I arched, offering my breasts to him, to tease, torment, and devour.

A low curse tore from his lips as his cell phone began to ring again. I couldn't help but giggle. Tony shot me a mock glare of warning, which I responded to by rolling my eyes. He shook his head and flashed a dazzling smile. The ease at which we teased one another warmed my heart. Still, Tony would make me walk the line for him, night and day and every second in between. I welcomed the challenge. It excited the hell out of me.

"Hello," he answered. A hint of perturbed frustration laced his tone. I caught a glimpse of unease flash across his face before he smoothed it away. "Ah, no. Not tonight. I'll be working as a Dungeon Monitor. I'll check with Shadow Master and see if he can scene with you, girl."

I knew right away it was one of Tony's regulars calling for a spot on his "hit list." The jealousy-guilt cocktail sluicing through my veins felt foreign and acrid. This wasn't going to be the last call of its kind. But if Tony's claims were true, I'd have to find ways to keep my knee-jerk jealousies at bay. It was his duty as a Dom to find replacement sadists to fulfill his play partners' needs. And his protective nature would ensure that every one of the subs was matched with a Dom they could trust.

"Yes, I'll let you know shortly," Tony replied before ending the call. Gazing down at me, he studied my eyes. "You know I feel obligated to help them, right?"

"Of course, I do. It doesn't mean I have to like it, though." I smirked.

He chuckled. "No, and I know you don't. But as long as you talk to me about all those insecurities running around inside your pretty little head, we'll be just fine."

I sobered and threaded my fingers in his. "I know you have a duty. You've helped a lot of subs achieve their submission, and even though they never wore your collar, they're going to still feel abandoned."

"Yes. I've taken care of some of them for a lot of years. They rely on me, just like you relied on Matt to take care of you."

The mention of his name made my blood turn to ice. "Tony, you can't compare your situation to mine with that sociopath."

"That's not what I'm getting at. We haven't talked about your feelings regarding Matt's death."

"And I really have no desire to start now."

"You need to, in order to find closure with that part of your life."

"It's in the past. He's dead. I'm still here, thankfully, so time to move on."

"You ran from him because you convinced yourself that he was a monster...a dragon you couldn't slay. I understand you feeling a great sense of relief now that he's dead, but the picture you have painted of him in your mind isn't the whole man. If you'd known about his ruthless side from the beginning, would you have let him take care of you?"

"No, I wouldn't have had a single thing to do with him."

"Even though he failed, I think Matt tried to shield you from his dark side. He cared a great deal about you, Leagh. Just like George did by naming you in his will. Why else would Matt take in a pregnant teen, pay your medical bills, feed, clothe, and house you? Just because he was a bad man, didn't mean he was a bad man fully."

"Why are you sticking up for him?" I asked indignantly.

"I'm not, angel. I'm simply giving you a sword to slay him with. Bring him down to your level and conquer the hurt he caused to your psyche. Purge the damage he did to you, come to terms with it, and *really* put it in the past. Don't just gloss it over. I want you to heal and find closure, sweetheart. I just know that it's sometimes harder to do with a ghost."

Everything Tony said made sense. I'd spent years molding Matt into a devil. I'd never let the consideration for all he'd provided me into my condemnation.

"Seeking closure with him while he was alive meant I'd have to face him again."

"Yes, and you were afraid of him. But now that he's gone, I want to help you work through the trauma and put those fears to rest. Will you let me?"

"Yes," I whispered. "But honestly, Tony, all I feel in regard to Matt is relief. A huge sense of relief, and it feels good."

He smiled and brushed his palm over my cheek. "I know it does, sweetheart. You have no idea how happy it makes me seeing the worry vanished from your eyes."

Staring at his erotic mouth, I licked my lips. "Will you please kiss me?" I whispered.

"Now you're getting the hang of it," Tony murmured. Bending low, he claimed me with a fervent kiss suffused with so much love I wanted to pull him into my arms and never let go. With a low growl, and much hesitation, he eased back. "I'm going to grab a shower. When I'm done, I'll help you get dressed, and we can head out to the dungeon."

"Yes, Sir." I smiled.

"Christ, Leagh," he growled as he rose from the bed. "You make my dick throb when you flip on your submissive switch."

I laughed and tossed a pillow at him. "So, all it takes is to say 'yes Sir' and you're ready to go?"

"Pretty much, you little minx." Tony smirked.

"I'll remember that."

"Just as long as you don't top from the bottom, I sure as hell hope so!" he exclaimed with a crooked grin as he swaggered into the bathroom.

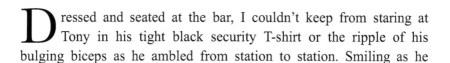

Dressed and seated at the bar, I couldn't keep from staring at Tony in his tight black security T-shirt or the ripple of his bulging biceps as he ambled from station to station. Smiling as he chatted with members while keeping a close eye on the subs at play, he took his duties seriously, and I respected him for that.

"We might need more of these, Mistress Sammie," Trevor taunted, dabbing my chin with a bar napkin. "Dahlia can't seem to stop drooling."

"Here, this should help." Sammie winked, slapping a stack of napkins onto the glossy polished bar.

"Very funny, Trevor," I chided. "I notice *you* squirm every time a certain Daddy Dom steps into the room."

"Yeah," he replied dreamily. "Even after all these years."

"And speaking of said Daddy Dom, here he comes," Savannah announced as she playfully poked Trevor in the ribs with her elbow.

As Drake approached, he arched his brows when he saw me sitting next to Trevor. A broad smile replaced his standard serious expression.

"Good to see you out and about, girl," he murmured, leaning in to give me a hug before turning his attention to Trevor. "March your sexy ass to the cross in the corner, and get those clothes off, boy."

Trevor squealed with glee. His eyes lit up, and a wide grin slashed across his lips. Jumping off the barstool, he scurried toward the St. Andrew's cross in the corner. Drake's eyes danced with pride as he watched the young man.

"You two have a good evening." The big Dom nodded to Savannah and me before following his sub to the station.

Trevor was naked and against the cross by the time Drake made his way to the corner. I watched as he sank a meaty paw into Trevor's hair and yanked the young man's head back. Their lips met in a soulful kiss, testament to the commitment they shared with one another. A tiny, knowing ripple skittered up my spine, and I turned my head to find Tony staring at me from across the room. A deliberate smile tugged his lips, and the strength and warmth of his love filled me.

"Please, tell me I wasn't as bad as you two when I first came here," Savannah giggled.

"You were worse. It was a constant double whammy when you looked at Dylan and Nick," I laughed.

"Yeah, I was afraid of that," Savannah sighed as she darted a nervous look toward the archway that led to the private rooms.

246

"How much time do you figure you've got until they come haul you away, sis?" I asked with a big grin.

"I don't know. I'm just worried about what they plan on doing to me. They've been *setting up*," she used her fingers as quotation marks, "for the past thirty minutes."

"You're worried that, what? Maybe you'll enjoy it too much?" I teased.

"They make sure I always do...eventually." Savannah beamed. "I'm just never sure what those two will think up next for me."

"And that's such a bad thing?" I teased.

"Not in this lifetime." She grinned.

"Can I ask you a personal question?" I murmured low.

"You can ask me anything, sis."

Leaning in close, I lowered my voice even more. "Do you take them both at the same time, you know, in the pussy and ass?"

Savannah issued a modest smile. "Yes."

"Did it hurt the first time...up the butt?" I whispered.

"No." She shook her head and leaned in close to my ear. "They spent days working with me down there, preparing me for the anal invasion."

We both started to giggle. Then I threw back my head and laughed.

"That is hilarious," I snorted, wiping the tears leaking from my eyes.

When Savannah finally regained her composure, she leaned in again and explained how Dylan and Nick had made her wear various sized butt plugs until she could accommodate their cocks.

"And it didn't hurt?" I whispered.

"There was no pain, just unimaginable pressure that I can't describe. It's euphoric, Leagh," she relayed in a soft voice. "I take it Tony is interested in..."

"Yes," I hissed. "And I'm terrified."

"Oh, don't be. That man would walk through busted glass for you. He'd never do anything to hurt you." Leaning in close to my ear, I felt Savannah suck in a deep breath. "Tony's not going to just shove his dick up there. He'll spend all the time it takes to get your ready. And when the time comes, concentrate on relaxing and breathe. If you tense up it *will* hurt. Let him guide you through it. Trust me, after the first time, you'll be begging for it."

I wrapped my arm around her and gave her a hug. "Thank you. You've eased my mind."

"I'm glad. Oh hell, it's show time," she whispered as Dylan and Nick stepped through the archway, their eyes locked on their prize —Savannah.

"Have fun," I chuckled.

"Always," she purred.

I smiled as Savannah slid off the barstool and rushed to the open arms of her Masters. The information she'd imparted rolled around in my head. Understanding what was entailed before the actual act made the thought of anal sex less intimidating.

"How much longer are you going to have to haul those casts around, Dahlia?" Mistress Sammie asked, placing a fresh soda on the bar for me.

"I'm praying the doctor will take them off tomorrow," I said, crossing my fingers.

"I hope so too, honey." She smiled and stepped away to take another drink order.

"Good evening, Dahlia." Master Stephen smiled before claiming the barstool Savannah had vacated. "You look stunning tonight."

I felt the heat rise on my cheeks. "Thank you, Sir. And may I say you look as dashing as ever?"

A huge grin spread over his mouth, and his seafoam green eyes sparkled. "You can, but we'd both know you were full of shit."

"Ah," I choked, my mouth falling open wide. "I beg to differ."

"I imagine you beg quite prettily, pet. Tony is a very lucky man." He winked.

"If you're trying to embarrass me to death, Sir, you're doing a fine job."

His laugh was deep and rich and perfectly suited for such an urbane man.

"I'm sorry to hear you uncollared Carnation, Sir."

The smile faded from his lips as a thoughtful expression lined his face. "Thank you, little one, but it was best for both of us."

248

I issued a slight nod and took a sip of my soda, unsure of what to say next.

"I'll find a girl that shares the same understanding of the lifestyle that I do, someday," Master Stephen assured. "But until that miracle happens, I'm quite content spending time here with my kinky family."

"And we're honored you're sharing it with us, Sir." I smiled, raising my plastic cup to toast the drink Sammie had set in front of him.

Stephen tapped the rim of his cup to mine. "Thank you for your endearing words, little one." He bent close and brushed his lips across my cheek, flashed me a devilish smile, and walked away.

Something about Stephen seemed more fluid. Relaxed, happy even. His demeanor was no longer edgy or stressed out. If letting Carnation go led to the abrupt change in him, he'd have done well to dump that nasty cat months ago.

Taking another long look at Tony, I grew anxious for the club to close. I longed to feel his rugged arms around me and breathe in that sensual scent I'd grown accustomed to. Just as my mind began to fill with visions of me beneath him, I blinked and jerked my head up as Carnation situated herself in front of me. Her eyes blazed in fury, and her face pinched in an angry scowl.

"Are you happy now? You got exactly what you wanted all along, didn't you?" Carnation spat with contempt.

"What are you talking about?" I asked, totally lost.

"Oh, don't play dumb with me, bitch. You've been trying to steal my Master for weeks!"

"Ex-Master," I corrected dryly.

Carnation's cheeks burned bright red, and her mouth opened and closed with an indignant snap. "You've wanted to fuck Master Stephen ever since that dusty old Dom of yours kicked the bucket."

"You're certifiably insane. You know that? I'm not the least bit interested in your ex-Master. I think you need to lay off the crack and get the hell out of my face." I gave her a dismissive wave of my hand.

"Liar! You've always wanted him. I've seen the way you look at him. I hate you, you fucking bitch!" Carnation screamed.

Members began turning their attention to the scene she created.

"I'm with Tony, you delusional player."

"Player? Player? You've got the nerve to call *me* a player? You're the b-brat of the club and... and everybody knows it." Sputtering and fuming, Carnation snatched my soda from the bar and dumped it over my head.

Gasping as the cold liquid spilled down my body, I jumped off the barstool, ready to knock her on her ass. My cast hit the wet tile and promptly slid out from under me. I hit the floor with a bone-jarring thud. Pain streaked from my hip to my knee and back again. Biting back of cry of pain, Carnation's ear-piercing laughter stabbed through my brain.

"You're such a pathetic attention whore," she bellowed.

Before I could pick myself up off the floor, Tony crouched by my side, his gentle hands caressing my shoulder. "Easy, sweetheart. I've got you," he reassured in a calm, steady voice. "Are you hurt?"

"No, thankfully, I landed on my good side and not on my casts. Get me off this floor, so I can kick her ass," I hissed.

"You. Out!" Drake thundered. I knew immediately he was talking to Carnation.

"But... but," she sputtered.

"Not another word, or I will drag you through this club by your hair and throw you out the front door on your ass," Drake bellowed.

"Everybody back," James instructed. "Give Tony and Dahlia some room."

Great. It wasn't bad enough I was on the floor, covered in cold sticky soda, but a crowd had gathered around Tony and me. Inwardly, I cringed.

"Are you sure you're not hurt, baby?" Tony asked, his worried voice rising through the commotion.

"Nothing but my pride, honest," I replied, dreading the look on the members' faces once Tony helped me off the floor.

"I've got this, Drake, besides, Trevor's still on the cross," James reminded the big leather Dom.

"I'll tend to Trevor for you, Drake, Sir, if you'd like?" I recognized the deep baritone voice of Mistress Ivory's submissive, Dark Desire.

"Yes. Thank you. Tell him I'll be right back," Drake instructed.

"Come on, angel. Let's get you off this hard floor." Tony tucked his arms around my chest and knees and stood up then gently eased me onto the barstool. Using his body to shield me from prying eyes, he cupped his hands around my cheeks.

"Move. Now!" Drake bellowed behind us.

Glancing past Tony, I narrowed my eyes on Carnation.

"It's not my fault she fell off the barstool and spilled her drink all over her. Someone should put her in a padded room, so she doesn't hurt herself even more."

"You fuc—"

"Leagh!" Tony's feral bark stopped me mid-sentence.

"But she's lying," I spat, staring into his furious eyes.

"I know. I saw the whole thing," Tony assured. "Drake."

I'd never sensed Tony so close to the edge. His entire body hummed in fury.

"Relax. I'm taking care of it. Consider it over," the big Dom vowed.

Carnation tossed her nose in the air and headed toward the front of the club. Members watched the nasty cow with scornful expressions. James and Drake stepped alongside her, guaranteeing she left the premises without causing any further drama.

"I'm so embarrassed," I whispered, shooting Tony an anxious glance.

"She's the one who should be embarrassed. What the hell happened?"

"I was sitting at the bar, and Master Stephen came over. We talked all of two seconds, and the next thing I know, Carnation is up in my face accusing me of stealing Stephen from her. I have no clue what crawled up her butt to think such a thing."

"She had to blame someone other than herself, I imagine." Tony frowned.

"Can I please go back to our room?"

"In a minute, I want to check you out first."

"Here?" I moaned.

"Yes. Here. Among your friends and the people who love you," Tony emphasized with a grin.

"You know I don't do humiliation well, Sir," I grumbled.

"But you'll do it for me. For my peace of mind, won't you, angel?" he cajoled.

"Yes, Sir," I replied with a soft nod.

"I've never wanted to whip someone's ass for vengeance before in my life. But I'd gladly make an exception for that little bitch."

"She's not worth it, Sir."

"Worth what?" Tony asked as he grabbed a handful of napkins and dabbed my cheeks.

"You losing your Dominant reputation over."

"Are you all right, sugar?" Sammie asked. Her pale blue eyes filled with concern.

"Yes, Ma'am." I nodded.

"I'm sorry, Dahlia. I was at the other end of the bar. If I'd have known she was up in your face, I'd have put a stop to it immediately," Sammie apologized, adding to the pile of napkins on the bar.

I grabbed a handful and started wiping the soda from my hands and hair. "It's okay. She's got…issues," I said with a frown.

"She's a hot mess of trouble is what she is," Sammie grumbled under her breath before stomping away.

While I cleaned myself up, Tony poked and prodded, bending my limbs and asking a dozen times if anything hurt. Thankfully, the members gravitated back to their places once the commotion was over. I watched Dark Desire smoothing his hand over Trevor's head as he whispered into the young sub's ear.

It wasn't long before Drake reappeared. His big frame taut with tension, and anger etched on his face. He shot an inquiring glance my way, and I flashed him a smile and gave him the thumbs up sign. Still wearing a ferocious scowl, Drake issued a curt nod and stormed back to the cross where Trevor patiently waited. Dark Desire stepped away, leaving Trevor in the capable hands of his Master.

Drake paused for a moment, as if to gather his wits, before he stepped up behind his sub. Trevor turned his head and smiled. Meshing his burly body against the man, Drake whispered something in Trevor's ear. Closing his eyes, the young sub opened his mouth, willing and pliant. I could almost see the ire leaving Drake's body.

After a long poignant kiss, the big Dom stepped back, picked up his whip, and began where he'd left off.

James approached Tony and me wearing a look of bewilderment. "Do you want to file charges?"

"No," I replied, adamantly shaking my head.

"Are you sure, angel?" Tony asked.

"Positive," I reaffirmed, darting a glance at the two scowling Doms.

"Okay. I have just one more question. Does trouble follow you everywhere you go?" James asked with a chuckle.

"Not anymore," I quipped with a saucy smile and stole a quick kiss from Tony's lips.

Chapter Thirteen

B right and early the next morning, Tony and I sat in Dr. Coleman's exam room anxiously awaiting the results from the x-rays he'd taken when we first arrived.

"So, what is the first thing you want to do when you get your casts off, angel?" Tony asked.

I flashed him an impish grin. "First, I want to take a hot shower. Lather my whole body in citrus gel and let the water beat down on me for hours."

"A shower, huh? Alone or with someone?" Tony's voice dipped low and sensual. I tried not to squirm.

"Someone very special, but first, I'll need to ask him if he'd be kind enough to join me."

"I'm sure if you ask properly, he will. He might even show you his special shower talents."

I swallowed tightly. "You mean there's more you haven't shown me?"

"Oh yeah, sweetheart, lots more," he growled, moving in close to the paper covered table I sat upon.

Staring up into his eyes, I slowly rolled my tongue over my bottom lip. Tempting. Teasing. "Don't you want to know what I want to do after that?"

A playful smile tugged his lips. "What's the second thing you want to do when you get your casts off, love?"

I leaned my lips close to his ear. "I want to wrap both my legs around your waist."

A labored groan rumbled from deep in his chest. Sliding his fingers around my nape, Tony skimmed them up my scalp and gripped a fistful of hair. Tilting my head back, he nipped my bottom lip. "I won't ever make you ask permission for that, angel."

My nipples drew tight, and blood rushed beneath my clit. For a split second, I wondered if there was a lock on the exam room door and if I could convince Tony that we had time for a quickie.

That's topping from the bottom. A little voice inside my head reminded. I knew that wouldn't get me what I wanted. I'd have to ask. *Right.*

The door swung open, and Dr. Coleman stepped in. Tony tensed, released me, and quickly backed away from the table, guilt written all over his face. He looked like a kid caught with his hand in the cookie jar. I tried not to laugh.

"Didn't mean to interrupt. I guess I should have knocked," Dr. Coleman smirked.

"We were just talking," I replied innocently. "Please, tell me you're not going to make me walk out of here with these casts on."

"Okay, I won't." The doctor smiled. "But you will have to wear a splint on your wrist for a couple more weeks. You can take it off to shower and to sleep, but I want you wearing it ninety-nine percent of the time, understood?"

The look he shot me was reminiscent of Tony's unhappy Dom scowl, and it raised my suspicions that Dr. Coleman harbored a little dominant kink of his own.

"Yes, Sir," I replied, fighting a grin as I shot a glance Tony's way.

"I'll make sure she's a good girl and keeps it on," he assured with a twinkle in his eyes.

A strange look passed over Dr. Coleman's face, and he opened his mouth to speak but quickly closed it. A few awkward seconds passed before he began cutting the cast from my leg. As he pulled the heavy plaster away, I looked down.

"Oh, good grief. I need to shave."

Both men laughed. "I'll get you a new razor, angel," Tony assured.

After being fitted with the splint, Tony and I headed back to Genesis. I felt a hundred pounds lighter. We pulled into the parking lot, and my cell phone rang. Tony cut the engine as I dug the device from my purse.

"Hello."

"Leagh, it's Reed. Do you have a minute?"

"Sure, Reed. What's up?"

"Couple of things, couple of big things," he replied cryptically. "Judge Bernard is in the process of being disbarred, and Sloane's challenge of George's will has been expunged. I know I'm asking a lot, but I'd like to set up a meeting with you and Paula next week."

"No," I blurted out in a knee-jerk reaction.

"Leagh," Reed soothed. "We need to settle his estate. You and Paula are the only surviving beneficiaries named. I'm working like hell to divide his assets between the two of you, but if I don't get this settled, we risk of it all ending up in probate."

Tony watched me with concern. He was my knight in shining armor. Ready and willing to slay dragons and monsters, move mountains and boulders or anything that blocked the path of my happiness or my submission—even when the barrier was me and my own stubborn pride.

Suddenly, it all became crystal clear. George had never been a real Master. He'd never corrected my rebellious streaks, never punished or praised, just allowed me to act out until *he* submitted to my demands. George wasn't able or willing to harness his own dominance, and I had floundered. Having absorbed the potent power exchange at the club, it had awakened my inner submissive. No wonder it chaffed so badly to be known as the 'brat' of Genesis, but topping from the bottom had been the only skewed way I knew to fill what was missing.

Until now.

A smile spread across my mouth, and I knew what I needed to do.

"I don't want George's money, Reed. Give it all to Paula."

Tony choked, and his mouth fell open in shock. "Wait. Are you crazy? Put him on speaker, angel. Now."

"Reed, can I call you back in a few?" I asked, startled by Tony's anger.

"Sure. Call me back."

When I hung up from the call, Tony glared at me.

"What?" I asked, wondering why he'd gone from stunned surprise to now shooting daggers at me.

"I told you to put him on speaker, not call him back," Tony growled.

"I want to talk to you about this, but I'd rather do it inside. I wasn't topping from the bottom," I explained, trying to remain calm.

With a grunt, Tony relented. I filled him in on the details as we made our way into my room.

"You really need to think about this, Leagh," Tony began. "This is a once in a lifetime chance at financial freedom. You'll never have to work another day in your life. You could live anywhere. You..."

He paused and looked away. The palpable wall he erected scared me.

"What's wrong?"

"I can't help you with this decision, angel. I'm sorry, but I can't. You're going to need to figure out what you want to do on your own."

"Wait a minute," I cried. "You've been all up in my shit for weeks."

"Language," Tony warned.

Ignoring him, I continued with my rant. "Now, all of a sudden, you don't care what I do?"

"That's not what I'm saying," he replied in a low, even tone.

"Then, what exactly are you saying? It sounds to me that since Matt's dead and my casts are off, you're washing your hands of me."

His placid expression turned to one of shock. "Seriously? What have I ever done to make you think that? Or are you just projecting the one thing you're most afraid of... me dumping you?"

"Don't start analyzing me, Tony."

"That's what I do, sweetheart," he taunted with a crooked smirk.

"Save it for your patients. Why do you suddenly have no desire to weigh in on a huge decision that affects my life?" I pressed my fists onto my hips. Dominant or not, the man forced me to put on my bitch wings. "Why, now, are you not chomping at the bit to stick your nose in my business?"

My last comment brought an impish grin to curl his lips. "I'd love to throw you down on the bed and stick my nose, mouth, and tongue all up in your business, angel. But Reed's expecting your call."

"Dammit, Tony! Answer my question," I cried.

Fire flashed in his dark eyes as a wicked laugh rolled off his tongue. "You're going to pay for your filthy mouth…later. And by the way, I think you're sexy as hell when you get all riled up."

I sent him a seething glare. Undaunted, he moved in closer. I bristled when he caressed my arms before gripping them tight.

"You want something from me, sweetheart? I suggest you do it the right way and stop trying to make me lick your heels." As he leaned his mouth close to my ear, I trembled. "Ask me from your heart, my love. Not from your fears."

Unable to help it, I melted against him.

"Why?" I whispered. "Why are you turning me away?"

"Awww, sweetheart, I'd never turn you away. I'm sorry if I made you feel that way, but I can't give you an unbiased opinion on whether or not you should take the money."

"Can you, will you tell me why, please?"

His cock jerked against my belly, and my pussy fluttered. Even at odds with one another, our bodies ignored the conflict and tangled in lustful harmony. It was impossible for me to stay angry with him while hungering for him at the same time. Both cursing and rejoicing at the claim he had over me.

Brushing the hair from my face with soft fingers, he lovingly gazed into my eyes. "I want you, Leagh. Today, tomorrow, forever. Now that your casts are off, I'd envisioned you coming to live with me. But when I thought of the freedom you could have with George's inheritance, I didn't see you in my future. I didn't like it, love."

My throat constricted, and tears welled in my eyes. I swallowed tightly, clearing the lump of emotion from my throat. "I don't care if I have five cents or a million dollars. I want to be with you, Tony."

A tiny shudder rippled through him. I physically felt the ball of tension leave his body. The magnitude of love reflected made my heart melt all over again.

"Kiss me," Tony commanded in a thick, raspy tone.

Leaning in, I pressed my lips to his, pouring my whole heart into that one glorious kiss. He ate at me like a ravenous animal, feral and uncompromising, and I embraced his dominance with a surrendering whimper.

Tony tore from my lips with a growl. "Call Reed. Tell him you'll meet him and Paula next week."

"Will you come to the meeting with me?"

"Wild horses couldn't keep me away."

My heart soared as I picked up my phone and called Reed back. I surprised him when I announced that I'd be at the meeting. He gave me the date and time.

"Now that the uncomfortable part is out of the way, there's something I need to talk to you about." There was a strange tension in Reed's voice. "Since the news report about the fire, I'd sort of been expecting this. The FBI contacted me. They're sending an agent here tomorrow. He needs to talk to you."

"I'm confused, Reed. Why would the FBI, first, contact you about the fire, and second, want to talk to me?"

"It's not just about the fire, Leagh. When they started investigating, they found the restraining order that I'd filed for you."

"No, that's not right. George told me it wasn't public record," I argued.

"Leagh, all court documents have to be recorded," Reed exhaled loudly. There was a long pause. "I'm sorry he lied to you."

"Again, you mean. You're sorry he lied again." I couldn't keep the contempt from my tone. "Well, I have nothing to say to the FBI. And the restraining order is worthless now. Matt's dead. He died in a parasailing accident in Belize."

"How do you know that?" Reed asked.

"Tony had a friend of his in California do some digging."

"That's a relief. I tried to pinpoint exactly what the FBI wanted to talk to you about, but the bastard wouldn't give me a crumb. I'm sure it has something to do with Sloane and the fire, but don't worry, I'll be there with you."

A strange buzzing in my ears grew loud, and my heart thundered in my chest. "They can't implicate me on anything Matt did, can they?"

"I don't know. They can try, but, look, do your best not to worry until there's something to worry about, okay?"

For a split second, I thought I was going to pass out. I sucked in a deep breath, then another while the phone trembled in my hand.

"What time tomorrow?" My voice quaked.

"Ten o'clock."

"Okay, I'll be there. Thanks, Reed."

When I hung up, Tony held my hand and gave me a puzzled look. "What's going on, Leagh?"

I looked at him and issued a weak smile. "I think I need a drink."

Sitting at the bar, I nursed a rum and coke as I filled Tony in on my conversation with Reed about the FBI. Even the liquor didn't calm my nerves. My hands continued to tremble.

"Come on, sweetheart," Tony urged as he took my hand and led me back to our room.

Once inside, he ushered me into the bathroom, where he silently removed my splint, and peeled away my clothes before shucking off his own. The sight of his strong, naked body calmed me. His turgid shaft—and knowing what was to come—swapped anxiety to hunger. Turning on the shower, he adjusted the water temperature before steering me inside with him, and when the hot spray cascaded down my body, I sighed in contentment.

"This was first on your list, angel. Close your eyes. Let me bathe you in suds and kisses."

"Mmm," I groaned, following his instruction. "Thank you."

A tiny chuckle resonated in my ears. "I'd like to say the pleasure's all mine, but I aim for both of us to enjoy this, sweetheart."

Tony didn't seem to be in a rush as he shaved my legs and washed and conditioned my hair, sliding his slick nimble hands and the sudsy loofah over every inch of my body. His warm mouth fused with mine as his fingers toyed with my pussy. Drowning in the smooth warmth of his skin, Tony ramped me up only to ease back, dragging me away from the cusp of release over and again. I wondered how many times he'd drive me to the edge before he'd grant me mercy and let me fly. Leading me in a maddening yet well-choreographed dance of denial seemed to be Tony's expertise. It was divine torture.

Crying out when he dragged his slick thumbs over my tight nipples, a mewl of want seeped from my throat. Gliding my hands over his sculpted chest, then lower along his defined abs, I wrapped my fingers around his hard, throbbing heat. Tony cupped my ass with both hands and pressed me against the tiled wall, aligning me with his massive erection. With a slow push, he seated inside me, all the way to the base.

Stretched full, I moaned, rolling my hips as he remained motionless inside me. Anchored to his chiseled body, I lifted my legs and locked them around his waist. Tony issued an approving growl, and I smiled beneath our tangled lips as he rocked up, driving into me even further.

Slow and sensual, he moved within my clutching tunnel. His deliberate rhythm felt intoxicating. Nipping, pinching, and laving my nipples, Tony coaxed me up the carnal path of pleasure. All too soon, I was poised on the precipice. The swell inside grew to a desperate level. My keening cries filled the air.

Tony unleashed the fury of need he'd kept wrangled so tightly. Slamming into my cunt, he shifted his hands and pinned my shoulders to the wall. His tongue invaded my mouth, driving in time with his demanding cock.

When the craggy peak beneath me gave way, I sank my fingernails into his broad shoulders and held tight. Tony swallowed my screams of ecstasy as spasms tore through me. Shuttling through my spasming channel, faster and harder, he froze and jerked his mouth from my lips. "Mine!" he thundered. Thrusting again, he roared as he jettisoned inside me.

My tunnel clutched around him as he exploded inside me. Electricity surged through my veins. My limbs trembled as the water splattered onto the shower floor, melding with our moans.

Tony stayed buried inside me until our ragged breathing returned to normal. Neither of us said a word. We simply clung to one another, absorbing the pulses of love and quivering aftershocks. Breaking the spell, I leaned forward and kissed him. His cock jerked deep inside me, and I moaned.

Suddenly, the hot water turned to ice. Squealing in surprise, I dropped my legs to the floor. Tony dipped and slid from inside me. Issuing a curse, he turned off the water, stepped out, and grabbed us each a towel. Securing his around his waist, he dried me off. When he knelt to rub the soft cotton up my legs, I leaned in and sipped the beads of water from his colorful tattoos. Tony froze, and his body grew taut. Rising quickly, I feared I'd broken some unwritten submissive rule as I watched him stand. His dark eyes were narrowed, and his jaw ticked.

Shit. Yep, you fucked up again.

"What possessed you to do that, angel?" Tony asked with a guarded expression.

"I don't know. I...the very first time I saw your tattoos, I wanted to run my tongue over them. I'm sorry."

"Don't be sorry, sweetheart," Tony replied in such a buttery timbre I felt my legs wobble. "It's one of the most submissive things I've ever felt before. I liked it."

Lifting me off the floor, he tossed me over his shoulder. I let out a yelp of surprise before I giggled at his caveman antics. Tony stormed to the bed and tossed me onto the mattress. I continued to laugh as he pounced on top of me.

"I love seeing you happy," he whispered.

Sobering, I stared up at him, noticing for the first time the tiny little lines at the corners of his eyes, the contour of his dark brows, the arch of his nose, and the plumpness of his well-kissed lips. For some bizarre reason, my mind tripped back to my high school history class and the weeks we spent studying European Mythology. Tony was exactly as I'd imagined *Anteros,* the God of love and passion, might look like.

"You make me happy, Sir. Happier than I've ever been in my entire life."

"Ditto, my *tesorino.*"

"What's a tesorino?" I asked with suspicion.

"It means little treasure. That's what you are to me, Leagh, a priceless little treasure."

And even when I thought it impossible, the man made me melt a little more.

"Please, Tony, make love to me again?"

"Please, who?" he asked in that deep, erotic voice of his.

"Please, Master," I replied in a shy whisper.

"How can I refuse, angel? You will call me that from now on, understood?"

"Yes, Master." I smiled softly.

As Tony reached for a condom on the nightstand, he stopped. His brows furrowed in worry. "We didn't use a condom in the shower, Leagh."

"I know."

"I'm clean, and I assume you are as well, but what about birth control?" he asked.

"I'm not on birth control. George was…he'd had a vasectomy when he was in his forties."

I could see Tony mentally counting the days since my last period. He exhaled a breath so deep it was as if he'd been granted a reprieve from a death sentence. "You're due to start any day now, aren't you?"

"Yes," I nodded, worried about his extreme sense of relief. "So, I take it you don't want kids?"

"Not nine months from now. But someday, after you walk down the aisle of the church I went to growing up."

"Whoa. I think you're getting the cart before the horse a little? Wait. Did you just ask me? No, you didn't, did you?"

"No, you'll know when I do, angel. I'm simply planting seeds in your head right now."

"You mean you're just fu…err… messing with my mind."

"Who? Me?" He chuckled. "And that reminds me. You owe me something, my little trash talking vixen."

"Great, me and my big mouth," I grumbled with an impish grin. "It was a little slip in the passion of the moment."

"So, I'm what? Supposed to say, 'don't do it again' and let it slide? Hmmm?"

"You'd actually do that?"

"Not on your life, angel," Tony laughed as he climbed off the bed.

Holding my silk robe on the end of his fingertip, he winked. "Put this on and follow me."

"Where are we going?" I gulped as I stood and wrapped the robe around me.

"No more questions or comments. You're now limited to only three responses: Yes, Master, No, Master, or protocol. Understood?" Tony instructed, adjusting his erection beneath a pair of black athletic shorts.

"Yes, Master," I replied as I tied the silky sash around my waist.

"Let's go," he grinned before walking out the door.

I followed him down the hall and into the empty dungeon. Glancing up at the two-way mirrors of Mika's office I wondered if anyone was up there watching. A shiver of anxiety rippled through me.

"We're all alone," Tony affirmed.

"Yes, Master," I replied, biting back the overwhelming urge to ask if he was doubly sure. My limited vocabulary was already proving to be a major pain in the ass.

When he stepped up to the St. Andrews cross in dungeon's corner, my eyes grew wide, and my heart clutched. Darting a gaze around the available toys, every one of them was way above my level of experience. Quirts, canes, cat o'nines, and dragon tails lined a long cloth-covered table. I bit my lips between my teeth and took a step back, still eyeing the pain inducing assortment.

"Do you need to talk to me before we begin, sweetheart?" Tony asked, stepping close to run his knuckle over my cheek.

"Yes, Sir." I nodded, focusing back on him.

"Permission to speak."

"I can't do this. I can't take the level of pain those things produce!" I exclaimed, pointing to the frightful collection.

"I never said I planned on using them, angel," he challenged with a crooked grin.

Walking to the wall near the cross, with an even larger selection of nefarious toys that had never come in contact with my lily-white ass, Tony plucked his favorite whip from the hook. I felt my eyes grow wide as I sucked in a ragged breath. "This is what I'm going to use."

"No," I squeaked, backing away in fear.

"No?" he asked, arching his brows.

"I mean, I don't want to be sliced open."

"What makes you think I'd do anything of the sort?" Tony frowned. "I'm sensing a lack of trust here, sweetheart."

Dammit. Why did he always have to play that fucking psychological card on me?

"You either trust me or you don't, my love. It's as simple as that." Tony squared his shoulders, spread his legs, and tucked his hands behind his back, thus hiding the wicked whip. Dominance rolled off him in a potent wave. "Lose the robe and step up to the cross or safeword out and go back to your room. It's time for you to decide if you're going to put yourself into my hands and let me mold you or not."

The knee-jerk reaction to fight or take flight slammed into me with a force so brutal I nearly doubled over. All the time Tony and I had spent together culminated to this one pivotal moment. It was time for me to take one step for Leagh—one giant leap for my submission.

Sucking in a fortifying breath, I peeled off my robe and stepped up to the cross.

Tony stepped in behind me to whisper in my ear. "I'm so fucking proud of you."

Tamping down the terror as he stepped away and secured the cuffs to my wrists and ankles, I tried to prepare myself for the first slice of searing pain. Trembling, I closed my eyes and listened as he took several steps behind me.

"We're all alone, angel. Feel free to scream out your safeword if you need to. There's no one but me to hear you."

Get on with it already before I change my damn mind.

"Did you hear me, Leagh?" Tony asked in an impatient tone.

"Yes, Master." I swallowed tightly.

Cringing, I squeezed my butt cheeks together and waited... and waited. Anticipation spiked, and I fought the urge to peek over my shoulder when a soft pop split the air. I whimpered, waiting for the pain to sink its teeth into my tissue and spread. Surprised when the only sensation I felt was a small gust of wind followed by a barely perceptible nip of... something, I couldn't even call it pain. I felt another and yet another. Where was the agony? The red welted slash marks? The blood?

"See, sweetheart. I can do amazing things with this lovely whip. I can make it bite so deep and hard you crave to crawl out of your skin. Or I can leave kisses upon your sweet flesh like the gentle caress of a lover's lips."

I exhaled a deep sigh and relaxed against the cool, polished wood of the cross.

"That's it. Let my whip, my lips, cover you in kisses, my *tesorino*," Tony spoke in a raspy growl as he threw the whip in soft, gentle whispers. "Your submission tastes like wine, angel, sweet and intoxicating and so damn delicious."

Within seconds, the static gray filtered in behind my closed eyes. The pinpoint of light glowed much brighter than ever before. Racing toward it, I surrounded myself in its blissful peace and eagerly sailed away.

When I opened my eyes, I was back in my room under the soft cotton sheets of my bed. Tony sat beside me, strumming his fingers through my hair, watching me with a sated expression lining his face.

"Welcome back, my love." He smiled, bending to brush a tender kiss upon my lips.

"That was..." I struggled for words to describe the depth of intensity that had carried me away. "Amazing. More than amazing."

"It was for me, too, sweetheart." Tony glanced down at his lap, tightening his fist around a silver metal collar; he raised it up to me. "This is for you, Leagh. You've earned it. And I want everyone to know, not only are you are under my protection, but in training with me as well. Sit up, my love."

Tears of joy streamed down my cheeks as Tony gazed into my eyes.

"Do you promise to strive to be the best submissive you can be and to represent me in a positive and respectful light?"

"Yes, Master," I sobbed softly.

"Do you desire to wear my training collar with all your heart and soul, angel?"

"Yes, Master."

"You may beg for it, sweet girl." Tony smiled.

Sliding from beneath the covers, I eased onto the floor, kneeling at his feet. Tony issued a sigh of delight and strummed his thumb over my lips before I cast my eyes to the floor.

"I beg for the chance to grow beneath your hands, Master. To serve you in all ways with an open heart and make you proud that you've chosen to guide me. May I please have the honor of wearing your training collar?"

"You make me proud every single fucking day. It will be *my* honor to have you bound to me. Yes, my love. You may wear my sign of training, of claim, of ownership."

Tony unclasped the silver band. Leaning forward, I lifted my hair while he placed the collar around my throat. When I heard the snick of the lock, I briefly closed my eyes and sighed, allowing the significance of this reverent moment to meld into my being.

Tony cupped his palm beneath my chin, lifting my face upward. He claimed my mouth with a fiery kiss. Soaring with joy, I floated to the heavens as his tongue delved deep. His promise, commitment, and love tasted sweeter than honey.

Rising from the bed, Tony tugged off his shorts before wrapping a sturdy fist in my hair. Guiding my mouth to his cock, he paused. Holding the moment, he kept me suspended in feverish anticipation. Raising my eyes, I looked up and gazed into his sinful, dark pools. Something about him was palpably different. His intense command seemed sharper, the passion in his stare hotter. My entire being clawed in desperation to prove my love, my commitment, and my submission to this magnificent man.

I strived to portray a vision of patience on the outside. But on the inside, I clawed at the need to prove myself to him and to feel his steely velvet upon my tongue.

"What is it you want, angel?"

I flashed him a saucy grin. "Permission to suck your big, bad cock, Master?"

A wicked grin crawled across his lips. "You may, my sassy little minx."

He let me tease him with my mouth and tongue for a long time before he pulled me to the bed and slid his glistening cock deep in my core. Tony took me on a rollercoaster ride of frustration that left me sweaty and ragged and begging for relief, which, of course, he adamantly refused.

I made an inward vow to never try to drive him out of his mind again. Tony achieved release twice before he allowed me to come. When he finally relented, I shattered into a billion shards of pulsating glass. Sated and boneless, I melted against his hot body. Tony had proven that hell hath no fury like a Master tormented by his sub.

Hours later, Tony pampered me with wine, cheese, and fruit. Little did I know. he was merely recharging my batteries for round two, three and—rousting me from sleep in the early dawn—four.

W hen we finally woke the next morning, Tony sent me to shower to get ready for the meeting at Reed's office while he fixed breakfast. The pancakes were fluffy and light, but once inside my stomach, they sat like a load of bricks. My nerves worked overtime, leaving me feeling unsure and jittery. Fingering the silver collar at my throat, a subtle sense of peace sprinkled over me. Whatever information the FBI sought, I knew I'd get through the inquisition with Tony by my side.

We made the drive to Reed's office in companionable silence. I glanced at the commanding man beside me concentrating on the road. Tony was lost in thought, no doubt mulling over the same billion what ifs I did. But once inside Reed's masculine office, I felt a shift in Tony's demeanor. He seemed more relaxed—or at least, I'd hoped so. But when Reed's secretary opened the door and a tall man with greying temples wearing a dark blue suit stepped inside, there was enough electricity in the air to light all of Las Vegas.

Reed stood and rounded his big, ornately carved desk. Just as he extended his hand to the man in the blue suit, Matt entered behind him and shut the door.

Chapter Fourteen

B linking twice, my eyes grew wide. I launched from my chair and raced to the corner behind Reed's desk. Shrinking into the crook between the wall and his bookshelf, erratic bursts of air vibrated from the back of my throat as my heart slammed against my ribs.

Tony jumped from his chair, rushing toward me as Reed turned with a confused expression.

"What the hell?" Tony barked, jerking a glance over his shoulder before turning a concerned look at me. Worry filled his eyes. "Leagh, what's wrong?"

"M-M-Matt," I stuttered, peering over Tony's wide shoulder at the man I thought was dead. A pained expression wrinkled his face at my reaction to him.

Tony spun around and stormed toward Matt. "Matthew Price? You son of a bitch! How dare you come in here and scare the living shit out of her like that? What the hell are you up to, motherfucker?"

"What the fuck?" Reed thundered, sidling up next to Tony. "Get the hell out of my office!"

"Easy, you two." The man in the blue suit held up his palms in surrender. "If you'll all just take a seat, I can explain."

"Explain what?" Tony shouted to the man before turning his full fury on Matt. "Is he some hired thug posing as FBI so you can get to Leagh? If you think I'm going to let you take her out of this office, you're fucking crazy! The only way you'll get to her is through me. So if you're here for her, asshole, bring it."

"Wait," Matt sighed and shook his head. "No, that's not why I'm here."

"Mister, what is your name?" the man in the blue suit asked as he stepped in front of Matt, trying like hell to calm the wild animal who looked ready to rip both their heads off, Tony.

"Tony Delvaggio."

"Delvaggio?" the FBI agent repeated with an inquisitive stare. "I know of an Enzo Delvaggio out on the west coast. You're not related to him by any chance are you?"

"I'm his nephew. Who the hell are you?"

"Huh," the man in the blue suit grunted. "Interesting. I'm Special Agent Jonathan Rizzo."

"Special agent for what division?" Tony pressed.

"WITSEC," the agent replied. "Now, if we can all just sit down, calm down, I'll explain why we're here."

A string of obscenities rolled off Tony's tongue as he returned to me and pulled me in his arms. "What's WIT, whatever?" I whispered.

"Witness protection," he murmured.

"I'm not going into witness protection for you or anyone else," I snapped at Matt. "I've spent the last six years looking over my shoulder. I won't do it anymore. I finally got a taste of what my life could be like over the past few days when I thought you were dead."

Tears burned my eyes as I looked at Tony. "They were the best damn days of my entire life." Pinning Matt with a taunting glare, I sucked in a deep breath. "So, if you're here to kill me, then just do it now and get it over with.

"Relax, Miss Bennett. No one is here to hurt you. Mr. Price requested this meeting. I'll let him explain. But first, I'd like to thank you, Judge Landes for allowing us yours and Miss Bennett's time. I'm sure once Mr. Price has explained everything; all the misunderstandings will be cleared up,"

Reed begrudgingly shook Special Agent Rizzo's hand as Tony led me to a chair far away from Matt. Once seated, Tony wrapped a protective arm around me. I could feel his heart pounding in his chest, keeping time with mine own. The whole damn thing seemed so surreal I wondered if it were just a bad dream and I'd wake up any second.

"That's all good and fine, Special Agent Rizzo, but if you don't mind, I'd like to see your ID. Considering the history of my client in regard to Mr. Price, I'm sure you understand." Leave it to Reed, suave and sophisticated, even when shoving a condescending knife in a guy's gut.

A bitter smile played over Special Agent Rizzo's lips as he pulled out his badge and handed it to Reed.

"Thank you. You may take a seat." Reed returned the badge and extended his hand at the vacant chairs and flashed me a wary look before he sat behind his big desk.

All eyes turned to Matt, who seemed suddenly nervous, his face ashen white. He opened his mouth only to close it again, swallowing what seemed a basketball lodged in his throat.

"First of all...kill you? I never want *any* harm to come to you, honey. You're like a daughter to me. Why did you think—Never mind. I know why you thought I'd come after you. I came here to tell you I'm so sorry for what I put you through."

My panic ebbed, but my temper spiked. I tried to bolt from the chair, but Tony's sturdy arm held me in my seat.

"You're sorry? You're sorry?" I screeched. "You son of a bitch! I've been waiting for you to find me since I was twenty years old. My head filled with visions of you stepping out from some dark alley and putting a bullet in my head or breaking in while I was asleep and putting a pillow over my face, suffocating me to death."

"No. No. No." Matt adamantly shook his head. "Honey, I could never do that to you. Please, let me explain."

My body trembled, and I sucked in a deep breath. Tony held me tighter, and I issued a curt nod toward Matt.

"I came here to ask for your forgiveness, so I need to start at the beginning. Some of this you're not going to want to hear, and I'm sorry, but you need to know. It might make some sense to you when

I'm done." Matt scrubbed a hand over his face, and as he lowered his hand to the table, I noticed he was shaking.

"I can handle it. Go ahead."

Matt chuckled softly and looked up at me. Funny, he didn't look like a monster, just a troubled old man whose eyes still reflected love when he gazed at me. "I know you can. You're a strong young woman."

I made a noise in the back of my throat. He was the one who had forced me to grow the rigid backbone, but I bit back that snarky retort.

"Twenty-eight years ago, your dad was out of town on a business trip. I dropped by to check in on your mom. This was long before they became so immersed in the church. She was wild and carefree, happy and full of life."

The woman he described was in no way, shape, or form the woman who had raised me, but I let him go on.

"There'd always been this underlying current between us that we tried to ignore, but that day..." Matt exhaled loudly. "It was a one-time thing, and she was so overwrought with guilt she threw herself into the church hoping that God would forgive what we'd done. I've always blamed myself for stealing her zest for life. I tried to apologize to her once, but she told me if I ever mentioned the affair to her again, I wouldn't be welcome in her home. So, I didn't. When you were born, she said it was a sign from God that he'd forgiven her sins. Unfortunately, she never was able to forgive herself or me."

"You had an affair with my mom, and she turned into a pseudo-cult member of the church, dragging my dad along with her? I get that you feel responsible for that, but none of that explains...why are you here with an agent from witness protection, Matt?" My tone was arctic. It was the only defense I could pluck from within that wasn't suffused in rage, hurt, and betrayal. Just the thought of my mother being a loving, happy woman at one time made tears sting my eyes.

"I couldn't handle the guilt much better, Leagh. Not long after you were born, I started using cocaine, but I soon realized I could make a hell of a lot of money distributing the stuff rather than using it. That's when I started building my empire," Matt snorted sarcastically. "After nearly twenty years, I'd amassed billions of dollars and was among the ranks of the biggest drug lords in the world. Guns, drugs, sex slaves, I had my hands in it all."

I closed my eyes and swallowed the urge to vomit.

"When I came home and found that you'd left me, the silence drove me insane. I missed your laughter and your vibrant spirit...you were gone and so was my chance at redemption. I knew then what I needed to do, but still I couldn't find the guts to do it. So, I continued to deal with the devils in hopes that I could fill the void inside me. But it didn't work, so a year later, I picked up the phone, met with the FBI, and cut a deal. I handed over names, locations, quantities, and a list of murders I'd committed. In return, they granted me immunity and witness protection. With my videotaped testimony from numerous safe houses, they were able to bring down most of the bigger players and corrupted government officials I'd been associated with."

The room was silent. Tony's thumb circled my shoulder in constant reminder that I wasn't alone. I knew in my heart he would always be by my side, supporting me. *My rock.* A sense of renewed strength filled me.

"I can't take back the things I've done or the lives I've destroyed. When I saw you on the news, I called Special Agent Rizzo and begged him to set up this meeting. I had to see you and tell you how very sorry I am. Not only for what I subjected you to, but for taking away the woman your mom used to be. Don't worry, Leagh. I'm not holding onto the pipe dream that you'll ever forgive me, but I hope you understand how important it was for me to apologize to you. I never meant to fuck up your life."

When Matt was done, I didn't know what to say. Part of my heart broke in two for the pain and guilt enveloping him. But my mind screamed that he'd done it all this to himself, and I was nothing more than collateral damage from the bad choices he'd made. Could I forgive him? I didn't know.

Tony cleared his throat. "Coming here to confess everything was very difficult for you."

"Yes," Matt whispered.

"I think Leagh understands that. But I also think she's going to need some time to digest it all. Don't you agree?" Tony asked.

"Without a doubt. I didn't come here today expecting a heartfelt reunion," Matt explained, looking at me once again. "Hell, I honestly didn't expect you'd even listen to me. I'm relieved and very happy that you did. I understand why you thought I'd hurt you, but trust me. I'd never physically harm you, Leagh. It breaks my heart that my stupid choices caused you so much pain."

His tortured expression almost made me weep. By confessing his deeds, Matt tore down the walls I'd erected, blocking childhood memories of the man. Not only had he bought me my first bike, but he ran alongside me to make sure I didn't fall and scrape my knee, teaching me to ride it. When I got invited to my first high school dance, he snuck me out of the house and took me dress shopping. When I tried on the coral-colored formal gown, Matt's eyes sparkled, and he repeatedly told me how beautiful I looked. He'd even insisted on buying the dress for me and showed up at the house the night of the dance to take pictures, like a preening father.

Tony had been right. I'd built Matt up to be a horrific monster in my mind. And I let the image feed my fears, so thoroughly, convincing myself that I'd lived with a maniacal Jekyll and Hyde, and I'd erased all the happy times and unconditional love he'd showered upon me.

"I appreciate you arranging this meeting and telling me the things you did today, Matt," I hesitantly began. "Maybe, in time, I can forgive you. Over the years, I let my imagination run wild, but I still have nightmares of blood on my hands, and... hopefully, they'll go away now."

"I'm sorry, honey, so damn sorry. I never meant for that to happen. I panicked. Never in a million years did I want you exposed to the shit I was involved in. But when I saw you come around the corner with that bucket, I took that as a sign of acceptance. That you were committed to me, even the dark, ugly parts I never wanted you to see. I'm sorry I've ruined your life the way I have. I'm so fucking sorry." Tears brimmed in his eyes.

"Please, stop saying you're sorry, Matt. I feel your remorse. I do. But I'm so overwhelmed right now. I-I do want to thank you for taking me in and standing by me when I lost Nathan. I loved you more than I did my own parents."

Matt closed his eyes and hung his head. Tears dripped from his cheeks and his shoulders shook in silent sobs. After several long moments, he pulled a handkerchief from his pocket, wiped his face, and lifted his head.

"I know I have no right to ask anything of you, Leagh, but would you please make an appointment to talk to someone, a professional who can help you past the damage I've caused you?"

I chuckled softly and darted a glance at Tony. "I'm already seeing someone."

"Good. Good." Matt nodded. "I am, too, and it's helping. He's the catalyst behind me coming here to see you."

"I think, in time, you're both going to be just fine," Tony announced with a soft smile.

Special Agent Rizzo turned to Matt. "Is there anything else you need to say?"

"No," Matt replied somberly. "I'm sorry doesn't come close to what I carry in my heart, but hopefully you know that now, Leagh."

"I do." I nodded.

"Judge Landes, thank you for allowing us this visit," Special Agent Rizzo announced as he stood and shook Reed's hand once more.

"It's been my pleasure to facilitate this for both Leagh and Matt," Reed replied.

When Matt stood, I gave Tony's leg a slight squeeze and rose from my chair. On trembling legs, I walked to Matt and wrapped my arms around him. A mournful wail gurgled from the back of his throat as he pulled me to his chest. Openly sobbing, he hugged me tight for a long time as tears spilled down our faces.

Pulling back, Matt wiped his eyes and sniffed. "Goodbye, my little munchkin."

"Wait. When will I see you again?" I asked, my voice trembling as I brushed at my tears.

He flashed a beseeching look toward Special Agent Rizzo.

"Never, I'm afraid, Miss Bennett. Mr. Price is a dead man. In fact, neither of us were ever here."

"But…" The finality of his words pelted me. "No."

"Mr. Price is in the witness protection program now. He has a new name and a new city," the FBI agent explained. "All ties to anyone in his past must be severed to protect him and those he loves."

I felt Tony move in close behind me, his body heat like a blanket of reassurance, one that I desperately needed. As he placed his hands on my arms, I knew he was there to help me say goodbye to Matt.

To help me heal the scars that marred my heart.

To catch me and never let me fall.

"Please, take good care of her for me," Matt murmured to Tony.

"It will be an honor, sir," Tony replied, his voice thick with emotion.

Matt pulled back, his eyes red rimmed and filled with tears, then bent and pressed a gentle kiss upon my cheek. As he and Special Agent Rizzo turned and walked to the door, Matt paused and looked back at me.

"I love you, munchkin. Always remember that."

"I love you, too," I sobbed.

When the door closed behind him, I broke down.

"I'll give you two some privacy," Reed whispered and left the room.

Tony held me in his arms as I cried uncontrollably.

"Let it out, angel. You've held so much inside you for so long. Just let it out. It's time to unburden all the fear and pain and misery."

"How could I think that he would ever have tried to hurt me?" I wailed.

"Because you were young and what he did was opposite of the man you believed him to be. None of us are perfect. We all make mistakes. Matt made some huge ones, but I don't want you blaming yourself for how his actions affected you or how you responded to what he did. You did the right thing by going into self-preservation mode," Tony assured, wiping my tears with the pads of his thumb. "Besides, running away ultimately brought you to me."

He captured my lips, inundating me with passion and so much love more tears spilled down my cheeks.

"Come on, angel, let's go home."

Snuggled tight against Tony's side, he drove to the club. Once back in our room, we laid in bed, my head on his chest, and his arms wrapped around me.

"I know today was an emotional rollercoaster ride for you, sweetheart. Tell me how you're feeling, what you're thinking?"

"Really? You already want to pull your scalpel out?"

"No time like the present." I could hear the smile he undoubtedly wore in his voice.

"All right, but if you think I'm going to pay you for this visit, you're crazy." I grinned.

"You'll pay all right but not with money," he rumbled.

In an instant, my nipples drew tight, and I ground my pussy against his thigh. "I'd rather play doctor, patient in other ways."

"I'm sure you would, and maybe we'll have to investigate your desire for medical play...later. Right now, it's time to talk."

I swallowed tightly, thinking about stirrups and speculums. "Okay, I really don't have any medical fantasies, it was just a metaphor."

Tony chuckled as he tugged a strand of hair clinging to my shoulder. "You're stalling, angel. Talk to me."

"The relief I feel now is totally different from what I felt when I thought Matt was dead."

"Explain that statement to me."

A small smile curled on my lips. Tony had three distinct modes: doctor, Dominant, and lover. And damn if I didn't thoroughly love them all.

We spent hours discussing every feeling, thought, and rationalization running through my mind. Tony's persuasive yet gentle questions brought a sense of closure and healing. Not only in regard to Matt but the deep scars I'd carried from the rape, the loss of Nathan, George's betrayal, and the resentment I felt toward my parents. When he was through, I felt emotionally and physically exhausted.

"I'm proud of you, angel. You're mighty strong for such a little wisp of a girl," Tony teased.

Leaning up on my elbows, I laughed and stared into his eyes. "Thank you, Tony. Thank you for everything."

"I love you, sweetheart. There's nothing on earth I wouldn't do for you."

"Or me for you, Master," I whispered before dipping to brush a soft kiss to his mouth.

When I tried to pull away, Tony gripped my hair and held me captive to his lips. Demanding. Untamed. His delving doctor side vanished, and his inner Dominant roared to life. My heart soared.

When he rolled me beneath him and began stripping off my clothes, my pulse raced and my body ached. Soon we were naked and panting. And when he thrusted inside my sodden cunt, I cried out, gripped his shoulders, and held tight as he drove into me with savage delight. Time blurred into a haze of explosive orgasms, adoring murmurs, and blissful embraces. Serenity enveloped me.

~

Three weeks later, Tony rubbed suntan lotion on my belly as I lay upon a chaise beneath the warm, bright sun of Palm Beach. Our private bungalow, facing the rolling, blue waves of the Atlantic Ocean, sat a few feet behind us. He surprised me with the romantic getaway, asserting that the change of scenery would do us both good. And as the sea gulls dipped and swooped overhead, I couldn't have agreed with him more.

We swam in the ocean, took romantic walks along the beach at sunset, and spent hours tangled in each other's arms, feeding our boundless appetite for one another. I could easily grow accustomed to the carnal splendor we'd cocooned ourselves in.

"I wish we could stay here forever," I sighed.

"We can if that's what you want, sweetheart," Tony chuckled. "You have the means now."

My mind shifted back to the meeting with Paula in Reed's office. I'd been so nervous, but Tony held my hand, and when she'd stepped through the door, Paula looked exactly as I'd pictured her. Tall with perfectly coiffed gray hair, the woman oozed poise and grace. She was a lady in every sense of the word. Controlled and direct, Paula declined Reed's offer of thirty-seven million dollars, half of George's estate. I was blown away at the figure but more curious as to why she would turn down such an obscene amount of money.

"I know it must come as a shock to you," Paula said, addressing Reed as if Tony and I were invisible. "After my husband's stroke, I was awarded guardianship over his holdings. The simple truth is, I don't need the money, nor do I wish to have my feelings for George reduced to a monetary number."

Then, Paula did a strange thing—she turned to face me. A warm, grandmotherly smile spread over her lips. "Take it, Leagh. Take it all. Donate to charities, support medical research, help those that need it, and live out your wildest dreams with the rest. All I ask is every once in a while, you lift your face to the heavens and thank George. Regardless of his duplicities, you held a special place in his heart."

I gazed up at the clear blue Florida sky and whispered a silent 'thank you' to George before turning and flashing a crooked smile Tony's way.

"What do you think about a winter home here?"

"I think it would be a marvelous place to thaw out when we're up to our ass in snow drifts." Tony grinned.

That night, he shooed me off to take a shower, telling me he had a surprise for me. Clad in a towel, I stepped from the bathroom to find the bungalow empty and a sexy red dress, matching thong, and a pair of low-heeled black sandals set out on the bed.

"Maybe we're going dancing," I whispered to myself.

After drying my hair and applying a dusting of makeup, I painted my lips with a shimmering red gloss and stepped into the silky, little dress. With a critical eye, I looked in the mirror and smiled. I felt like a princess. The dress Tony picked out for me was beautiful and showed just enough skin to be tempting. Just as I began to wonder where my sneaky Master had run off to, a knock came from the bungalow door.

I opened it, expecting to find Tony, but was instead met by a forty-something man dressed in a black tux and snow-white gloves.

"Miss Bennett?"

"Yes?"

"I've been sent by Mr. Delvaggio. If you would allow me to escort you, he requests your presence on the beach."

I couldn't imagine what Tony was up to, but I agreed by slipping my arm through the stylish man's elbow. He led me down the palm shrouded path and into a clearing. That's when I spied Tony, standing at an elegant, candlelit table for two, right there on the beach. He was dressed in a black tuxedo, sans the gloves, wearing the broadest smile I'd ever seen.

"Oh goodness," I whispered in surprise. He'd gone to all this trouble for me? My heart flip-flopped in my chest, and I found it hard to draw in breath. As I made my way to him, warm sand spilled between my feet and sandals, but I didn't care. All I could think of was tearing away that pristine tailored tux with my teeth and devouring his sexy ass. Tony held me with his shimmering dark eyes, and I could see the lust burning bright within them. The way he looked at me, coupled with the hunger rising inside me, it would be a miracle if we even ended up eating the dinner he'd arranged.

As the older man handed me off to Tony, he tipped his head with a smile, turned, and walked up the beach toward the main hotel. We were all alone.

Tony stood staring at me, undressing me with his eyes, before he stepped in close, wrapped his arm around my waist, and pulled me tight against his steely chest.

"Forget dinner," he growled. "I want to lay you out over this table and feast on your slick, hot cunt, sweetheart."

My knees turned to jelly, and I purred against his ear. "Anything you desire, Master."

"Fuck," he cursed under his breath. His cock pressed hard and hot against my belly. "Anything?"

"And everything," I murmured, arching my hips and grinding my mound against his erection.

"Oh, already topping from the bottom, are we, my little minx?"

"Oh no, Master. Never," I replied with feigned innocence. "I just wanted to make sure you remembered where to put that when the time comes."

Tony reached and swatted me on the ass. "Like I could ever forget?"

"I sure hope not," I giggled.

"Let's eat. My cock is already screaming to be released from these trousers."

"I don't mind a little sand on my knees, Master."

"I'll remember that. Maybe you can have dessert beneath the table...If you behave."

My mouth watered as Tony turned and helped me into the chair. As soon as he sat, a young man appeared carrying a bottle of champagne. He filled the empty flutes next to our plates, then turned and left.

Tony lifted his glass as I did mine. "To the beautiful full moon, the relaxing music of the waves, and the most breathtaking woman I've ever laid eyes on sitting before me."

I felt the heat rush to my cheeks as Tony brought the rim of his glass toward mine. "And to the most amazing Master on the planet," I added before chinking my glass to his.

The sweet champagne exploded over my taste buds. "Mmm," I moaned as I swallowed. "I like this. What it is?"

"It's Italian. A favorite of mine. I'm glad you like it."

"I love everything about this night, Master. It's perfect."

Course after course, the waiter brought our dinner. It was the most decadent and delicious meal I'd ever tasted. When dessert came, I shot Tony a coy smile; he threw his head back and laughed.

"Maybe in a little bit, angel," he replied, wiggling his brows. "Did you enjoy the food?"

"Oh yes. It was...I don't know what to say, Tony. This has all been so amazing. Thank you."

A strange expression fluttered over his face before quickly disappearing. Rising from his seat, Tony stepped in close beside me. When he eased down on one knee, I sucked in a tiny gasp.

"There's only one thing I want you to say, angel."

Reaching into the pocket of his tux, Tony pulled out a red velvet box, lifted the lid, and placed it in my trembling hand. I stared at the enormous, shimmering square-cut diamond in the center. Smaller ones surrounded it; tears began to blur my vision.

"Will you make me the happiest man and Master in the world? Marry me, angel."

"Yes, yes...a million times, yes!" I choked past my sobs of pure joy.

Through my tears, I watched Tony lift the ring from the box and slide it onto my finger before he stood and lifted me into his arms. Leaving the remains of our dinner behind, he carried me back to our bungalow. He set me down in the middle of the room before taking a seat in the wingback chair in the corner. A mischievous smile tugged his lips.

"Hand me the toy bag, angel, then I want you to stand in front of me and strip. Nice and slow. Can you do that for me?"

"Yes, Master."

Strip for him? Like a stripper? Oh, this is going to be fun!

After delivering the toy bag, I took a step back and pouted my lips. Gazing at him with a seductive stare, I slowly slid one thin strap off my shoulder. Licking my lips, I traced my fingertips over the swell of each breast invitingly before lowering the other strap with a languid sweep of my hand. Cupping my breasts, I caught the silky fabric before it could slide down my body.

Tony's eyes darkened and his lids fell heavy in that familiar lustful way. Without looking away, he unfastened his pants and released his zipper. His thick erection sprang free, and an audible purr rolled from the back of my throat. Tony wrapped a fist around his ready cock, gliding his hand up and down in long, slow strokes. It took all the strength I had not to fall to my knees and swallow him up.

"Don't start something you can't finish, sweetheart," Tony warned in an edgy growl.

"Oh, I can finish this for you, Master. Trust me," I countered with a playful wink.

"I wouldn't be so sure about that, pet. You have no idea how deeply I can crawl inside your mind."

I let the dress puddle to the floor and eased to my knees. Skimming my palms on the carpet toward him, my ass resting on my feet, I stretched my neck upward and looked into his eyes.

"Show me, Master. Seize all of me."

Thank you for reading ***Seize Me***. I hope you enjoyed Tony helping Leagh heal and spread her wings. If you did, I'd love for you to leave a review and recommend this book to all your friends.

And if you'd like to be the first to hear about my upcoming releases and read exclusive excerpts, please sign up for my **newsletter**. Oh, and if you want to let your hair down, get a little rowdy, and grab some freebies, join my private Facebook group **Jenna Jacob's Jezebels**. I'd love to see you there!

Ready to see what's happening next at Club Genesis?

AROUSE ME

A sizzling one-night stand ignites obsession and forbidden cravings while a dangerous stalker threatens to destroy the future.

AROUSE ME
Club Genesis - Chicago, Book 4

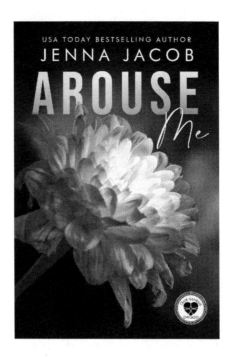

He compelled the surrender I didn't want to give...

I'm **Mellie Carson**—bold, ambitious, career-driven, independent woman. When I hook up with sexy-as-sin sculptor **Joshua Lars** for a one-night stand, he totally blindsides me. I never expected his skilled hands and commanding presence to awaken the forbidden desires hiding inside me. The passionate night we share reshapes my definition of pleasure.

To save my sanity, I try to forget him. But fate—and a killer—have other plans.

Determined to save my life, Joshua hides me away. Safely protected in his loving arms, he steals my heart while doing everything in his power to...*Arouse Me.*

Previously published as *Saving My Submission.*

Here's a sneak peek of *AROUSE ME*...

Joshua Lars kissed my lips like he owned them. His capable hands —those of a famed master sculptor—swept over my shoulders, sending my red designer dress down my body, past my hips to spill like a puddle at my feet. Languid and thorough, he made love to my mouth as if I were a masterpiece he sought to mold.

As he unfastened my bra and tossed it to the floor, his intoxicating scent made me dizzy. I clung to him, trembling with anticipation, as he lashed his tongue up the column of my neck before devouring each pebbled peak and the aching flesh around them.

From the moment he'd pressed me up against the door of his studio and kissed me breathless until he'd lowered me onto his bed, Joshua's jade-colored eyes held a piercing command. And as his body hovered over mine, all sinewy and taut while his bicep muscles bunched and rippled, I quivered beneath his steely erection pressed against my belly.

As a shock of his wheat-colored hair fell over his brow, I reached up to brush it away, but he clasped my hand. Then, with a barely perceptible shake of his head, he raised my arms over my head and pinned my wrists to the mattress.

My pussy clenched.

My heart skipped.

His Dominant gesture stole my breath as the need to submit surged through my veins. I hadn't let a man command me for years. I wasn't about to start now.

I struggled to break free, but Joshua shook his head.

"Easy, Mellie. I'm not going to hurt you." His voice was smooth, like fine-aged brandy. "Tell me, little one, are you what I hope you are?"

His actions, his ragged whisper, put a chink in my armor and made the burning pulse of surrender rise higher. "What exactly is it that you hope I am?"

"Don't play innocent. You know what I'm talking about. Earlier tonight, while you were staring at my sub statue, the glow on your face aroused my suspicion. But when you started to cry, it was as if you'd opened a window to your soul. I keep catching glimpses of your true nature, but it's elusive, like smoke. There and smoldering one second, then floating away on the wind the next. It's as if you're trying to deny your feelings."

What. The. Fuck? Out of all the men I'd been with—and there had been plenty—not one had ever sensed the sleeping submissive inside me. Yet, ninety minutes with the world-renowned artist Joshua Lars, and his Dominant radar saw right through the thick, sturdy walls I'd painstakingly constructed.

His lips brushed mine in a feathery-light kiss. "I'm dying to taste your surrender."

His words unnerved me. "I-I don't know what you mean," I lied. "Stop talking and fuck me."

To throw him off my submissive scent, I arched my hips and rubbed my pussy against his cock, aiming to coax him into a down-and-dirty, dazzling, one and done that I could handle. Diving into BDSM waters—especially with Joshua—would be like jumping off a cruise ship without a life vest. I didn't want or need to take my chances in those shark-infested waters again.

Lifting my head, I tried to force him to kiss me. He reared back with an arch of his brows. Disapproval lined his face. I'd never have the upper hand with the man, and it should have scared the hell out of me. Instead, it turned me on even more.

This is going to be tricky.

"Ah ah ah, play nice, pet. I won't allow you to top me. We're going to take the path that's got you so skittish, because it's the same one that has you wet and ready." He bent and nuzzled his lips close to my ear. "I can smell your cunt, little one. It makes my mouth water."

I didn't know what to say. He pinned me with a dissecting stare. His breath fluttered over my lips. Unable to look at him without wanting to melt in surrender, I cast my gaze to the golden patch of hair between his flat nipples. I couldn't risk him seeing those submissive parts of me I'd hidden.

"Yes, that's the one. My, my, what a gorgeous little thing you are."

His low, raspy praise sent lashes of fire dancing up my spine. It felt as if the devil himself had licked me with his scorching tongue.

Cinching both of my wrists into one hand, he skimmed his other down my body, pausing to roll each of my beaded nipples between his fingers and thumb. Shards of electricity shot south and gathered behind my already throbbing clit.

"Your safeword is *fantasy*, because that's what you are—a fantasy that's been plucked straight from my dreams."

Lord help me. The man had seduction down to a science. Combined with his potent Dominance, I didn't know whether to laugh, cry, or run for my life.

Desperate to keep this encounter as vanilla as possible, I scoffed. "What the hell is a safeword?"

Joshua narrowed his eyes. "Don't lie to me, pet. Lie to yourself all you want, but I've already seen everything I need to."

He bent and pressed his lips to mine with a kiss so explosive it stole my breath. Surrender, like a long-lost blanket, enveloped me, and for one brief moment I didn't care if he saw through my mask or not. The need to please him cracked my walls, and the stroke of his demanding tongue had my submission seeping through.

My mind was still spinning when I felt the cool tip of his latex-shrouded cock slide between my heated folds.

"Yes," I gasped, arching in willing compliance.

With a feral growl, Joshua thrusted deep inside me as a cry of pleasure-mixed-pain tore from my throat. Blessedly endowed, he filled and stretched me with a captivating burn. Struggling to relax my passage, he withdrew, only to impale me once again. My packed pussy fluttered and rippled around his shaft. A low groan of delight rolled off his tongue and vibrated onto mine. Squeezing my wrists—almost to the point of pain—he emphasized his control, and it sent my heart soaring.

Joshua plunged in and out of my clutching cunt in a slow and steady rhythm. Arching to meet his thrusts, I held nothing back. The sounds of gasps, grunts, and slapping flesh filled the room. Tearing his mouth from mine, he gazed down at me. Sweat dotted his brow and his red, swollen lips glistened. The epitome of rugged beauty and command, Joshua drew me in even deeper with the fiery lust dancing in his eyes.

"Are you going to be a good girl and ask for it, little one? Beg nice and pretty for me?"

When I nodded sharply, he drove even deeper. Crying out, I wrapped my legs around his waist as every thick inch of him throbbed inside me. His glorious torture was sublime. Exhaling a savage hiss, he began dragging his bulbous crest over the sensitive bundle of nerves in a slow, decisive rhythm. As if orchestrating a symphony, the swell grew to a turbulent crescendo, sending lightning ricocheting through my cells. I cried out again, letting the sinful blaze burn me alive as he unleashed his potent sexual skills.

"Harder, Joshua. Please, fuck me harder!" I begged.

And he did. Hard...fast...and unrelenting, like a freight train thundering down a mountain slope. Joshua drove in frenzied thrusts as if his life depended on it. Sweat dripped from his face, mixing with mine as our harsh animalistic sounds echoed in the room.

Wedging a hand between us, Joshua strummed my clit with just the right amount of pressure. My moans turned to screams, morphing into keening pleas that he'd allow the swell to pull me under and annihilate my blistering need.

"Now," he bellowed. "Come for me, Mellie."

Right on cue, as if eight years had been but yesterday, I responded —like I'd been trained—and shattered at his command.

Rocked by the force of my powerful orgasm, dark spots formed behind my eyes. Pounding into my channel like a man possessed, Joshua suddenly froze. Fixed deep inside me, he let out a deafening roar before pummeling my cunt in a torrent of erratic strokes; he followed me over.

Releasing my wrists, he dropped to his elbows. Panting, he pressed his face against my neck. Our coupled muscles twitched and pulsed until the sexual buzz faded. Easing from my pussy, Joshua collapsed to the bed alongside me. Both of us covered in a fine sheen of sweat, the heady scent of sex lay like a heavy blanket around us.

It took several long minutes before our ragged breaths slowed and evened out, and all the while I lay staring at Joshua. His eyes were closed, and a serene, sated expression lined his face. I wanted to pinch myself.

I just had sex with Joshua Lars.

Sex, my ass! The man fucked your brains out. And did a righteous job of it, too.

The little voice in my head was right. No lover before him had been capable of enticing an orgasm of *that* magnitude. Clearly, Joshua had more impressive talents besides gifted hands. Studying the sharp features of his handsome face, his rugged jaw line and the light blond scruff covering his chin, I smiled. His golden hair, now dark and wet, lay plastered to his head. Still, he looked like sin on a stick, and I'd have no trouble whatsoever taking him on for round two.

As if reading my mind, he opened his eyes. A quirky smile played over his lips. "Oh yeah, we definitely need to do that again, but give me a minute. I'm not as young as I used to be."

I laughed. "You're not the only one, Sir."

Sir? Sir? Where the fuck did that come from?

Joshua didn't bat an eye at my reply. Obviously, he was accustomed to being called 'Sir' by someone—maybe a whole lot of someones. The inward prick of jealousy surprised me, but I was more concerned at how easily the honorific 'Sir' had rolled off my tongue. Unnerved, I realized Joshua had picked the lock and opened the Pandora's Box of my submission. A knot of fear began to unravel, and a surge of panic-laced adrenaline exploded through my veins. I leapt from the bed as if it were on fire.

"Where are you going?" Shifting, he raised up on one elbow. A quizzical expression lined his face as he watched me race around the room.

"Bathroom," I replied curtly. Gathering up my dress, thong, purse, and shoes, I raced away.

"Wait," he called to me. "I thought we were going to—"

Before he could finish his sentence, I slammed the double doors of the bathroom shut and locked them. On shaky knees, I stepped into my dress, clutching the sink to steady myself. Catching a glimpse of my reflection in the mirror, I froze. My lips were red and swollen. My cheeks flushed in a 'just fucked glow.' Still taut, my dusky nipples tingled from all the attention Joshua had bestowed with his fingers and teeth. The elegant, coiffured bun I'd worn to his showing was now

293

wild and disheveled in the vivid aftermath of how his urgent hands had snarled through my mane. Outwardly, I wore all the markings of a woman well satisfied, but gazing at my eyes, I could see the terror stamped within. A new, more potent wave of alarm slammed through me. I'd allowed Joshua Lars and his Dominant charm to touch me too deeply.

"Dammit, what the fuck are you doing? Get your shit together and get the hell out of here," I mumbled to my reflection in the mirror.

Stepping into my thong, I grabbed my purse and pulled out my cell phone. Scrolling an online search engine as I tugged the tiny scrap of material to my knees, I dialed the number of a local cab company. Tucking the phone against my shoulder, I fumbled through my beaded clutch, plucking out the invitation as a gruff man answered. Rattling off the address, I swiftly ended the call, shoved everything back in my purse, and finished yanking up the thong still abandoned at my knees.

A thunderous knock landed on the other side of the door. Jumping, I yelped in surprise.

"Mellie, open up," Joshua demanded.

"Just a sec," I called out, my voice cracking with anxiety.

"Mellie?" He pounded once again. "Don't make me break this fucking door down. We need to talk."

Talk? Oh hell, no. There was absolutely nothing I wanted to say to the man.

"Open. Up. Now."

I bit back a whimper. *Shit! Why did he have to use that imposing Dom voice on me?*

"Okay," I snapped. Cursing under my breath, I chided myself for letting him awaken my dormant submissive longings.

Slipping on my fiery red stilettos, I yanked the door open and instantly wished I'd kept the sucker shut. Joshua stared down at me, wearing nothing but his black tuxedo pants and a nipple-hardening scowl. His commanding mien nearly took me out at the knees.

When he opened his mouth to speak, I raised my hand and pushed past him, surprising him into silence.

"Thanks for a wonderful time, Joshua. I had fun." The tone of my voice was so dismissive I couldn't help but cringe inside. I couldn't even look at him. *Coward.* Plucking a business card from my purse, I held it out to him. "If you're ever in Phoenix, give me a call."

AROUSE ME
Club Genesis - Chicago, Book 4

<u>CLUB GENESIS - CHICAGO</u>
<u>Awaken Me</u>
<u>Consume Me</u>
<u>Seize Me</u>
<u>Arouse Me</u>
<u>Ignite Me</u>
<u>Entice Me</u>
<u>Expose Me</u>
<u>Bare Me</u>
<u>Unravel Me</u>
<u>Command Me</u>
<u>Tame Me</u>
<u>Tempt Me</u>

Are you aching for another smokin' hot BDSM romance?

THE BREAK
The Unbroken Series: Raine Falling, Book 2

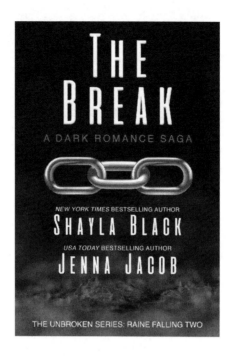

One woman. Two Rivals. Countless secrets...

Raine Kendall has everything a woman could want—almost. Sexy, tender Liam O'Neill is her knight in shining armor, but is he too good to be true or could their growing connection actually last a lifetime? To complicate matters, she can't shake her feelings for her commanding boss, Macen Hammerman, especially after the mind-blowing night he stopped fighting their attraction, took her to bed, and ravished every inch of her.

Now there might be consequences.

While Hammer can't stop coveting Raine and counting the days of her cycle with glee, Liam resolves to keep her for his own. But she stubbornly refuses to open the corners of her scarred heart. Determined to win her for good, Liam risks everything. Though once he puts his plan in motion, she proves as elusive as smoke. It's a bitter pill when he needs Hammer's help to bring her home. And Liam can't help but wonder…will Raine ever be his again or will he lose her to his ex-best friend for good?

ABOUT THE AUTHOR

USA Today Bestselling author **Jenna Jacob** paints a canvas of passion, romance, and humor as her alpha men and the feisty women who love them unravel their souls, heal their scars, and find a happy-ever-after kind of love. Heart-tugging, captivating, and steamy, her words will leave you breathless and craving more.

A mom of four grown children, Jenna, her husband Sean, and their furry babies reside in Kansas. Though she spent over thirty years in accounting, Jenna isn't your typical bean counter. She's brassy, sassy, and loves to laugh, but is humbly thrilled to be living her dream as a full-time author. When she's not slamming coffee while pounding out emotional stories, you can find her reading, listening to music, cooking, camping, or enjoying the open road on the back of a Harley.

CONNECT WITH JENNA
Website - E-Mail - Newsletter
Jezebels Facebook Party Page

ALSO BY JENNA JACOB

CLUB GENESIS - CHICAGO

Awaken Me

Consume Me

Seize Me

Arouse Me

Ignite Me

Entice Me

Expose Me

Bare Me

Unravel Me

Command Me

Tame Me

Tempt Me

CLUB GENESIS - DALLAS

Forbidden Obsession

BAD BOYS OF ROCK

Rock Me

Rock Me Longer - Includes Rock Me Free

Rock Me Harder

Rock Me Slower

Rock Me Faster

Rock Me Deeper

COWBOYS OF HAVEN

The Cowboy's Second Chance At Love

The Cowboy's Thirty-Day Fling

The Cowboy's Cougar

The Cowboy's Surprise Vegas Baby

BRIDES OF HAVEN

The Cowboy's Baby Bargain

The Cowboy's Virgin Baby Momma - Includes Baby Bargain

The Cowboy's Million Dollar Baby Bride

The Cowboy's Virgin Buckle Bunny

The Cowboy's Big Sexy Wedding

THE UNBROKEN SERIES - RAINE FALLING

The Broken

The Betrayal

The Break

The Brink

The Bond

THE UNBROKEN SERIES - HEAVENLY RISING

The Choice

The Chase

The Confession

The Commitment

STAND ALONES

Small Town Second Chance

Innocent Uncaged